WATCH ME BREAK

WATCHED IN DARKNESS BOOK 1

V.E. HUNTLEY

Published in the United States by V.E. Huntley

The Cataloging-in-Publication Data is on file at the Library of Congress

Paperback ISBN 979-8-9907982-8-1

Ebook ISBN 979-8-9907982-7-4

Book Design by V.E. Huntley

Book Cover Design by C. David Photography & Design

First Edition 2025

This is for all my dark romance girlies out there —the ones who aren't afraid to admit they want to be tied up, completely at someone's mercy, and taken to the edge of sanity and back again.

You know who you are. You're the ones who dog-ear the filthy pages, who stay up way too late reading "just one more chapter," and who've definitely Googled "Is it normal to be attracted to fictional psychopaths?"

So here's my advice: Find yourself a Damien.

He's the kind of man who'll take you right to the edge, hold you there while you're gasping and begging, and have the audacity to look smug about it the entire time.

Because let's be honest—vanilla is great for ice cream, but we're here for the dark, decadent, deliciously twisted stuff.

And trust me, Damien delivers. Every. Single. Time.

Enjoy Your Surrender

If reading lots of hot, intense, ridiculously spicy sex isn't your thing, don't read this book.

If crude language, graphic violence, and characters with a very questionable moral compass aren't your thing, don't read this book.

If men who take exactly what they want with zero apologies aren't your thing, definitely don't read this book.

But...

If you enjoy sensually surrendering to a dark, masked stranger who will absolutely ruin you—body, heart, and soul—before piecing you back together and dragging every one of your deepest, darkest desires into the light?

Then buckle up, my lovelies.

And enjoy your surrender...

Content/Trigger Warnings

This is not a full list, just the most triggering.

Please visit my website (https://vehuntley.com/) for the entire list of TWs.

This story contains the following dark themes, situations, and kinks that may be triggering for some readers: stalking, spying, primal play, fear play, knife play, breath play, non-consent/very dubious consent between the main characters, obsessive behaviors, bondage, torture, graphic violence, explicit sexual situations, animal neglect and cruelty (off page), medical treatment of abused/injured animals (**NO** on page animal abuse), on page death of an animal from natural selection (**NOT** abuse or injury, **NOT** graphic). This death occurs in Chapter 32, and sensitive readers can skip this chapter without losing the plot, but you will miss a very poignant moment in Luna's journey that is referenced later in the story.

If any of these (or the additional TWs listed on my website) are potential triggers for you, please do not read. I won't be offended.

Your mental health matters—do what's best for you.

Despite the content/triggers and dark elements in this series, it is a story full of love, laughter, desire, passion, found family and loyalty. At its core, it's a love story about two people destined for each other.

So, for those who still want to take this ride with me, enjoy.

He's always watching.
She's starting to want him to.

Chapter One

Damien

The amber liquid burns as it slides down my throat, but the heat pales against the fire building in my chest. My heart pounds as I face the massive stone fireplace, watching the flames writhe over blackened wood. The thirty-year Macallan tastes different tonight. Sharper.

Beside me, Athena stretches in her sleep, her blue-gray coat painted silver by moonlight creeping through the cracked transom above. She's the only creature on this earth that sees gentleness from these hands.

I flex my fingers, studying them in the firelight. Two hours ago, these same hands dragged Dale Nash out of his truck at that shithole puppy mill in Fort Lupton. Hundreds of dogs crammed into wire cages, living in their own filth.

Not anymore.

The look on his face when I stepped out of the shadows...

Fuck, that was beautiful.

I drain the glass and let my gaze drift across the room. What was once a grand Victorian study now lies half-shrouded in dust and shadows, its carved mahogany panels warped and water-stained from four decades of neglect.

This place called to me the moment I saw the listing. Five hundred acres of Colorado wilderness, far from prying eyes and closer to God's judgment than man's law. The real estate agent kept dancing around the property's history, but that history is the reason I bought it.

I chose this place because isolation breeds opportunity. No neighbors to hear screams, no streetlights to cast unwanted shadows, and no city noise to mask the sounds of justice. The nearest house, a wildlife sanctuary tucked in the valley to the west, is a mile down a winding mountain road that becomes almost impassable in winter.

The empty whiskey glass sits heavy in my palm, each facet sharp against my skin. The cut crystal belonged to my grandfather and is one of the few possessions I kept when I shed my old life. Everything else about Damien Wolfe is carefully constructed theater. But here, surrounded by decay and darkness, I can stop pretending and be what I am.

The monster they created.

A log shifts in the grate, sending sparks spiraling up the dark throat of the chimney. Athena's ear twitches, though her eyes remain closed. The scars along her muzzle have faded to thin white lines, souvenirs from the fighting ring I saved her from two years ago. She was scheduled to be bait for a champion fighter, thrown into the pit to be torn apart for entertainment. Instead, she found her way to my home and is the only living thing I let close.

I set the empty glass on the mantel and reach for my mask. I catch my reflection in its polished surface. Eyes burning bright. Pupils dilated. The face of a man ready to christen his new killing ground.

The silver titanium wolf mask covers half my face, spanning from the top of my head to above my upper lip. Cade calls it my death wish, a calling card that will eventually hang me. But the moment that metal touches my flesh, I shed my human limitations. The mask doesn't just hide my identity; it reveals my true nature.

The floorboards protest under my boots as I move toward the office door. This mansion settles and sighs like a living thing, its bones creaking with the weight of accumulated sins.

Athena lifts her head as I pass, dark eyes following my movement. She yawns, and I stop to scratch behind her ears. Her fur is warm from the fire, soft against my palm.

"Sleep, girl. This part isn't for you."

She settles back into the warmth with a satisfied grunt.

Beyond my office, the hallway fades to shadow, wallpaper peeling in curling strips, exposing layers of faded florals and the gray plaster beneath. Most of the mansion has remained untouched since I bought it. The decay serves as a testament to what happens when evil takes root.

The door to the basement sits at the end of the hall, heavy oak that's absorbed decades of secrets. I pause before it, savoring the anticipation clawing at my chest. This moment, crossing from hunter to executioner, never loses its power over me.

The ancient wooden planks creak and shift as I descend the stairs. Good. I want Nash to hear me coming, to count each footstep like the slow beats of a dying heart.

The cool basement air is heavy with moisture that seeps through the stone foundation. When I reach the bottom of the stairs, the smell hits me. Earth and the lingering copper scent that never quite faded from this place.

The single bulb above throws sharp shadows around the room, lighting up the cold metal table in the center. The kind used in morgues. It came with the property, along with the rickety wooden workbench rotting in the corner, both abandoned by the previous owner, a serial killer from almost forty years ago. Jeremiah Morrison carved his name into local legend with the blood of seven teenage girls before they caught him in 1984. Their deaths left this place cursed and untouchable.

Until I came along.

Nash lies strapped to its surface, awake now, his eyes wild and bloodshot. They snap to me as I step into the pool of harsh light. His chest strains against the restraints. Tendons stand out in his neck, and sweat beads on his forehead despite the basement's chill.

Behind the duct tape, Nash's breathing turns to panicked snorts through his nose. The sound makes something warm unfurl behind my ribs. He jerks against the straps, his wrists already raw and bleeding where they cut into his skin.

I step closer. The mask gleams in the bulb's glare, and Nash's eyes widen with terror.

I move to the workbench against the wall. The serrated blade is still there, reflecting the faint light. My fingers wrap around the handle, leather worn smooth from use, molded to my grip like it belongs there.

"Do you know what separates us from animals, Dale?" I turn the knife, watching light dance along its edge. Each syllable hangs in the air, carrying the weight of coming judgment. "It's not intelligence. Not morality."

Nash thrashes against the leather straps binding him, the metal table legs scraping concrete in a rhythm that matches my pulse.

"It's our capacity to understand suffering before it arrives."

The blade hovers above his chest, not quite touching. Nash freezes, every muscle locked. Even his breathing stops.

The tip touches his skin below his collarbone. Cold metal against warm flesh. I press down, and the skin parts in a clean, shallow line. Blood wells, a perfect crimson thread against his flesh. Nash's body arches off the table, his muffled scream vibrating through the duct tape. The sound echoes off stone walls that have heard worse. Much worse.

The cut throbs with his heartbeat, weeping fresh drops with each pulse. It's beautiful in its simplicity, like an artist's first brushstroke on virgin canvas.

Outside, wind rattles the basement's single boarded window. The storm that's been brewing all night finally breaks, the rain hammering against the glass like desperate fingers trying to get in. Perfect weather for what comes next. Nature's fury will swallow any noise that might escape this tomb.

The scent of urine assaults my nose as a dark stain spreads across the front of his jeans.

"Already?" Disappointment colors my voice. "We've barely started."

Nash's eyes squeeze shut, tears leaking from the corners. His whole body shakes—fear, adrenaline, or maybe just the cold seeping into his bones.

I select a different knife from my array of tools, smaller and more precise. The handle fits between my thumb and forefinger like it was crafted for my grip. I test its edge against my thumb. A thin line of blood appears.

I press the tip against Nash's shoulder, above where the first cut weeps crimson. His entire body goes rigid as the metal bites through his skin, opening a parallel line that mirrors the first, only deeper. Blood flows in twin streams down his chest.

His scream tears through the duct tape, his body convulsing against the restraints. The straps creak under the strain but hold. They always hold.

I walk back to the workbench and lean against it. Nash's frantic eyes track my every movement. Time to let anticipation do its work. Let him marinate in the knowledge that those two cuts are only the beginning of a very long night.

His muffled cries, a prayer for mercy, will go unanswered.

Justice has no ears for the pleas of monsters.

Chapter Two

Luna

I hold my breath as I secure the splint around the eagle's fractured wing, my fingers steady despite my racing heart. The smell of antiseptic fills the treatment room, mixing with the underlying musky scent of feathers.

Working with raptors isn't easy. There's something about their gaze that strips away all pretense until you're left exposed. This magnificent creature doesn't understand that I'm trying to help. All he knows is captivity and pain.

"Almost done," I murmur, checking the alignment one more time.

The eagle remains still beneath the towel draped over his head and body, with only his injured wing uncovered. Maren's hands keep his legs and talons secured.

Then he mantles. She adjusts her hold, but I still step back. Adrenaline spikes through my system, a primal response to a predator's threat that no amount of veterinary training can override. My pulse hammers, a reminder that no matter how many wild animals I treat, I'll never be completely immune to fear.

"How about we drug him up a little more?" Maren whispers to avoid startling our patient. "I'm not in the mood to get my face rearranged. I like my face."

I edge closer. "It's a good face."

"JT thinks so too. He's especially fond of the expression it makes when I'm coming on his cock."

"That's not something I needed to know, but okay."

"Oh, please." She snorts but cuts herself short when the eagle's head turns toward the sound. We both freeze until he settles again. "It's not like you don't know what my orgasm face looks like. We shared a dorm room for four years.

There's no way you were always asleep when I brought a hookup home. No one sleeps that deep."

"Selective hearing was the only way I could survive all that grunting and groaning without losing my mind."

"Try not to choke on that imagined chastity belt, Dr. Foster."

I blow her a kiss across the examination table. Without missing a beat, she flips me off while maintaining her grip on the eagle's powerful legs. I have to admire her dexterity. Few people can deliver obscene gestures while restraining a bird of prey.

The eagle shifts again, testing her hold. The muscles in his legs ripple beneath her gloved hands, reminding us both that we're dealing with a predator capable of snatching salmon from rushing rivers.

"So you're sure he doesn't need any more drugs?"

"No, he's been incredibly cooperative. Even during the X-rays." I smooth the last piece of tape, ensuring the splint is secure without being restrictive. "I think he knows we're trying to help."

"Or he's plotting our demise and waiting for the perfect moment to strike. You know, when we least expect it."

I bite back a chuckle. "Your optimism is truly inspiring."

"I prefer realism. This bird could fuck up a small aircraft if he put his mind to it."

"He could wreak havoc if he wanted to, that's for sure." I tuck the injured wing against his side. "Let's move him to recovery."

When he's inside the sanctuary's avian recovery enclosure, I remove the towel, and those fierce golden eyes lock onto mine, unblinking and intense.

For a moment, I feel oddly seen, like this wild creature is reading my thoughts. There's intelligence in those eyes that seem almost human, an ancient wisdom that makes me feel small and young by comparison.

"You're going to be okay. Six weeks, and you'll be back where you belong."

He tilts his head, studying me with what feels like curiosity rather than fear. Something passes between us, an understanding, maybe, or mutual respect.

Some days, I wonder if I'm crazy for choosing this life, patching up creatures that would as soon tear into me as thank me. The doubts creep in during late nights when funding is tight and the workload seems endless.

But the indescribable rush I get when I release a healed animal into the wild, when wings spread or paws hit dirt and instinct takes over, when captivity ends and freedom begins. I'd never want anything else.

This is who I am. Who I was always meant to be.

I drape the cage with several large blankets, providing the darkness that will help reduce the eagle's stress. Even through the fabric, I can sense him still watching me.

A knock interrupts my thoughts. Tate, our intern from CSU Fort Collins, stands in the doorway holding Ricky, one of our two resident raccoons, as he nibbles on a banana.

"I can't get him back into his cage." Tate's face floods with relief as he hands Ricky to Maren. "This is the third banana I've tried to bribe him with."

"Ow." She pulls Ricky's paw away from her breast, wincing. "Stop it, you perverted little shit."

Ricky has a boob fetish, so I can only allow the male interns, my part-time volunteer vet Ethan, myself, or Maren to handle him. Otherwise, I'm asking to get slapped with a sexual harassment suit.

"Don't you have to mail those grant applications?" Tate asks. "The deadline is Friday, right?"

My stomach drops. "Shit. I was going to take those to the post office this morning, but then our friend here came in, and—"

"You hyper-focused on the immediate crisis while the rest of the world continued to go about its day." Maren wrestles with Ricky's wandering paws. "Tate, she does this. A lot. It's like she has selective awareness disorder."

"That's not a real thing," I protest, already moving toward my office, where the envelopes sit buried under everything else that needs attention. "Stop that, Ricky." I remove his paw from Maren as I pass.

"With you, it should be in the fucking DSM. Right between 'chronic lateness' and 'inability to remember anything that isn't bleeding or broken.'"

Tate clears his throat as he and Maren follow me. "The post office closes at five. It's already four-thirty. Do you want me to drop them off?"

I glance at the wall clock. Thirty minutes. I can make it if I leave now.

"No, I'll do it. I need to pick up some supplies at the general store." I yank off my lab coat, almost catching the loose knot at the back of my head. "Can you finish the evening meds? The chart's on the—"

"—wall." Maren's eye roll is so dramatic, I'm surprised they don't fall out of her head. "Contrary to what you seem to believe, I don't actually need you to function. I've been keeping this place running despite your organizational chaos for five years."

The truth of her words hit home. Maren is the backbone of this operation, while I'm the beating heart, the dreamer who sometimes forgets practical realities. She's been my best friend since freshman year of college, and after almost fifteen years, she still hasn't given up on me.

I tuck the envelopes under my arm. "That's why you get the big bucks."

Maren snorts. "Oh yeah, my enormous salary. I'm practically drowning in cash. Try not to get distracted by any wounded butterflies on the way. And for the love of all that's holy, don't stop to rescue anything else."

"Can't promise that." I head toward the door. "Put Ricky in his cage and give him some Gabapentin. That'll chill him out."

"It's like living with a Disney princess who went to veterinary school." Maren's voice floats down the hallway, followed by Tate's laughter. "Ow, Ricky, damn it."

I pause at the threshold and look back to see Maren tussling with him. She's his favorite, but then again, she has the bigger boobs of the two of us. As she traps both his paws in her hands, she turns her head to glance at me. Sun streams through the windows, bathing her in golden light, her brown hair pulled back in its usual ponytail, shining like shimmering chocolate. My heart swells with affection for this woman, who puts up with all my flaws and sexual harassment from my animals.

"Thank you, Mar. Seriously. I'd be lost without you."

"Yeah, yeah," she calls after me as I step out the door. "You'd be late to your own funeral, too. But somehow you'd still show up with a three-legged fox that 'needed your help real quick.'"

"It's my superpower!" I shout back as the door closes behind me.

The early September air hits my face, still somewhat warm, but hinting at the approaching autumn underneath. I pause, drinking in the view of Sage & Summit Wildlife Sanctuary.

My sanctuary.

Sprawled across forty-seven acres nestled against the Rocky Mountains outside Estes Park, the property has been in my family for generations. After my parents died, my grandfather raised me here, and this place became a refuge for every stray, sick, and wounded animal I found. But it wasn't until I inherited it from him five years ago that I turned it into a haven for injured wildlife.

The late afternoon sun slants low across the sky, painting everything in shades of gold, as purple shadows begin to creep over the eastern hills. A comforting sense of belonging washes over me as I breathe in the air, heavy with pine and sage. This is home in the truest sense of the word.

I'm halfway to my truck when I remember Shadow, my seven-year-old gray wolf. He lifts his head as I approach the wolf enclosure, his amber eyes bright with recognition and curiosity.

"Hey, baby." I stop at the fence. "Wanna come to town with me?"

His tail thumps against the ground. I've raised him from a pup after poachers killed his mother, and he remains the one creature, besides Maren, who seems to understand me completely.

"Come on, then. But you have to promise to behave. Eleanor likes you, but you freak her out a little."

I grab his leash and harness, and we head to my ancient blue truck. It's older than I am, patches of rust blooming across its once-vibrant paint like abstract art. Grandpa taught me to keep it running, and something about its reliable unreliability feels comforting.

I turn the key, and the engine coughs, then sputters to life with a noise that sounds suspiciously like protest. I pat the dashboard, my hand lingering on the worn surface. "Just to town and back."

Shadow settles his head against the window as we turn onto the main road. I rehearse my apology to Eleanor, the postmistress who's watched me sprint through the doors seconds before closing too many times to count. Maybe I should bring her cookies next time as a peace offering. Would that be a bribe?

The truck's engine groans as we climb a steep section of road, and I pat the dashboard again in encouragement. "Almost there, I promise."

Twenty-three minutes. We'll make it.

We always do.

The small town of Aspen Ridge comes into view as I round the final bend in the road. Main Street encompasses a handful of buildings clustered together against the backdrop of the mountains. A general store, the town library, Nancy's Diner, a gas station, and the post office—a white clapboard building that hasn't changed in eighty years. I pull into a space in front with five minutes to spare.

Shadow lifts his head from the passenger window. His harness shifts as he stretches, the reinforced straps designed for his impressive frame.

"Come on, baby."

I clip his lead to it before we climb out. Envelopes in hand, we head toward the entrance, Shadow padding beside me. He's a hundred and eighty pounds of pure wolf, and even though people have gotten somewhat used to seeing us together, he still draws stares. The harness and leash can't disguise his undeniable wildness.

I'm reaching for the door handle when it swings open toward me. I jerk back, startled, nearly dropping my envelopes as a tall figure emerges from inside. My breath catches as I look up—way up—into the most intense pair of blue-gray eyes I've ever seen.

Whoa!

The man is imposing, at least six-foot-something, with broad shoulders that seem to fill the doorway. Everything about him radiates an intensity that makes me want to step further back, but I find myself frozen, caught in that penetrating gaze.

"I'm sor—"

An unmistakable growl rumbles from deep within Shadow's chest, cutting off my smile and apology. He shifts forward, positioning himself between me and this stranger, his energy coiling with readiness.

"Easy, boy." My hand drops to his head. I grasp his harness and pull him back. When I look up again, the man is already walking across the street, his back to me. No apology for almost running me over. He doesn't acknowledge me at all.

Well, that was rude.

Shadow's hackles settle as the distance between us increases, though his ears remain pricked forward, tracking the stranger's movement.

I shake my head and push through the door, the little bell above it announcing our arrival. The post office is small, just a service counter at the back and a wall of brass mailboxes to the left. Eleanor Jenkins looks up from behind the counter, her rhinestone-rimmed glasses perched on her nose.

At seventy-eight, Eleanor, who still dyes her hair jet black, has been running the post office since before I was born. She's all up in everyone's business and makes it her mission to keep tabs on the entire town, but Shadow still makes her nervous despite our frequent visits. I can't blame her. He's intimidating even when he's being his sweetest self.

"Cutting it close as usual, aren't you, Luna?" She smiles as she sees me, but stiffens when she spots Shadow.

"Hi, Eleanor." We approach the counter. The tension that had gripped Shadow's body moments ago has melted away with the stranger's departure, leaving him alert but calm. "Eagle with a compound fracture came in this morning. Please tell me I'm not too late."

"You're in luck. Mail truck is behind schedule." She takes my envelopes. "What's this? More animal mysteries for the lab coats in Denver?"

I push a stray lock of hair behind my ear. "No. Grant applications. I have to resubmit every two years to keep our state and federal funding."

"Frank, honey, add this to the outgoing." She stamps the first one.

A grunt comes from behind the mail slots. A few inches shorter than Eleanor, Frank Jenkins, a round, balding man with graying hair around the sides, walks out of the back with a grin on his face. Unlike his wife, Frank's always been unfazed by Shadow because he grew up hunting and understands predators.

"Hi, Luna. Still running that sanctuary all by your lonesome?"

"I have Maren. She's worth ten regular people."

Frank pushes the mail trolley toward the back door as Eleanor's eyes light up with that familiar gleam, signaling incoming gossip. "Oh my goodness, you just missed meeting our newest resident! Did you see that tall, dark, handsome man leaving as you came in?"

"You mean the rude one who nearly knocked me over and didn't even apologize?"

Eleanor gasps, her hand on her throat as if reaching for nonexistent pearls. "Honey, that was Damien Wolfe! Billionaire tech mogul and Denver's most eligible bachelor. Did you see those sexy little silver streaks at his temples?"

"Can't say I did."

I couldn't make it past those penetrating eyes.

"He bought the old Morrison estate a couple of months back."

The Morrison estate. My stomach does a little flip. Five hundred isolated acres bordering the national forest, east of my sanctuary. Vacant for over forty years after the eldest son was convicted for the disappearance and death of a handful of local girls. I've always loved the wild, untouched property, despite its morbid history.

"I heard someone bought it, but I haven't seen anyone."

"How could you miss him?" Eleanor fans herself with one of my envelopes. "That man is a walking invitation to sin. And that voice? It's like dark chocolate. Smooth enough to make a nun reconsider her vows."

I choke out a laugh at her gushing. "Eleanor!"

"I can hear you," comes Frank's dry voice from behind her.

"Oh, hush, Frank." She stamps my second envelope. "I know there's some distance between your places, but how did you not notice him walking out of here? The man takes up a lot of space."

"You know Shadow doesn't like most men. He got a little growly. Besides, he seemed kind of abrupt."

"He's a billionaire. They're always abrupt, mysterious types. But I'll tell ya, if I were thirty years younger, I'd climb that man like a tree."

"Still hearing everything," Frank calls, his voice laced with amusement.

Eleanor brushes him off with a wave. "You know you're the only man for me, Frank. But I'm old, not blind." She leans across the counter, her voice dropping to a near whisper. "Let me tell you something, Luna Foster—a rich, brooding, handsome man like that doesn't come along every day. If I were you, I'd march right over there and welcome him to the neighborhood properly."

"We live in the middle of nowhere, Eleanor. He, Old Man Henderson, and I are the entire neighborhood. And I'm not in the market for—"

"Nonsense! You're young, you're beautiful, you're smart, and you work too hard. A little romance wouldn't kill you."

Frank appears again. "Eleanor, leave the poor girl alone. Not everyone needs your matchmaking services."

"Frank Jenkins, romance makes life worth living! Look at us. Fifty-four years of marriage and still going strong."

"That's because I learned when to keep my mouth shut."

"You mean unlike now."

I can't help but smile at their banter and obvious adoration for each other. "I should get back. Maren's handling evening meds, and I've left her alone too long already."

"I mean it, sweetie." Eleanor gives me a pointed look as she runs my credit card. "You're so busy caring for all those animals, you have no time for yourself. Taking some time for a romance with a man who looks like he stepped out of a magazine would be good for you."

"I'll add it to my to-do list. Right after vaccinating foxes and before monthly inventory."

Eleanor's laughter drifts after us as Shadow and I push through the door. The sun hovers over the horizon now, bleeding orange and pink across the sky, while a light breeze carries the promise of night. We make our way toward my truck, Shadow's tail swishing as he sniffs at interesting scents along the sidewalk until it goes still.

His ears prick forward, that subtle shift in posture that I've learned to read like a book. He's alert. Focused on something my human senses haven't detected yet.

I slow my steps. "What is it, baby?"

A prickling sensation starts at the nape of my neck and crawls down my spine. It starts small, a whisper of awareness, then spreads until my entire body feels like it's under a microscope.

I'm being watched.

I roll my shoulders, trying to shake off the feeling, telling myself I'm being paranoid. This is Aspen Ridge, for crying out loud. The most exciting thing that happens here is when Nancy burns a batch of her famous apple pie. But the crawling sensation persists, growing stronger with each step toward my truck.

My gaze sweeps the street, trying to find the origin. Nothing seems out of place, except for the sleek black Range Rover parked at the curb in front of the diner, its dark-tinted windows making it impossible to see inside. My gaze scans the buildings and the shadowy alleys across the street, but nothing catches my eye.

Shadow's body trembles with an almost silent growl. He shifts closer to me, his massive frame tense and ready. He feels it too, whatever this is.

"Easy."

The sensation of being watched lingers as I open Shadow's door, making me more aware of my movements than usual. It's not frightening, just... uncomfortable. Like having an itch I can't quite scratch. I glance around once more, but the street is still empty except for a few parked cars and the stillness of late afternoon.

I climb into the driver's seat, and Shadow settles beside me with a soft huff. Whatever had caught his attention seems to have passed.

As I back onto the road, I glimpse a tall figure emerging from the diner in my rearview mirror. Even from this distance, I recognize that imposing silhouette as the one that almost ran into me earlier. He was inside Nancy's the entire time.

Could he have been watching me?

I shake my head, shrugging off the lingering unease. Maren's going to have a field day when I tell her about our new neighbor.

As I pass the Morrison property, I wonder what drove Damien Wolfe to buy it. The sprawling Victorian mansion sits on the mountain beyond my property line, abandoned for decades. I explored its overgrown grounds as a child, before the stories about the family's dark history made it a place to avoid.

Now, out of nowhere, it has a new owner. A rude, brooding one who makes Eleanor gush like a teenager with her first crush.

I'm pulling into my long driveway when I remember I forgot to stop at Hansen's for supplies.

"Damn it." I glance at the clock on my dashboard. The store will be closed by the time I get back to town. I reach over and scratch behind Shadow's ears. "We'll have to make another trip tomorrow, won't we?"

I pull up next to Maren's SUV and climb out, unclipping Shadow's harness as he jumps down.

"Go on." I give him a gentle pat on his flank. "Take your before-dinner run. Work off some of that energy."

He takes off behind the house, disappearing into the trees without a sound. He'll be back in twenty minutes, tired and ready for dinner.

In the meantime, I head inside to help Maren with the evening rounds.

Chapter Three

Damien

I toss the bag with my burger onto the passenger seat and lean against the Range Rover, watching her ancient blue pickup disappear down the winding road in a cloud of dust. The sight of it vanishing around the bend sends an unexpected jolt of loss that carves itself into my ribs.

I hadn't planned on eating at the diner, but after what happened in the post office doorway, I needed time to think. To process. To figure out why the hell a simple glance and smile would affect me this much.

The moment she looked up at me, everything faded.

Gone.

Just her, standing there with blonde hair escaping from a messy knot and eyes that... *Christ.* Hazel with flecks of gold. I've been with beautiful women, stunning, perfect women who knew how to use their looks.

But this? This is different.

It's not only her beauty, though she's certainly that. It's something else entirely. Something that makes my chest constrict and my thoughts scatter like I'm some inexperienced teenager instead of a man who controls billion-dollar deals without blinking.

I've heard rumblings about the beautiful local wildlife vet and her infamous wolf, and glimpsed her silhouette in the rain a month ago, but seeing her up close was a shock I won't soon forget.

I'd been pushing through the door, my mind already on the evening's plans, when she appeared. For a heartbeat, we were suspended in the same space, close enough that I caught the scent of peaches and something uniquely her. Her eyes lifted to mine, startled, and that crooked smile curved her lips before she stepped aside, murmuring a soft apology I barely heard over the roar in my ears.

I should have said something. Apologized. Instead, I walked away without a word because another second in her presence and I might have done something that would have revealed what kind of man I am. The urge to reach out, to grasp those shimmering blonde strands and yank her head back until her eyes met mine, had been almost impossible to resist.

So I'd fled to the diner, ordering food I didn't want, positioning myself at the front window so I could watch the post office. Waiting. Needing to see her again with a desperation that makes no fucking sense.

When she exited with that massive wolf at her side, I couldn't look away. The way she handled an animal that outweighed her by at least forty pounds was...

Impressive doesn't begin to cover it.

Her beauty isn't conventional. It's raw, unpolished, and natural. And that light she carries—it's like she radiates something I can't name but yearn to touch. So contradictory to my own nature.

She possesses the kind of body that haunts dreams. Lean muscle beneath soft curves, strength wrapped in femininity. I curse myself for not studying her face longer, but now my mind conjures a different image—her descending to her knees, those mesmerizing hazel eyes never leaving mine, that crooked smile promising wickedness as she reaches for my belt. Her mouth enveloping me in wet heat, those perfect lips stretched taut, her throat working as she takes everything I have to give.

Fuck!

My ironclad self-control is the only thing that keeps me tethered to reality. No woman has ever shattered my carefully constructed facade with one look.

Until her.

My isolation is deliberate, my darkness born of a violent childhood and cultivated through years of hunting those who prey on the helpless. I don't form attachments, and I don't experience this instant, all-consuming obsession with people, least of all women who represent everything I'm not.

Yet here I stand, already imagining how I might draw her into my orbit, how her light might look when bathed in my darkness.

I want her.

Not merely in the physical sense, though that desire burns hot enough. I want to possess her spirit and mark her in ways that leave no room for escape.

I shift, my cock pressing against the zipper of my black pants. I've been semi-hard since I laid eyes on her. My mouth waters at the thought of how she'll taste—her skin, her cunt. Even her fear. Especially her fear. I want it all. Want to drown in it. And her.

The post office door swings open, and Eleanor Jenkins steps out, ruining my daydream and my erection.

She spots me, her weathered face breaking into a knowing smile that makes me want to get in my car.

"Well, now," she says, crossing the street. "Most folks don't watch empty roads unless they're expecting something."

I remove my sunglasses, studying her. I don't like most people, but there's something about this little old bitty that I find endearing. Maybe it's the way she doesn't flinch from my stare.

"She's quite something, isn't she?" Eleanor follows my earlier line of sight.

I keep my expression neutral. "Who?"

Eleanor snorts, a sound startlingly undignified from a woman her age. "Don't play coy with me, young man. I saw that little dance you two did at the door."

"I don't know what you mean."

"Luna Foster. Our local wildlife vet. Your new neighbor."

Luna Foster.

Her name is stunning. It's perfect. Wild and beautiful, like her.

"She seemed... distracted."

Eleanor's eyes narrow behind those ridiculous rhinestone glasses, less friendly than she was a few minutes ago inside the post office. "Luna's got a lot on her plate. She's the best wildlife rehabilitator in three states. That sanctuary of hers is more than a full-time job." She pauses. "Poor girl thinks you were rude. Said you nearly knocked her over and didn't even apologize." Her tone of disapproval is obvious.

Rude? She doesn't understand. I couldn't speak. Couldn't think. Could barely breathe.

"I was... distracted myself." An understatement, but the closest to the truth I'm willing to give her.

"I bet you were." Eleanor tilts her head. "I know that look."

"What look?"

"The look men get when they spot something wild they think they might want to tame." Her expression grows serious. "Word of advice, Luna Foster isn't tameable. Best remember that."

I bristle. Most people find me unreadable and intimidating, despite the affable billionaire persona I project in public. But Eleanor Jenkins isn't like most people. And she's wrong. I don't want to tame Luna. I want to possess her, wildness and all.

"I'm not interested in taming anything. I was merely observing." I brush some lint from my sleeve. "Neighborly interest. Her sanctuary borders my property."

"Mmhmm." Eleanor's expression betrays her disbelief. "Luna's special, Damien. That girl has more heart in her little finger than most folks have in their whole bodies."

"I would never suggest otherwise."

"You didn't have to. Men like you always have an angle. Especially with women who look like every man's fantasy."

The muscle in my jaw ticks at the thought of other men fantasizing about Luna.

She's mine.

Mine to take.

Mine to break.

The thought should disturb me, but it doesn't. It feels right. Natural. Like a fundamental truth.

I bury the fury, masking it behind a calm expression as I lift a curious eyebrow.

"Men like me? That's a rather swift character assessment coming from someone I've only met twice."

"Please. I've been reading people longer than you've been alive. You walk into a room like you own it, like you own everything in it, which you probably do in most places you go. Your reputation precedes you, Damien. You've got secrets written all over you." She squints up at me, crossing her arms. "The question is whether they're the dangerous kind or the brooding, mysterious kind that sells romance novels."

A dark chuckle escapes my lips. "Which have you decided I am?"

"Jury's still out. But I'll tell you this much. Luna has buried herself in her sanctuary for years, healing every broken creature that crosses her path. Girl's got a sixth sense about damaged things. She doesn't need to add a damaged man to her collection."

Her words strike a nerve. This woman has no clue how damaged I am. I let my gaze drift to the empty road, composing myself before looking back with a disarming smile.

"Eleanor, I assure you, my interest in Dr. Foster is purely neighborly."

She barks out a laugh. "Save that smooth talk for someone who might believe it. Though I must say, it works like a charm."

"Would Frank approve of your flirting with the mysterious newcomer?"

"Frank knows exactly who he married. Besides, he's secure enough not to worry about a handsome face." She gives me an appraising look. "And it is a handsome face, even with that scowl permanently etched onto it. Ever consider smiling occasionally? Might make you look less like you're plotting world domination."

"Perhaps I am."

"Well, do be a dear and spare the post office when you take over. I've just gotten the filing system the way I like it."

"What can you tell me about the sanctuary?" I'm curious, desperate even, for more information about Luna's life. "Sounds like a substantial operation for one person to manage."

"Luna's grandfather raised her out here after her parents died. Taught her more about animal behavior than most university professors know. Girl could track a deer through a blizzard by the time she was fifteen. Not that she'd ever shoot it, unless it was for mercy. He left it to her when he passed."

"She lives alone out there?" The edge in my voice surprises me. The sanctuary is remote and isolated. Anything could happen.

"Luna can handle herself. Why so interested? Planning a visit to see the wildlife?"

Something in her tone suggests she isn't talking about the animals. I straighten to my full height, rebuilding the careful walls that had slipped as I check my watch.

"As I said, neighborly interest. I should go."

"Don't forget about Elk Fest next month," Eleanor says as I turn toward my car. "Good opportunity to get to know those neighbors."

"I don't do festivals."

"Shame. Luna always has a wildlife education booth. She brings several animals from the sanctuary. Big draw for the kids." She starts back across the street, then pauses. "But I understand. A man planning world domination probably doesn't have time for a small-town festival."

I watch her go, amused by her tenacity. "Eleanor." She looks back, eyebrow raised. "What time is this festival?"

"Ten to four, both Saturday and Sunday. Luna's usually there by eight to set up." She lowers her head, meeting my gaze as she peers at me over the top of her glasses. "She's not what you'd expect, Damien. None of us in Aspen Ridge are. Small town doesn't mean simple people."

With that, she disappears, leaving me alone with thoughts I don't want to examine too closely. I pull out my phone, scrolling to the familiar contact.

Cade answers on the first ring. "Yes?"

He's at his desk in my Denver offices, looking every inch the polished, professional COO who runs my empire, not the man who disposes of my bodies.

"I need information. Luna Foster. Wildlife veterinarian. Complete background."

"Your neighbor?"

"Yes."

"Timeline?"

"Twenty-four hours." I pause. "I have something I need to do first, but I'll be finished up by midnight."

"I'll be on stand by."

"Update the list of targets in the immediate area." My fingers tighten around the phone. "I want to know if anyone's ever threatened Luna Foster or her sanctuary."

"Okay." There's suspicion in Cade's usually neutral tone, but I end the call before he can ask.

As I pull onto the main road, my hands steer themselves toward the longer route, the one that winds past the entrance to Sage & Summit Wildlife Sanctuary.

I need to see where she lives, to glimpse the world she's created. As the carved wooden sign comes into view, I slow, heart pounding with unexpected intensity. Down the long driveway, I can make out several buildings clustered together in a half-circle at the end. Somewhere in there, Luna Foster is tending to damaged creatures, making them whole.

I want to show her my darkness, wrap it around her like a cloak. In my fantasies, already vivid and insistent, she doesn't run from the monster I am. She recognizes it as the necessary counterpart to her own saving nature. The shadow that makes her light possible.

I accelerate past the entrance, gripping the steering wheel until my knuckles whiten.

The Morrison estate had been a strategic purchase. Isolated, with extensive land bordering the national forest, perfect for my other activities. I didn't come here for distractions, no matter how bewitching they might be. Getting entangled with a local veterinarian would be foolish at best, dangerous at worst.

But none of that matters now.

As I navigate the half-mile between our driveways, the memory of those hazel eyes and breathtaking smile lingers, taking root in my chest like something I can't shake.

Beautiful. Unstoppable. Transforming everything in its path.

Chapter Four

Luna

I kick off my shoes and collapse onto the sofa in my office, my body sinking into the cushions.

"You made it back in one piece, I see," Maren says without looking up from the computer, her fingers flying over the keyboard. Her long dark hair cascades around her shoulders now, freed from her earlier ponytail. "Eagle's resting. Gave him the pain meds on schedule."

"Thanks." I rub my temples, the tension of the day settling into my skull. "How are your boobs?"

"Ricky got me with his claws. At least it wasn't my nipple this time, but he's due for a nail trimming."

"How's the baby bobcat doing?"

She turns to face me, her expression darkening. "Still refusing to eat. Tried the new wet food blend you ordered. He looked at it like it was poison."

My heart sinks. "The psychological damage runs deeper than the physical."

"Those bastards beat and starved any hope of trust out of him. If I ever get my hands on the sick fucks who did that to him..."

"I'll hold them down while you use those perfectly manicured nails to scratch their eyes out." The bite in my voice catches me off guard, and something foreign shifts in my chest, sending my heart racing.

Where the hell did that come from?

Maren snorts, but her eyes light up with amusement. "Dr. Luna Foster advocating violence? Holy shit, I'm impressed. Maybe there's hope for you yet."

"I'm not advocating anything." The sofa's springs creak as I shift. The darkness in my thoughts feels too natural, too appealing. "I'm just tired and frustrated."

"It's been a long week." Maren leans back in her chair. "And it's only freaking Wednesday."

"I ran into the new owner of the Morrison place at the post office. Well, he ran into me."

She swivels to face me, interest sparking across her features.

"And? Is he the mysterious billionaire everyone's been gossiping about?"

"He definitely has that vibe."

"Hot?" The question comes with that mischievous grin I know all too well.

"We only passed each other in the doorway. He almost knocked me on my ass."

"That's not a no. How old is he?"

I shrug, even as my mind drifts back to those piercing eyes. "Hard to say. I didn't notice from our brief run-in, but Eleanor said he has some gray at his temples."

"Ooh, silver fox. Luna Foster's kryptonite."

"Older men are not my kryptonite."

"Tell that to your post-Caleb rebound. What was that guy? Like a hundred?"

I shoot her a scathing look as she leans back in her chair again. "In his late fifties somewhere. And he looked younger. I didn't know how old he was when I agreed to go home with him."

"Yeah, until you saw the pictures of his wife and grandkids on his fireplace mantel while he was railing you over the sofa."

"I had no idea he was married either. I don't fuck married men."

"Not on purpose."

"Maren!"

"What?" She shrugs. "If you want to bang married guys, go for it, but come to think about it, I never properly lectured you about that shitshow. I'm all for rebound dick, but you don't go to some random old guy's house after knowing him for two hours. That's how pretty girls end up in shallow graves. You make him spring for a nice hotel where you can call security if he goes all Silence of the Lambs on you and tries to 'rubs it with the lotion'."

"That's not even the right quote, you know."

"I made my point. Don't make me bury your stupid ass because you're thinking with your vag instead of your brain. I'll be pissed as hell at you."

"I'll come back to haunt you." My words are meant to tease, but I catch the vulnerability flickering in her eyes. Fear of abandonment—that's Maren's weakness, hidden beneath all the crude jokes, inappropriate sex humor, and bravado.

"Empty promises. But back to the billionaire, he's rocking that hot older guy vibe, huh?"

"I told you. I don't know. He has incredible eyes, though. Blue like the ocean after a storm."

"You're blushing!"

"I am not." I stand, shoving my feet back into my Skechers.

"Sure you're not," she says with a knowing chuckle. "And I'm the good little Catholic granddaughter Estella Rodriguez wishes I was."

I head for the door. "I need to check on the bobcat before dinner, then call Shadow in."

"His name is Titus, by the way." Maren turns back to the computer. "I named him this morning. He needed a strong name."

I pause, my hand on the doorframe, and turn back to her. "Titus. I like it. Want to stay for dinner? I've got leftover pizza and enough veggies to throw together a salad."

There's one mom-and-pop pizza shop in downtown Aspen Ridge, but it has pretty decent pizza for a hole in the wall. Aside from Nancy's Diner on Main Street, it's the only restaurant in town, other than a small Chinese place that opened a year ago. Family-owned by a couple from Boston, it's the only restaurant in the state that serves Polynesian-fusion Chinese food. I'm addicted to it. We get it at least twice a month.

"Hell yes to the pizza, hell no to the rabbit food." She's already back to typing. "Stop trying to make everything healthy. Carbs are to be enjoyed, not counted."

Though I've never needed to watch what I eat, Maren is very curvy and has struggled with fluctuating weight most of her life. But she's comfortable in her own skin and is so strikingly beautiful, with sultry brown eyes, chocolate brown hair, and a smile that stops men in their tracks, that she's never had an issue attracting them, as long as they can get past her potty mouth. JT, her current boyfriend of two years, adores her the way she is. And I love him for that.

She shoos me away. "Go check on your patients, Doc, and let me finish these notes before I forget what happened today."

The recovery den is quiet as I pull the small package of organic chicken liver from the fridge. It's not exactly pleasant to the human nose, but sometimes it's the only thing that tempts a reluctant eater.

"Hey there, Titus." I soften my voice as I approach his cage. Those intense eyes watch me from the back corner where he's huddled, wary and broken. "Maren tells me you're being stubborn about dinner." I crouch, keeping my movements slow. "We're not like those people. You can trust us."

The chicken liver makes a wet sound as I place it on the dish and slide it through the feeding slot. "This is the good stuff. No medicine, no tricks. Just food."

His nostrils flare—progress, maybe—but he doesn't move from his corner. The silence stretches between us, heavy with his fear and my hope.

"I'll leave you to think about it." I rise to my feet. "Nobody's going to force you to do anything here. That's a promise."

It's one I might not be able to keep much longer. If he doesn't start eating, we'll have to consider a feeding tube, but I want to give him every chance to choose.

As I turn to leave, a soft rustling behind me reaches my ears. When I glance back, Titus has moved forward, his body language less defensive as his nose twitches.

I'll accept small victories like that.

Darkness has settled over the sanctuary by the time I head out to get Shadow. The familiar gravel path crunches under my feet as I make my way toward the wolf enclosure by moonlight. He materializes from the shadows beside the fence.

"Hey, baby." I kneel and press my hand against his head. He nuzzles into my palm, warm and solid. "Did you enjoy your run?"

Though Shadow's not as large as wild wolves, he's still oversized for what most people would consider a pet. Not that he's domesticated. Wolves can't be. But he watches me with those intelligent eyes, like he understands every word I say. Sometimes I swear he does.

I scratch behind his ears as the tension of the day starts to ease. "You know what? I think Titus might eat tonight. He moved toward the food when I—"

Shadow's head tilts, his attention shifting away from me, toward the darkness beyond the trees. The growl starts low and builds in his chest, a sound that's pure animal. The vibration passes through my hand like a current and makes my skin come alive, raising every hair on my arms.

I push myself to my feet. "What is it, baby? Is there an animal out there?"

The other wolves are already settled in their den for the night, but Shadow's fur bristles along his spine, his entire body rigid. It could be anything out there—a mountain lion, a bear, or even a deer. But this isn't his typical response to forest sounds or animal movement. He's positioned himself in front of me, his concentration holding the razored edge reserved for threats that walk on two legs instead of four.

I peer into the darkness but see nothing except shadows and trees and the whisper of wind through branches. Still, the feeling creeps over my skin like ice water. That same feeling I felt on the street in town earlier. Like invisible eyes raking across my skin.

My heart hammers against my ribs. I've lived alone on this property for years, surrounded by wild creatures and constant forest sounds. I don't scare easily. But this isn't the rustle of nocturnal animals or the crack of settling trees.

This is different.

"Who's there?" My voice is steady, out of sync with my racing heart. "This is private property."

Silence only increases the uncomfortable sensation. Eyes in the darkness, watching me, raising goosebumps on my skin. Shadow maintains his protective posture, confirming I'm not imagining things. His growl deepens, and I trust his instincts more than my own.

"Come on, show yourself." My bravery surprises me. My hands are shaking, but anger overrides fear. "What do you want?"

Nothing.

Just wind through the trees and Shadow's continuous growling.

"This is stupid, standing here like bait," I murmur under my breath. I back away from the fence, my eyes never leaving the tree line. "Come on, Shadow. Time for dinner."

He hesitates, reluctant to abandon his vigil, but follows me along the fence line, keeping himself between me and whatever lurks in that darkness. My devoted protector.

"Good boy. Always looking out for me." I run my fingers through his thick fur as we head back to the house. The contact grounds me and reminds me I'm not alone.

I'm being paranoid. It's probably a curious bear or something.

But even as we walk away, I can't shake the feeling of those unseen eyes following my every step.

⸻ ◆ ⸻

Shadow and I slip through the front door of the main house, my fingers fumbling with the lock before I manage to secure it. I move to the front windows, drawing the curtains closed with more force than necessary.

I'm used to the symphony of the wilderness—branches creaking in the wind, the rustle of creatures moving through underbrush, and the occasional crack of a twig under a deer's hoof or mountain lion's paws. Hell, last week I watched a bear lumber down the driveway like he owned the place.

But even as I repeat this internal mantra, the prickly sensation between my shoulder blades refuses to fade. I'm hyperaware, every nerve ending on high alert. The adrenaline coursing through my veins refuses to abate as I smooth down the curtains.

Tonight, the familiar awareness of wildlife nearby has shifted into something else.

"Pizza's ready!" Maren's voice from the kitchen cuts through my spiraling thoughts, and I exhale a breath I didn't realize I was holding.

We head to the kitchen, Shadow rushing ahead of me, no doubt already calculating his chances of scoring some pizza out of her.

She'll cave. She always does.

Maren stands at the counter, sliding a cookie sheet from the oven where she's reheated our dinner. The kitchen is warm and bright, with the smell of pizza filling the air. Shadow lopes over to where Maren has already set out his dinner of raw meat beside the back door.

Before I reach the island, three feline shapes materialize around my ankles like furry little magnets.

"There are my other babies." I bend to stroke each one. The simple act of touching their soft fur calms me, pulling me back from the edge of the panic simmering under my skin.

Juniper, the largest with her long, fluffy gray coat, meows. Willow, slender and black with white paws and belly, leaps onto the counter. Sage, my tiny calico runt, presses against my leg, her purrs so loud they vibrate through my jeans.

"They've been absolute pains in my ass." Maren slides a plate of pizza toward me with a theatrical sigh. "Juni knocked over that stupid vase I keep telling you to move, but you ignore me like I'm talking to myself over here."

"What?" I scoop up the gray culprit, cradling her substantial weight against my chest. Juni kneads my shirt with her paws, her claws catching in the cotton. "You're not usually my troublemaker, baby girl. That's Willow's job." I shoot a pointed look at Willow, who's now sniffing Maren's wine glass. "Why are you being so naughty today?"

Juni responds by head-butting my chin with enough force to make me blink, her purr rumbling against my ribs. I nuzzle into her fluffy belly, breathing in, and the tension in my shoulders eases. "I think you're getting fatter, Juni. Has Maren been sneaking you extra treats?"

"Hey. I'm not the only one who gives her treats." Maren drops into a chair at the kitchen table and takes a generous bite of her veggie pizza. A string of cheese dangles from her lip, and she slurps it up with zero shame. "And yes, before you ask, I weighed her the other day. She's put on a quarter of a pound. Time to put the chunky monkey on a diet."

I grab my plate and settle at the table beside Maren, Juni still in my arms. The normalcy of it all—pizza, my animals, Maren's easy chatter—makes the fear lurking at the edges of my mind seem almost foolish.

"She's going to hate us for it, but you're right." I take a bite of my chicken and mushroom pizza and pick off a piece of the meat. Juni's eyes lock onto the morsel as I slip it to her under the table.

"That's exactly why she's turning into a furry bowling ball, you know," Maren says without looking up from her plate.

I shrug, not bothering to look innocent. "Oh, I gave Titus some liver. He seemed interested, at least."

"Progress. But should we plan for a feeding tube if he doesn't eat in the morning?"

I sigh. "Yeah, I think so."

She nods with a frown. She hates it when animals won't eat, and we have to help the process along. We both do.

"So, what had Shadow all worked up? I heard him growling when I walked over here."

The question brings the crawling sensation back, an almost tickling along my spine. I hesitate, unsure how to explain the odd feeling without sounding paranoid.

"Not sure. He sensed something in the woods. Probably something wild moving around."

"But?" She always knows what I'm not saying.

I take a breath, debating how much to say.

"It felt like someone was watching me. It was strange. Not just passing through or foraging, but deliberately... observing."

Maren's eyebrows shoot up. "Observing? That sounds ominous and a little creepy."

"It felt a little creepy at first, but then it felt different," I say, not wanting to alarm her because I'm probably imagining it. "We're so far out here that anything human would have to really want to be here, you know? It's not like someone's going to stumble onto the property by accident."

"True. We are in the middle of bum-fuck nowhere." Maren gestures toward the windows with her wineglass. "Too much effort for casual creeping. Unless it's those wolf poachers again, but they tend to be loud and obvious about it."

"It wasn't poachers." I hold out a piece of crust to Shadow. "This was quieter. More intentional. It was probably nothing. My imagination after a long day."

Maren studies my face for a moment, then a slow, mischievous smile spreads across her lips.

"Maybe you have a stalker. That could be kinda hot."

I choke on my bite of pizza and take a gulp of wine to wash it down. "Only you would immediately jump to that conclusion or find the idea of a stalker hot."

"What?" Maren gets up to grab another slice of pizza and the wine bottle. "I'm not talking about a creepy stalker, but a hot one, you know. The kind that makes your panties wet thinking about what he might do if he caught you out there in those dark woods?"

A strange sensation coils in my belly, and my pulse races for reasons that have nothing to do with fear. Being wanted with that kind of intensity—the sort that compels someone to lurk in the darkness, to memorize my movements, to make themselves invisible while making me the center of their universe—awakens something reckless in my core.

Sweat breaks out along my hairline and slides down my neck like fingertips against heated skin. "You're ridiculous."

"I'm just saying, if someone's going to watch me from the woods, I'd prefer it be someone who knows what to do when they make their move. Make the stalking worth both our times, you know?" She takes a sip of wine, unbothered by the outrageousness of what she's suggesting. "Like, if you're going to go through all that effort to creep on me, at least have the decency to be fuckable when you finally catch me."

A soft laugh slips out, even as my imagination fills with what she's describing. Strong hands, intense eyes, the thrill of being pursued.

Jesus, I'm losing it. I need to get laid.

"Though knowing your luck, it was probably Old Man Henderson looking for his goat again."

"Let's talk about something else. Did the lab results come back for Winston?" I redirect before she can elaborate further on her stalker fantasies. The last thing I need is more fuel for the inappropriate thoughts that have no business being in my head.

But Maren's grin only widens. She's filing this conversation away for future teasing. That's who she is—crude, direct, and shameless about turning every conversation toward sex. She's the only thirty-two-year-old woman I know with the dirty mind of a teenage boy.

It's also why I love her so much. Her irreverence, her ability to make even my darkest fears seem manageable through sheer audacity.

Willow jumps onto the table and sits beside Maren's plate, fixing her with reproachful eyes for not sharing. Sage has climbed onto Shadow's back, using him as her personal heated bed, and Juni's warm weight in my arms is comforting as Maren launches into an elaborate fantasy about what my hypothetical sexy stalker would do. She's fine with me being stalked as long as he's hot, and he pins me down and fucks me senseless when he catches me.

Why am I not surprised?

As I let her drone on, laughing at her absurdity, I can almost convince myself that whatever I felt out there was nothing more than my overactive imagination.

Almost.

Chapter Five

Damien

She enters the house, the door closing behind her and that wolf of hers. My entire body tenses, every sense heightened as she disappears from view. She felt me watching. Even before she called out, the subtle stiffening of her shoulders, the careful tilt of her head, and the deliberate slowness of her movements told me everything.

She felt my eyes on her.

The wolf sensed me first, and despite my efforts to stay hidden and the considerable distance between us, the animal knew my exact location.

Wolves are such remarkable creatures.

He didn't come rushing out to investigate. He stayed by her side, sensing the potential danger I posed to his owner. And make no mistake, I am a threat to her.

Be careful, Dr. Foster. Your guardian has good instincts.

I move closer while staying concealed within the trees that border her sanctuary. I pull up satellite imagery of her property on my phone, my eyes tracking each detail, committing buildings, enclosures, and camera placements to memory.

Amateur security.

The basic cameras, there only to track wildlife, cover the main buildings but leave blind spots I can bypass in my sleep. The tall fences might keep animals in, but they won't keep someone like me out. She needs a lesson in proper security.

Perhaps I'll give her one.

My mind once again drifts back to our encounter at the post office. The way she captured my attention felt like gravity reversing—sudden and inescapable. I went from being a man with a purpose to being a man with only one purpose.

Her.

Something primal within me recognizes her as mine, but the intensity of this possession is startling. I want to claim her like the wolf I've become through years of hunting. I've crossed too many lines and shed too much humanity to pretend I'm anything other than the predator she's awakened.

I've felt nothing resembling genuine emotion in so long that I forget what it feels like. I'm incapable of feeling anything more than the satisfaction of ownership. And I want to own her. Claim her. Brand her.

I check my watch, and my pulse kicks up with each passing minute as I wait for her vet tech to leave. The lights inside the house glow through curtained windows, each one hiding her private world from my view. A world I'm going to step into whether she invites me or not.

I don't have to wait long. Less than half an hour later, the door opens and both women step out onto the porch. Luna's hair is down now, spilling over her shoulders in waves. My hand curls into a fist. I can feel it already—those strands wrapped around my knuckles, silky and tight. Her on all fours, spine curved, and ass in the air. Pulling her head back as I thrust into her. That blonde hair giving me something to hold onto while I fuck her hard enough to make her voice break.

They embrace at the doorway. Luna's laughter drifts through the night air like a melody, and a hunger to be the one who coaxes that sound from her lips stirs in my chest.

She releases her friend, unaware of the wolf watching from the shadows. I'm not close enough to hear what they're saying, but her lips mouth the words, "thank you."

Her friend walks to her car, and Luna kneels next to her wolf, speaking to it with an intimacy I rarely witness between humans, let alone across species. Her hand scratches behind its ears, and it accepts her touch with a trust that seems absolute. It's distraction enough that the wolf doesn't sense me still here.

Invisible bands wrap around my ribs. I've spent my life studying predators, understanding their nature because I recognize it in myself. Yet Luna Foster handles this apex predator with a gentleness that would typically register as weakness to me. Instead, I see strength in it, a power of a different kind than I'm accustomed to wielding. It's this contradiction that calls to me. How can someone so soft survive in this world of teeth and claws? How has her light not been extinguished?

Luna and the wolf enter the house again as her friend drives away. The pain of losing sight of her is swift. Even in the dark of night, her light is like a beacon that calls to me. Perhaps it's how she embodies everything I'm not. Light to my darkness, mercy to my judgment, and healing to my destruction. The thought of corrupting that purity, of watching her light flicker and dance as I introduce her to my shadows, sends electricity racing up my spine, tightening every muscle.

The lights on the first floor turn off behind the curtains as I wait for Luna to head upstairs. My patience pays off when only her bedroom light remains, illuminating the oversized window on the second floor. A balcony runs the entire length of the front of the house, creating a roof for the porch below. It's strange to have a balcony with no door access.

The curtains are open, offering me a perfect view as Luna enters the room.

The hunter in me awakens, recognizing its prey. But it's different this time. I don't want to destroy her. I want to possess her.

This unfamiliar yearning is dangerous. Distracting. I should eliminate it and focus on my reason for buying the Morrison property. To hunt and kill without prying eyes. But as I watch her, I know I won't.

Can't.

Won't even try.

She approaches the window, her gaze sweeping the tree line, but I'm positioned far enough back that she can't see me. A cat sits in the window, and Luna's lips move, speaking to it before reaching for the curtains. She pauses mid-motion, pulling the fabric across the window but leaving a deliberate gap that feels like an invitation.

My breath snags as she undresses, peeling away layers with unhurried movements, unaware of her audience. Her skin glows in the soft lamplight, and I move closer, abandoning the trees to cross her yard as she turns and disappears through the door to a bathroom.

I wait for her to return with bated breath, the image of hot water sluicing over her pale skin nearly unbearable. Blood pounds in my ears, in my cock, turning everything into a dull roar. It takes all my self-restraint not to burst into her house, join her under that spray, and pin her to those tiles. Feel her wet and slick under my hands, and give her what's been building since the moment I laid eyes on her.

When she emerges, she's wrapped in a towel. She releases it, and the fabric drops to the floor. My throat goes dry. The glimpse of her nude body is brief—smooth skin, the dip of her waist, and the swell of her ass—before she pulls on a tank top. Then shorts that barely qualify as clothing. But it's enough to have my cock surging in my pants, hardening until the pressure becomes almost unbearable.

Fuck!

For the first time in my life, I'm hunting prey I have no desire to kill. In mere hours, she's become my obsession. Though every instinct honed through years of training screams at me to retreat, recalibrate, and regain control, I remain rooted to my spot, captivated by the woman who has somehow, without even trying, thawed something I thought permanently frozen within me.

As the light in her room turns off, plunging it into darkness, I force myself to turn away. I slip back into the trees, covering the short distance to my Range Rover, parked in a secluded turnout off the main road to the right of her driveway.

I want nothing more than to scale that balcony and watch her all night, but I have a target to kill.

⸺◆⸺

The first bead of blood wells and trickles in jagged red rivulets past Brixton's belly button.

My hands are steady after all the years of doing this. Still, every drop sparks something feral inside me, and a hot rush of sensation floods my veins. I lean closer, breathing in the metallic, coppery scent, and a shiver of excitement skitters down my spine.

I relish every involuntary flinch, every desperate whimper, every roll of his panic-stricken eyes, and the muffled screams vibrating through the duct tape that covers his mouth.

Social niceties were never my forte, but bodies—flesh, tissue, and bone—I understand. I excel at inflicting pain, torture, and punishment. After twenty-five years of delivering justice to monsters, I've mastered the art of retribution. The anticipation of each cut, each scream, feeds a hunger within me.

This basement is musty and damp, heavy with the scent of wet earth, blood, and death. I take a deep breath, savoring the stench that defines my sanctum of reckoning.

My target for tonight lies strapped to the metal table. He strains against the straps and duct tape that bite into his flesh, his muscles bulging like gnarled tree roots beneath skin slick with sweat. Panic burns bright in his eyes, the same wild fear that consumed him when he first opened them in this dank chamber to find my mask looming above him like death incarnate.

Tommy Brixton is a heinous monster, torturing cats and dogs on video and posting them to social media and dark websites. People think men like him are just evil and broken, some fuckup of DNA or a bad childhood. Sometimes they're right. Sometimes, though, it's not a mistake so much as the world's natural decline, the slow rot inherent in the very nature of the species itself. No therapist or priest will cure that. Only pain and vengeance can.

He's been pleading for mercy through the tape for the better part of an hour, eyes rolling, and snot bubbling out his nose. I ignore his pleas, drawing out his suffering, savoring every moment.

I want him to suffer like the animals he tortured. Every yelp, every cry, every ragged breath those innocent cats and dogs took with collapsing lungs—I want

Brixton to echo. I want him to see the world flickering away at the margins and know, without a doubt, that he deserves this.

I started his torture tonight with my mini blowtorch, using it on the soles of his feet, like he did to his victims, watching them blister and blacken under the intense heat. He bucked and writhed, screaming behind the duct tape, trembling at the edge of unconsciousness until he blacked out. I've revived him with smelling salts and the shock of my knife plunging into his gut.

I'm only getting started.

My phone rings, a harsh intrusion on my meticulous work, and I pull it from my back pocket with a sigh. I hate being interrupted. Cade's face flashes on the screen. I turn away from Brixton as I answer the call. Cade appears, dressed in his black fatigues, ready for cleanup.

"I'm not done yet."

My mask doesn't surprise him. I only remove it right before I take their sight, revealing my true face to them in their final moments.

"I'm heading up that way in a few, anyway. It'll take me almost two hours to get there."

I glance over my shoulder at Brixton, the ten-inch knife plugging the hole it created in his stomach, blood seeping through the edges of the wound and onto the handle.

"Why not bring the chopper? It's the middle of the night, and I'm in the middle of nowhere. That's why I bought this place."

Cade steps into the private executive elevator at my Denver headquarters. "Yes, but animals are sensitive to vibration and sound, and the wildlife sanctuary is only half a mile away. We don't need to attract any attention at this time of night."

A shiver of excitement runs through me at the mention of Luna and her sanctuary, so close to my own.

Only mine is one of suffering, not healing.

"Let me fucking get back to it so I'm done by the time you get here. You're throwing off my entire goddamn rhythm."

I end the call before Cade can respond, a habit he's grown used to over the twenty-five years he's been by my side. Longer than anyone else has survived in my world. Trust is a luxury I can't afford, but Cade has earned it with blood and silence. Almost ten years my senior, he's the only one who knows I live for this. The only one who understands the depth of my mission, who sees beyond the CEO facade to the predator beneath.

I turn back to Brixton, stepping up beside the table, my heart pounding with anticipation. He lifts his head, chest heaving, and I can almost taste his fear.

"Now, where were we?"

His wide, frantic eyes follow my movement as I wrench the blade from his abdomen. Blood sprays upward, splattering my clothes and mask with shiny droplets. He screams, and the raw, panicked sound vibrates through my bones like a drumbeat of triumph.

More blood flows from the wound, forming spiderweb-like patterns across his pale skin. The wound isn't fatal. I've avoided vital organs. He doesn't get a fast death. That would defeat the purpose.

My mini blowtorch hisses to life again, a blue flame dancing across the gaping hole, sealing seared flesh with a muffled sizzle. Brixton's whole body convulses, spasms rippling down his torso as his eyes flutter. Strangled curses tear from his throat, fighting against the tape that seals his mouth. His head whips from side to side, plastering slick strands of sweaty hair across his forehead.

"Tommy." I let his name roll off my tongue, a chilling prelude to the events about to unfold. "I'm sure you're wondering who I am and why you're here."

His eyes, wide, black pools, drown in panic. His fingers, bound at his sides, claw at nothing as his body shudders with each fractured breath.

I switch back to my trusted knife, drawing the blade along the inside of his elbow, severing tendons in one smooth cut. The flesh parts like silk, the subtle give under the steel sending a thrill up my arm. His body arches off the table, thrashing so violently I have to brace him with my knee. Each muted shriek feeds the electric thrill coursing through me.

The concrete walls seem to pulse with the history of this place. Forty years ago, another monster stood in this same space. His victims were innocent. Mine are not. I'm aware of the irony—a killer living in a killer's house. But we're nothing alike.

My darkness adheres to a code and burns with righteous fire. It serves a purpose. Every life I take balances scales that the law abandoned.

I move around the table to his right thigh, and the knife slips in with little resistance. My strokes are steady and measured. I savor every millimeter of red opening beneath my blade. I taste it on my tongue—the metallic tang of retribution. His muffled screams grow weaker as tears streak down his cheeks.

The human body is such a fragile thing, held together by skin and a vast network of muscles and nerves. It's so easily breached.

I pause, my fingers slipping beneath the mask to wipe sweat from my brow.

Once more, I cauterize the cuts with the blowtorch, the sharp smell of burning flesh stinging my nose. My heart thunders, and I tilt my head, watching his convulsions with perverse delight.

I'm not a sadist. Not in the clinical sense. I don't get off on pain. But watching monsters break—watching them realize, cell by cell, that judgment exists beyond badges and gavels—there's satisfaction in that.

Brixton's eyes search mine through the mask's eyeholes for a trace of mercy, but he won't find any. I show no mercy to my victims. The same way they showed no mercy to theirs.

I drive the knife into his chest; the resistance of skin, muscle, and cartilage is a little bit of a nuisance as the blade plunges through his right lung with a sickening squelch. A violent jerk racks his body, his eyes bulging with shock, and he gasps, a single, shuddering inhale that rattles the metal table beneath him. The high-pitched hiss of air escaping around the blade reminds me of a punctured bicycle tire.

The duct tape over his mouth balloons out with each failed attempt to draw air, then sucks back against his lips. His nostrils flare wide, working overtime, but it's not enough. The wheeze from the wound is music, a sound that grows more frantic with each passing second.

"Not so easy to breathe now, is it? Now you know how scary it was for those animals, fighting for every breath." I lean closer, savoring the wet, sucking sound that accompanies each failed breath. "That's it. Fight for it. Feel the fear, Tommy."

I twist the knife handle to widen the wound. Fresh crimson spills across Tommy's skin, pooling in the hollow of his collarbone.

"Do you know what happens when a lung collapses? The air that should go into your lungs is now filling your chest cavity. Pressing against your other organs."

He's fading, pupils dilating as his oxygen-starved brain begins to shut down. It's time to end it.

Before I shove the knife into his left eye, I raise my mask and let him see my face, the last face he'll ever see.

"My name is Damien Wolfe, Tommy. And I'm your judge, jury, and execution-er."

Chapter Six

Luna

"This poor girl's been living on nothing but scrub brush."

I run my hands along the goat's ribs, each one protruding through her dull, matted coat as I rub the medicated salve on her skin irritations. The months of neglect are written across her body like a heartbreaking story.

"Her owner claimed she was 'fine' when animal services showed up."

Maren adjusts the IV line, delivering much-needed nutrients and antibiotics. "Yeah, I've got a few choice words for Mr. Anderson's definition of 'fine.'" Her voice drips with fury. "Like how feeding an animal only three times a week and never cleaning their living space somehow equals responsible ownership."

I bite back the surge of anger that always comes when facing cases like this. It's not the violent rage I have toward true abusers. This is more like a slow burn of frustration edged with disgust. Mr. Anderson wasn't evil, just negligent and ignorant. Still, this sweet goat's condition makes my teeth grind together.

"At least he surrendered her willingly when Deborah explained the situation," I say, trying to find some good in the mess.

As one of our first sanctuary volunteers, Deborah is constantly on the lookout for instances of mistreatment and neglect. She has a unique talent for convincing owners to surrender animals they otherwise wouldn't, with a finesse I lack. As Maren often reminds me, my emotions can get the better of me, despite my calm nature. But Deborah has single-handedly helped rescue dozens of animals before neglect turned into something worse.

"True. But I still want to kick his ass." Maren checks her cracked, overgrown hooves. "This girl's got good bones under all this poor condition. With Dr. Foster's tender care and more than enough food for her belly, she'll be fine."

Gertie, as we've named her, tolerates our attentions with surprising calm. She's probably just grateful for gentle hands and real food. I stroke her neck, feeling the way she leans into the contact, starved for affection as much as proper nutrition.

"I didn't tell you about my drive up this morning, did I?" Maren applies salve to an angry-looking sore.

"No. What happened?"

"There was a freaking antelope in the middle of Devil's Gulch Road, holding up traffic. That's why I was twenty minutes late."

"Was it hurt?" I check Gertie's IV site, but I don't know why I bother. Maren is a master of IV placement.

"No. Just taking a stroll."

"Well, at least he wasn't hurt."

"But he was holding up traffic, Lu. He can't do that on narrow two-lane roads."

"I think he can do whatever he wants."

Maren scoffs. "Of course, you'd take his side."

"I think we're done for now." I pull off my gloves and step back from Gertie, who looks better than when we started. "She'll need the same treatment regimen for another week, but she'll be okay. Let's put her in the recovery den for the night, and then we can move her to the deer enclosure tomorrow. She and Buttercup can share for a day or two."

I smile, satisfied with another successful treatment. This is what grounds me. The healing and the purpose. The tangible good I can do in the world. Everything else is noise.

Once she's settled with a bowl of water and a mineral block, I roll my neck to work out the kinks. Maren's hands on my shoulders, digging into the knots that formed in the last two hours, draw a long, low moan out of me.

"Hey now, no moaning allowed when my man's out of town. You know what that does to me."

I snort out a laugh as her firm hands trace my spine, pressing all the right spots, and I swear my knees almost buckle. "You staying up here tonight since he's gone?"

"I can't. I promised Estella I'd come for dinner. I haven't seen her in a week because she was away at a church retreat."

"Oh, no. She's always a little wacky when she gets back from one of those."

"Yeah, I know. You want to come with me so I don't have to listen to a two-hour lecture about how I'm going to burn in hell for living in sin with JT before marriage?"

"My being there won't stop her from lecturing you."

"No, but she'll spend at least half the time fretting over your failure to find a good Catholic boy to marry."

Maren hits a spot on my right shoulder that makes my eyes roll back. "I'm not Catholic."

"And that's why you're gonna burn in hell, too. But at least we'll be together. So you wanna come? She's making spinach enchiladas."

"Why didn't you lead with that? Hell yeah, I'll come."

Maren looks relieved. As much as she loves her grandmother, Estella Rodriguez can be a handful. But she took me under her wing when I met Maren in college. Without the two of them, I wouldn't have made it through losing Grandpa. I love her as much as I love Maren.

"Come on." I step away from the massage even though it's the last thing I want to do. "Let's do final rounds before calling it a day. Do you think Estella will let us make margaritas?"

"Not if Dr. Luna is driving home later. But that doesn't mean we can't have a couple before we go."

⋅•◦•⋅

When I get back from dinner, I'm stuffed and tired and properly lectured for still being single. Thirty-two is considered nearing spinsterhood according to Estella.

She sent me home with enough leftovers for three days. I check on Gertie, who's resting comfortably, and head toward the house.

A shiver runs down my spine. The unsettling sensation of being watched creeps over me again, like an icy wave. I pick up the pace, and as soon as I'm inside, I lock the door and check the windows before closing all the curtains on the first floor.

I'm greeted by Shadow and the girls, each of them demanding attention after I dared to leave them alone for over three hours. I drop to the floor and cuddle them all, glad for their presence, especially Shadow. He'll keep me safe from the eyes in the woods.

Juni tries to open the pan of enchiladas with her paw before I swat her away.

"Don't even think about that, missy. You'll explode in the litter box if you try to eat that."

I put the food in the fridge and double-check the back door lock before turning off all the lights and heading upstairs to take a shower. The warm water feels good after the day I've had, and I don't get out until it cools. I slip into a tank top and some sleep shorts before walking to the window, my body heavy with exhaustion. I glance outside, my eyes scanning the treeline. Juni jumps up onto the windowsill, and I pet her as I search for any movement. I know something or someone is watching me again.

I know it.

The darkness beyond the glass seems alive somehow, watching and waiting. A rational part of my brain urges me to lock the window and close the curtains. Instead, I again leave them open, with a wider gap than last night. A small act of defiance against the fear, or perhaps an acknowledgment of the strange, curious thrill that accompanies it.

I glance at Shadow's bed in the corner. It's empty. He must be curled up in the one beside the fireplace. I leave the door cracked in case he wants to come in during the night, then I climb into bed. Willow curls against my side while Sage nestles at my feet. Juni remains in the window, her silhouette alert against the moonlight. Does she sense what I sense? This invisible presence that seems to press against the glass?

I close my eyes, but sleep feels impossible. The darkness beyond my window pulses with secrets I'm not sure I'm brave enough to uncover. Yet I lie, curtains open, as if inviting whatever watches to come closer.

I adjust the pillow beneath my head and try to relax. Minutes pass, but sleep still doesn't come.

I shift beneath the covers, but the damage is done. Maren's teasing keeps echoing in my ears, overshadowing the fear that's brewing inside me. My body responds to the illicit idea of someone watching me, my skin warming, and a low hum of longing stirring in my abdomen.

When was the last time I had a good fuck? Over a year, at least. Not since that one-night stand Maren reminded me of last night.

My work at the sanctuary fills my days, but my nights? My nights are empty.

I stare at the ceiling, tracing the shadows with my eyes. This is insane. The idea of a stranger stalking me and taking me shouldn't turn me on this much, but my body doesn't care about logic. I'm aware of each breath and each subtle shift of the sheets as I move, and it sends ripples of sensation across my sensitized skin.

I close my eyes and let my fingers slip beneath my tank top. My palm cups my breast, thumb brushing over the taut peak in the center, until a faint moan slips out. The fingers of my other hand drift beneath the waistband of my shorts, tracing the hollow of my stomach. The movement is slow and teasing, an echo of hands I imagine pressing into my flesh. Goosebumps erupt along my skin.

My fingers find that sensitive bundle of nerves, and I circle my clit in small strokes. My back arches as an answering wave ripples through me. There's no face to the stranger in my head, only eyes the color of storm-driven seas, the promise of strength in each slow touch.

I part my thighs and sink a finger inside, the slick slide sending a shock through my core. I add another, winding my hips into a steady rhythm, pressing against my own hand as if he were here with me. In my mind, the faceless man settles his weight on me. Strong hands on my hips, lips at the nape of my neck, trailing fire across my collarbone, a body pressing mine into soft sheets.

I roll my nipple between my fingers. My body hums in response, the tension coiling tighter with each flick and roll of my fingers.

I whisper into the darkness, "Come for me," as though he might step out of the shadows to claim me.

Silence fills the room save for the slick slide of flesh and the harsh rasp of air through my throat. The sensation consumes me, and my breath hitches. I sink my teeth into my lip to trap the sound, but Willow skitters away. She knows.

My walls shudder, and a single gasp tears free as I tumble over the edge in an explosion of warmth. Stars burst behind my closed lids, every nerve ending singing.

For a moment, the world outside vanishes—the sanctuary, the animals, Maren's jokes. There's only this. Me, my pulse pounding, and the hollow aftermath of pleasure that leaves me trembling in the quiet.

Chapter Seven

Damien

"That's it, beautiful, come all over my cock."

The words escape my lips as I erupt, my vision blurring as thick ropes of come splash onto Luna's window. I watch her fall apart so fucking beautifully beneath her covers, rocking and writhing in sync with the movements of her fingers. Hips lifting off the bed, her thighs trembling, and her mouth falling open as pleasure rolls through her in waves.

This private moment belongs to me now.

The splashes of viscous, milky ejaculate slip down the glass as my thighs tremble. My cock jerks in my hand, my fingers shaking around my shaft as the last of my orgasm fades. My vision clears, and I see the cat sitting in the window, watching me with unblinking eyes.

A witness to my depravity.

I meant only to peek in the window and watch her sleep for a few minutes. Her open curtains were an invitation I couldn't resist. But imagine my surprise when I climbed up the side of her porch, onto the balcony, looked between those open curtains, and found her with her fingers buried in her cunt.

I give my cock a few last jerks, debating whether I should wipe the window, but I decide against it. It's my gift for her, a token of my obsession. When she looks out her window again tomorrow, she'll find proof of my desire.

Let her wonder what it is and how it got there. She's brilliant from what I've seen and heard of her so far. She'll figure it out.

The only question is, will it frighten her to know someone was outside her window, someone who left their come on the glass while watching her?

Or will it thrill her?

My eyes return to Luna as her hips lower to the bed and she throws her arm above her head, gasping for air. What was she thinking about as she touched herself? Was she picturing me, her billionaire neighbor she ran into yesterday?

My thoughts are so vivid, I can almost touch them. Her yielding to me, melting under my hands, begging me to claim her, to show her how completely I can consume her. I imagine her pleading, thighs wrapped around my hips, nails digging into my back as I fuck her. Rough and hard and deep, stealing her breath and her voice as she screams herself hoarse, coming on my cock over and over. There's no gentleness. Only punishing, unrelenting need. Fucking at its most primal as I claim her until she surrenders to me, offering me her life along with her body.

Fuck! I'm getting hard again thinking about it.

My gaze lingers on her for a few more minutes, not wanting to leave. She's panting, her breasts rising and falling under that little scrap of fabric she considers a top, her arm still thrown over her eyes.

Then she rolls onto her side, facing away from the window, pulling the sheets around her. My hands grip the window frame. I want to tear through the glass, shred those sheets, rip that fabric off her skin, and bury myself inside her.

I could watch her forever, but I pull myself away. As I land on the ground in front of the porch, I spot Luna's wolf watching me through the front window. He growls, the sound vibrating the glass, but he stops short of howling and doesn't alert his mistress to the man who watched her come apart by her own hand. We regard each other with mutual recognition, two predators acknowledging each other. I allow him his territory for now. Soon enough, he'll understand that Luna belongs to me.

I slip into the woods, the dense trees welcoming me back into the darkness as my phone vibrates in my pocket. It's Cade. He's the only one who has this number.

"Report."

"Background check complete on Luna Foster."

"You're four hours late."

"Cleanup last night took longer than normal. You left quite a mess."

"Fucker deserved it. Now give me the info on Luna."

"Thirty-two years old, wildlife rehabilitator for the past five years. Attended CSU Fort Collins for undergrad and D.V.M. doctorate. Inherited the sanctuary land when her maternal grandfather died during her second year of residency. Clean record, pays her taxes on time, no significant debt besides a fifty-thousand-dollar mortgage on the property for which she used the proceeds to expand the sanctuary two years ago, and a little over one hundred thousand in student loans. Payments are in deferment status until next year."

I navigate through the underbrush. "And before? Family history?"

Cade pauses. "Orphaned at ten. Parents died in a pedestrian bridge collapse outside a Celtic festival in Wyoming. She survived only because her father's body broke her fall. She was hospitalized in the ICU for several weeks with a broken arm, broken collarbone, two broken legs, and a brain bleed. Two years of intensive rehabilitation. After recovery, she lived with her grandfather, an eccentric wildlife photographer, until college."

Fuck! I almost lost her before I even found her.

"Anything else? What about men?"

The question sends fire through my veins. I picture gutting every man she's been with, every bastard who dared lay hands on her skin.

"A couple of high school boyfriends. Nothing serious. Appears she lost her virginity on prom night junior year."

Hot, quick rage surges through me.

"What's his name?" I grit my teeth, failing to appreciate the modern technology that allowed Cade to gather this intel, despite it being my primary business.

"Billy Smith."

"Smith? Are you fucking serious? Where is he now?"

"Joined the Navy after high school graduation. Currently stationed in Guam. Married with two kids."

Fuck! That means I can't kill him. I don't like to leave children orphaned, unless their parents are pieces of shit abusers, and their kids are better off without them.

I want to tear Billy fucking Smith's throat out for being the first to touch Luna, but all that matters is that no other man but me will ever touch her again. I halt in my tracks as that fundamental truth takes root inside me.

Luna Foster is mine.

"Any others?"

"A couple of hookups in college, but no serious boyfriends that I could find. After she opened the sanctuary, she dated a Caleb Hunter for two years but broke it off last year when he became abusive. There's a current restraining order in place."

"He laid his fucking hands on her? What kind of abuse?"

Now, Caleb Hunter, I will kill. Without batting a fucking eye, even if he's Mike fucking Brady from the Brady Bunch.

"One hospital visit with a couple of broken ribs and several bruises a few times before she kicked him to the curb. He only seemed to become abusive later in their relationship, after developing a cocaine problem."

"Where is he?"

"That's the million-dollar question. After Dr. Foster ended things, he lost his job, reputation, law license, and went off the grid. No technological presence for over a year. No credit cards, no banking, no phone. Nothing. I'll keep looking."

"Find the fucker, Cade."

"Damien, remember your code. Only those who deserve it."

"He fucking deserves it."

"Damien—"

"We're done talking about this. Anyone else?"

Cade sighs. "A one-night stand a month after she ended things with Hunter. He was fifty-nine and married. She hasn't seen or spoken to him since."

"I want all their details, every fucking one of them, uploaded to my private server."

"Damien, I won't help you kill every man who has ever touched Luna Foster."

"I don't need your assistance, Cade, just the information. Now what about the abusers?" I need an outlet for my rage. "Any locals?"

"I've identified eleven individuals who've been reported for animal abuse in the county in the last six months. The most recent is Daryl Rawlings, age forty-one. Three prior arrests for animal cruelty, released each time with minimal consequences. Latest victim was…" He hesitates, and I know what he's going to say. "A shepherd mix found starved and beaten. Local authorities issued only a fine."

Daryl Rawlings has become my next kill.

"Dr. Foster nursed him back to health a few months ago, and a family in Platteville with a menagerie of animals adopted him. They're frequent fosters for Luna and often keep the animals she sends their way."

Of course, she finds the best homes for her damaged souls.

"Rawlings frequents the Broken Antler Bar most evenings. Lives alone on an isolated property three miles northeast of town. I've sent the details to your secure server, along with the information on the other ten subjects."

"He's next on the list. Have any of them threatened Luna?"

"A few. Though she's well-liked and respected in the community, she's not favored by the local abusers."

One more reason they deserve to die.

"Pay off her mortgage and student loans tomorrow. Make sure it can't be traced back to me."

"Done."

"Now find me Caleb Hunter."

I end the call, then stop at the forest's edge and glance back at Luna's house one last time, though it's too distant to see.

What is it about her that draws me so powerfully?

Is it her gentleness with creatures others would fear or discard? The hint of hidden pain behind her smile? The way she moves through the world as if she believes in its essential goodness, despite evidence to the contrary?

Perhaps it's all of those things. Or maybe it runs deeper, a crack in her that matches the fractures inside me. Something in her calls to my darkness, not to shy away from it, but to recognize it as a necessary counterpoint to her light. I want to surround her with my shadows until she understands their power and protection. I want to watch her eyes as she realizes that true freedom comes not from hiding from the monsters, but from belonging to one.

Tomorrow, I'll hunt for her and remove one of the stains from her world. But tonight, I carry the image of her pleasure with me, the sound of her ecstasy on her lips through the thin glass, and the beauty of her face as she came.

My beautiful Luna, so unaware of the wolf who now has her in his sights.

Chapter Eight

Luna

"Y ou hoo... You up yet?"

Maren's voice comes from the hallway, and I almost drop my towel. It's not even seven, for crying out loud. I cinch my robe around my waist as steam from my shower still clings to the bathroom mirror behind me. Three raps echo against my bedroom door, and I step out of the bathroom as it swings open.

"I hope you're decent, babe. But honestly, if you're not, that's fine by me, too." Maren's grin is audible in her voice as she strolls in uninvited. "Half the freshman class at CSU got an eyeful during rush week, anyway. What's one more peek between besties?"

"Are you ever going to let me live that down?"

"Not until the day I die. Maybe not even then." She drops onto my bed with theatrical flair, making Willow hiss in displeasure. "I might even have it put on my headstone: 'Here lies Maren Rodriguez, best friend of Luna Foster, infamous streaker of rush week.'"

"Why are you here so early?"

"JT called wanting some morning video sex. I couldn't go back to sleep. So, I grabbed you a Starbucks on my way up. It's on the kitchen counter, but you'll probably need to nuke it."

The drive from Estes Park to Aspen Ridge takes thirty minutes on a good day, longer when the mountain roads decide to be temperamental. In the winter, the road often closes because of snow, isolating Aspen Ridge and its five hundred and twelve residents from the rest of civilization.

"You didn't have to do that."

I pull open my dresser drawer and grab a bra and underwear.

"Course I did. You helped me fend off Estella last night. I owe you one. Maybe ten."

Maren's been my best friend and the sister I never had since we met at CSU Fort Collins. I attended because they have one of the top three veterinary doctorate programs in the country. We were both fish, wildlife, and conservation biology majors, our love for animals apparent even back then. I went on to veterinary school, and she earned her accreditation and became certified as a vet tech, but she's almost as knowledgeable and skilled as I am.

She's the only vet tech within a hundred miles willing to make the drive up here. I've given her one of the bedrooms, and she often spends weeks living here during the winter.

"Yeah, you do owe me. She was pretty rough on me last night." I grab a pair of scrubs from the closet.

"You and me both." Maren shimmies across the bed, closer to Willow and Sage. "Morning, my lovelies."

Sage melts under her attention, purring as Maren scratches under her chin. Willow, however, fixes her with a death glare. She's my cranky cat and doesn't appreciate having her beauty sleep interrupted, even by her second favorite human.

"Are we releasing Buttercup today?" Maren ignores Willow's obvious annoyance as she continues petting and snuggling her against her will.

"Yeah." My voice cracks on the word. "It's time to set her free."

Three months ago, Buttercup was hit by an SUV, badly fracturing her right hind leg. The driver had stopped and called animal services. She followed Roger when he brought her to us, crying the entire time about how sorry she was. It took weeks of careful treatment and months of rehabilitation to get the doe back to full health.

"That's great news." Maren's voice goes soft with understanding, and she meets my eyes over Willow's twitching ears. "She's been asking for it. I saw her pacing in her enclosure yesterday like she was planning a jailbreak."

"Wild animals always know when they're ready. She's been watching the tree line for days now, wanting to get back to her territory."

Deer need their freedom, their natural habitat, and their herds. Keeping her longer than necessary would be cruel, even if saying goodbye will break my heart.

Willow swats Maren's hand away and jumps off the bed. "I'll keep the wolves in their enclosure, then. So they can't track her scent and follow her."

"Thanks."

I head toward the bathroom to change, leaving the door cracked. Privacy between Maren and me went out the window years ago. As I pull my hair into a ponytail and brush my teeth, my mind drifts back to last night.

What does it say about me that my fear of someone watching me from the woods drove me to leave my curtains open and get myself off at the thought of it?

Not that I ever need to close my curtains. I live on an isolated property in the Colorado mountains, with my nearest neighbor a half-mile away. No one can see the sanctuary or any of its buildings from the road, so I could leave the curtains open and prance around naked in front of them, and no one would know.

Not that I'd do that. But I could.

But for the past two nights, I know I felt someone watching me, eyes piercing the darkness beyond my window. Last night, my fear curdled into desire, a per-verse longing that sparked heat between my thighs. A hunger that left me aching.

I need therapy. Seriously. There's something wrong with me.

"Hey, Juni bug." Maren's voice carries from the bedroom. "Are you sunning yourself in the window, pretty girl? Wait a hot minute. What in the actual fuck is this?"

I spit out my toothpaste, wiping my mouth with the back of my hand. "What's what?"

I walk out of the bathroom to see Maren leaning close to the window, the curtains wide open, her forehead crinkling.

"There's some kind of... something on your window." Maren peers closer, then turns to me with wide eyes. "On the outside of the glass. It's all streaky and white, and frankly, Luna, it looks suspiciously like come."

I grab a pair of socks and my Sketchers from the closet. "You're insane."

"I'm not kidding! Come see for yourself." She beckons me over. "This looks like premium grade A jizz if I've ever seen it. And honey, I've seen plenty."

"It's probably bird shit." I sit on the chair beside Shadow's empty bed. He must have bolted when Maren made her grand entrance. "Or tree sap. We're surrounded by forest."

"Lu, I know what bird shit looks like. And this is not avian in origin. I also know what jizz looks like." There's a hint of amusement in her voice now. "How did you get male ejaculate on your second-story bedroom window? Did your stalker bring a ladder and climb onto the balcony? Is he out there every night cranking one out while watching you sleep like some perverted Peeping Tom?"

"I worry about where your mind goes sometimes."

I walk to the window, and there it is. Unmistakable white, filmy streaks coating the glass in a haphazard pattern. Long, thick trails that catch the morning light.

"I told you it looks like come," she says with a laugh before scooping up a protesting Juniper. "Come on, pussies, time for breakfast." She heads toward the door. "Oh, and Lu, that's one thing I'm not helping you clean up."

After she leaves, I stand frozen, staring at the streaks on the glass. Could someone have been out there?

No. That's crazy.

The rational part of my brain screams that it's impossible. But as I trace one of the white streaks with my fingertip, I can't shake the memory of how aroused I got. How hard I came from just imagining an elusive, watching presence taking me in the dark.

What if he came to my window, watched me, and ejaculated on it?

What kind of sicko would do that?

"Ricky, come on, buddy. You have to leave my boobs alone."

I pull the raccoon's hands away from my chest for what feels like the hundredth time. Checking his back paw should have taken five minutes, but here we are, locked in this ridiculous battle of wills where he's determined to cop a feel and I'm equally determined to maintain some semblance of professional dignity.

He chitters at me, his dark eyes gleaming with what I swear is mischief. He's been pawing at my breasts since the moment I took him out of his cage, and I'm starting to wonder if he's doing it on purpose to mess with me. His fingers are dexterous and persistent, and every time I move his hands away, he goes right back to his favorite target.

Behind me, Maren snorts as she enters the main exam room. I don't have to turn around to know she's wearing that shit-eating grin of hers.

"Don't you hate it when you have to fend off a raccoon's advances in the morning?" Her voice drips with amusement. "Though I gotta say, Luna, at least you're getting a little action."

Ricky chooses that moment to make another grab for my left breast, and I have to twist away from him while still trying to examine his injured foot.

"Ricky!"

I catch his hand. This raccoon has become my most challenging resident, and not because of his medical needs.

I've never encountered a raccoon with such a specific fascination with women's breasts. Having to handle all his care so he can't assault any of the female volunteers is becoming a chore, but the liability alone of letting him loose on them would probably shut us down. The only reason Maren tolerates his wandering paws is because I have enough dirt on her to ensure her cooperation. Estella would have a heart attack if she knew what her precious little Maren was really like.

"Speaking of action..." Maren crosses to the sink to wash her hands. "Have you figured out yet what that weird shit was on your window this morning? Looks like someone had a really good time watching you sleep. Might be kind of hot if you've got yourself a sexy stalker. Better than the dating apps."

My hands freeze on Ricky's foot. I've been thinking about it all morning. It really did look like come, but how is that even possible?

Ricky takes advantage of my stillness to investigate the collar of my scrubs, his fingers working their way under the fabric. I bat his hands away without taking my eyes off his paw.

"Right at eye level too." Maren dries her hands on a paper towel, then moves to the supply cabinets. She yanks open the top drawer, metal instruments clinking as she rummages through them. "Either you've got yourself an admirer, or someone's got really weird taste in places to jerk off."

"Maren, if I have a stalker masturbating outside my bedroom window, that's not a good thing. It's a very bad thing. I'll have to start sleeping with Grandpa's shotgun next to me at night."

Ricky seems to interpret my distraction as permission to explore. He grabs a loose thread on my scrub top and tugs. I intercept his fingers and redirect them to his own grooming.

"Eh, you always have to ruin my fun." Then, a frown creases her forehead, her eyes reflecting a hint of worry. "It's kinda creepy though, isn't it?"

"Yes."

"Maybe you should call Sheriff Mills."

"And say what? I found what I think is ejaculate on my bedroom window? She'll think I'm working too hard and need to get dicked down properly."

"Well..." Maren draws out the word with a meaningful look as she crouches, pulling open a lower cabinet door to check inventory. "She wouldn't be wrong."

"Don't start." I point at her while keeping one hand on my furry groper.

"You could always tell her you've been getting this feeling lately, like someone's watching the house. Why don't you start there?"

"Because it's crazy. I've lived up here alone for how long, and now someone starts watching me? What the hell for?"

Ricky's attention shifts to my stethoscope, dangling from my neck. He grasps it with both hands and gives it an experimental tug, trying to pull me toward him.

When I resist, he abandons the stethoscope and makes another lightning-fast grab for my breast. I catch his hand again.

"You don't think it's Caleb, do you?" Maren stands, closing the cabinet with her hip.

"God, I hope not. The restraining order's supposed to keep him at least five hundred yards away."

"When has a piece of paper ever stopped a determined asshole? It's been over a year, but you know how those psycho types can be. They lie dormant like herpes, then something triggers them, and bam—outbreak."

I shake my head, trying to dismiss the chilling thought that my ex is lurking in the woods.

"I don't think it's him. Caleb isn't the stalker type. He was sweet until one day he wasn't."

Ricky abandons his quest for my anatomy and instead nuzzles against my neck. For a moment, he's almost sweet. Then, he uses the proximity to grab a fistful of my hair, trying to use it as an anchor to climb higher on my body.

"Seriously though, babe, all kidding aside." Maren picks up her tablet and swipes the screen. "If you really feel like you're being watched, we need to call the sheriff. Especially after your window wanker. Because that's some next-level creepy shit if someone is climbing up and watching you through the glass."

I untangle Ricky's fingers from my hair.

"Did you figure out what he could have cut his foot on inside his cage?"

We call it a cage, but it's a combo indoor/outdoor enclosure that houses both Ricky and our other resident raccoon, Zorro. It's large enough for them to move around, climb, and play, mimicking a natural outdoor habitat, including live plants, ramps, platforms, hammocks for sleep, and a separate section for their litter boxes. Zorro tends to stay inside the enclosure, while Ricky jumps at any chance to get out. After all, there's no boob access in there, unless we're inside cleaning it.

"I couldn't find anything. And Zorro is fine. But there was some blood on the floor outside. Very mysterious."

"What did you get up to last night, Rick?"

He ignores me, deciding my earring looks interesting. He reaches up and gives it a little flick with his finger, his head tilted in curiosity. I redirect his hand before he can yank it out of my ear, then look back at his back paw.

"I don't think he needs a bandage on this. It's only a small cut."

Maren sets her tablet down and crouches again to check the supplies in the opposite cabinets. "We'll never be able to release him back into the wild, will we?"

I pull Ricky's hand away because it's creeping down my chest again and give his fingers a gentle but firm tap like I would an errant child. He's been with us for almost six months, since he was only two weeks old. He was injured after he and his mom were both hit by a car. She died, but by some miracle, he only got clipped. Animal services got him to me in time, but it was touch-and-go for a few days, and I had to amputate two of his back toes.

His will to live was impressive, which is matched only by his determination to grope every woman he encounters. Maren blames me because in those first few weeks nursing him back to health, I'd lay his little body on my chest and tuck him into my shirt to soothe him with my heartbeat. So did she.

"No, he's too domesticated now. He's unafraid of humans and might wander up to the wrong person and get shot."

"Yeah, because that's totally the reason and not because you've gone soft on another patient."

She knows me too well. Or perhaps I'm that predictable. I hate to let any of the animals go, even when I know it's best for them. I do it, but it breaks my heart. Like Sassy, the squirrel who lost her tail to a weed whacker. I cried for an hour after I released her last week.

Ricky shifts, angling his body toward Maren, and starts chittering. He stretches toward her, his arms reaching as if he wants to transfer his affections to a new victim. Maren shakes her head. She recognizes the con artist beneath the cute exterior.

I set him down on the floor, and he scurries across the room toward Maren, like a furry missile with a very specific target.

"Oh, no, you don't—" Maren's hands come up too late. Ricky launches himself at her, grabs her right breast with both hands, and then dives under the desk in the corner. "You heathen." There's no real heat in her voice. Despite her protests, she's as fond of him as I am.

I let out a muted snort. "At least he's consistent."

"Yeah, consistently inappropriate." Maren brushes imaginary raccoon prints off her shirt as Ricky pokes his face out from under the desk, dark eyes bright and alert, chittering.

"Are you ready to behave, Rick? If we give you another chance?"

He responds by making a beeline for my ankles, climbing up my leg with surprising speed and agility. I manage to catch him before he reaches his usual target.

"I'll take that as a no." Maren stands and grabs her tablet again. "Maybe we should get him a little raccoon girlfriend. Work out some of that pent-up energy."

I shoot her a pointed look.

"What? It's a legitimate therapeutic suggestion. Sometimes animals need to get laid, too. And if you'll remember the show we watched in your backyard last year, raccoons like gettin' freaky."

I look down at Ricky, who's settled into my arms and is purring softly, his hands occupied with grooming his own fur again. My eyes trace over the silver in his mask, and I'm struck by how beautiful he is, how perfectly designed for his life in the wild.

But I think I might have ruined him with my propensity for getting attached to those in my care.

⸻ ⚬ ⸻

"Luna! Sheriff Mills is on line one," Maren calls from the front office. "Tell her about feeling watched."

I turn from my computer screen and pick up the phone extension. "Hi, Karen, what's up?"

"Got a situation. Fish and Wildlife found illegal wolf traps on public land near your western border. Dangerous to your releases. Can you check if any tracking collars show animals in that area?"

My grip tightens on the phone. "Poachers?"

"Looks that way. There's something else. The trap setup is similar to the one that killed Shadow's mother."

I close my eyes as memories flood back to the bloody scene, the mother wolf's mutilated body, and tiny Shadow hiding nearby. The authorities never caught the poachers.

"I'll send the tracking data." Anger bleeds through my voice despite my efforts to hide it.

"Thanks. I'll get Roger and his crew to scatter any animals if the trackers show them in the vicinity. How are things over there these days?"

"The usual. Too many animals needing help and not enough me to go around."

"Well, hang in there."

"Thanks, Karen."

I hang up and brace my hands on my desk, drawing a breath. Something dark unfurls inside me. A protective rage that runs deeper than compassion. I've never told anyone, but I sometimes imagine taking justice for these animals into my own hands.

"Luna?" Ethan, the vet who volunteers here once a week, appears in the doorway, concern on his face. We were classmates at CSU. He and his brother own a practice in Estes Park, but he's volunteered here since I opened the sanctuary. "Everything okay?"

I straighten, pushing the darkness down. "Fish and Wildlife found illegal traps. Similar to the one that killed Shadow's mom."

His expression darkens. "Want me to check the collar data?"

"Thanks, that would be great. Can you also send it to Sheriff Mills and Roger?"

"Sure thing." He squeezes my shoulder before walking away.

He's a nice guy, recently married. We went on a single date, the first week of vet school, but there was no spark. Friendship suits us better. His help has been invaluable to me, giving me at least one day a week to myself. Not that I take it often. I always seem to find my way over here, unable to stay away.

I try to shake off my anger, but my thoughts keep returning to the feeling of being watched. Is there a connection? Are poachers surveilling the sanctuary before setting their traps?

If someone is targeting animals under my protection, they'll learn that Dr. Luna Foster is more than the compassionate healer everyone sees on the surface.

Chapter Nine

Damien

I stand motionless among the pines, the scent of their needles sharp in my nostrils as I watch her. My breath slows to match the rhythm of the forest. Deliberate, patient, and invisible. Luna leads a small doe on a leash across the sanctuary grounds toward the tree line.

Luna.

Even her name feels sacred. I've never been a man who believed in fate until the other day when she looked up, those hazel eyes meeting mine for the briefest moment. Something shifted inside me then, a tectonic movement in a soul I'd long believed was fixed and immovable.

Now I can't stay away.

She doesn't know I'm here, but something in her posture suggests awareness. A slight tension in her shoulders, the occasional glance toward the shadows where I stand. Instinct, perhaps. Prey animals develop that sense when predators are close. The thought brings a smile to my face.

My little doe.

The nickname feels right on my tongue as I whisper it.

I lift my binoculars to my face, bringing hers into focus. I'm close enough not to need them, but I want to see her more clearly. High cheekbones, full lips, and that cascade of blonde hair catching the afternoon light. She's beautiful in a way that transcends the physical, radiating a gentleness that makes my chest ache.

What would it be like to be the recipient of such tenderness?

She's speaking to the animal, her lips moving in gentle encouragement as they approach the forest's edge about ten yards from my position. I've chosen my vantage point carefully, close enough to see her expressions, far enough to remain undetected.

"It's time, Buttercup," she says, her voice carrying on the breeze. "It's time for you to find your family and go home."

The tender way she speaks to the doe stirs something uncomfortable within me. I'm not accustomed to this... this fascination, or this pull toward another person. In my forty-six years, I've perfected the art of detachment. People are a means to an end, an occasional distraction at most.

But Luna Foster is different.

She kneels beside the doe at the edge of the trees, removing the simple halter and running her fingers through its dappled coat.

"You're all healed up now, but you can always come back if you need me, okay? I'll be here."

Something about those words, "I'll be here," strikes me. People have never been constant in my life. I've preferred it that way. Attachments are vulnerabilities. I've eliminated them as methodically as I've eliminated those who deserve my particular brand of justice.

Yet, despite not even having met her, I find myself wanting to be a permanent part of her world.

I lower the binoculars, weighed down by this unusual desire. My pulse races as I remember standing in the darkness outside her bedroom window. The memory floods back with visceral intensity. Her silhouette beneath the covers as her hand moved and her hips rocked, her body arching as soft gasps escaped her lips.

I couldn't tear my eyes away.

My body responds to the memory, blood rushing southward, my cock hardening in an instant. I shift my stance, reaching down and pressing the heel of my hand against my erection.

This isn't like me. I don't fixate on women this way. Sex has always been transactional for me, a biological release with willing partners who know nothing of my true nature. I've never needed it to be more.

But with Luna... I want to consume her. To possess her. To show her the darkness that lives inside me and watch her accept it, accept me, rather than run from it.

I wonder if she found my gift on her window this morning?

Luna's fingers linger on the doe's coat. The sadness in her expression catches me off guard, mirroring something I've felt my entire life but never acknowledged.

A loss that cuts to the core.

"Go on," she urges the doe. "Be free."

It hesitates, then takes one tentative step away from her. Then another. Luna remains still, her body tense. Only the tremor in her shoulders gives away what the pain of letting go costs her. But this is what she does. She heals broken creatures and returns them to the wild, resisting the urge to keep them for herself even when she wants to.

My little doe.

The nickname truly does suit her. She's as gentle as the creature she's releasing. Delicate, cautious, and pure.

And I am Wolfe. Not just by name, but by nature. The name defines me. The silver wolf mask I wear when I hunt sits in my car, a reminder of what I am.

I chose the symbol when I chose my name. An homage to the image of a massive gray wolf mid-leap through snow, its amber eyes blazing with primal fury and intelligence. Those eyes held something untamed and uncompromising. Something that could never be collared, beaten into submission, or held back by fear or heartless restraint.

And wolves hunt deer. They chase them through forests, relentless in their pursuit until their prey surrenders to exhaustion or fear. The idea of hunting Luna, of watching her run from me only to surrender, fuels another rush of excitement within me, my cock throbbing in sync with my heartbeat.

The doe hesitates again at the forest's edge, stopping to look back at Luna. She waves at it, like she's sending a child off to school.

"Don't forget to visit. And tell your friends this is a safe place."

I shake my head. Like her wolf, she speaks to it as if it understands complex human language. Yet there's something in how they both respond to her that makes me wonder.

The fawn finds its courage and bounds away into the deeper forest, disappearing into the dense underbrush. Luna watches it go, her eyes fixed on the wall of green, her shoulders falling. The loss is there, written in every line of her body.

Sadness.

She misses the animal already, despite knowing release was the right choice. This is what I don't understand. Her capacity to connect and release, to care without possessing.

My own nature runs counter to hers. When I find something of value, I claim it.

One hand rises to wipe at her cheek.

Is she crying?

My chest tightens. Why does her pain affect me? I've witnessed countless people in states of emotional and physical distress. It's often one of the last things they experience, second only to pain, before I deliver judgment for their crimes. But their tears have never reached me.

Hers do.

She stands, brushing dirt from her pants, and turns back toward the sanctuary. For a moment, she pauses, her head tilting as if sensing me again. Her gaze sweeps across the tree line, and I'm certain she's looking right at me, though the dense foliage makes that impossible.

I don't move. Don't breathe. The distance between us feels both vast and nonexistent at the same time.

"Hello?" Her voice carries through the trees. "Is someone there?"

Her instincts are remarkable. Another reason she fascinates me. Those who work with animals often develop a heightened awareness, an ability to sense danger or presence that others lack.

"I know you're out there," she says a little louder. "If you're here to harm any animal under my care, you should know I protect what's mine with whatever is at my disposal."

Her bravery is as impressive as her capacity for kindness.

After a long moment of silence, she turns away, walking back toward the main sanctuary building. Her hips sway with each confident step.

She represents everything I'm not. Yet something tells me there's darkness in her too. I'm certain of it. Not like mine, never like mine, but a shadow nonetheless. Perhaps grief or loneliness that she hides beneath her compassionate exterior.

She doesn't know yet, but we're connected by something deeper than chance or circumstance.

I retreat further into the trees, allowing myself one last look at her sanctuary before I leave. I have preparations to make for tonight's hunt.

Tomorrow I'll return. And the day after. And the day after.

I'll watch over her, a silent observer from afar, until the time is right to reveal myself.

Chapter Ten

Luna

I climb through my bedroom window onto the balcony with a cup of Sleepytime tea. Shadow follows, his massive frame making the window opening look tiny as he squeezes through. The familiar ritual should be relaxing, settling into one of the two Adirondack chairs I placed out here, with the small bistro table within arm's reach and the chamomile scent rising from my mug.

But tonight, nothing feels familiar.

I never understood why someone removed the French doors that once opened onto the balcony, replacing them with this one oversized window. Grandpa told me his great-great-great-grandfather had them replaced after a fugitive used them to break into the house. He always intended to install new doors, but he never got around to it before his death. I plan to do it myself when I have the time and money, but everything goes into the sanctuary for now.

I love the tranquility of this place. The isolation and privacy it provides. The quiet from being miles from the closest neighbor. It's always been my refuge.

But something has shifted. The same isolation and silence that used to wrap around me now press down. The trees, once a barrier, now hold something, or someone, behind them.

Watching.

Goosebumps erupt across my arms and won't fade no matter how many times I rub them away. The unease coils in my stomach and twists itself into a knot. My body hums with an anticipation I refuse to name, a dark excitement that makes me feel sick even as it draws my attention back to the tree line again and again. I shove the feeling down deep and try to pretend it isn't there at all.

I take a sip of tea and pretend I'm not straining to catch every sound from the darkness beyond. Shadow's ears perk up, twitching at each rustle from the surrounding forest. I mirror his alertness, my shoulders rigid, unlike the usual ease I feel out here.

The main house sits at the edge of the sanctuary property, offering seclusion and a sense of being part of the wild landscape I love. Usually, this remoteness is comforting. Tonight, it amplifies my awareness of how alone I am out here. How vulnerable.

The other night could have been nothing. It could have been an animal in the woods. This afternoon could have been the same thing. But I have no explanation for how ejaculate got on my window. When I scrubbed it clean this afternoon, the evidence was undeniable. It was come.

Beside me, Shadow lets out a low growl and rises, walking to the railing. He rests his head on it, every line of his body taut with attention, eyes fixed on the tree line.

My heart thumps in my chest as I stand and follow his gaze. At first, there's nothing except shadows shifting in the breeze, but then that familiar sensation crawls up my spine. Electric, invasive, like invisible fingers trailing across my skin.

Something catches my eye as I start to turn away. A glint of something that looks like metal at the forest's edge. I freeze, my breathing shallow and rapid. My heart pounds so hard I can hear it in my ears, drowning out the night sounds. The mug trembles in my grip, tea sloshing dangerously close to the rim.

Stay calm. You're stronger than this. You've faced down wounded predators many times. This is—

Then I see it. The outline of a figure among the trees, motionless and watching.

Shadow's growls increase in volume, his whole body vibrating with them, and terror floods through me. My knees threaten to give out. But my vision sharpens, hunting for movement in the dark. Every instinct screams at me to dive into my window, hide, and get away from those eyes watching me. My throat constricts, and I have to force myself to breathe through my nose.

Grandpa's shotgun. It's in the cabinet at the end of the hall. How long would it take me to get to it? Faster than whoever that is to reach the house?

I blink hard, squeezing my eyes shut for a moment, and when I open them...

Nothing. Only trees and shadows and the ordinary darkness of night.

"Shit."

The word escapes before I can stop it. My hands are shaking now, a fine tremor that makes me clench my fists.

Get it together, Luna. You imagined it. You had to have imagined it.

But my body doesn't care what I tell it. My pulse hammers in my ears, and my palms are slick with sweat despite the cool night air.

I grip Shadow's collar, needing the solid warmth of him to anchor me. "Come on, baby. Time for bed."

He resists, still focused on whatever we just saw, and I have to pull harder than usual. The effort makes my muscles tremble with leftover adrenaline. When he relents, I scramble through the window, panicked and clumsy.

Shadow squeezes through behind me, and I close and lock it, my fingers fumbling with the latch. I press my face to the glass, searching the darkness beyond the yard for any sign of that metallic glint, that human silhouette. My breath fogs the window, and I wipe it clear with my sleeve, but there's nothing there.

The absence of a visible threat doesn't calm the storm in my chest. My heart pounds a rhythm against my ribs that won't slow, and my stomach twists and untwists in a relentless churning. Fear drives most of it. The raw, animal kind that floods your veins and screams at you to run. But underneath the terror, threaded through it like dark ribbons, is a sickening pulse of excitement.

My fingers hover over the curtain's edges, and I'm caught between two opposing forces. The rational part of my brain, the part that's kept me alive through years of working with dangerous animals, pounds a warning through my skull. Danger. It could be the poachers Karen warned about. Or worse, maybe Maren's right. It might be Caleb.

I should close the curtains. Double-check the locks downstairs. Maybe even swallow my pride and call Karen, like Maren suggested.

But another part of me thrills at this game of watcher and watched. If someone is out there, hidden in the dark, who are they? What do they want?

The gap I left in the curtains the last two nights was a whim, a reckless invitation to what? The possibility of whoever, or whatever, was watching? Tonight, knowing there is actually someone out there, I'm torn between pulling them closed and leaving them open.

"This is how people die in horror movies," I say to Juni as she leaps onto the windowsill. She responds with a judgmental meow that somehow manages to sound disapproving of my life choices. "Fine, compromise it is."

My hands shake as I adjust the curtains, leaving the largest gap yet. Enough to see out, and enough to be seen. Especially if someone were to climb onto the balcony again.

What the hell? Why am I even contemplating that as a possibility?

I consider getting Grandpa's gun, but I can't stand the thought of leaving a loaded weapon out with Shadow and the cats in the room. Instead, I force myself through my bedtime routine on autopilot—showering, brushing my teeth, and snuggling my babies. All the while, my mind keeps returning to that figure and the metallic gleam in the forest. The absolute stillness of whoever was watching me.

Was it real? Or a figment of my imagination?

I slip into bed, and when I reach for the lamp, I see my phone charging on my nightstand. I pick it up and pull up Karen's number. My finger shakes as it hovers over the call button, but for some reason, I can't bring myself to dial.

I set it down again, and my gaze returns to the window and the gap in the curtains. The forest beyond reveals nothing but darkness. Yet as I settle against the pillows, my pulse slowing, I can't shake the bone-deep certainty of what I saw.

Someone is out there.

Someone is watching me from my woods.

Chapter Eleven

Damien

The digital clock on the dashboard of my blacked-out Range Rover reads 11:43 PM, but time has long since become a fluid concept. I've been sitting here since 10 PM, after a brief visit to Luna's, my second of the day.

She was on that balcony with her wolf when I crept up to the treeline, tension coiling through her body like a loaded spring. I could have watched her all night, but then her wolf sensed me, his growl rattling the air. I should have melted back into the shadows and used the trees for cover, but my mask concealed my face, so I stood my ground.

I'm not sure why I wore it tonight. Did part of me hope she would see me?

And she did. The way her body froze, her eyes locked on the spot where I stood... *Fuck!* The air itself seemed to vibrate with her panic. Dark, twisted satisfaction pounded in my chest, stirring my cock to life.

I wanted to step out of the trees and let her see all of me, but she's not ready for that yet. Neither am I. I need more of that beautiful terror first. It will make her surrender that much sweeter when it comes.

So, I backed away, leaving her to wonder if I was real or just another shadow in her mind.

Now, I'm tucked in an alleyway between two buildings, out of sight, observing every detail of the Broken Antler Bar's exterior, including Daryl Rawlings' shitty old F-150 pickup parked out front.

The rundown bar is a testament to small-town desperation. A weathered wooden exterior with neon signs, their erratic flickering casting fragmented shadows across the parking lot. The kind of place where secrets fester beneath the surface.

Athena lies beside me, her muscled frame resting in the passenger seat, her dark eyes locked on me. Her breathing is slow and controlled. She understands the art of waiting, often acting as my co-pilot on nights like these. Her presence calms me, centers me, and reminds me why I do this.

My hand strokes her head, my touch gentle. My fingers trace the scars along her neck. With Athena, the monster in me goes quiet.

She nudges my hand, her warm brown eyes looking up with a mixture of loyalty and understanding that no human could comprehend.

My phone vibrates on the console between the seats. I press the steering wheel button, and Cade's face appears on the dashboard screen.

He sits rigid behind his office desk, that military bearing locked into his spine even after all these years. Again, he's traded his business suit for dark fatigues, ready to clean up and dispose of whatever mess I leave behind.

"Everything all set?"

"Yes, he's been inside for hours. I'm ready when he comes out."

Cade nods, understanding implicit in his movement. He knows the drill. It's always the same. I never deviate from my routine. It's how I've kept my actions concealed for two and a half decades.

"I'm heading to the chopper in thirty. I'll meet you at your place."

"I thought you said it's too loud for this late at night."

A rare smile curves his lips. "New toy. A contact at the DOD pointed me to the manufacturer. Covert Flight Systems. They're letting us test it, see if it fits our needs. We like it, they'll custom build one for us."

"Two days and you've got military-grade stealth tech?"

"I have my ways."

"Do I want to know the price tag?"

"Nope. All you need to know is we can make an almost silent approach to your estate."

"Good. Let me know what you think of it."

"I'll leave it at the house. You can fly it back to Denver yourself tomorrow."

Silence stretches between us while my fingers work through Athena's fur. She leans into the touch, content.

A war plays out behind Cade's eyes for almost a full minute.

"You want to spit out what's eating you? You're fucking with my focus."

"Damien..." His tone is part warning, part concern. "I'm getting—"

"What? You saw what this bastard did."

This one is personal. He knows why.

"I wasn't going to say anything about Daryl Rawlings. He's earned what's coming to him."

"Then spit it out already. Since when do you hold your tongue?"

"Dr. Luna Foster."

Her name is all he needs to say.

"Don't fucking start with me, Cade."

"I know you've been watching her."

"I said, don't start."

A heavy silence settles between us, the tension growing thicker. "This isn't like you. Should I be worried?"

"No."

He nods, but doubt flickers behind his eyes. "Fine. I'll see you in a few hours."

His image vanishes, and now I'm fucking pissed. How dare he question me about Luna? What I do in my personal life is my own business. His concern is well-intentioned, but it doesn't fucking matter.

It won't change the fact that Luna Foster is mine.

⸻◦✦◦⸻

It's almost midnight when the last of the bar's stragglers stumble out, including Rawlings. To my surprise, he's a functioning drunk. The kind of intoxication that lowers inhibitions while maintaining just enough control to be dangerous.

He gets into his truck and pulls out of the parking lot. I follow at a distance, close enough to see but far enough to remain unseen.

The Range Rover's engine is a whisper as I drive with my headlights off. The night vision goggles paint the world in shades of phosphorescent green. Fish Creek Road stretches before us, Rawlings swerving in only the way a drunk can.

This fucker better make it home alive because I won't be denied the pleasure of his death.

My hands are steady on the steering wheel as Rawlings almost misses the turn into his long dirt driveway. Having staked out the place earlier when he was drowning in his pathetic existence at the bar, I know there is a small turnout tucked off to the left side of the driveway about halfway up.

Perfect for my purposes.

I park and reach for my gloves, then my mask. As soon as the cool metal slides over my face, the transformation is immediate. Damien Wolfe, respected billionaire CEO, ceases to exist. In his place, something ancient and predatory. A creature of shadow and purpose.

I pet Athena and get out, striding the last few hundred feet up the driveway. Rawlings stumbles from his truck toward the porch, fumbling with his keys and muttering to himself.

He reaches his front door. As he grasps the doorknob, I step up behind him and clamp my right hand over his mouth as my left arm wraps around his neck. The chokehold restricts the blood flow to his brain, compressing his carotid artery and jugular. The right pressure is all it takes to obstruct his airway, cutting off his oxygen.

I want to snap his neck and fucking kill him right here, but he needs to suffer for what he's done. A quick death is too good for him.

He struggles in my grasp, with muffled shouts against my hand, but it's pointless, futile, because I'm much larger and stronger. He claws at my arm, trying to create space to breathe, but I don't ease up.

It takes ten seconds for his struggles to weaken. Another three for his fingers on my forearm to loosen. Another four until his body goes limp.

Seventeen seconds was all it took to render this piece of shit insentient.

I lift him, tossing him over my shoulder. He smells rancid, like booze and body odor, and I want to gag. I load his body into the back of the Range Rover, zip-tying his wrists and ankles and duct-taping his mouth. Athena looks back at me from the passenger seat, a low growl emanating from her chunky body.

"I know, girl. You can sense evil as well as I do."

I leave no trace evidence of myself or what happened here. No drag marks. No signs of a struggle in the dirt driveway. Just boot marks that could belong to anyone.

I remove my gloves and climb into the front seat, tossing them to the floor before rubbing Athena's head. I remove my mask and set it on the seat beside her, inhaling a deep breath.

It's just shy of 1 AM.

It takes almost forty minutes to drive to the Morrison estate. I should probably start calling it the Wolfe estate, but it isn't a home. It's a place to take care of my brutal business.

Five hundred secluded acres of forest.

With no neighbors.

And no witnesses.

Rawlings lies spread-eagled on the steel table, stripped bare except for his boxers and socks. I rarely strip my prey, but his stench was so foul I ripped everything off. As it turns out, the odor was all him. Removing his clothes didn't help.

My favorite torture implements line the workbench—knives, needle-nose pliers, a ball-peen hammer, and my mini blowtorch. And a rusty tire iron, courtesy of Rawlings. It will be my most useful tool tonight.

I thrust smelling salts under his nose. His body jolts, and his eyes snap open. He blinks, confusion flaring to terror as he registers the restraints biting into his wrists and ankles. He strains against the bonds, grunting, but the straps hold firm.

I move around the table, my pace unhurried. Rawlings' eyes follow me, wide and wild with terror, fear pouring off him like heat. My boots scrape against the stained concrete, each step reminding him I'm here, even when out of his line of sight. I rip the duct tape from his face, taking strips of his stubbled skin and a howl of pain with it. Wet crimson streaks run down his cheeks.

My blood pounds and my body hums with excitement.

"Please... I don't know what—"

"Shut the fuck up!"

My fist connects with the right side of his jaw. A sharp crack echoes in the room as his head snaps sideways, his scream ricocheting off the stone walls.

The smell of piss fills the basement, mingling with the acrid, burning scent of bleach, searing my nostrils. I sneer at the wet spot spreading across his dirty underwear, his fear and desperation laid bare.

They all do this when the terror takes hold.

I continue my slow, stalking movement. My unhurried demeanor amplifies their fear because they have no idea how long I plan to torture them. Taking my time is part of my ritual. It's what brings me pleasure. Sometimes it turns into an all-night event, which is hard on Cade because he has to postpone disposing of the body until the next night. But I refuse to be rushed.

"You're the worst kind of filth." Tears pool in his eyes, carving streaks down his dusty cheeks. "Animal abusers and child abusers. You all belong in hell, and you'll be there soon." I lean over his face so he can see my mask up close, the wolf that embodies the predator within me. "But make no mistake, Daryl, you won't die quickly tonight. Though by the time I'm through, you'll wish you had."

"Please."

I deliver a second blow to his other cheek. Bone breaks with a sound that bounces off every surface down here. Two yellow teeth shoot from his lips, skittering across the basement floor like tiny, grotesque dice.

"I said, shut the fuck up. I'm not here to listen to your apologies, pleas, or promises that it will never happen again. Pieces of shit like you don't change and will always take out your anger and hate on those smaller and weaker than you."

"But, I don't—"

"Do you ever fucking listen? Shut. The Fuck. Up."

Uncontrollable sobs rack his body as I step over to the workbench and lift my favorite knife. Its serrated edge grabs on and grips not only the flesh it slices but also the tissue, organs, and blood vessels beneath, extracting the maximum amount of pain.

My pulse thunders in my ears.

The blade glints as I press it to his skin and carve a slow arc through flesh and muscle. He screams, a chorus of agony that sets my heart racing faster. I'm struck by how fantastic the acoustics are in here. The space swallows and amplifies every note of agony. No wonder Jeremiah Morrison picked this place for his kill room.

I think about what he did to them. Those girls. The ones who never made it home. My teeth grind together as the thought burns through me. They didn't deserve to die that way. The state executed him for his crimes, but lethal injection was far too easy. I wish I could have gotten my hands on him.

Blood wells around the fresh cuts. The thick, cloying scent assaults my nose. By the time I'm through carving into Rawlings' chest, Buddy's name is emblazoned across his skin like a gushing bloody tattoo. His voice is raspy and raw, and uncontrollable twitches seize his body.

"Now, let's talk about Buddy." My voice is soft. Dangerous. "Remember him?" Images from my past flash in the back of my mind—the first death I witnessed—and a wave of nausea rolls over me. "Two years old. A shepherd mix. First, you starved him. Then you beat him with a tire iron, fracturing his skull and breaking his back legs."

I plunge the blade into his stomach, avoiding any vital organs, for now, and stride back to the bench. His scream of pain follows me. I lift the tire iron, test its balance, and then step forward. Rawlings' eyes widen, recognition flickering before his expression breaks. My lips curve into a menacing smile.

I pause above his right shin before bringing the iron down. Bone shatters with a wet, satisfying crunch. He strains against the restraints, an agonizing howl of pain tearing from his lips. I raise the iron again—above his left leg this time—and bring it down with a sickening thud. Another splintering fracture. Another scream of agony.

Fury surges through me. Over and over, the tire iron cracks bones, a sound that punctuates my hard recounting of Buddy's injuries.

Blood and bits of flesh splatter on my clothes and mask. By the time I'm done, I'm drenched in it, clinging to me like a second skin. My breath is ragged, and sweat pours off me, dripping onto the table, mixing with the blood on the cool metal.

Rawlings' legs are a gruesome mess of mangled bone, muscle, and sinew. I close my eyes, take a deep breath, and center myself again as stifled sobs break the silence.

"Luna nursed him back to health." My voice softens at the thought of her, an angel in this hellish world. "Saved his life and found him a loving home."

I shake off thoughts of her. Her light has no place here. Even thinking of her in here is blasphemous.

But a lightbulb goes on.

I pull my phone from my pocket and dial Cade. He's upstairs in my office, waiting for me to finish, but this is easier.

"Done already? That was quick."

The sight of me covered head to toe in blood doesn't even faze him.

"No, I'm just getting started, but you can leave. I'll dispose of him myself."

"Why?" He looks confused. "I'm here."

"Because I plan to do something special with this fucker's body."

"Damien—"

"Go home, Cade. I've got this."

I hang up. Let him stew. He'll be fucking pissed, but I'll deal with that tomorrow.

My decision feels right, and a calm spreads through my limbs as I turn back to Rawlings. He's barely coherent now, his screams having died down to whimpers.

I grab the pliers, clamping onto one of his yellowed teeth, and yank. He screams as the root tears free, blood pouring from the gap. I drop the tooth, and the ping as it connects with the floor brings a smile to my lips.

"One down. So many more to go."

I extract each tooth, his screams rising and falling like tidal waves. The sound is so beautiful, a testament to his pain, it makes me shiver with satisfaction. Blood streams from his mouth, onto the table, and down his throat, gagging him.

I lose track of time, and it's almost 3 AM when I glance at my watch. Morning's first light will be here soon, and I'm running out of time. I'll have to just wrap his body and deal with cleaning the basement later.

I step back to admire my handiwork. Rawlings' body is unrecognizable as he clings to life. I was careful not to smash his face. I need him to be identified, after all. With one hand, I force his eyelids open. I lean down to meet his glassy stare. He trembles, silent and broken.

My mask comes off. His pupils dilate in helpless terror. I raise my blade high as I prepare to shove it into his eye.

"Remember my face, Rawlings. Because I'll find you in hell again someday."

I bring the knife down, driving it into the socket with a final, merciless plunge.

<hr>

It's almost morning when I pull up in front of Luna's house. The pre-dawn light paints the landscape in ethereal shades of gray and silver.

Everything is quiet. The kind of quiet that holds its breath. I sit for a moment, hands gripping the steering wheel, and let the anticipation build. Luna is sleeping in that house, curled up in her bed. She works so hard. She deserves a peaceful sleep.

For now.

She needs to see that the creatures she saves have a guardian beyond her. This is the only way I can show her.

I step out of the truck. My eyes scan the treeline, cataloging the positions of her wildlife cameras. None point toward the driveway. Luna's focus is on protecting her animals, not monitoring her own front door. Still, I'll need to loop back and scrub any footage before I leave.

I also have micro-cameras to install in and around the main sanctuary buildings so I can watch her in her environment. I'll eventually get them in the house, but she spends most of her time in the other buildings. It's more important that I start there.

I heft Rawlings' dead body over my shoulder. The plastic crinkles. His dead weight settles against my spine. Heavy. Heavier than he was alive.

This is for you, Luna. This is what happens to monsters who hurt what you love.

I stride toward the porch, the gravel crunching beneath my boots. Everything about this place radiates her gentle spirit. The carefully tended flower beds, the weathered birdhouses hanging from tree branches, and the hand-painted signs on all the buildings. She's built something pure here. Something worth protecting.

I climb the five wooden steps of her porch. Movement in the front window catches my eye, and I pause. Once again, her wolf watches me through the glass. His eyes lock with mine across the darkness, and something passes between us. Recognition.

Wolf to Wolfe.

Again, he doesn't howl or alert Luna to my presence. He only growls. Loud enough to carry through the glass, but quiet enough not to wake her. His tail is still, neither wagging nor bristling. We understand each other, Shadow and I.

We both know what it means to claim someone as ours, to stand between them and the world. We both understand that protection sometimes demands blood. It's about being willing to turn violent when the moment calls for it, keeping that capacity for destruction ready and honed. We both guard what belongs to us, and we won't hesitate when the time comes to prove it.

"Good boy."

He blinks. His gaze changes, and the wildness dims. What's left behind is trust, or close enough to it that the difference doesn't matter right now.

I drop Rawlings' plastic-wrapped body at the top of the stairs, positioning him so she'll see him as soon as she opens the door.

Presented. Like the gift he is.

On top of his corpse, I lay a Rocky Mountain Columbine, Colorado's state flower, its velvety purple petals shimmering under the overhead porch light. Something pure and beautiful to contrast with the ugliness of what Rawlings represented.

I head toward the sanctuary buildings. The micro-cameras in my jacket pocket feel like tiny promises of connection, ways to stay close to Luna even when I can't be here.

The main building sits about ten yards to the right of the house. Its wooden exterior, like all the other buildings, is well-maintained. Luna's touch is everywhere—in the careful repair work, the fresh coat of stain on the trim, and the small wind chimes that hang silent in the still air. I step up to the front entrance's porch, where she keeps a spare key hidden beneath a ceramic garden gnome. She used it when she returned from her hike the other morning. So trusting, my little doe. So naïve about the dangers that lurk in the woods.

I step inside. The small lobby area greets me, moonlight streaming through the large windows, illuminating the reception desk. The first micro-camera goes beneath the windowsill, behind a fern, its lens hidden among the green fronds. Perfect line of sight to the entire lobby.

My heart pounds harder as I move deeper into the building. This is her domain, her sanctuary within the sanctuary. Every step feels like a deeper invasion of her privacy, and the thought thrills me more than it should. She'll understand eventually. When she realizes how far I'll go to protect her and what she loves, she'll see that this was necessary.

Luna's office door stands ajar, and I push it open. The space embodies her, all organized chaos with stacks of files and medical books on the desk, framed photos of animals she's rehabilitated covering the walls, and a coffee mug with a chip in the handle sitting on the arm of the sofa. A cardigan sweater hangs on the back of her chair, and I give in to the urge to bury my face in the fabric, to breathe her in.

The scent goes straight to my cock. That light scent of peaches that hit me like a brick when we almost collided outside the post office.

Focus, Damien. You're here for a purpose.

The second camera goes on top of her bookshelf, hidden behind a small ceramic owl. From there, it has a clear view of her desk. I imagine she spends hours in this room, and now I'll be able to share those quiet moments with her.

The main treatment area is beyond her office, a clean, sterile space filled with medical equipment and examination tables. This is where the real work happens. The thought of watching her, of seeing that focused intensity up close, makes my cock even harder.

I place the third camera on top of a cabinet, angled down toward the treatment tables. The lighting here is harsh and clinical, but it will provide perfect visibility. I can already see Luna's face in the camera's feed, biting her lower lip when she's worried about a patient, and the gentle murmur of her voice as she soothes frightened animals.

Then I head into the back area, where Luna houses the animals too injured to be released and her permanent residents. I learned all of this from the images and text on her website. This is the heart of her sanctuary, the reason she built this place. The cages and enclosures are larger than most facilities would provide, each one designed with the specific needs of its inhabitants in mind. Even in the dim light, I can make out several sleeping forms.

A soft chittering sound draws my attention to a medium-sized enclosure to the right. Two raccoons sway in hammocks in the far corner, but one of them has noticed my presence. It comes forward, hands gripping the wire mesh, its masked face tilted up toward me with curiosity.

"Who are you?"

I crouch to the raccoon's level. It studies me with dark, knowing eyes, the chittering continuing in a soft conversational sound that somehow doesn't seem alarmed.

I mount the fourth camera on a support beam nearby, positioned to capture the entire space. The raccoon watches my movements with interest, its head tilting back and forth as I work. When I'm finished, it gives one more soft chitter before retreating to rejoin its companion.

Movement catches my eye in the next cage. A baby bobcat crouches in the shadows, yellow eyes reflecting the dim nightlights scattered around the room. Unlike the curious raccoon, this one radiates wariness, every muscle tensed and ready for a fight.

Its eyes never leave mine as I approach. There's intelligence in that gaze, and something else. Pain, maybe. The lingering trauma of whatever brought it here.

"You're lucky, you know." I settle back on my heels to appear less imposing. "You have Luna taking care of you. She'll make sure you heal. That you're strong enough to return to the wild where you belong."

The bobcat's ears twitch at the sound of my voice, but it doesn't move.

"She saved you. The same way she saves all of them. That's what makes her special."

The bobcat blinks, then turns away, deciding I'm not a threat.

I finish installing the cameras throughout the back area, each one strategically positioned and concealed. The animals seem to tolerate me with the calm patience of creatures used to human handlers. They don't know that I'm not supposed to be here, that these cameras represent an invasion of their sanctuary's privacy. They simply see another figure moving through their domain.

When the last camera is in place, I make my way back through the building, double-checking each installation. The feeds will go to my private server, accessible only by Cade and me, for round-the-clock access to Luna's world. The thought sends a thrill through me. Soon, I'll be able to watch her work, interact with the animals she loves so much, and witness the compassion that makes her so extraordinary.

The morning light is growing stronger as I step back outside, locking the door behind me and replacing the key beneath the gnome. I walk across the driveway to the treeline on the opposite side, where I tuck two more micro-cameras into crevices of two tree trunks across from the house, providing a perfect view of the front door.

I attach the last camera to the roof trim of the screened back porch. It covers the entire backyard and rolling foothills to the rear of the property. When I'm done, I make my way back to the front.

Now for my final task—the wildlife cameras.

I know where they are, having studied this place for over a week. Luna positions them to catch poachers and trespassers, not realizing that the real threat comes from someone who's learned to move through her sanctuary like a ghost.

As I work, the wolves stir, sensing my presence the way animals always do, but they don't sound the alarm. Maybe they recognize my scent from previous visits, or maybe they understand I mean no harm to them or their sanctuary. Either way, their silence is a gift I don't take lightly.

Luna will wake soon and step out to check on her animals as she does every morning. She'll find my gift waiting, but she'll have no way to trace it back to me. When the time is right, when she's ready to accept my presence in her life, then I'll reveal myself. But not yet.

Until then, I'll be watching.

Chapter Twelve

Luna

Three cats tumble around my ankles in a dangerous dance that threatens to send me sprawling as I descend the stairs. I manage to reach the bottom without incident, but pause when Shadow is absent from his usual morning greeting spot. Instead, he's sitting rigid by the front window, nose pressed to the glass, his gray fur standing on end.

"Shadow? What is it, baby?"

His ears twitch at the sound of my voice, but he doesn't look back. Doesn't move. Only stares through the window at something I can't see.

"Come on, breakfast time." I head toward the kitchen. Usually, the word "breakfast" has him bounding after me, but not today.

I fill the coffeemaker with fresh grounds and water. The cats wind between my legs as I reach for their food bowls.

"Patience, ladies." I set down three dishes, measuring out their breakfast. I watch them eat for a moment, then glance toward the living room. Shadow still hasn't moved.

"Shadow!" I call again, more firmly this time, setting down a bowl of raw meat. "Come get your food!"

Nothing. Not even a flick of his tail.

Coffee drips into the pot, its rich aroma filling the kitchen, but Shadow's behavior is triggering all my alarms. He's not alert; he's frozen. Fixated.

All night, images of watchers in the woods plagued my dreams. So much so that I bolted awake, heart pounding, sweat beading on my forehead, thirteen minutes before the alarm. A quick shower washed away the dream-sweat but not the memory of that masked figure inside the trees. I pulled on a pair of worn jeans and one of Grandpa's old flannel shirts that still hangs in my closet five years after his death. The fabric is soft from countless washes, and sometimes I imagine I can still detect his scent. Pine, tobacco, and something uniquely him that made me feel safe.

Nothing makes me feel safe that way anymore.

I pour myself a mug and take a sip, trying to convince myself there's a simple explanation for Shadow's odd behavior. Maybe a deer wandered into the yard. Or maybe a bear. I hope it's not a bear. I'm not in the mood to chase one away before I even eat breakfast. Yet Shadow's stance speaks of something more ominous. What could be more ominous than a bear?

"What are you looking at, huh?" I cross the room toward the window and place a hand on his back. His muscles are tight beneath my fingers.

I lean forward, peering through the glass, as I squint in the early morning light.

There's something on my porch.

My stomach drops like a stone. The coffee mug slips from my fingers before I even register letting go. It shatters against the hardwood, hot liquid splashing across my bare feet. The heat should sting, but all I feel is cold spreading through my chest.

No. No. That can't be what I think it is.

My hands shake as I fumble with the deadbolt, my fingers clumsy and uncooperative. Shadow whines behind me, pressing against my legs. The lock gives way with a hollow click, the sound jarring in the morning quiet.

The door swings open. I step onto the porch, and my worst fears crystallize into horrifying reality.

A body.

Wrapped in clear plastic like some grotesque package, lying motionless on my welcome mat. The plastic clings to still features, and through the transparent barrier, I can make out the pale, gray complexion of death. A bright purple Rocky Mountain Columbine bloom sits centered on the torso like a sick calling card.

My knees buckle. The world tilts sideways, and I grab the doorframe to steady myself.

"Oh God! Oh, my God!"

I've seen death before. Countless times. Wounded animals that didn't make it, creatures that arrived too late to save, Grandpa. But this is different. This is deliberate. This is wrong in ways that make my soul recoil.

Shadow tries to push past my legs, his nose twitching at the scents carried on the morning breeze. I snap back to my senses, my protective instincts kicking in despite the shock freezing my blood.

"No, Shadow. Stay back." I push him back inside, my voice stronger than I feel. Whatever happened here, whatever this means, I won't let my animals near it.

I step closer, my legs unsteady but moving anyway. I need to be sure. I need to confirm what my mind is already screaming at me. The plastic wrap crinkles in the breeze, and bile rises in my throat. The face is obscured, turned away, but there's no mistaking the stillness, the absence of breath, and the waxy pallor of skin that will never warm again.

A shudder runs through me from head to toe. I stumble backward through the doorway, slamming the door shut and turning the deadbolt with shaking fingers. My back hits the wall beside the stairs, and I slide down until I'm sitting on the floor, Shadow pressed against my side.

My hands tremble as I fumble for my phone in my pocket. The screen blurs through the tears I didn't realize were forming.

"911, what's your emergency?"

"Hi. This is Luna Foster at Sage & Summit Wildlife Sanctuary." My voice cracks, and I swallow hard, forcing myself to speak. "I found a dead body on my front porch."

The words sound absurd, impossible, as they leave my mouth, like something from a nightmare I should wake up from. But with that sickly, sweet smell still in my nostrils and the way Shadow whines and presses closer, it's all horrifyingly real.

"Your address, ma'am?"

"1472 Mountain Pass Road."

"Sheriff is on her way. Stay inside and don't touch anything. Are you alone?"

I glance down at Shadow, then at the cats who've wandered over, drawn by the commotion. Sage rubs against my leg, sensing my distress, while Willow settles in my lap with a soft purr. Juniper, ever the independent one, hops onto the windowsill and begins taking a bath as if dead bodies on porches are perfectly normal Saturday morning occurrences.

"Just me and my animals."

"Do you want to stay on the line until the sheriff arrives?"

"No. I'll be fine."

But it's a lie. Nothing about this is fine. Nothing will ever be fine again.

I end the call and let my head fall back against the wall. My whole body trembles now, not just my hands. Shock. I'm going into shock. I've seen it in injured animals enough times to recognize the signs in myself.

Shadow tucks his face into my armpit, his warm breath against my ribs anchoring me to the present. Sage and Willow's purrs are a steady vibration against my legs. Even Juniper pauses in her bath to look at me with those knowing green eyes.

"It's okay," I whisper the words like a mantra as I rock back and forth. "Everything's going to be okay."

⁕

The sheriff's cruisers have been parked in my driveway for over an hour now. Yellow crime scene tape flutters in the breeze around the porch, transforming my sanctuary into something tainted and foreign. I stand at the front window, trying to ignore the body still there, as officers move around the property, taking photos, collecting evidence, and turning my peaceful morning into a goddamn nightmare.

No. The dead body on my front porch did that.

I grip the mug of fresh coffee, though it's long grown cold. I can't remember the last time I took a sip, but at least my hands are steady again. The taste of bile rises in my throat, and I close my eyes. I can't look at that plastic-wrapped form any longer, lying there like some sick present.

Shadow hasn't left my side since I discovered the body, even though all the men around are making him agitated. He doesn't so much mind people as men. Men killed his mother in front of him. But he keeps close to me, protective, pressing against my leg. Even now, as I stand frozen at the window, he leans against me, as if he can sense the tremors I'm fighting to control.

I open my eyes at the sound of a commotion outside.

"Luna?" Maren's voice breaks through my trance as she bursts through the front door. "I came as soon as I got your text. Jesus Fucking Christ, Luna. That's a freaking body I stepped around out there."

I whirl toward her. Relief crashes over me, and I sway on my feet at the sight of my best friend's familiar face, even pale with shock as it is. Maren's wild brown curls are more disheveled than usual when left out of her signature ponytail, like she ran her hands through them during the drive, and she's wearing mismatched socks visible above her untied boots. She came running. She always comes running when I need her.

I nod, unable to form words.

She barrels into me, wrapping me in one of her magical Maren hugs, and I sag against her. There is nothing like a Maren Rodriguez hug when the world is falling apart around you.

"Do they know who it is?" She pulls back, dropping her voice to a whisper even though we're alone inside the house.

"They haven't said." I take a shaky breath. "They haven't unwrapped it yet. They're waiting for the medical examiner."

"Luna!" Karen enters the house. "I need to speak with you again."

"I'm gonna grab a cup of coffee." Maren squeezes my arm. "I didn't have a chance to make any. I threw myself out the door so fast, I'm lucky I've got pants on."

Only Maren could make me laugh at a time like this.

"Can you grab the treat bag? Shake it for the cats?" I gesture toward the back door. "They bolted when everyone showed up. All these people and noise have all the animals freaking out. But I'd like to get the cats back inside before they run off too far. Or Sage ends up stuck in a tree like last month."

"On it."

She walks toward the kitchen before she pauses, glancing back at Karen with a look I recognize—protective and territorial. Maren's never been one to trust authority figures.

I sink onto the couch, Shadow plopping onto my feet. Karen pulls out a notepad and takes the armchair across from me. The professional lines on her weathered face do little to hide her concern. At sixty-something, with silver threading through her dark hair, Karen has been Aspen Ridge's sheriff for as long as I can remember. She was friends with my grandfather before he died and used to stop by for coffee and to complain about the tourists. Her familiar presence should comfort me. Instead, I feel exposed.

"Walk me through it again. From the beginning."

I rake my fingers through my hair. I've done it so many times, it must resemble Maren's, sticking up in every direction. My reflection in the window shows someone I barely recognize—unhinged and fraying at the edges.

"I came downstairs around six. Shadow was acting strange, staring out the window. I went to see what he was looking at, and..." I swallow. "And there it was. I called 911 immediately."

Karen nods, jotting something down. "You didn't hear anything during the night? No cars, no voices, nothing that woke you?"

I think back to the figure I swore I saw standing in the trees before bed. The way the moonlight seemed to glint off what looked like a metal mask. But how do I tell her about that without sounding insane? How do I explain the feeling of being watched, of eyes tracking my every movement from the forest's edge for the past week, without her thinking I've finally cracked under the pressure of living alone in the middle of nowhere?

"No. The usual noises. That's it. The wild animals. The wind."

Why am I hiding this?

Karen gestures to the body outside. "You've never seen this person before?"

"I have no idea who it is. I haven't seen the face at all. The plastic—"

"Right." Karen sighs. "Look, Luna, I have to ask, has anyone been giving you trouble lately? Disgruntled former employees or volunteers? Hunters or owners pissed off about you being... you?" Her voice softens on the last word. "Anyone who might have a grudge?"

I shake my head. "No one specific. I mean, you know how some of the locals feel about me and what I do here, especially my reporting of animal abuse when I witness or hear about it. But no one's made any direct threats or anything like that. Not lately anyway."

"What about your ex?" Karen asks, as if reading my mind. She was the one who helped me file the restraining order against Caleb last year. "When's the last time you had contact with him?"

"Over a year ago. Why would you—"

"Covering all the bases. Domestic situations have a way of escalating, sometimes years after the fact."

"It's not Caleb."

But even as the words leave my mouth, doubt creeps in. Is it? Could it be?

Deputy Wilkenson appears in the doorway, his young face grim. "Sheriff? We've got a problem with those wildlife cameras."

Karen turns, her expression sharpening. "What kind of problem?"

"They've been wiped. All of them. Memory cards are blank."

A chill runs down my spine as Karen's eyes narrow. "All three of Luna's cameras? That's not a coincidence."

"I checked them two days ago." My voice sounds far away and disconnected. "They were working fine then. I downloaded footage of a family of skunks playing near the north fence line."

Karen turns back to me, her expression hardening. "Someone planned this, Luna. Someone who knew about your cameras and how to erase them." She turns back to Deputy Wilkenson. "Have them brushed for fingerprints."

Maren chooses that moment to emerge from the kitchen. "The pussies are treated, and hanging in the enclosed porch." Her steps falter. "What's happened now? Did they find another body? Please tell me there's not a whole fucking cemetery buried under your driveway."

"Someone erased my wildlife footage." My mind reels from the knowledge that someone tampered with my cameras.

"Well, that's not disturbing at all." Her attempt at sarcasm falls flat. She moves to sit beside me on the sofa, her thigh pressed against my leg. Her hand finds mine, squeezing until my bones ache in the best possible way. "What kind of sick fuck would do something like this?"

"The kind who leaves a dead body on my porch."

Karen stands, slipping her notepad back into her pocket. "Luna, you need to think about getting a proper security system. Not wildlife cameras. You need more coverage for the whole property, not just areas where the foxes and raccoons like to sneak in."

I nod. Maren has been saying it for a while.

"I'm going to have a deputy drive by regularly for the next week. And I want you to be careful. Lock your doors, all of them, every time you go in or out. Call if anything seems off."

A voice calls to her from somewhere outside. "I need to go. The ME is here. We'll talk more after they've examined the evidence."

After she leaves, Maren turns to me and hisses, "Why didn't you tell her about feeling watched?"

"Because I think I'm being paranoid." The lie tastes bitter on my tongue.

"But what if you're not? What if this is connected?" She pauses, studying my profile. "What if this is Caleb?"

"Why would Caleb come back now? He hasn't tried to contact me for a year."

"Because he's a creep who hit you."

"I don't think it's him. I think it's my imagination going wild."

Why am I not telling her about last night?

"Well, your imagination didn't conjure up that corpse outside. If it keeps happening, you need to report it. If you don't, I will. You know I'll make it sound way more dramatic than it is. I'll probably tell her you've been having wet dreams about mysterious stalkers or some shit."

My mouth twitches. Leave it to Maren to work sex into a conversation about murder. "You're terrible."

"I'm worried about you." She bumps my shoulder with hers, a concerned frown creasing her forehead.

I lean over and plant a kiss on her cheek. Shadow, not to be left out, stands up and licks her other cheek with his enormous tongue.

"Ugh, gross." Maren makes exaggerated wiping motions across her face, but she's smiling. "There's nothing better than getting sloppy kisses from my favorite weirdos. But they won't stop me from ratting your ass out."

She wraps her arms around Shadow's neck, and we fall into silence, watching through the window as men in white suits gather around the porch, preparing to process the scene.

"Who do you think it is?"

I swallow hard, my throat tight with a mix of fear and confusion over why this is happening to me.

"I don't know. And I'm not sure I want to."

Chapter Thirteen

Damien

"Are you out of your fucking mind?"

Cade strides into the room, his eyes blazing and bulging, his usual calm demeanor now replaced with the rage beast that rarely comes out to play. He stalks right up to the front of my desk as my office door slides closed.

The glass walls of my Denver office reflect the city's late afternoon light, casting stark angles across the polished surfaces. Screens surround me, on both the desk and walls, a digital fortress of my own design. Multiple monitors display Luna's sanctuary from the micro-cameras I hid this morning.

"You left the body on her front porch. Like a fucking gift. We have protocols for disposal, Damien. This is not how we operate."

I glance toward Tiffany's desk on the other side of the glass. She's already gone for the day.

"How we operate?" I lean back in my chair and glare up at him. "Last I checked, I'm the one who decides how this works."

Cade crosses his arms, that military stillness never leaving him, even now. "You've been watching her for over a week. Stalking her like she's prey instead of—"

"Instead of what?" I surge to my feet, letting him see the beast beneath my surface. "She's not prey, Cade."

"Then tell me what she is to you. Because this isn't you, Damien. You don't get obsessed. You don't get reckless. You sure as hell don't drop bodies like twisted love letters."

Love letters. The words don't sit right. I walk toward the window and look out over the city.

"He hurt one of her rescues. She needs to know he paid for it."

"And you needed to be the one to tell her?"

"Yes."

Cade shakes his head and moves to stand beside me. "You've never been this way about a woman before. What do you really want with her?"

Her face flashes in front of my eyes, and my pulse changes rhythm. The thought of her makes my chest burn with something that shakes me to my foundation. That night I stood outside her window and watched her touch herself in the moonlight. The hunger that tore through me wasn't simple lust. It was deeper. Darker. The need to mark her. Keep her. Make sure no one else can touch what's mine.

"I want all of her. I want to claim her. Own her. Brand her."

"Jesus Christ, Damien. Are you listening to yourself?" Cade stares at me like I've lost my mind. Maybe I have. "You need to get laid and leave the doctor alone."

The words are barely out of his mouth before I have him by the throat, slamming him against the window. His eyes widen, but he doesn't fight back.

"This isn't about fucking her." My grip tightens.

Though I will. I'll fuck her until she screams and begs me never to stop. But it's more than that.

"Damien—"

"Yes, we have protocols for disposal, but Luna, what I do for her is off-limits. You don't get to question it."

I release him, and he rubs his throat. "You're not thinking clearly."

"I've never been clearer in my life. For over twenty-five years, I've lived in shadows, Cade. Hunting. Killing. Then I saw her, and it's like someone turned on a light I didn't know I needed."

Athena jumps off the sofa where she was napping and ambles over, her brown eyes taking in the tension between us.

"Hey, girl." I kneel, and she nudges my hand with her head. I stroke the fur around her ears.

Cade watches the interaction in silence, his expression unreadable except for the slight relaxation in his jaw. We both know Athena is my weakness. My connection to something pure in a world I've painted in shades of violent gray.

Her tail wags as she looks between Cade and me, sensing the conflict but trusting me to handle it.

The office is silent except for her contented breathing. Cade studies me with the calculating gaze that's kept us both alive for decades.

"Are you sure you left no DNA evidence behind?"

I give him a withering look. "Have I ever left DNA behind?"

"No. But that's because I clean up after you."

"From this point forward, I'll handle the entirety of the kills, including cleanup, related to Luna's sanctuary. You'll handle all the others."

He's silent for a long time, debate warring in his eyes over whether he should fight me on this.

"Just be careful. Whatever this is, don't let it destroy everything we've built."

My hand stills on Athena's head. "It won't destroy anything."

Cade leaves my office. I stand up and look out the window again. Athena remains by my side, her presence a comfort I've never found with another living being.

Until Luna.

I was only in her presence once, for mere seconds, but that single encounter with her was enough to know her power both to arouse and calm the beast within me.

Chapter Fourteen

Luna

Shadow and I cut across the backyard with Maren trailing behind us, all three of us heading toward the screened porch. With cooler weather approaching, it's time to install the glass panels for winter. I hate having to enclose it, but it's too cold in Colorado not to. Otherwise, I wouldn't be able to use it all winter. I make a mental note to call Eddie, the sanctuary's handyman. The panels are too heavy for Maren and me to install alone.

I barely slept last night after the body I found on my porch. The forensics team was here half the day, throwing off the sanctuary's usual rhythm and schedule. Maren told all the volunteers to take the day off. Neither of us wanted them dealing with the shitshow the day turned into. Maren stayed last night, and I've never been more grateful for her presence. She made spaghetti and meatballs, and we watched a mindless comedy, both of us trying to forget. I double and triple-checked the locks on all the windows and doors before bed and stared out the window for hours, looking for anyone lurking in the trees. I saw nothing unusual, but I still found it impossible to sleep.

As the sun started to rise, I gave up and decided a hike would help me shake off this incessant fear pulsing through me. I intended to go alone, but Maren must have heard me leave my bedroom because a few minutes later, as Shadow and I were about to head out the back door, she came traipsing down the stairs, grumbling about stupid dead bodies fucking with her sleep schedule.

The hike started slow, my fatigue weighing me down, but I found my stride. Now my legs are tingly and pleasantly tired, but Maren's dramatic groaning suggests she's having a different experience.

"Oh, come on. A hard, brisk hike is good for you in the morning."

"So's a good hard fuck. But you don't have the equipment to give me the railing I need."

I open my mouth to respond with a sarcastic comeback, then the feeling crawls across my skin. Invisible eyes watching, tracking our movements. I slow my pace, scanning the treeline. I stop walking. "Do you feel that?"

"What? My legs? No, not after that hill you made me traverse like some kind of mountain goat."

"No, I'm talking about that." I look around. The feeling is stronger now, more focused. "Like someone's watching us."

"Again?" Maren's body stiffens as she follows my gaze toward the forest. "Wouldn't Shadow be freaking out if someone was out there?"

"You'd think so, but—" I stop mid-sentence and point, directing Maren's attention to Shadow.

He's on full alert, ears pricked forward, body tense as he stares toward the dense forest, his growls growing louder with each passing second.

"Well, that's not creepy as shit. Come on, let's go inside. You need to call the sheriff."

Tate pokes his head out the back door of the main sanctuary building, interrupting the argument forming on my tongue. He's one of our early volunteers, often showing up before I head over. He's not usually here on Sundays, but he offered to come in today when we canceled him yesterday.

"Luna, Roger's on the phone. Said he's got a case he needs you for."

Shit. We detour inside, forgetting about who might be watching, and I pick up the extension. "Hey, Roger, what's up?"

"Got a call about a wolf hybrid chained up at an abandoned property about twenty miles east on Highway 34, outside town. It's bad." The last two words come out clipped, bitten off at the edges.

My heartbeat stutters. "How bad?"

"Worst I've seen in years. Animal's barely alive. Owner left town. Neighbor called it in. I'm texting you the address. Can you come?"

"I'll grab my emergency kit and head out now." I end the call and rush to gather supplies.

Maren looks up from petting the rabbits as I burst into the treatment room. "What's happening?"

"Wolf hybrid, severe abuse case." I'm already filling my medical bag with extra IV fluids. "Can you handle things here for a few hours?"

"Of course." Maren's expression darkens as I zip my bag shut. "Take the truck. I filled it yesterday."

I nod, grabbing my keys. "If I don't call in an hour—"

"I'll handle everything here and be ready when you bring the patient in."

I jump in the truck and speed down the driveway. As I pull out to the main road, my phone rings. It's Karen. Damn it, what now?

"Hi, Karen. What can I do for you?"

"We've identified the body from your porch."

"Already? Who is it?"

"Daryl Rawlings."

The truck swerves. I yank the steering wheel hard, wrestling it back onto the asphalt. "Are you kidding me?"

"No."

"Who would kill Daryl Rawlings?"

"He wasn't well liked around here, but you're the only person I know of who threatened to kill him."

Oops. I did say that, didn't I?

"Karen, that was said in the heat of the moment, in anger, when we were at his place, taking Buddy from him."

"I know, Luna. I don't think you killed him. But you did threaten him in front of me and half a dozen other deputies and county animal services employees. Now he's found dead on your property. It looks suspicious."

I slow the truck to avoid interfering with a family of elk crossing the road ahead. "How is that suspicious? Do you really think that if I killed him, I'd call it in? No, I would've buried him in a shallow grave and been done with him."

"I'm going to pretend you didn't say that."

The elk wander into the meadow beside the road, and I speed up again. "I don't get it. Who would do this? Who would want to leave me the dead body of a person tied to one of my abuse cases?"

"I don't know, but I'm going to figure it out. I just wanted you to hear it from me."

"Thanks. I didn't do it, Karen. But I'm not sad he's dead."

I want to regret my words, but there's a sense of freedom in the honesty.

Karen is quiet for several beats. "I'm not either."

It's almost as good when she agrees.

"Stay vigilant, Luna. Get those cameras, and call if anything doesn't feel right."

"I will."

※

Twenty minutes later, I pull my truck onto a dirt road leading to a dilapidated single-wide trailer, still in shock over Karen's call. Roger's county-issued truck is parked in front. I push Daryl Rawlings and my unexpected and confusing happiness that he's dead to the back of my mind as I grab my bag and jog around the back, following the sound of Roger's low, soothing voice.

The sight steals my breath. A massive white wolf hybrid, with one amber eye and one blue, lies on its side in mud mixed with its own waste. A heavy chain attached to a crude collar has rubbed the animal's neck raw. Its ribs protrude against matted fur, and flies buzz around several infected wounds. A large paper plate sits in front of him, scattered with kibble crumbs.

Roger kneels a few feet away, keeping his distance from the weakened but still dangerous animal.

"Jesus." I crouch beside him, unzipping my medical bag.

"Been chained here for at least a week, from what the neighbors say." Anger threads through Roger's voice as he runs a hand through his hair. "Owner skipped town, left it to die."

"Has it had any water?"

"Dirty puddle from yesterday's rain. That's it."

"Did you give him that food?"

Roger nods. "A cup of kibble. I didn't want to overdo it. Poor thing wolfed it down in seconds."

The animal's eyes track my movements with a dull wariness. Not aggression, just the exhausted vigilance of something that expects only pain from humans.

"I'll need to sedate him to get him back." I open my drug kit and start preparing a syringe. "Can you get a catchpole ready? I don't want to approach until he's under."

Roger nods and walks around the house.

I creep forward, pausing between steps to gauge his reaction, my voice a gentle murmur. "Hey there, handsome. I know humans have been nothing but terrible to you, but we're going to help now. Hold on a little longer for me, huh?"

The hybrid's ears twitch at my voice, his breathing labored.

With Roger's help, I manage to administer the sedative via a long injection pole. We wait in tense silence as the drug takes effect, the hybrid's mismatched eyes closing as its body goes limp.

I pull on my gloves and approach him. Up close, the damage is even worse. Deep lacerations across the animal's haunches suggest beatings. Cigarette burns dot its muzzle, and the pads of its paws are cracked and bleeding. I clench my jaw, examining the crude metal collar embedded in infected flesh.

"A week on this chain? What kind of monster would do this? And why did it take the neighbors that long to call it in?"

"Don't go there." Roger helps me lift and place the unconscious animal onto a tarp. "Focus on saving him."

I insert an IV line and begin pushing fluids. He's severely dehydrated and malnourished. "We need to get him to the sanctuary. I'll need to surgically remove this collar."

Roger's hand on my shoulder is some comfort, but I don't need it. This animal does. Together, we lift the tarp into the back of his truck and secure him. I administer another dose of medication to keep him sedated for the drive back.

"I'll follow you."

My eyes sweep over the weathered shed beside the spot where the hybrid was chained. The name "DEMON" is crudely spray-painted on the side.

"Did you get the owner's name?"

"Thomas and Bertha Meyers. Sheriff's already looking for them."

"Good." The single word carries the weight of all I can't allow myself to say. "Thanks for calling me, Roger."

"If anyone can heal him, it's you, Luna."

My vision blurs as I nod and climb into the truck. During the drive back, tears carve hot tracks down my cheeks as I punch in Maren's number.

"Prep the surgical suite," I manage between hitched breaths.

"Already done." Her voice carries that familiar calm that keeps me anchored.

My knuckles go white against the steering wheel, my mind filling with images of what I would do to the Meyers if I ever see them again. The violence of these thoughts should horrify me. Instead, they bring a disturbing comfort. My mind drifts to Daryl Rawlings, and I can't help but hope whoever killed him finds the Meyers before Karen does.

⸻ ◆ ⸻

I stare at the sweet, injured animal on my surgical table, fighting to stay clinical, to keep my hands steady.

"Blood pressure's dropping." Maren's usual humor is absent in the sterile intensity of the operating room.

"I see it."

I work to free the embedded collar. It's grown into his flesh, the skin healing around the metal and leather in grotesque ridges.

"Saline."

Maren hands me the syringe. We've done this dance too many times.

The hybrid wolf-dog, part Alaskan husky from the look of him, doesn't even twitch under the anesthesia. His body is so worn down and depleted, but I refuse to accept the possibility of him not making it.

"Oh, I didn't tell you, I got a call from Karen earlier." I break the heavy silence as I separate another section of collar from raw flesh. "They've identified the body."

Maren's hands pause. "Yeah? Who was it?"

"Daryl Rawlings."

"Are you fucking kidding me?" Maren's mouth drops open. "Good fucking riddance to him, I say. Piece of shit deserved it. Like the piece of shit who did this."

"Careful with the suction here." I reach over and guide her hand.

Two hours crawl by, my back aching, fingers growing stiff, but I refuse to rush. This boy deserves my best, my most careful attention after everything he's endured. By the time I place the final suture, my scrubs are drenched with sweat and spattered with pus and blood.

I step back from the table, overwhelmed by exhaustion. "Let's get him to recovery."

Together, we transfer his limp body to a soft bed in the recovery den. I arrange warm blankets around him, careful not to disturb the fresh bandages around his neck. His breathing is shallow but steady. The blood-matted and waste-covered fur we've cleaned reveals patches of beautiful silver-white coloring. He's going to be stunning once he heals.

I collapse into a chair beside his bed, unable to take my eyes off his sleeping form. I should be documenting the procedure and updating his chart, but I can't seem to move. Maren disappears and returns a few minutes later with a steaming mug she presses into my hands.

"Drink."

The familiar smell of Earl Grey mixed with a healthy dose of whiskey hits my nostrils. I take it without argument, letting the burning liquid slide down my throat.

Maren pulls up a chair beside me. "What did his owners call him again?"

"Demon."

"Assholes." She shakes her head in disgust. "What are you going to name him? You've obviously claimed him already."

As usual, she's right. He's now a permanent resident here.

I study him. Despite everything—the starvation, the abuse, the neglect—there's a dignity in his face. A resilience in his very survival that takes my breath away.

"Ghost. His name is Ghost."

"Fitting." Maren's expression grows serious. "Luna, whatever you're thinking... Don't."

My head snaps up. "What are you—"

"I know that look." Her voice is gentle but firm. "I've seen it every time we get one of these cases. But this time it's different. You're not only angry. You're planning."

I look away, my chest tightening. "If you'd seen where he was kept, Maren. The chains. The filth. How those monsters treated him..." My voice catches, and I blink back tears. "Thomas Meyers and his wife don't deserve to be walking free after what they did."

"I know. And they'll face charges. The sheriff—"

"The sheriff can't do shit, and you know it." I surprise myself with the vehemence in my voice. "It's the courts. They'll get a fine, maybe. Animal abuse isn't taken seriously enough in this state."

Maren sighs and reaches for my hand. "That may be true, but your job is to heal them, not to deliver justice."

My shoulders slump as the fight drains out of me. "I wish..." I trail off, uncertain if I should voice the darkness swirling inside me.

"Wish what?"

I stare into my mug. "I wish whoever left Daryl Rawlings's body on my porch would find Thomas and his wife before Karen does."

There, I said it. The words hang in the air, dangerous once spoken aloud, a confession I can't take back.

Maren's eyebrows shoot up. "Whoa, Luna 'Do No Harm' Foster actually wishing harm on someone? Now I've heard everything." Her tone is light and teasing, but she can't hide her concern. Not from me.

"I know, I know." I take another sip of the spiked tea. "That's what scares me. That I don't just think it. I want it."

"Look, I'm not saying I disagree." Maren stretches her legs out in front of her. "Those people deserve a special place in hell. But this isn't you, Lu. You're the person who once spent three days hand-feeding a baby squirrel every two hours. You cried when we couldn't save that elk with the broken back."

"Maybe I'm changing." I watch Ghost's chest rise and fall.

"Maybe we all are." Maren nudges my shoulder. "Hey, if it helps, I'll totally hold the Meyers down while you tattoo 'animal abuser' across their foreheads. Much more ethical than wishing vigilante justice on them, right?"

"You're on."

"For what it's worth, I get it. These cases... they chip away at you. Make you question humanity. But you can't let them change who you are at your core."

I nod, knowing she's right, but I'm not quite ready to let go of my anger. It wraps around me like armor, protecting the parts of my heart that break a little more with each case like this one.

And maybe, just maybe, that armor is what I need right now.

Chapter Fifteen

Damien

The three monitors in front of me display different angles inside the sanctuary. The central screen captures Luna moving between treatment areas. Every movement—from her breath to the way she watches the sleeping hybrid, and every new line of worry on her face—is so captivating, I can't look away.

Her reaction to my gift the other day was not what I had in mind. I expected the fear and the horror, but the gratitude I hoped would come with it never materialized. Though her words to her vet tech during Ghost's surgery were music to my ears. They were what shot Thomas and Bertha Meyers to the top of my kill list.

"You've been watching those cameras for three days." Cade slams a coffee cup onto the desk, hard enough to rattle my keyboard. "It's a good thing you have me to run your business, or you'd go bankrupt."

I don't look up because I can't. Luna's kneeling beside the animal now, changing its bandages. Her movements are gentle, and there's something about the careful way she touches him that makes heat pool low in my stomach. I want her to touch me with that gentleness.

"She's different."

"You've said that before. Different how?" Cade folds his arms across his chest in that disapproving way that usually amuses me. Right now, it irritates the fuck out of me. "Because from where I'm standing, she looks like a potential complication we don't need."

We. As if Cade gets a say in what I need. As if anyone does.

"She saved that animal two days ago. A wolf hybrid. Owners tortured it. Left it to die on a chain."

Cade's expression hardens.

"And this owner is now on your list, I assume?"

"Top of it. Thomas and Bertha Meyers." He walks around the desk as I pull up another screen showing driver's license photos of a heavyset man with a receding hairline and dead eyes and a woman with purple hair and a mouthful of teeth so crooked, it's clear she's never seen a dentist. "Already located them. They're holed up in a motel outside Pueblo."

"You don't often hunt women."

"Only when they deserve it."

"Did she abuse the animal too?"

"Even if she didn't, she stood by while he did. She deserves death as much as he does."

I'm reminded of my mother and the price she paid for her inaction.

Cade nods, knowing I won't be deterred from my course. I never am once I've made up my mind. It's one of the things he both respects and fears about me.

"And the doctor?" His sigh tells me he's been building up to this question. I was expecting it because even though I threatened him, Cade won't let a subject drop if he thinks it might harm me. The protective bastard. "I know you told me to back off, but what's really your interest there? She's an attractive woman, I get it, but—"

I swivel in my chair, meeting Cade's questioning gaze. "You should have seen her face when she was treating that animal. The rage she tried to contain. It was beautiful. She has darkness in her." I turn back to the screens, needing to see her again. "She wants justice as badly as I do. She just hasn't embraced it yet."

"Damien." Cade's shoulders square, his chin lifting in that familiar way that means a lecture is coming. "Leaving that body for her was a mistake. You cannot drag a civilian into this. Especially not one with an obvious moral compass."

"I'm not dragging her anywhere. I'm simply curious."

"Your curiosity usually comes with a body count."

The comment pulls a rare smile from me because he's not wrong. My curiosity does tend to be lethal. But not with her. Never with her.

"Not her body. Not yet, anyway."

Cade walks to the window and looks out over the Denver skyline. "This is what I was afraid of."

I detect the resignation in his voice, the way he's already calculating damage control.

"Nothing you say is going to change my mind."

He's processing my words, trying to find an angle that will talk me out of this. Good luck with that.

He turns from the window to look at me. "Damien, you know I think of you as a son."

The words scrape against old wounds I thought were long scarred over.

"You're not my fucking father, Cade. I killed my father. Besides, you're barely ten years older than me."

"Regardless." His expression doesn't change. My outbursts stopped affecting him years ago. "I care about you too much to let you go down this path. You don't have the emotional capacity for a relationship with this woman. You'll only hurt her. Maybe even destroy her."

I know my emotional capacity. Cade isn't wrong about that either. I'm not capable of love. But I am capable of obsession. And I'm obsessed with Luna. From the moment I laid eyes on her.

"I'm not going to destroy her." But honesty compels me to add, "But I'm going to ruin her for anyone else. No one else will ever have her. Not while I'm breathing."

Cade sighs, the sound heavy with years of watching me make choices he can't approve of but can't stop either. "Remember your code. We don't involve innocents."

"She's not as innocent as she appears." I click through more surveillance images, stopping on one that captures Luna's face as she examines the wolf's wounds. The raw fury in her eyes is unmistakable. "She has dark thoughts. I can see it."

"Thoughts aren't actions. Most normal people have dark thoughts they never act on. That's what separates them from people who are—"

"Like me?"

"I was going to say wired differently."

"Same thing." I zoom in on Luna's face, studying every line, every shadow. She's so fucking beautiful.

Cade pushes away from the window with the frustrated energy of a man who knows he's fighting a losing battle.

"Do what you need to do with the Meyers, but dispose of them properly. And please leave the doctor alone. I'm begging you, Damien."

The plea in his voice would have moved me once. But that was before Luna, before I understood what it meant to want something so completely that breathing becomes secondary.

"No. Wrap your mind around it, look the other way if you have to, but I will have her."

Cade leaves without another word, and I continue watching Luna through the cameras. She moves between patients, her every gesture displaying competence and care. Then she returns to the wolf hybrid's bedside and settles beside him, her hands stroking his beautiful silver-white fur, and there's something so tender about the gesture that it makes me want to reach through the screen and touch her.

I switch camera angles until her face fills the frame. My fingers tighten on the mouse as I zoom in, and white-hot rage explodes behind my ribs. Blood roars in my ears, and my skin burns as if someone lit a match to my veins.

There are tears in her eyes. She's crying for the hybrid, like she did for the deer. She reaches up and swipes her cheeks when a male volunteer approaches, trying to hide her emotions, but I can't unsee it.

The Meyers will pay for it.

Unable to watch her cry any longer, I switch screens. The cameras I hacked outside the motel show Thomas and Bertha walking up to their room with a six-pack of beer and a bucket of KFC. The planning part of my brain calculates entrances, exits, and the familiar ritual before a hunt as a plan comes together.

But my mind drifts back to Luna.

Would she be horrified? Or would she understand that sometimes the only answer to cruelty is more cruelty?

⸻◆⸻

Athena snoozes on the office sofa as I prepare to leave the estate. I've only completed renovations on two rooms in the vast mansion so far, my bedroom and the office, but they're all I need for my purposes, except the basement for my kills.

Before Luna entered my world, I never slept here, but now I do most nights because I can't bear to be far from her. The decay I once embraced, the crumbling plaster and rotting floors, now seems unworthy. Luna deserves to see this house as it was meant to be, restored to the grandeur that existed before evil poisoned it. My designers will have free rein everywhere except the basement.

I came up here tonight before heading to Pueblo because I need to see her and not just through a monitor. The thrill of what's to come spreads through my bones. It's twofold. The thrill of seeing her and of knowing tonight is the night the Meyers will take their final breaths.

I glance over at Athena. She's staying here tonight. Having two marks at once will make juggling her presence too complicated, and these two require my full, brutal focus. Not only because of what they did to that hybrid, but because they committed an even greater sin in my eyes.

They made Luna cry, and no one makes my little doe cry. Except me.

I drive toward the turnout on the main road between our properties, parking behind the pines that conceal my vehicle. The silver wolf mask sits in the center console, its empty eyes reflecting the dashboard lights. I trace a finger along its contours, feeling the cool metal beneath my fingertips.

I want to wear it for her tonight. In case she sees me again.

I move through the trees, my black clothing blending with the darkness. I don't need night vision anymore. I could find my way to her blindfolded. She's become my beacon, pulling me through the wilderness with an invisible thread I never want to break.

Her house appears through the treeline, warm light spilling from the windows. Her vet tech's car still sits in the driveway, its presence an unwelcome complication.

Why is she still here?

They pass through the living room, turning off the lights as Luna shuts the curtains. Her friend must be staying the night again. Frustration bubbles up inside me. I need cameras inside that house. The blind spots in my surveillance are maddening.

Luna's bedroom light turns on, and she closes her door. One of her cats, the fat one, jumps onto the windowsill as she approaches, with a slight stumble in her walk.

Is she drunk? Did her grief over the hybrid drive her to alcohol? My fists clench. The Meyers have a lot to answer for.

She reaches the window and looks out, straight in my direction, before leaning down and snuggling the cat as her eyes scan the forest's edge.

Is she looking for me?

I step out of the treeline, my footsteps measured and slow. The moonlight barely illuminates me, but she squints, tilting her head as if questioning what she sees.

I take another step forward, emerging from the shadows.

I'm here, little doe.

Her mouth opens in surprise, a gasp I can't hear but imagine perfectly. She grabs the curtains, and every muscle in my body tenses.

Don't you fucking dare close them.

The internal debate plays across her beautiful face, a conflict between fear and curiosity as she wrestles with which one she'll let win. Her fingers grip the fabric, ready to shut me out, cut me off from this view of her private world, but she doesn't. She steps back, dropping her hands.

Leaving the curtains wide open.

A smile spreads over my lips.

Perhaps she's beginning to understand how this dance between us works.

Then her fingers find the hem of her shirt, playing with the edge. Testing. Teasing. Deliberating.

Is she really going to...?

She lifts the fabric, revealing skin inch by inch. The smooth plane of her stomach, the curve of her ribs, the swell of her breasts. Higher and higher until she pulls it over her head and tosses it aside with a casualness that belies the significance of what she's doing.

Blood rushes in my ears. My body responds, and pressure builds behind my zipper, threatening to burst, steel fighting against swelling flesh.

This is different from when she dropped her towel. She knows I'm watching.

Is this a challenge? An invitation? Or is she testing how far she can push before I break?

I step closer, deeper into the yard and into the moonlight. She sees me now. Her posture shifts, shoulders back, and chin lifted. A new confidence emerges. She's playing a dangerous game without understanding the rules.

If her friend wasn't here, I'd storm that house and fuck her to within an inch of her life. Show her what happens when you tease a wolf.

Who knew she could be this bold? This fiery? It makes me want her even more. Not just her body, but her spirit. I want to capture that flame and keep it burning only for me.

She stands backlit by her bedside lamp, a silhouette of perfect curves and hidden promises. Beautiful doesn't begin to describe her. She's magnificent. A goddess who doesn't know her own power.

Or maybe she does.

Because when I think I can't get any harder, she reaches up and flicks open the front clasp of her bra. The fabric parts, her breasts spilling free. Even from this distance, I see her chest expand and contract with each breath. Then she shrugs, and the garment slides down her arms and onto the floor.

And I'm granted another glimpse of her exquisite perfection.

Her breasts are round, generous, and hard-tipped. Luna cups herself, filling her own hands, thumbs brushing across peaks that respond to her touch. Her neck arches back, lips parting in what must be silent pleasure. Lightning races down my spine as she explores herself, her touch growing bolder with each caress.

The world narrows to this single window, my lungs forgetting how to work. The mask clings to my face, too confining, the night air too thick. My muscles tense with the urge to scale that balcony again or kick through her door regardless of who might hear. Her friend can watch or run. I don't care. I want to discover every sound Luna makes when hands know exactly where to touch. I want to map her body with my mouth, worship every inch, until she breaks apart beneath me.

Before I can act, she steps forward and, with one final challenging look, pulls the curtains closed.

She vanishes behind them, leaving me hollow, rooted to her lawn with hunger eating me alive from the inside. My jaw hangs open, catching night air, while my jeans have become a torture device.

And it's all from the simple sight of her fucking tits. All from watching her hands claim what should be mine.

You're playing with fire, little doe.

My feet carry me backward through the grass, each step a war between leaving and staying. Her window holds me like a magnet even as the distance grows between us. My hands shake with the need to claim what she's offered, to teach her the consequences of this torture. She's started something tonight that won't end with closed curtains and locked doors. But the Meyers have expiration dates stamped on their foreheads, and I won't let them slip away while I'm drunk on her performance.

The trees swallow me whole before my hands attack my zipper, releasing what she's awakened. Oak bark bites into my forearm as I brace against a tree, working myself with savage pulls, the image of her curves burned behind my eyelids.

Minutes blur together until release explodes through me, her name ripping from my throat, shattering the silence as I empty myself onto earth that will keep my secrets.

I stuff my cock back into my pants and drag out a handkerchief, wiping my hand as I head back to the SUV. The pressure has lifted. For now.

She's dismantling me piece by piece, turning discipline into dust. The careful balance I've maintained for years tilts toward chaos with every breath she takes.

Dawn will bring her two new gifts. Then we stop playing games through glass and cameras.

But first, I have an appointment with Thomas and Bertha Meyers. They've been breathing borrowed air long enough.

Chapter Sixteen

Luna

Consciousness hits me like a sledgehammer to my temples. Morning sunlight streams through the gap in my curtains, thanks to Juni claiming her usual spot on the windowsill, and each ray feels like it's stabbing into my brain. I groan and burrow deeper under the covers, surrounded by Sage and Willow's warm weight. Why can't Juni stay in bed with the rest of us?

My tongue sticks to the roof of my mouth, which tastes like I licked the floor of Ricky and Zorro's cage.

I'm never drinking again.

The words taste like lies. Maren and I always say that when the bottles are empty and the sun rises.

Last night comes back in disjointed flashes. Chinese food, way too much of it, because Maren always orders enough to feed an army. Then, bottle after bottle of wine as we tried to drown out the stress from the past few days. Daryl Rawlings' dead body, Ghost's injuries, and that poor donkey dragged behind his bastard owner's truck for five miles. I should drag that asshole behind my truck and see how he likes it.

We sat on my living room floor, drowning in our glasses, as we passed sentences on monsters who tortured innocent animals. Death by fire. Death by blade. Death by their own methods turned back on them.

And then... *oh, fuck.*

Bile rises in my throat as another memory surfaces. Standing at my bedroom window after Maren and I stumbled upstairs. Seeing the tall figure in my yard, moonlight catching that disturbing mask of what looked like a wolf's face. My watcher. My stalker. The stranger who's been watching me for almost two weeks now.

Do I really have a stalker?

I should have called Maren into my room the second I saw him to prove I'm not losing my mind. Then, I should have called Karen. Instead, the alcohol hijacked my brain and body, twisting terror into dangerous desire.

I press my face into the pillow. I'd stared right back at him through the window, daring him to look away first, as I pulled off my shirt, unhooked my bra, and let everything drop to the ground.

He'd turned to stone when I started stripping, his gaze tracking my every movement through the window. I let him look his fill, knowing he'd never get closer than the glass between us, letting him watch what he could never have.

What the hell is wrong with me?

I'm a thirty-two-year-old doctor and a respected member of my small community, not some hussy who strips in her window for masked strangers.

But I can't deny the thrill. Electricity still crackles under my skin at the memory. The raw excitement of being the center of someone's universe, even a stranger's dangerous attention. Of taking control of the fear I've been feeling for days in the most unexpected way.

Then, the spell had shattered like glass. One second I was putting on a show like some kind of slutty exhibitionist, and the next I was yanking fabric across the window while my heart tried to beat its way out of my chest.

A knock at my bedroom door jolts me from my mortifying memories.

"Rise and shine, Doc!" Maren's voice is far too cheerful and far too loud. "It's almost seven, you lazy ass!"

She barges in, looking annoyingly put-together in jeans and a faded Sanctuary sweatshirt, hair in a messy bun that somehow looks intentional. The only signs of her hangover are slight shadows under her eyes and the death grip on her coffee mug.

"I hate you," I groan, pulling the comforter over my head. "Go away and let me die in peace."

"Not a chance." The edge of my bed dips as she sits down. Willow meows in protest at being disturbed. "I made coffee. And I found some stale bagels that might be salvageable with enough cream cheese."

"How are you even functioning?" I peek out from my fabric fortress, squinting at her. "We killed at least two bottles of red."

"Three." She smirks. "And I'm dying inside, trust me. I just handle my liquor better than your lightweight ass. Advantages of my extra padding."

I push myself up with one arm, my skull pounding with each heartbeat, while Maren slurps her coffee.

"Come on, get up. We've got animals to check, and you're useless until you're vertical and caffeinated."

"No."

I don't care how petulant I sound.

"I'll make you French toast if you get your ass out of bed in the next five minutes."

"With bananas," I grumble, but I'm already contemplating the monumental effort of sitting up.

"Sure. I want blueberries too. This room is like a cave." She stands and walks toward the window. "Let's get some light in here."

"No!" I yank the covers over my head again. "The light will literally kill me."

"When did you become such a drama queen?" Maren snorts and I hear her pull the curtain aside. "Where's Juni? There she is. Hello, beautiful." Juniper purrs, the little traitor. "How's my favorite pus—"

The unexpected scream replacing the softness of her words sends me bolting upright, my hangover forgotten.

"What? What is it?" I scramble out of bed, tripping over Willow in my haste.

Maren points out the window, her face drained of color. "Luna... there's... What the fuck is in your driveway? Are those fucking bodies?"

I rush to her side and look out the window, the sun shooting through my skull like a laser beam. Then my blood turns to ice.

Two human shapes lie motionless on the gravel, bodies wrapped in plastic that glints in the morning sun.

Just like Daryl Rawlings.

"Oh, fuck. Not again."

"More dead bodies?" Maren grabs my arms, sending Juniper scurrying off the windowsill with a hiss. "Why the hell are there more dead bodies in your driveway?"

For one wild, irrational moment, I think of the wolf-masked stranger, of my watcher, and of what I did last night. The two thoughts collide in my brain with horrifying clarity.

He was here last night.

Now, there are dead bodies in my driveway.

⊷◆⊶

"I know I said this before, but you need security, Luna."

Karen crosses her arms, and her chin lifts. I recognize that look. She's not letting this go.

I lean back in Grandpa's ancient desk chair, grimacing as it squeaks in protest, the sound echoing through my small office. I stroke Shadow's fur as he presses against my leg, the familiar comfort anchors me when everything else feels like it's spinning out of control.

"Karen, I appreciate the concern, but—"

"Three bodies, Luna. Three. Dumped on your property, wrapped up like presents." She winces, but frustration etches her face. "Whoever's doing this has an unnatural interest in you that concerns me."

There is someone who has an interest in me, but I don't know who he is or why.

Ghost fingers crawl across my skin, the phantom weight of his gaze still burning through glass and memory, leaving invisible marks that pulse with every heartbeat. My skin flushes with a combination of shame and something darker. And I try to piece together why some buried part of me had craved his attention even as fear clawed at my lungs.

The woman who'd peeled away her clothes for a masked stranger feels like someone else. Someone I don't recognize but can't quite disown, a mystery wrapped in wine and reckless desire.

Karen's eyes search my face. I should tell her everything right now. Instead, my voice dies somewhere between my brain and my mouth. He's the one leaving these bodies. I know it like I know my own name. But why is he doing it? What kind of psycho leaves dead bodies on a person's doorstep?

"All three people are connected to cases that came to your sanctuary." Karen's voice interrupts my spiraling thoughts. "That's Thomas and Bertha Meyers out there."

I force my features into an impassive mask. "Are you sure it's them?"

"Yes, I recognize their faces."

My teeth grind together while something bright and terrible blooms in my chest because the Meyers got what they deserved. The euphoria lasts three heartbeats before shame turns my stomach inside out. This version of myself, the woman finding joy in their death, terrifies me more than any masked stalker.

"I understand the impulse not to care." Karen's voice is softer now. "God knows I've wanted to throttle these monsters myself. But someone's targeting these people and using your sanctuary as a dumping ground. That makes you either a target or a suspect, Luna. And you're not a suspect."

I tug on my messy blonde knot, releasing the strands and running my hands through them. Even the small movement makes my eyes hurt, my hangover lingering despite two cups of coffee, three Advil, and the greasiest eggs and bacon Maren could cook up because I was out of bread for French toast.

"You need protection. Security cameras at a minimum."

"I run a wildlife sanctuary in the middle of nowhere, Karen. My budget barely covers medical supplies and feed."

She places her hand on the handle of her holstered gun. "I'm not asking you to install Fort Knox. But something more than those useless wildlife cameras. Besides, it's not only for you. What about Maren? The volunteers? The animals?"

Irritation burns through me as I narrow my eyes. She's trying to manipulate me, and we both know it.

Shadow's head jerks toward the window, ears up. I follow his gaze, but the treeline looks empty.

"Fine. I'll look into some options."

Karen nods, satisfied. "Good. Now, I'll check back with you later, but be careful. And have someone stay here with you. I know you can't leave the animals, but get someone, preferably someone big and male. With a gun."

"I have a gun, Karen. I can take care of myself."

"I mean it, Luna. Whoever's doing this is fixated on you, and that's never a good thing."

After she leaves, I let my head fall onto the desk. Pain explodes through my skull, but the cool wood feels good against my skin.

"Okay, spill." Maren drops into the chair across from me. "That's the second time you didn't tell Karen about feeling watched? Why not? And don't give me that 'it's probably nothing' bullshit. You never called her after our hike the other day, did you?"

I cringe and lift my head. "No."

"Luna." Her voice is incredulous and irritated all at once. "Three dead bodies on your property, and you think feeling watched isn't worth reporting to the sheriff? Who are you, and what have you done with my smart, level-headed best friend? What's really going on? What aren't you telling me?"

That I have a stalker. I am being watched, and I stripped for him. And some dark, twisted part of me wants his attention. I'm terrified, but I can't stop replaying how it felt when he was staring.

But I can't say any of that. Instead, I sit up and meet her gaze. "I don't know, Mar. Maybe I'm losing my mind."

Sane people don't strip for their stalkers. Sane people call the police the second they see a masked stranger watching them from their yard. Sane people don't feel this perverse thrill alongside the bone-deep terror.

"You're not losing your mind. But you are being an idiot if you don't take this seriously. Karen's right. You need security. And you need to stop keeping secrets that could get you killed."

I trace the wood grain on my desk with my finger instead of looking at her. "I know."

"Did I overhear Karen say that was Thomas and Bertha Meyers out there?"

"Yeah."

"Fuck!" She exhales a long breath. "I guess you got your wish. And whoever did this to them is a hero in my book. Those assholes had it coming." She rubs her temples. "So, about this security system?"

"I can't afford a fancy security system, Mar. I'd rather spend the money on medical supplies or the enclosure we need for Titus."

"You can't help animals if you're dead, Lu."

I turn away and start shuffling papers that are already organized. "I'll research some systems tomorrow."

"No need." Maren tosses an elegant business card onto my desk with a flourish. "Eleanor asked me to give you this when I picked up the mail. Mr. Damien Wolfe owns a security company. And Eleanor won't shut up about him or how hot he is. Although I don't know if I trust Eleanor's opinion of what defines hot. She is married to Frank, after all."

"Be nice. Frank is a sweetie."

"Oh, he is, but he looks like the old man from UP."

A small laugh escapes before I can stop it, making my head pound so hard I half expect my eyeballs to pop out like corks from champagne bottles.

"God, he does, doesn't he? Poor Frank."

"Anyway, you said Mr. Billionaire is a hottie silver fox, too."

"No, I didn't. You inferred that when I told you Eleanor said he has gray at his temples."

"Whatever. Point is, you need to call him. Eleanor said one of his companies specializes in custom security. And since he's loaded, maybe he'll cut you a deal for the sanctuary."

I pick up the card, running my fingers over the heavy stock and minimalist design. WOLFE GROUP embossed in matte black against slate gray, superimposed over the face of a silver wolf. Beneath it: Damien Wolfe, Chairman and CEO.

I trace the raised lettering with my thumb. "I'll think about it."

She pushes to her feet. The skepticism's written all over her face. She's heard this exact promise before.

"Your call, but you need to get something. You know you do." She turns toward the door. "I'm tired of seeing dead bodies at work. I'm going to ask for hazard pay if it keeps happening."

⚬

A low growl rouses me from sleep. Moonlight filters through the curtains, illuminating Shadow's silhouette at the window. He presses his nose flat against the cold glass, nostrils flaring, as he peers into the yard. My heart kicks like a caged animal trying to break free.

I'd gone to bed relieved when my watcher didn't show, but my relief evaporates the instant realization dawns.

My pulse hammers against my throat as I fling the covers aside.

"Is he out there, baby?"

The cool air hits my skin, raising goosebumps along my arms and legs. I fumble for my robe, tying the knot as I edge toward the window.

Shadow's growl rolls low and continuous, a sound that comes from deep in his chest. But he makes no move to bark, no sudden lunge toward the door or down the stairs. He watches, waiting, as if he knows something I don't.

I press my palm to the glass and peer out into the yard, squinting through the darkness. At first, nothing. Then a shadow shifts, separating itself from the darkness beneath the trees.

My watcher.

My heart slams against my ribs, the sight of him stealing the breath from my lungs. I can't breathe. Can't think. Fear floods every cell. But beneath it, excitement that has no business existing pulses. Dark and hungry. It crackles under my skin like a live wire, scattering my thoughts until I can't hold on to a single one. Am I losing my mind? The fear makes sense, but what is this dark current running parallel to it?

I should move, run for Grandpa's shotgun, or do something other than stand here like a deer caught in headlights. But I'm frozen, eyes locked on the figure below, the man who's turned my yard into his stage, looking up at me wearing an eerily beautiful silver wolf's mask covering the top of his face.

I square my shoulders, forcing steel into my spine.

"I think it's time we stop this game, watcher."

My voice is steady, though every hair on my neck stands up. I pivot away from the window and slip out of the bedroom. In the hallway, I turn right, moving toward the cabinet at the far end, between the bathroom door and Maren's room.

I step on a loose floorboard, and the groan is deafening in the otherwise silent house. Stopping in my tracks, I look back, half-expecting to see him materialize behind me.

My fingers shake as they find the lock on Grandpa's gun cabinet. Sweat slicks my palms, making my grip uncertain, but I manage the combination. Numbers burned into my brain from age twelve, when he first put a rifle in my hands.

I lift the shotgun, surprised by how natural it sits in my palms despite the tremor running through my arms. The weight of it grounds me, solid and reassuring. Like a promise of protection wrapped in cold steel.

Grandpa's voice echoes somewhere in my memory, gruff and certain.

Never point unless you're prepared to shoot, LuLu.

Am I?

The stairs creak under my weight as I descend, the cool wood a shock beneath my bare feet, sending shivers up my legs that have nothing to do with temperature. Shadow waits by the front door, his eyes reflecting what little light seeps through the windows. He doesn't whine or pace but gazes at me with eyes that seem to imply this moment was always inevitable.

I slip my feet into the boots waiting by the door. The lock turns with a soft click, and I take one last breath of safe, enclosed air before pulling it open.

Chapter Seventeen

Luna

I exhale and step onto the porch, lifting the shotgun, the barrel trembling in my hands.

Shadow slips out beside me, his fur warm against my bare leg. Instead of charging ahead like he would with any other intruder, he plants himself between me and the yard. His growling resumes, but absent is his usual aggressive behavior toward male strangers.

My watcher is closer now, standing less than twenty feet away. My lungs seize, forgetting how to draw air, the automatic rhythm of inhale and exhale vanishing.

The wolf mask he's wearing is some sort of metal that transforms his face into something beautiful and unsettling, all sharp angles and predatory lines. It covers him from his hairline down to above his mouth, wrapping around the sides of his head. Dark shadows obscure his eyes, but their piercing intensity feels like hot coals burning me in the dark.

They hold me captive, and I can't look away.

The sound rolling from Shadow's throat turns darker, more threatening. His ears flatten, and the fur on his back bristles.

"Don't move!"

My voice sounds normal, nothing like the panic eating me alive inside. I'm amazed anything comes out with the terror clawing at my throat. The shotgun shakes in my grasp.

He takes a step closer, and I catch the hint of a smile curving beneath his mask. Even that slight movement seems calculated and predatory, like a wolf testing the boundaries of wounded prey. My mouth goes dry, and my skin tightens, pulling against my body until I want to claw it off just to breathe.

The mask gleams in the moonlight, and it's both fascinating and terrifying. There's something almost mythical about him—part man, part beast, but wholly dangerous.

Those hidden eyes never leave mine. The intensity of his stare peels away every defense, leaving me exposed. He's memorizing my terror, cataloging every tremor, every quickened breath.

My finger tenses on the trigger.

"What do you want?" The words come out breathless, betraying my panic.

He closes more of the distance in three silent strides. The way he moves, like he owns the night, makes my hands quake. My brain shouts orders—move, retreat, get to safety. But my body won't listen. My feet might as well be nailed to the porch. Shadow launches himself down the stairs, and fear for my wolf cuts through my paralysis.

"Shadow, no!" I shout, the click of the shotgun echoing as I cock it.

My watcher holds up one hand, palm facing out, and Shadow, who trusts no one outside of Maren and me, freezes mid-charge. He sits back on his haunches, looking up at the masked figure with something that looks disturbingly like deference.

The masked man examines me with the focus of someone cataloging weaknesses. His gaze peels away every defense I've built, burning through my clothes, my skin, and straight into the fear I'm trying so hard to hide.

"Your security is inadequate." His voice is rough and deep, the sound of it making my skin crawl and burn at the same time.

I blink, thrown by the mundane observation, sputtering, "Ex... Excuse me?"

"No real cameras. Blind spots a child could exploit. I could bypass the lock on your back door in under thirty seconds." He gestures toward the sanctuary building. "And the medication storage has no alarm system."

I raise the shotgun higher, my mind racing. How the hell does he know all this?

"Thanks for the security audit." The words come out sharp. My stomach twists itself into knots beneath the false bravado. "Now tell me who you are and why you've been stalking me."

"You're beautiful."

The simple words, spoken with quiet sincerity, send confusion crashing through my fear. My hands tighten on the gun. A red haze of anger clouds my vision, replacing the confusion.

"Are you kidding me?"

He takes another step closer and reaches down to scratch Shadow's head. My fierce protector grunts and headbutts his hand like an overgrown puppy.

"Really?" I shoot an incredulous look at my traitorous wolf. "I've raised you since you were a pup, and you betray me for the first creepy masked guy who comes along?"

Shadow's tail thumps against the ground once, a gesture that seems almost like an apology, but he doesn't move from his position.

My eyes return to my watcher.

"I asked you a question." The words come out thin and reedy, nothing like the authority I was going for. "Why are you watching me? What do you want?"

"You."

That single word should send me running, bolting into the house. Instead, something deep in my core clenches. Fear and arousal tangle together in my belly like liquid fire, scalding and dangerous.

What the hell?

"I'm not interested."

My finger tightens on the trigger, and I stand my ground as Shadow abandons his post and returns to my side, positioning his body half in front of me.

"Yes, you are, little doe." The endearment rolls off his tongue like honey, a warm and seductive sound that infuriates me as my heart pounds in response.

"You were watching me when I released Buttercup?"

I knew I felt eyes on me.

"I'm always watching you, little doe."

"Don't call me that."

"Why not? It suits you. Does are gentle, beautiful creatures." His voice drops lower, more intimate. "And you're my perfect prey."

My heart hammers so hard it hurts, like it's trying to punch through my chest. I clutch the shotgun tighter, my arms trembling, threatening to give out, as his words wrap around my throat and squeeze the air from my lungs.

"You're the one leaving those dead bodies, aren't you?"

"Do you want it to be me?"

"That isn't what I asked."

"They were monsters. They got exactly what they deserved." His voice carries a cold satisfaction and no hint of remorse.

Part of me agrees, though I won't admit it. The other part is terrified by his casual confirmation.

"But why are you leaving them on my porch?"

"Most of them were in the driveway. And they're gifts, little doe."

"I told you not to call me that."

"And I told you, it suits you."

Why haven't I shot him yet?

"You need to leave." Terror turns my legs to jelly, but I plant my feet and square my shoulders like Grandpa taught me. "And stop dropping corpses on my property. I don't want your gifts."

He tilts his head, short tendrils of dark hair falling in loose strands around the mask's edge as it catches the light at a new angle. The sight of it is hypnotic, but everything about his posture screams danger. My body wants to retreat, but I dig my heels into the wood.

"Your wolf recognizes what I am." He nods toward Shadow. "Why can't you?"

I glance down. Shadow is stretched out next to me, at ease, his tail thumping against the porch boards. Everything about him reads comfort and trust, the same way he acts when it's just me and him. As if he has no worries about this predator being near me.

When I look back up, my watcher has moved closer.

"Take one more step, and I'll shoot."

The words die in my throat, ending in a whimper as he surges forward, striding up the stairs, two at a time. Panic roars in my ears, and training kicks in before thought does. The gun jumps in my grip, and I fire, the blast hammering through my body and rattling my bones.

But he's faster than me. His hand shoots out, fingers wrapping around steel, jerking the barrel aside. The shot misses him by inches, echoing across the property, and tearing into an aspen tree across the driveway. Smoke curls from the muzzle.

The gun disappears from my grip before I can blink, and I stagger back. It crashes onto the porch swing with enough force to make the chains rattle. His expression turns to stone, and the air around him crackles with the kind of energy that comes before storms break.

I shake so hard my vision fractures, the trembling coming from somewhere deeper than muscle. My feet stumble backward while my heart tries to choke me, hands scrabbling for distance, but he seizes my wrist in an iron grip. An electric shock runs up my arm.

Shadow surges to his feet, fur standing on end, teeth bared as he snarls, a sound that makes the night air tremble. My wolf is back, my protector returning, whatever hold this stranger had on him finally broken.

"Sit!"

The command slices through Shadow's growl. His body goes slack, and he drops onto his haunches like he's been trained his whole life to respond to this voice.

The tsk-tsk sounds almost amused, paired with the slow shake of my watcher's head. He's too close, but my body has forgotten how to move. I tried to kill him and failed. Now all the power sits in his hands.

"Naughty little doe." He lifts his hand to brush his finger down my cheek.

"Don't touch me." I jerk my head back and yank at my arm. He lets go, but his hands find my hips instead, thumbs pressing into my flesh. His grip burns through the fabric. My palms slam against his chest, pushing with everything I have, shoving against solid muscle. It's like trying to move a mountain.

"Let me go."

"If you wanted me gone, you wouldn't stand at your window every night looking for me."

He nudges Shadow to the right with his knee, then guides me backward despite my struggles, his grip almost painful until I'm pressed against the front door. His body forms a wall of heat, and my pulse gallops into a wild rhythm, panic and arousal colliding until I can't tell one from the other.

"Get off me." I choke on a sob.

My fingers claw at his chest, finding only unyielding muscle beneath the fabric. Everything in me is begging me to push him away. So why do my fingers cling to his shirt like a lifeline?

"You wouldn't have stripped for me, teasing and tempting me with your body."

He steps closer, too close. His voice, low and deep, filters through the minute space between us, his breath warming my face. His gaze drifts to the delicate curve of my collarbone, where heat blooms under my skin.

He towers over me, the top of my head only reaching his chin, and I'm trapped. The rational part of my brain shrieks at me to fight, to run, but my body has other ideas, caught in some chemical response that has nothing to do with self-preservation.

"I didn't—that wasn't for you."

Black ink peeks above his collar. I trace my eyes upward, over his neck and the hard line of his chin, until I'm looking into the wolf mask.

Up close, the metal of his mask looks expensive and custom-made. It's flat but looks three-dimensional, with intricate etchings that give it texture and depth. What little I can see of his face only makes him more intimidating. His jaw is strong and angular, covered with dark stubble. His mouth—the only feature fully visible—curves in the barest hint of amusement, as if my fear entertains him.

Those lips look dangerous, like they could whisper sweet promises or devastating threats with equal ease.

His dark hair is longer than I'd realized, the ends touching his collar where they escape the mask's coverage. It's thick and tousled, as if he's been running his hands through it. The contrast between the sleek metal covering the top of his head and those unruly dark strands makes him look like some ancient god of war.

But it's his sheer size that makes my body shake in terror, the chilling grip of fear seizing me. From my bedroom window, he looked tall, but up close—*God*—he's massive. I press my spine harder against the door, trying to melt into it. His body promises destruction with every breath. Mine whispers of how easy I'd be to break.

He's hard against my stomach. Fire races under my skin, and my heartbeat slams into my throat. My hands find his forearms, muscles like steel cables under my palms. I grip them, torn between pushing him away and pulling him closer. His fingers sink deeper into the curve of my hips, anchoring me in place.

The heat between us could ignite the air. My breathing comes in short bursts, matching the chaos in my chest. His grip tightens, possessive and demanding, as if he knows the war that rages inside me, the battle between fear and something darker and more dangerous that whispers I should let him have me.

"Please," I whisper, not sure what I'm begging for.

He ignores me, his warm palm sliding over my hip, as he leans down, bringing his masked face closer to mine. His scent wraps around me, flooding my senses. Rich leather and smoky firewood, wilderness and danger, and something clean and male that makes my head spin. I want to press my face against the crook of his neck where the scent is the strongest and breathe him in.

The air between us thickens. With each breath I take, my lungs fill with him until I can't tell where his presence ends and mine begins.

"You leave your curtains open for me, Dr. Foster."

My name on his lips unravels me thread by thread. I dig my fingernails into the leather of his jacket in a futile attempt to ground myself. His mouth travels the line of my jaw, then down the column of my neck. Cold metal from his mask's edge drags across my skin, leaving goosebumps in its wake. My head tilts without permission, offering him the vulnerable curve of my throat. His lips find that tender hollow where my pulse beats wild and exposed, and my breath catches and holds.

"It's an invitation, Luna."

My first name, in that low, gravelly tone, sounds even better. The syllables roll off his tongue with an intimacy that shouldn't exist between us.

Heat pools low in my belly as the sound echoes in the narrow space between our bodies. I've heard my name spoken a thousand times, but never like this. Never like a secret. Never like a promise.

His hand drifts down, a whisper between our bodies, before sliding beneath my robe. Terror floods my veins. I twist away, but the door blocks my escape. His other hand locks onto my hip, fingers branding my skin through the fabric.

His fingertips find the edge of my sleep shorts and slip beneath the silk. My breath dies in my throat as he sweeps his fingers through my soaked core.

"No." My voice cracks, but my body betrays me, yielding to his touch.

His fingers move against me, tracing patterns against my swollen clit that make the world narrow down to just his hand, finding spots that make my vision blur. Heat spreads through my pussy with each stroke. My legs tremble, and each breath comes ragged and desperate. I sink my teeth into my lower lip, trying to hold back the moan building in my chest, hating that my body responds to him this way.

His teeth scrape across my clavicle. I whimper, hips lifting against him. Then he sinks his teeth into me, biting hard enough to bruise. The initial pain makes me gasp before it twists into a dark, desperate, clawing hunger for him to hurt me more, to use me harder, to take whatever he wants. Tremors ripple through me, each one pulling me deeper under his control. Slick warmth coats his fingers, evidence I can't hide, and the sound that escapes me is part sob, part moan, and all damning.

"So wet for me."

His tongue follows the path of the bite, tracing the mark rising on my skin. Sharp pain melts into a low, shivering ache that radiates from the wound, settling deep into my bones.

I wish he'd speak louder. I want to hear his voice.

He slides his fingers lower, sinking two of them deep inside me. A cry tears from my throat as my back bows against the door. My body stretches to accommodate him, but it betrays me, clinging to the intrusion. I'm tight, but I've been celibate since I broke up with Caleb. And this man's fingers are huge. If his fingers are this thick, what will his...

No! The word slams through my skull. This is assault, not seduction. My body's physical response means nothing.

"So fucking tight." His words tumble around me, his voice, now a low growl, setting off a flurry of electric tingles that cascade through me. "But we need to get you stretched, or you'll never be able to take my cock."

My body's reaction to his words is instant, unleashing a fresh wave of slick arousal, amplifying the pleasure of his thrusting fingers.

He groans, a deep, rumbling sound, and I'm lost in the tide of his assault. With each thrust of his fingers, each unyielding push of his thumb against my clit, heat sparks along my spine. My vision wavers, white-hot pleasure colliding with icy terror.

"Stop."

The word catches in my throat, my body again arching against him, a traitor to my command.

His fingers move quicker and deeper with each plunge, each movement driving me to a point where arousal, confusion, and fear become indistinguishable. My body ripples with feverish heat as it climbs closer to sweet release.

I come with a cry that echoes through the night, muscles clenching in spasms, the orgasm tearing through my body like wildfire. He holds me there, waves of ecstasy washing over me, his fingers moving, prolonging the ache of my release until I sag against him, breathless and shaking. A whimper escapes as I turn my face, pressing it against his, the cool mask a balm against my heated cheek.

His fingers are relentless, and the second climax builds before the first one ends, crashing through my already shattered defenses. Reality dissolves as sensation drowns out thought, sight, and sound. Everything but the fire between my legs.

The pleasure turns to agony. My fingers find his wrist and squeeze, nails digging crescents into his skin as I try to drag him away, but he's too strong.

"Please." The plea tears free, broken and breathless.

His fingers still. My body quakes with the aftershocks, while my knees threaten to fold. Without him holding me up, I'd melt into the floor.

He lifts his head from my neck and pulls away. I look up at him as he steps back.

"I'll take you up on that invitation very soon, little doe. So, be ready for me."

My body trembles from head to toe, shaking everywhere at once, soaked with need that I hate myself for wanting. Confronted with the truth of my own behavior, I look away.

"Did you come on my window while you were watching me?"

The corner of my vision catches his lips curve into a dangerous and satisfied smile.

"As hard as you came on my fingers." He lifts those fingers to his mouth, and my head snaps to look at him. His tongue traces each one with the patience of a man savoring wine, a low growl vibrating in his throat. "Next time I'll be deep inside you."

I believe him. God help me, I believe him.

I gasp at the sight of his palm, an angry red burn in the shape of the shotgun barrel scorched into his skin.

"Oh my God, your hand."

I touched a shotgun barrel once when Grandpa was teaching me how to shoot. The steel can get hot enough when fired to cause third-degree burns. I still have a scar on the inside of my index finger from the first-degree burn I suffered that day.

He smirks beneath the mask. "Worth it."

I reach for his hand, my instincts as a doctor overriding everything else. "Let me see it."

He retreats down the steps, his gaze never leaving mine. "I'd endure any burn to touch you again, Luna."

Who is this man?

"What do you want from me?" I ask again, searching his eyes through the mask.

"Everything."

My chest tightens, and I swallow, pressing myself harder against the door, desperate to put distance between us.

"I'll see you again soon, little doe."

His words are both a threat and a promise.

"Wait!" I stumble forward, my body moving before my mind can catch up, chasing after someone I should run from. "At least tell me your name."

Moonlight catches the contours of his mask as he turns and heads toward the trees, leaving me trembling on the porch with Shadow's warm fur at my side and the echo of his touch inside me.

His voice floats back to me.

"You can call me the wolf."

Chapter Eighteen

Luna

As I drag myself into the bathroom the next morning, I try and fail to convince myself that the entire night had been a stress-induced hallucination. The evidence of my orgasm in my underwear is from a vivid erotic dream, nothing more. Yet, his touch lingers, like an undeniable brand.

And the bite mark on my collarbone—one of the cats must have bitten me in my sleep. That is, if one of them has a human-like bite radius and tooth structure, with incisors and canines similar to those of a human.

Shit.

By the time I walk downstairs for breakfast, having covered the bite mark with concealer and a turtleneck under my scrubs, my pretense of denial has disappeared. Only a crazy person could deny the reality of what happened last night. Still, I decide to enjoy my coffee on the front porch, the scene of the crime, before Maren arrives and the hustle and bustle of the day begins.

The impression of the silver wolf mask pressed into a patch of dirt at the base of the porch steps steals my breath. Tangible proof that what happened was real.

Oh god...

I let my watcher finger me to orgasm on my front porch last night. I came on his fingers, moaning like a whore, letting a complete stranger fuck me with his hand while he pressed me against my front door. A hand he burned on the barrel of the shotgun I tried to shoot him with.

The memory floods back with startling clarity. My nipples tighten against the fabric of my shirt, and heat pools between my thighs, soaking my panties. I press my legs together, knowing I'll need fresh underwear at this rate.

Sure, I've had one-night stands a few times in my thirty-two years. I fucked guys I only knew for a few hours. I even had a one-time, not-so-ethical sexual encounter with the TA in my applied clinical medicine class. Not the best decision I ever made, considering his apparent girlfriend walked in on us on the lab table. Thank God, all she did was dump him and not report us to the department supervisor. I could have been expelled from the program.

Then there's the married man Maren never lets me forget.

But my watcher, or—let's just call him what he is—my stalker is a stranger.

We didn't get to know each other over a date or a couple of drinks. We didn't exchange names, though he knows mine. We hadn't even spoken until last night.

And he's a serial killer.

Yet, I let him slip the same fingers he used to kill Daryl Rawlings and the Meyers into my panties, with barely an attempted no.

What kind of person does that?

I stare at the imprint in the dirt for a long time, until Maren's SUV comes up the driveway and pulls to a stop between the house and the main building. I smooth out the wolf impression with my shoe, erasing the proof of his visit. The last thing I need is for Maren or one of the volunteers to find it and ask questions I don't want to answer.

"Morning, lovely."

"You're chipper this morning." I fall into step with her as we approach the sanctuary's main entrance.

"I got myself a little something-something last night, so Maren is a happy girl today."

Her sigh is dramatic as I unlock the door, and we step inside the lobby.

"Don't tell me whatever deviant things the two of you got up to. I don't want to know."

Maren snorts, but the subtle blush creeping up her cheeks is unmistakable.

"You need to engage in a little deviant behavior yourself, Dr. Foster. It'll dry up if you don't use it."

I stiffen, then let out an awkward laugh that Maren seems to miss as she turns on the lights and boots up the reception desk computer.

What happened last night—his breath on my neck, my body's betrayal, the way I came apart under his touch—wasn't that deviant?

The urge to tell her everything burns on my tongue. But she'll have Karen on the phone before I'm even finished, insisting I tell her about the murders, at least, and I can't do that.

The truth settles like lead in my stomach. I'm protecting him. But why?

Why shield a man who violated me and kills people?

Ghost is improving, eating small amounts of food, and tolerating gentle handling. Despite everything humans did to him, he's choosing to trust again. Cautiously, but choosing nonetheless.

"You're a better soul than I am," I murmur, checking his neck wounds. The stitches look good and clean, with no infection, though I doubt the fur will ever grow back over the scars.

"Talking to the patients again?" Maren appears in the doorway. "First sign of veterinary madness."

A smile tugs at my lips. "Just having a philosophical discussion about forgiveness."

"With a wolf? Only Luna Foster can wax philosophical with wild animals."

"Ghost is only half-wolf, and I spend most of my time with them. Who else am I supposed to talk to? They keep me sane."

"I won't take offense at that because I'm in too good a mood." Maren sets two manila folders on the counter. "But speaking of things that'll make you question your sanity, your mortgage statement came today."

I cringe as I stand up. Though I've kept up with the payments, the most recent ones were a few days late.

"What does it say? How much are they hitting me for in late fees?"

She pulls out the statement and waves it at me. "That's the thing. There's no balance."

The air leaves my lungs in a rush. "What do you mean, no balance?"

"I mean zero. Zilch. Nada. Paid in fucking full." She hands me the paper. My eyes scan the numbers, or the absence of them. Where there should be a soul-crushing amount owed, there's a zero.

"That's impossible."

"That's what I thought, so I called the bank. Turns out some anonymous benefactor paid off the mortgage. Just like that. Poof."

"Anonymous? Who would—"

"Wait, it gets better." Maren grins and pulls a piece of paper from the other folder. "Your student loan statement. Also zeroed out. Someone paid off your college and veterinary school debt."

The room tilts, and I grab the counter for support, staring at both statements. Over a hundred and fifty thousand dollars.

Gone.

"Jesus Christ, Luna, you look like you're about to pass out. Sit down before you face-plant onto Ghost."

I sink onto a stool, my mind racing. "I don't understand. Who would do this? Who even knows my financial situation?"

"Honey, you run a nonprofit wildlife sanctuary in Colorado. It doesn't take a genius to figure out money is tight." Maren crosses her arms, studying my face. "The bank said they can't reveal who made the payments because it was all done anonymously through some fancy legal trust or something."

"This is insane."

Who has this kind of money? And why would they help me?

"Why do you look like you're gonna puke? You should be doing a happy dance right now."

"It's… overwhelming. I don't want to owe anyone. A bank loan is one thing, but not something like this."

"You don't owe anyone anything if it's anonymous. Maybe some rich asshole you hit up for money in the past finally developed a conscience and decided to help."

"Those are my debts. Not the sanctuary's."

"The mortgage was in the sanctuary's name, but, yeah, the student loans were personal. I don't know what to tell ya, Lu. Count your blessings and move on."

My relief is tangled with dread. I can breathe again, but at what cost?

Tate appears in the doorway, his usual cheerful grin missing. "Uh, Luna? Sorry to interrupt, but Sheriff Mills just pulled up outside. She's heading this way, and she looks… intense."

I look at Maren. "Did you call her?"

"Why would I call her?"

Shit. I didn't tell Maren about last night. Of course, she'd have no reason to call her.

Get a grip, Luna.

Maren turns toward Tate. "What's she want?"

"No idea, but she's got that same expression she had when the dead bodies showed up. Want me to tell her you're busy performing life-saving surgery or something?"

"No, I'll go talk to her. Maren, can you finish—"

I nod toward Ghost, who's shrunk into himself, trying to become one with the wall.

"Sure. I'll stay here, and Ghost and I will contemplate your mysterious benefactor while you go deal with whatever police shitstorm is brewing."

"What benefactor?" Tate asks as I head out to the lobby, my mind still reeling from that financial bombshell. The timing is strange and unsettling. Nothing in my life happens by coincidence anymore.

Karen enters the front door, removing her hat as the door swings shut behind her. "Afternoon, Luna."

"What can I do for you, Karen? Do you have more questions about the bodies yesterday?"

"No. But do you remember Raymond Davis? Emaciated horses, about eight months ago, up off Highway 14?"

My blood pressure spikes, heat rushing through my veins as his name settles in my gut.

"Yes. Only one of them survived. Cotton is still here. I kept him instead of adopting him out."

If that bastard has been allowed to own horses again, I'm going to lose what's left of my mind.

"He was found dead near the trailhead at Emerald Lake this morning."

Air abandons my lungs. "What does that have to do with me?"

"He was found wrapped in plastic with a Rocky Mountain Columbine taped to his body."

Shit!

"Another one?"

"I'm afraid so. He was starved before being killed. The medical examiner said he likely hadn't eaten for at least a week."

My mouth goes dry. "That's... horrible." But part of me doesn't think it's horrible at all. Remorse wars with something uglier in my chest, because underneath lurks vindictive satisfaction that he died the way he'd made those animals suffer. "Why are you telling me this?"

"Because they found a note with his body." Karen reaches into her pocket and pulls out a plastic evidence bag containing black note-sized card stock. Through the plastic, the typed words shout at me.

This is for you, Dr. Foster. Justice for the victims the law fails.

The room tilts for the second time today. "Jesus."

"Where were you last night between midnight and 4 AM?"

"I was home. Sleeping." Technically true, if I omit the confrontation with my masked watcher.

"Anyone who can verify that?"

"Are you seriously asking me that, Karen? While I'm not helpless, I weigh one hundred thirty-eight pounds. Raymond Davis weighed two hundred, easy. Do you really think I could kill him and drag him up to a trailhead at Emerald Lake?"

"No. But the last time you and Raymond Davis were seen together, you threatened him with bodily harm if you ever saw him again for what he did to those horses."

Heat flashes across my cheeks. I'd lost it that day, yelling at him while county animal services loaded his horses into our trailer. The memory makes me cringe. It's why they don't ask me to assist with pickups when owners are present anymore. Now, they just call to tell me they're bringing an animal in.

"Karen, come on. It's the same thing as Daryl Rawlings. Words said in the heat of the moment. You don't seriously think I meant them?"

"Again, no, Luna, but I have to ask. So, can anyone verify where you were this morning between midnight and four?"

I point to Shadow, curled up in a bed in the corner. "I was alone except for four animals who lack the power of speech."

Karen sighs, tucking the evidence bag away. "Luna, I've known you almost your whole life. I know you're not capable of this kind of violence. But in light of the other bodies found here, and that note…" She shakes her head. "It makes you involved, whether you want to be or not."

"This is ludicrous. I didn't kill him, Karen."

"I believe you. But someone with knowledge about you and the animals you treat has made this personal." Karen's shrewd eyes study my face. "Are you sure you haven't noticed anything unusual lately? Anyone paying too much attention to the sanctuary or to you?"

My watcher's masked face invades my thoughts. He said those bodies were gifts for me. I demanded that he stop dropping them on my doorstep. So, was this his pivot? Dumping the bodies elsewhere?

But how could he have killed Raymond Davis last night when he was here? Did he have Raymond's body with him? Had he already killed him? Or did he do it after he left me trembling on my porch?

Shit! What time did he come by?

"Luna?" Karen's impatient voice draws me back to her question.

"No." It's frightening how easily that word slips off my tongue. I'm grateful Maren stayed with Ghost. She would have spilled everything by now. "Nothing unusual."

"There's a level of expertise involved in this. Not only the killings themselves, but also transporting the bodies. And the scenes are meticulous. No DNA to be found anywhere. We're dealing with someone dangerous. Someone who's done this before."

A chill runs down my spine. No kidding.

"What are you saying?"

Karen touches my arm. "I'm saying be careful. There's no telling what he might do. Or who he might kill next. We have no leads, Luna, and I'm worried about you. Your safety."

I head to my office after Karen leaves and close the door, needing a few minutes alone to clear my head. I sink into my chair and pick up the mortgage and student loan statements, running my finger over the beautiful zeros. The relief hits me in waves so strong it makes my eyes burn. The weight that has been crushing me has lifted for the first time in years.

But who did this and why?

My watcher kills for me. Someone else pays my debts. What kind of life have I stumbled into where anonymous strangers are orchestrating such dramatic interventions?

I set the statements down with shaking fingers. The gratitude is there, warm and overwhelming, but it's tangled with fear and confusion. Someone out there, someone I've never met, cared enough to lift this burden from me. The thought is both humbling and terrifying.

I lean back in my chair, my thoughts spinning between the mysterious payments, Raymond Davis, and the masked watcher who's taken up residence in my head. He killed Davis. I know it in my bones. And last night, I surrendered to his touch.

Later that night, after all my resident animals are fed and settled in, I curl up on the sofa in the living room, with Shadow at my feet, drinking a cup of tea. No more wine for me for a while.

Maren wanted to stay with me again after the news about Raymond Davis, but I made her go home because JT's only in town for a few days.

But there's a chilling unease about being here alone now that my watcher has revealed himself and promised to return.

Damien Wolfe's business card sits on the coffee table in front of me. With a sigh, I pick up my phone and dial the number.

A smooth, deep voice answers on the second ring. "Wolfe."

I hesitate. "I—um... I'm calling about security services."

"I see." His tone shifts, becoming more attentive. "May I ask who's calling?"

"Luna Foster. I run Sage & Summit Wildlife Sanctuary north of Aspen Ridge. We're neighbors."

A pause, then a warmer, friendlier voice comes through the phone. "Yes, I've heard of you, Dr. Foster. Eleanor at the post office is quite fond of you."

I shift in my seat. Of course, Eleanor mentioned me to him. "She gave me your card. I've had some incidents on my property recently."

"I'm familiar with the reports. Three bodies discovered in the past week."

I tense. "How do you know?"

"I watch the news. And I make it my business to know what happens where I live. Security is about anticipating problems, not reacting to them."

I can't decide whether that's reassuring or disturbing. "Can you help or not?"

"I can offer a consultation tomorrow. 9 AM?"

"Can we make it 11? I have morning rounds with the animals."

"11 AM it is." Another pause. "And Dr. Foster? Perhaps keep your doors locked tonight. You never know who might be lurking in the woods around your property."

The line goes dead before I can respond.

I stare at my phone, unsettled by his words, which echo Karen's earlier warnings. I need to shake this off. I've always been safe in my home. There's no reason for me to feel unsafe now.

Except for the steady stream of corpses tied to my sanctuary.

And the masked man stalking and watching me from the woods, who also happens to be the killer.

Chapter Nineteen

Damien

I slip around the side of Luna's house, the cool night air whispering against my skin. The taste of her release still lingers in my memory, intoxicating and addictive. It's haunted me since last night, along with the echo of her gasps and moans playing on a loop in my head.

Cade thinks I've lost my mind for pursuing Luna like this, but he's wrong. I knew from the first glimpse of her what this would become. Both of her responses last night confirmed my belief.

A smirk tugs at my lips. She almost took my head off with that shotgun. Her aim was perfect. If I'd been a fraction slower, the slug would have found its target. Good thing she uses slugs instead of buckshot, or I'd be decorating her porch right now.

I flex my left hand, the skin raw and tender from the burn on my palm. I'll need to conceal that somehow when I meet her tomorrow. At least it's my non-dominant hand, so I won't have trouble shaking hers.

Fuck, this woman is something else.

When she confronted me, all fire and fury, she was magnificent. It took everything in me not to drop to my knees and worship her, and I'm not the kind of man who kneels. But her bravery while trembling with fear—I have to see that fire burn again.

The sounds that spilled from her throat, and the way she curved into me like she was made for it... *Fuck!* It's been driving me insane ever since.

She's dying to be claimed, her body confessing what her lips won't say.

The back door lock gives way at my touch with a soft click. Thank fuck she reached out to me for one of my systems. She needs better security, and now I'll get my cameras inside her house. She has no idea she's inviting another wolf into her home.

I step inside, and the warmth and scent of cinnamon and apples wrap around me. It's homey and inviting. The house is quiet, except for the gentle hum of the night. Moonlight filters through the windows as I move through, memorizing the layout. A knitted blanket drapes over the back of the sofa, books stacked on side tables, and cat-friendly plants crowd the windowsills. This is a home where someone lives, not just exists.

I reach her bedroom doorway and pause, drinking in the sight of her.

Luna lies in bed, wearing her usual pajamas. A thin tank top and tiny sleep shorts that leave little to the imagination. She's kicked off the covers, and they tangle around her calves, along with those three cats. The moonlight streams across her skin, turning her into something otherworldly. Untouchable.

But I'm going to touch her.

I'm going to finish what we started on her porch.

I step into her room. Her wolf lies curled in a bed tucked into the corner. His head snaps up, his eyes fixing on me as a rumble builds in his chest. He rises and pads toward me, sniffing, reading my scent while that low warning growl rolls between his teeth. Then he snorts once—dismissal, not threat—and returns to his bed.

That's it, boy. We're going to get along fine.

Luna stirs. Her eyes flutter open and widen in shock when she sees me. But there's something else there too. Like she knew this moment would come. Like she's been waiting for it.

She bolts upright, her breath catching as her eyes lock on my face.

On my mask.

Her fingers grip the sheets with a tremble she can't quite hide.

"How the hell did you get in here? I locked the doors." Her voice quivers despite the defiance in her words. She's trying to sound strong, but her fear bleeds through. Her body betrays her. The way she shrinks back against the headboard and how her knuckles go white where she clutches the bedding.

I let out a dark chuckle, savoring the mixture of terror and anticipation radiating from her.

"Locks won't keep me from you."

"I'm getting a security system. That'll keep you out."

Her effort to appear brave is endearing but not quite believable.

"No security system will keep me out."

"You can't just break into my house."

"And yet, here I am." I take another step, my voice dropping lower. Her eyes track my movement, a tremor in her jaw visible as she swallows hard.

"Did you kill Raymond Davis and dump his body at Emerald Lake?"

Her voice is steady, but her eyes—those beautiful, expressive eyes—betray her fear.

"Yes. You told me to stop dropping the bodies here."

Her chin juts forward, and her eyes flash. "Get out."

The words come out clipped, almost desperate, and she scrambles to pull the covers higher, creating a pitiful barrier between us.

"No. We both know you don't want that."

"You're delusional."

"Am I? Then why didn't you call the sheriff last night?" I move closer, and her breath comes faster. "Or tell her today? Why do you still leave your curtains open?"

Her mouth stays shut, but the answer lives in the silence.

"You've been thinking about what happened between us. How good it felt to surrender."

"I didn't surrender to anything. You violated me."

"Liar."

I stop at the foot of her bed, reach down, and pick up all three cats. Her eyes go wide as she drops the covers, lunging forward to reach for them.

"What are you doing? Leave them alone."

"Relax, Luna. I'm getting them out of our way so I can spread you out."

I set them on the floor in the hallway before turning to Shadow. With a single snap of my fingers, he's at my side.

"Out."

Luna's mouth falls open as her loyal protector exits without protest. I close the door and turn back to her.

"What did you do to him?"

"Nothing, but he doesn't need to see what I plan to do to you."

She pulls the blanket over herself again, clutching it to her chest, her eyes wide with a mix of fear and curiosity. Her fucking eyes are going to be the death of me.

"Why would he listen to you?"

"He's a predator, Luna. Like recognizes like. And his instincts tell him he doesn't need to protect you from me."

"You'll have to excuse me if I don't believe you."

I step closer to the bed, pressing my shins against the side of the mattress. Her breath hitches, her body tensing as I lean closer.

"Why the mask?" Her eyes dart between mine. "Why hide who you are if you plan to kill me?"

"I'm not going to kill you, Luna."

Relief spreads across her face, but her chin lifts higher as she looks at me, her eyes filled with defiance. "Again, excuse me if I don't take your word for it."

I chuckle, enjoying her fear and her resistance as her breasts rise and fall in quick succession.

"So, why the mask?" She asks again.

"Isn't it more exciting this way?" I step around the side of the bed. "To be touched by a masked stranger?"

She flinches. "That was a mistake. I shouldn't have... I shouldn't have let you touch me."

"Let me? I thought you said I violated you." My tone is mocking. "But you're right; you had no choice, little doe. You couldn't have stopped me even if you'd tried." I tilt my head, drinking in her fear. "And we both know you loved it. I can still taste how much."

Her face flushes crimson; whether from embarrassment or anger, I can't tell.

"That's not—no." She pauses. "How's your hand?"

She looks as surprised by her question as I am.

A smile pulls at my mouth. She's terrified and shaking. And she's asking about my hand. The one her shotgun burned. The one I used to make her shatter.

I hold it up and wave at her. "It's fine. Barely feel it anymore."

In truth, it's a little tender, but not bad. And it won't stop me from touching her.

She straightens her spine and hardens her expression. "I said, get out."

I lean over the bed, and she scrambles backward, feet tangling in the sheets as she tries to put distance between us. She nearly goes over the edge, catching herself at the last second and staggering upright on the far side of the mattress. Her chest heaves with each breath, and the heady, intoxicating scent of her fear floods the space between us.

"Where do you think you're going, little doe?" I unsheathe the knife at my hip. It was a spur-of-the-moment decision to bring it. I'll never use it to hurt her, but the fear it draws from her is a potent aphrodisiac.

The blade catches the moonlight as I draw it out, and Luna's eyes go wide. A small gasp escapes her lips, and she takes an involuntary step backward.

"Please."

She said it several times last night, and it didn't affect me, but tonight that single word does something to me. A flicker of doubt tries to take root, but I crush it down. This is necessary. She needs to understand that she has no choice.

She bolts for the door, and I'm on her before she takes three steps, spinning her around and pinning her against the wall. Her hands come up and push against my chest, trying to move me, but she lacks the strength.

I raise the knife and press it against the delicate skin of her throat. She freezes, her whole body rigid.

"Shhh."

Tremors wrack her body now, full-body shakes that vibrate against my chest. Her breathing collapses into short, panicked gasps, and her beautiful eyes blow wide with fear.

"Please don't."

"Luna, look at me." When she doesn't, I press the blade a little harder against her skin. "I said, look at me."

Her eyes drag upward and meet mine through the mask's eyeholes, tears she's trying not to shed collecting on her eyelashes.

She's so fucking beautiful.

"I don't want this." The words come out steady, but her voice cracks at the edges.

"Your mouth says no." My free hand traces down her side. She trembles where I touch her. "But this... this is telling me yes."

Her eyes tell two stories at once—terror wrestling with hunger. Something dark and wanting lurks beneath the surface, matching the need that burns through my veins. She presses against the wall behind her, but her hips tilt forward, a contradiction her body can't hide.

The steel of my blade rests against her pulse. A reminder of the rules we're playing by. Her terror should satisfy me, and part of it does. But the light fracturing in her eyes claws at my chest, and the contradiction tears at me because while her fear sets my blood on fire, something deeper recoils from the damage I see there.

I push the unwanted hesitation away. I want her complete submission to me, and if fear is the key that unlocks it, then so be it.

Because sometimes fear is just the beginning of surrender.

Chapter Twenty

Luna

The cold steel edge of the blade bites into my skin, sending a shiver of paralyzing dread spiraling through my body. I've faced down dangerous predators multiple times in my life, but none of them scared me the way this man does. Not even the three-hundred-pound grizzly that almost mauled me last year, nor the lion that attacked our safari camp while Grandpa and I were celebrating my acceptance into the CSU Fort Collins' veterinary program. Five people died that night before one of our safari guides put it down.

So, I consider myself pretty courageous when it comes to fear, most of the time, as much as anyone can. But I've never had a knife pressed against my throat before. One wrong move could be fatal.

He lets the knife fall away, just enough for my shoulders to slump in relief, before his cock presses hard and unyielding against my stomach, reminding me that safety is a lie.

"How tonight goes is entirely up to you, little doe."

Cold spreads through my limbs. My legs shake, threatening to give out.

That silver wolf mask, both beautiful and terrible, hovers above me, its hollow eye sockets swallowing whatever emotion might lie behind them. His gaze, though unseen, carves into me with the promise of violence.

His hand clamps around my hip, dragging me from the wall, spinning me around. Each backward step brings the bed closer. The knife flashes again, lethal and sharp under my chin, forcing my head up. Blood roars in my ears, my pulse so savage I half expect it to spray crimson all over him.

"You're much too smart to try anything foolish."

My mind races like a frantic squirrel trapped in a cage as I grasp for any escape. Shadow's betrayal stings, a hot lash of confusion and pain. Why would my protector trust him? Can't he sense the malice rolling off this man in waves?

The backs of my knees hit the mattress. He shoves me, and I collapse onto the bed, my arms flailing for purchase and finding only tangled sheets. He's on me before I can scramble away, one knee digging into the mattress between my thighs. The springs groan, and I twist away, but he's too strong, his grip unyielding as he seizes my wrists, pinning them above my head. I thrash beneath him, legs kicking out, but it's useless. His grip is unyielding.

He leans down until cold metal brushes my cheek, his lips hovering beside my ear.

"I said, don't do anything stupid."

His scent fills my nostrils—clean, musky, and male. It's the same as last night, a dark pull beneath the fear. I thought it was cologne, but now I don't know, and even through my terror, I can't resist its lure.

But I push back against the want, feeding on fear and fury instead.

"I'm not going to let you rape me without a fight."

Tears threaten to spill. I force my eyes shut, building walls behind my lids. I won't give him my tears.

He laughs, and it's a low, vibrating sound that skitters down my neck. "When the time comes for you to take my cock, you're going to be begging me for it."

"Not likely, asshole."

I twist my wrists against his hold, but his grip only tightens. The blade whispers along my jaw, tracing a path down my throat. Every muscle locks. My stomach revolts, but I choke down the nausea. I won't give him that satisfaction either.

He moves his hand down the front of my body, the blade leaving a trail of heat across my skin and over my collarbone. It reaches the top of my tank top and slices through the fabric with ease, down the center, slow and careful, never so much as nicking my skin. It's surgical, almost tender, the way he exposes me, inch by slow inch, the soft hollow between my breasts laid bare. Each millimeter of skin makes me burn with humiliation. Using the tip of the blade, he spreads the fabric, dragging it across my nipple until my flesh responds against my will. I swallow a cry that's more tremor than rebellion.

Behind that mask, his stare sears itself into every revealed inch of skin. Each second of his focus leaves marks I can't see but feel everywhere.

"So fucking beautiful."

His voice sounds almost reverent as a knuckle brushes the hardened peak.

He leans down, his breath warming my skin before his mouth closes around my other nipple. His teeth graze the sensitive tip before he bites down. My breath hitches, a moan spilling out before I can trap it.

When he sucks, the sensation detonates through my body, sending tremors rippling through my core. Pain fuses with pleasure, both tangled with terror, creating a brutal cocktail of sensation that overrides the fear.

"Stop!" My demand sounds weak, even to my own ears.

He hums and chuckles around me before releasing my nipple, giving it a quick flick with his tongue.

"Are you sure that's what you want?"

My stomach knots. I jerk and twist my body, tugging against his grip, but it's futile. He presses the tip of the knife to my nipple, a sharp reminder he's the one with the power.

"Don't." My voice breaks. "You don't have to do this."

He releases my wrists, but the steel of the knife remains pressed against my nipple, a silent promise that keeps me still.

His other hand slips beneath the waistband of my shorts. I clamp my legs together, but he's stronger, and when I fight, he twists the knife, pressing a fraction harder. Not enough to break the skin but enough to make my thighs fall open.

His fingers brush against slick flesh, and more horror floods through me when heat blossoms beneath his touch. Fear never aroused me before this man started watching me. Confusion tangles with self-loathing, not because of what my body craves, but because it's craving it from a killer.

"Fuck."

He drags his fingertip over my clit in slow circles, and my hips jerk upward before I can stop them. The motion rips a sound from my throat. Something between a groan and a sob that I'm unable to swallow back down. My legs tremble with the effort of staying still while heat pools low in my belly, uninvited and undeniable. I want to clamp them shut, want to kick him away, but instead my thighs spread wider. Heat builds where his finger presses, spreading through my core in waves I can't fight back.

He pulls his hand away and brings it to his mouth. His tongue sweeps across his fingertip, collecting what he's drawn from me. His eyelids flutter closed, and a muscle in his jaw twitches. When his eyes open again, they've gone dark, hunger consuming everything else in his expression, his eyes fixing on me like I'm the only thing that exists.

"I'm going to fucking devour you."

His damp fingers lift to my wrists, suspended above my head like a sacrificial offering. His powerful hand surrounds them again, and a jolt of horror streaks through me. My chance to escape has slipped through my fingers like sand through an hourglass. When his attention shifted, I could have tried to grab the knife. I could have slashed or stabbed or done anything to get free. Even a cut would have been worth it. A slice across my breast, or a gash on my ribs. I would have healed. Scars fade and pain passes, but that chance won't come back, and I can only lie here knowing I let it slip past while I did nothing. Lost in every tiny pulse of unwanted pleasure.

With my wrists secured again, he pulls the knife away and slides it down my stomach, dipping the blade beneath my sleep shorts. The sound of fabric tearing fills the air as he slices through them with the same ease he cut through my top.

He tosses the knife onto the bed, where it lands with a soft thud beside me. His one-handed agility is terrifying as he maneuvers me out of my shorts and underwear, even as I twist and kick against him, leaving me naked and shivering, with only the useless shreds of my own dignity. I whimper, and he glances up, his dark eyes glinting through the mask.

"You're so fucking stunning, Luna. And you're all mine."

He hauls me up the mattress. My heels scrape against the sheets, searching for purchase that isn't there. This man's strength—I'm no match for it. The fabric of my torn underwear cuts into my wrists as he winds it around the headboard slats, looping it tight so that wriggling free is impossible. The knife finds its new home on the pillow beside my temple, its constant threat thrumming with every frantic heartbeat.

He vanishes below my line of sight, his hands gripping my knees, forcing them wider. Then, his tongue is on me—hot, relentless, and all-consuming.

The first touch makes me gasp.

The second makes me forget why I should resist.

By the third, my back arches off the bed, the horror of my captivity melting into pleasure I don't want to feel.

A sob racks my body, and I choke out, "Stop, please— don't—" but all he does is hum, the sound vibrating through my flesh. Every part of me wants to recoil, but every inch of me is also awake, sparking and overloaded. I squeeze my eyes shut and try to transport my mind anywhere else.

But my body betrays me. His mouth is ruthless, and my hips buck before I can hold them back. I'm trying so hard not to feel, but sensation crowds in, taking all the oxygen, crushing me beneath it.

"Please."

I'm unsure what I'm begging for anymore. For release, for mercy, for anything that will end this torment.

The cool edge of his mask presses against my skin, a jarring reminder of how wrong this is. A killer is between my legs, and all I can do is lift my hips and press myself against his mouth.

"You taste like heaven." His growl, lost in the folds of my pussy, sends a surge of heat through me, a wildfire that consumes everything in its path.

His hand moves to my hip, pinning it to the mattress as the other slips between my legs to join his mouth. His fingers brush over my clit, a whisper of a touch, as he thrusts his tongue inside me, and a shudder engulfs my whole body.

I'm close already, embarrassingly so, my body a tightly wound coil ready to spring. His efforts intensify, and I shudder, already on the brink. He feasts on me, ravenous, driving me to the edge of oblivion. When he wraps his lips around my clit, I choke on a gasp, a drowning woman pulled under by a riptide of sensation.

"Don't." The word tears out of me. "Don't, don't—"

My head thrashes against the pillow. I pull at the restraints holding my wrists, feeling them bite into my skin. My nails dig into my palms until the skin threatens to break. My heels press into the surface beneath me, trying to push him away, but my hips roll forward instead. The contradiction splits me in two. Another sound bubbles up from my chest, and I bite down on my lip, trying to trap it inside, but it escapes anyway—broken and wanting.

His tongue is everywhere at once, and I come so hard my vision bleeds white at the edges, stars exploding behind my eyelids. A cry rips from my throat. I sob through it, the tears I've been holding back finally spilling, and when it's over, I sag against the mattress, spent and wrecked.

He gives me no time to catch my breath. His hands run up the insides of my thighs, thumbs pressing against my sex, working me open again. My skin is raw and fevered, but I can't stop my hips from tilting into his touch. I can't stop wanting. I loathe myself for it.

He tugs me against his face. "More."

He slips two fingers inside me, a stretch that makes me groan, his tongue working against me with devastating skill. The oversensitivity borders on pain, but he doesn't stop, pushing me toward a second peak that builds higher than the first.

"I can't," I gasp, even as my body contradicts me, tensing around his fingers. "It's too much—"

He thrusts harder, deeper, his teeth sinking into my clit. Pain flares, but it only fuels the inferno. He bites again.

"Ow." The sensation makes me jolt, but the pain only adds to the pleasure.

He releases me, kissing the tender bundle of nerves, making my body jerk. Then he rises, grabbing the knife glinting beside my head in the moonlight—a reminder of my helplessness—and presses the blade against my lips.

"You wanted this, little doe."

That nickname. Little doe. I should hate it, but the sound of it coming from his lips makes my clit throb.

His mouth descends again, and it's different this time, slower, more deliberate, as if he's savoring every twitch and gasp I make. He teases me until I'm shaking.

Trembling.

Shattered.

When I break, the second orgasm crashes through me like a tsunami, tearing sobs from my throat. He continues his merciless assault on my flesh until I'm a pleading, sobbing mess.

He pulls away, wiping his mouth with the back of his hand. I'm splayed out, wrists bound, eyes blurred with tears, and hair plastered to my temples. He traces the knife down my side, following the curve of my hip, and over my belly as my body trembles from both aftershocks and the terror of what he'll do now.

He doesn't cut. He teases, playing with the idea of pain. Keeping me terrified. Keeping me present.

The dark chuckle he lets out rumbles through my entire body, like thunder that resonates within my soul.

Then he's over me, resting the tip of the knife against my mouth again.

I look at him through the swollen, sticky, salty haze of my eyelashes, and a violent urge surges through me. I want to bite him, sink my teeth into that wicked mouth, and taste his blood as he's tasted me. Instead, I open my mouth and let him slide the knife's flat edge along my tongue.

I blame it on the brain fog still lingering from two powerful orgasms in less than ten minutes. I stare him down, swallowing my fear, and I don't miss the small smile playing on his damp lips as if he's tasting victory.

He leans over me, checking my restraints. His scent envelops me again, mixed with the heady scent of my arousal clinging to his skin. And I give in, breathing him in, filling my lungs with us, and, God help me, my core clenches in response.

He cocks his head. "Are you going to be good, or do I have to tie your ankles too?"

"Let me go. I won't tell anyone about this. I won't call the sheriff. I can't identify you anyway, so please just untie me and leave, and no one will ever know."

His lips curve into what one could only describe as a sinister smile beneath that beautiful mask, a grin that sends a chill down my spine.

"Oh, little doe, we're only getting started."

Chapter Twenty-One

Damien

Her eyes flare wide, pupils dilating until only a thin ring of hazel remains. Hunger flashes in those depths. Wild and untamed hunger that matches my own. Yes, there's fear woven through it, but desire dominates, the kind of loose-limbed heat that only comes after multiple orgasms and the body's greedy anticipation of more.

The scent of her arousal saturates the air and clings to my skin, wrapping around me until my head spins.

"I'm about to feast on you, Luna."

"Isn't that what you just did?"

The words tumble out breathless and disbelieving as she tugs at her restraints. Her spine curves, the line of her body taut and beautiful, her legs jerking around my hips.

"No. That was an appetizer."

I watch her face as her mind catches up with my words.

"This is insane. You're insane."

I toss the knife to the side. "I've been called worse."

I trail my fingers down her throat, tracing a path between her breasts, and her breath quickens. Her skin pebbles beneath my touch.

She turns her head away, but I catch her chin, my grip firm, forcing her to look at me. Her eyes hold mine for a heartbeat before something shutters closed behind them. The muscles in her face tighten.

"Don't hide from me, Luna." I lower my face to her neck, murmuring against her damp skin, as her pulse flutters beneath my lips.

Her skin burns beneath my mouth—flushed and slick with sweat, radiating heat as I drag my tongue down to the hollow at the base of her throat. Her breath stutters out uneven and desperate while I continue lower, following the curve of her collarbone and passing over the bite mark I left on her last night. My teeth graze her skin in the barest touch, and she whimpers in response.

Silk couldn't feel smoother than this. Her breasts rise and fall with each ragged breath, nipples tight and dark pink. Hunger coils in my gut. I lower my head and seal my lips around one nipple, sucking until her body shudders beneath me. My fingers capture the other, rolling and pinching until her spine curves and lifts her off the bed.

I bite down without warning, and her cry splits the air. The silk panties binding her wrists pull taut, the fabric straining and sliding against her skin as she yanks against them. Her shoulders lift off the mattress with the force of it.

"So responsive." My words come out muffled against her nipple as I flick my tongue over the hardened peak, and her hips roll upward in a rhythm she can't control, seeking friction that isn't there yet.

My lips travel lower, tracing the curve of her ribs and the plane of her stomach before I dip my tongue into her navel. She jerks with a breathless laugh that transforms into a moan as I bite the soft skin below it.

I hook her calves over my shoulders, her thighs trembling against my ears. Between her legs, everything is pink and slick, her flesh swollen and sensitive from what I've already done to her. I press my nose against her and inhale deep, letting the heady musk of her arousal fill my lungs. The thin strip of coarse hair tickles my upper lip as I brush my mouth against her with the lightest touch.

"Tell me you want my mouth on you again." I turn my face and let my warm breath caress her inner thigh.

"No." Her pride wars with her desire.

"Say it, Luna."

"No."

She twists her body and yanks at the silk around her wrists again, but there's no real fight in it anymore. The desperation that was there before is gone. I exhale against her swollen flesh, and frustration pours out of her in a choked groan. My lips brush her inner thigh, trailing kisses up and down the soft skin while avoiding the one place that's aching for attention. Her legs tense against my shoulders.

"Come on, little doe." I trace my tongue along the crease where her leg meets her body, my stubble dragging along her thigh until she shivers beneath me. "Tell me you want my mouth."

"Screw you."

I smile against her skin before sinking my teeth in, hard enough to make her cry out and jerk her leg away. My mouth follows, soothing the tender bite with my tongue.

"All you have to do is ask, and I'll make you feel so fucking good."

She lifts her head and glares down at me, her eyes a tempest of conflicting emotions. There's still fear, like a lingering shadow, but the overwhelming terror has receded.

"Please." The word tears from her throat.

"Please, what?" I blow on her wet flesh again, my fingers teasing her folds.

"Please let me go."

She just can't let go of that stubbornness.

"Wrong answer."

I sink my teeth into her thigh again, a little harder, and this time the cry she releases is more pain than pleasure.

"Forget what I said. I will call the sheriff. And I'll enjoy watching them arrest you for both murder and rape."

"No, you won't. Now beg me, little doe."

Her chest heaves as she stares down at me, her teeth catching her lower lip before they press into a hard line. She blinks, her eyes blazing, but then the fire in them flickers, the armor she's built showing its first crack. Desire and stubborn pride war, and when desire wins, it's a breathtaking and unforgettable sight.

She surrenders, her back curves, and her hips tilt towards my face, seeking what she's been fighting.

"Please..."

I blow on her clit again. "Please what?"

"Please put your mouth on me."

I lower my mouth to taste her again, a groan rumbling through me as her flavor explodes on my tongue, sweet and musky. The moment my tongue touches her swollen clit, she cries out, hips rising off the bed, her body betraying every protest she's made. I slip my middle finger inside her, all the way to my knuckle. Her walls grip me, throbbing around the digit.

My cock presses hard against my jeans. It takes everything in me, every ounce of self-control I possess, not to climb on top of her and bury myself inside her tight cunt.

She's mine. Her pleasure, her pain, her life—all of it.

Her next orgasm hits. Her back arches off the bed, her head thrown back, and her throat exposed. Around my finger, her inner walls pulse—once, twice, three times—as a broken cry tears from her lips. I don't stop. I keep up the pressure until she's sobbing, until every last tremor has wracked through her body.

But it's not enough. I need more.

I slip my fingers from inside her, my thumb circling her clit. Her stomach muscles jump. Tears leak from the corners of her eyes, tracking wet lines down her temples.

The salt-sweet taste of her makes my head spin. Her thighs quiver against my palms as I press them wider, relentless in my pursuit of her complete surrender.

"Too much." Her body twists and thrashes. "I can't—"

"Yes, you can."

Her fourth orgasm comes harder and deeper. Those hazel eyes, usually so sharp, roll back, her lips parted in a silent scream. My own breath catches. The sight of her, all fierce pride and defiance stripped away, lost to pleasure, is the most erotic thing I've ever seen.

It's still not enough.

I press three fingers into her slick heat. A hiss escapes through her clenched teeth, her inner walls clamping around the intrusion. The lightest flick of my tongue makes her jolt as if shocked. I alternate between gentle licks and firm pressure until she doesn't know whether to push toward me or pull away.

Her fifth orgasm builds slower but hits the hardest. Her breathing changes first—shallow, then ragged. When she finally breaks, she turns her face and screams into the pillow, tears streaming down her cheeks, as she comes apart.

I soften my tongue, each lap gentler than the last, bringing her down, soothing her battered flesh. Her violent tremors subside to shivers. Her sobs turn to whimpers, then soft, exhausted sighs.

I rise to my knees, my fingers working at the knot around her wrists before slipping her panties into the pocket of my jeans.

Her limbs sprawl across the sheets, chest still heaving with each breath. Her wet, heavy-lidded eyes track me as I stand. The metal of the knife catches the moonlight as I slide it into the sheath at my hip. Her gaze drops to the front of my jeans, to the visible outline pressing against denim. Her lips part.

"Aren't you going to—"

"Not tonight." I bend until my mask is inches from her face. Her nostrils flare, inhaling the unmistakable scent that clings to my lips and my chin. "I want you thinking about what comes next. Every time you close your eyes."

Her breath hitches. Moonlight streams through the window, illuminating the rush of color that spreads up her neck.

"I'll be back soon, little doe. Be waiting for me."

"Can you please stop calling me that?" Her voice is raspy, like worn velvet.

"No."

I lean down and kiss her nipple, and she groans, her back arching off the bed as her exhausted body craves more. My eyes never leave hers as I back away toward the door. "I'll see you again, Luna."

"Wait. Why me? Why are you doing this?"

I pause with my hand on the doorknob.

"Because from the moment I saw you, there was no one else."

I open the door to find the cats and her wolf waiting for me to vacate, their combined gazes heavy with judgment. Luna inspires such devotion from everyone around her. Especially the animals she saves.

They rush past me, Shadow growling at me before loping over to the bed, resting his head on the mattress beside hers. She's pulled up the sheet, and the cats all pile on top of her. She rubs her hand against the side of her wolf's face, forgiveness reflecting in her eyes as she looks at him.

Perhaps one day she'll give me the same look.

I slip back through her house, the taste of her still on my tongue, her complete surrender echoing in my mind.

Chapter Twenty-Two

Luna

I settle on the porch steps of the main sanctuary building, Ghost's medical charts spread across my lap. Ricky perches beside me on the wooden step, his masked face tilted up as I reach into the bowl of apple slices.

"Here you go, Rick." I hold out a slice. He chitters like he's trying to tell me something important, though his dark eyes keep drifting to my chest with unmistakable intent.

I flip open the folder, squinting at the white blood cell count. The numbers blur as my thoughts drift back to last night. My body still hums, my clit still pulses, and the bite on my inner thigh still throbs with the memory.

He came again. My dark watcher. My masked... what? Stalker? Hunter? Wolf?

The words jumble in my head, none of them quite fitting the man who watches me and, now, comes into my room in the dead of night, his face concealed behind that beautiful, disturbing mask.

God, that mask.

It haunts my thoughts—cold metal against heated flesh, the contrast of sensations as intoxicating as the man himself. Long after he left, I traced my fingers over my thighs where the edge of his mask left faint impressions, physical proof that he'd been real, that he'd claimed me, that I'd let him.

It was the most mind-blowing and terrifying experience I've ever had. When I woke and realized he was there, terror flooded my system. When he pulled out his knife, I expected him to cut, rape and then kill me. I didn't expect him to bring me to orgasm five times and then walk away without getting off himself.

What kind of man does that?

Fear and panic held me captive for most of the encounter, but desire and arousal bled into and then overrode them.

What kind of woman does that make me? The kind who spreads her legs for a masked serial killer?

"Ricky, no!"

I jerk sideways as his paws dart out quick as lightning, aiming straight for his target. The charts scatter across the porch.

He chitters in what sounds like protest, then sidles closer and nuzzles against my arm. The sweet gesture almost makes me forgive him until those sneaky paws creep toward my breasts again.

"I said, no!" I scramble to gather the scattered papers while holding up another apple slice as a distraction. "Food first, boob-grabbing never."

He accepts the bribe, settling back on his haunches to eat, but those dark eyes never leave their prize.

Part of me is horrified by what happened last night. All of me should be horrified. A killer touched me, made me come apart beneath his mouth and hands, and I let him. More than let him. I begged for it by the end.

But there's another part of me, a dark place I don't like to recognize or admit exists, that whispers he's doing what the law won't. What I can't. Those monsters got what they deserved, and if my masked watcher is the one to deliver that justice...

The thoughts I sometimes have would horrify my parents and grandfather if they were still alive, but I can't help it.

It contradicts everything I stand for. I save lives. I don't celebrate death. But when I think about Ghost's broken body, about every broken animal that comes through these doors because of human cruelty, that dark part of me grows a little stronger, a little more satisfied that their abusers are gone.

And the man who kills them is the one I let touch me.

I fought and begged him to stop. Until I didn't. Until I arched into him, pressing against his face, pleading for his touch.

No one has ever made me come like that from oral sex, so hard and fast the first time that I swear I nearly blacked out. Then, building me back up for a second before wrenching three more orgasms from me, leaving me wrecked, wishing I knew his name so I could have screamed it.

The irony isn't lost on me—a wolf mask, when today I'm meeting Damien Wolfe about a security system. I can't help but wonder if there's some cosmic joke at play. Still, the coincidence is peculiar.

Ricky finishes his apple slice and eyes the bowl. I hand him another piece, watching him settle into a more relaxed position. For a moment, I think he might behave. Then he abandons the fruit and scrambles into my lap, his warm body curling against me.

"That's better." I stroke his fur. "See? You can be sweet when you want to—" Those determined paws make another grab. "Seriously?" I catch his hands, redirecting them to the apple slice. "You're worse than a horny teenager."

He chitters indignantly but accepts defeat. For now.

"You look like you're about to spontaneously combust out here."

I jump, nearly sending Ricky tumbling off my lap as Maren emerges from the front door, carrying two cups of coffee, navigating around the scattered charts as she approaches. She glances at Ricky, then hands me a cup before settling in the rocking chair at the far end of the porch, well out of his reach.

"Thanks. Why are you sitting over there?"

As if on cue, Ricky makes another grab, but I catch his paws. "Jesus, Ricky, you're relentless today."

"And that's why I'm sitting way over here." Maren smirks. "I had my fill of raccoon molestation yesterday." She takes a sip of her coffee. "So Ghost's bandages are all changed, and get this... Titus ate his breakfast."

My heart leaps. "All of it?"

"Every last bite. I gave him seconds."

Relief floods through me. "Thank God. If he keeps this up for another couple days, we can remove his feeding tube. He's going to be fine, but we need to find a permanent place for him here. He's too skittish to go back into the wild."

Ricky, bored with having all his advances redirected, climbs out of my lap and scampers across the porch. He pauses at the railing, testing its height before hauling himself up to balance on the narrow wooden beam.

"Careful, Rick," I warn, but he ignores me, walking the railing like a tightrope performer.

Maren's expression turns serious. "Yeah, about that. Have you figured out how we're going to afford to build another permanent enclosure?"

"Now that my mortgage is paid off, maybe I can take out another one."

"Don't even think about it." Maren points a finger at me. "Let's do a fundraiser or something. I'll start calling around to old donors and try to hit them up. We'll figure it out, but no more mortgages."

"Yes, Mom." Her reprimand makes me smile. She's so bossy sometimes. "Speaking of figuring things out. I called Damien Wolfe last night. He's coming today at eleven to consult on a security system."

Maren's eyebrows shoot up. "Halle-fucking-lujah. Three dead bodies showing up is more than enough as far as I'm concerned. I was starting to think you enjoyed having psycho killers wandering around."

If only she knew.

I can't tell her what happened, as much as I want to. And I can't call Karen. I should have the second he left, but how can I report what he did to me without confessing that I gave in? Not because he forced me, but because I wanted it.

Ricky loses his balance for a moment, windmilling his arms before catching himself. He chitters, as if he meant to do that.

"Yeah, well, better late than never. I'm just glad he agreed to come out."

I need to keep my watcher from coming into my home. I hope Damien's system is able to do it.

"Mmhmm." Maren's grin turns wicked. "It doesn't hurt that he's your hottie, billionaire neighbor, does it? Hey, maybe he can help fund that enclosure for Titus while he's at it."

"I don't know how we're even going to be able to afford this system, so let's start with that before you try to hit him up for something else."

"He has more money than God. He should share it."

I believe in asking for help. The animals depend on it. But I'd invite him to see what we do first, let him fall in love with the cause. Maren's already mentally spending his fortune. I can see it in her eyes. She'd ask the Pope for donations at his own funeral.

Ricky completes his circuit of the railing and scrambles back down, deciding the floor offers better opportunities for mischief. He scurries over to investigate Maren's chair, but she's ready for him.

"Oh, no, you don't," she says, pulling her legs up. "Back away." Ricky gazes up at her with his sweet masked face, but she holds firm. "That look won't work on me, mister. Oh, by the way, have you seen my keys?"

I chuckle at her abrupt topic change. "No. Why?"

"I can't find them. They disappeared yesterday."

"How'd you get home last night?"

"I keep a spare set in my desk now, after the time I accidentally locked them in my car. But my main set is missing. I don't know what I did with it."

Ricky climbs back into my lap, this time with what I swear is a strategic gleam in his eyes. He settles against me, purring, lulling me into a false sense of security. I enjoy the brief moment of peace. Then he makes his most ambitious grab yet. I catch his hands. "That's it. It's time for you to go back into your cage."

"Maybe he's picking up on all the sexual tension you're putting into the universe, waiting for Damien Wolfe to arrive." Maren lowers her feet to the floor now that it's safe. "Animals are sensitive to that shit."

"That's ridiculous."

"Is it, though?"

Maybe she's right, especially considering what happened last night. I woke up still swollen and tender this morning, but I swear to God, also still aroused.

I should have fought harder. I can't believe I didn't. My passivity haunts me more than his touch. By all rights, I should be dead for that weakness, but my gut tells me I don't need to fear him. Not that way. My instincts are usually right, and Shadow agrees.

His reaction baffles me the most. He's always so protective of me. And though he growled before my watcher revealed himself and stood between us on the porch, Shadow seems to have accepted him now. Every cell in my body wants to trust my wolf's instincts, but this whole situation is insane.

"Can we not discuss my sex life, or lack thereof, in front of the animals?" I gesture to Ricky, who's now grooming his belly.

"Right, because Ricky here is so innocent," Maren snorts. "Oh, by the way, Ethan treated that peregrine falcon that came in early this morning. Wing fracture, but it should heal clean. You might want to check on him, though. He's been pretty agitated."

I glance at my watch, dislodging Ricky's questing paws again. "Let me do that before Damien gets here." I stand, scooping Ricky up, and he curls against me. "Here." I deposit him in Maren's lap. "Your turn."

"What? No! Luna, don't you dare—"

But it's too late. Ricky wastes no time, reaching for Maren's boobs with impressive speed and determination.

"Son of a bitch!" Maren catches his paws while trying not to spill her coffee. "This is exactly why I was sitting way over here! You're evil, you know that?"

"Payback for the sex comment." I gather up Ghost's charts and head for the door.

"Don't forget to freshen up before your billionaire boyfriend arrives!" Maren laughs as Ricky makes another strategic strike. "And maybe change into something that shows a little cleavage. Give the man something to work with!"

My body still hums with the memory of last night, and the thought of meeting Damien Wolfe while my skin still carries the phantom touch of my masked watcher makes my pulse flutter.

As the door closes behind me, Maren's creative cursing fades away, and I can't shake the feeling that today is going to bring more complications than a horny raccoon and a security consultation.

Chapter Twenty-Three

Damien

"You're starting to sound like a broken record, Cade."

He's been chewing my ear off for the past ten minutes, and I'm about to hang up on him as I turn into the sanctuary's driveway.

"You assured me you'd dispose of the Meyers' bodies properly."

His voice carries an edge, but on the dashboard screen his face remains smooth, his jaw relaxed, expression neutral, and not a muscle out of place.

"I did no such thing." My voice stays level, but the warning is clear. "Just because you demanded I do it doesn't mean I will. I told you, I'll dispose of the targets tied to Luna as I see fit." I pull into the parking space in front of the sanctuary building, cutting the engine. "But don't worry, I won't leave them on her property anymore. She asked me not to, and I'll respect her request."

Her request. The one that matters.

"You've had contact with her?"

"I texted you last night about meeting her today. Do you even read my texts?" The question comes out sharp, but Christ, sometimes dealing with Cade is like managing a paranoid parent.

"I mean, as the wolf." His jaw ticks, and he exhales. "How and under what circumstances was she able to ask you not to drop dead bodies on her property?"

"That's none of your business, Cade."

"Does she know your real identity?"

"Of course not." I let my eyes sweep across the building in front of me before returning to the dashboard screen to see a calculating look creeping into his expression. "And don't even fucking think about hacking into my micro-cameras. Now I have to go. I'm here."

I sit for a moment, observing Luna's sanctuary from behind the tinted windows, cataloging security vulnerabilities. I've already done this a dozen times, but it's a professional habit when I arrive for consultations.

I exit my Aston Martin Vantage at precisely 11 AM. The suit I chose is tailored to downplay my imposing build. No tie—this is rural Colorado, after all.

Different cologne than I wore last night.

Different posture.

Different hairstyle.

Different man.

I even shaved, erasing the stubble that might remind her of rough lips and a wolf's mask in the darkness.

Perhaps wearing my wolf mask was a mistake. It's too close to my real identity, but it's what puts me into my predator persona. Those unfortunate enough to see the mask up close never leave the encounter alive.

Until Luna.

I need to hide my true identity from her, but she's a smart woman. Since I intend to know her body even more intimately than last night, is it possible to keep the truth from her? I push the thought aside and focus on the situation at hand, installing my security system on her property so I can watch her unencumbered.

The sanctuary is larger than it appears from my usual vantage point in the surrounding forest. I've studied the layout from both county records and satellite imagery. Several outbuildings surround the house and main sanctuary structure, which houses both the offices and medical facilities. Enclosures of various sizes dot the property, each designed to mimic natural habitats. Luna built something here that works. A place where damaged animals can finally rest.

I approach the main building. The entrance smells of animals, antiseptic, and bleach, evidence of Luna and her team's meticulous cleanliness.

I wait for someone to greet me, letting my posture settle into something approachable. In the light of day, I'm Damien Wolfe, billionaire businessman, technology innovator, and respectable citizen.

Her vet tech emerges through a swinging door that leads to the main treatment area, eyeing me like I'm a piece of meat, and I suppress a smile.

"Mr. Wolfe. Welcome to Sage & Summit Wildlife Sanctuary."

"Ms. Rodriguez, I assume." I offer my right hand. She hesitates before shaking it.

"Luna's finishing up with a patient. She'll be out in a minute." Maren crosses her arms, sizing me up. "I'm surprised you came yourself. Don't billionaires usually send minions?"

A smile tugs at my lips. I like her already. "I prefer a hands-on approach for initial consultations. Especially in special circumstances."

"Special circumstances," Maren repeats with amusement before her face and voice harden. "You mean the dead bodies?"

Yes. I like this woman a lot.

"I mean Dr. Foster's safety and her important work here. That includes her team and the animals."

Something in my voice must reassure her because her posture eases. The door behind her opens, and Luna appears, pulling off latex gloves. My heart forgets its rhythm. Seeing her up close, in daylight again, is so different from watching her through windows, cameras, or binoculars from afar. It's different from seeing her from behind a mask, inches from her beautiful face. The overhead lights catch gold threads in her blonde hair, and her hazel eyes are even more striking in the light.

She is so fucking beautiful it hurts.

Her face is free of makeup, but she doesn't need it. She's stunning, dressed in jeans, boots, and a green high-necked sweater that hides the mark I left on her. Shadows pool under her eyes. The stress of my visits and gifts and how thoroughly I used her last night are all etched in her fatigue. The impulse to gather her close and smooth away the weariness until she melts hits me unaware.

The want ambushes me, and my chest does this strange thing. It tightens and squeezes, like a fist closing around my heart. Not painful, just there when it shouldn't be. Out of place. I don't cradle or soothe, but her obvious exhaustion makes me want to be her refuge instead of her storm. I step forward.

"Dr. Foster. It's a pleasure to meet you." My voice is pitched higher than she knows, polished and impersonal, bearing no resemblance to the deep one that owned her in the dark.

Luna wipes her palms on her jeans before accepting my handshake. Her smile is genuine, a slight tinge of pink blooming on her cheeks. "Mr. Wolfe. Thanks for coming on short notice."

The moment our hands connect, electricity arcs between us. Her eyes go wide, her fingers trembling against mine. I know what she feels. The same current that surges between us with every touch.

I keep my expression neutral even as satisfaction blazes in my chest. Her gaze sweeps across my face, lingering on my eyes, then my mouth, like she's searching for something familiar. I savor the flash of confusion in her eyes as pink spreads deeper across her skin.

"Please call me Damien." I release her hand, my fingers trailing away from the warmth of her skin.

"Then call me Luna." A small line appears between her brows, and I have to resist the urge to smooth it away with my thumb. "I hope you don't mind touring the property first? I'd like you to understand what we're protecting before we discuss systems."

"Of course."

Maren clears her throat. "I'll just get back to whatever it is I've gotta do."

Luna tears her eyes away from me to look at her friend, and I miss the weight of her attention the instant it's gone.

"Thanks, Maren. We'll be fine."

Luna leads me outside. I fall into step beside her, careful to maintain a professional distance when the wolf howls at me to crowd closer, breathe in her scent, and touch her.

"Let's start with the wolf habitat. It's our largest enclosure and the most frequent target for trespassers."

"Trespassers were a problem before the recent incidents?"

"Occasionally. People hear we have wolves and want to see them up close." She shakes her head, frustration clear in her voice. "They don't understand these aren't pets. They're wild. Most have been injured or orphaned. Human interaction is stressful for them."

"Except with you."

The comment earns me a pointed look. "I've spent years earning their trust. Even then, I respect their boundaries. Unlike most humans."

We reach the wolf enclosure, where three wolves pace near the opposite fence, but my attention fixes on the fourth, lying on a patch of grass, relaxed.

"That's Shadow." Luna's voice goes soft and warm. "He's the exception. I raised him from a pup, and he's imprinted on me."

At the sound of her voice, my new beta wolf approaches, ignoring me as he presses against the fence beside Luna. She crouches, murmuring endearments as she slips her fingers through the slats to touch him. He nuzzles her hand, then goes rigid, his nostrils flaring.

I tense. The wolf stares at me, a low growl vibrating in his throat as Luna tries to shush him.

"It's okay, baby. He's a good one. He's here to help us." She looks up at me. "He's leery of most men. Poachers killed his mother in front of him."

Her reassurance amuses me. If she only knew the real reason for his reaction.

The growling fades away as he stares at me, then he does something unexpected. He tips his head, almost in a gesture of acknowledgment, before returning his attention to Luna.

Most people don't understand how intelligent wolves are. Studies have shown they possess superior cognitive abilities, connecting cause to effect in ways that shame their domestic cousins. They're also known for their strong familial bonds, and Shadow has bonded with Luna, adopting her into his pack of one. She belongs to him now with the totality that wolves reserve for family. Protective, possessive, willing to die defending what's his. I can hardly blame him.

But wolves aren't just killers—they're smart killers. He knows the difference between enemies and complications.

I'm the latter.

Luna rises, confusion on her face. "His reaction to you is unusual. He must recognize your scent from the post office last week."

I shrug, feigning ignorance. "Animals often sense intent. Perhaps he recognizes I'm here to help."

"Perhaps." The skepticism in her voice is impossible to miss. "The wolf enclosure backs up to the forest. It's our most vulnerable point, almost impossible to secure without making it feel like a prison."

"There are options. Perimeter sensors that won't disturb the animals but will alert you to intruders."

To anyone but me.

The tour continues, and every minute feeds my obsession. She shows me barns, rehabilitation spaces, medical facilities, and enclosures housing everything from eagles to foxes. Though not all, most animals have a story of abuse or abandonment that she recounts with clinical detachment, but I see through the mask. Her hands clench when describing cruel cases, pain flickering across her expression despite her professional composure.

I catalog each reaction, each sign of the darkness that lives beneath her compassionate exterior. She's light and dark, opposites that can't exist without the other. Except in me.

"And this is my office." She leads me into the small, cluttered space I know better than she realizes. "Not much, but it's where I handle administrative work when I'm not with the animals."

My eyes flick to the ceramic owl on the shelf that hides my micro-camera.

"Your home is separate?"

"Yes, it's about ten yards that way." She points in the direction I know by heart. "I can keep an eye on things from there, but it's far enough that I can sometimes pretend I have a life outside this place."

"Do you? Have a life outside?"

Luna raises an eyebrow, moving to lean against her desk. "Is that relevant to my security needs, Mr. Wolfe?"

"Damien," I correct. "And yes. Understanding your routines helps identify vulnerabilities."

"My routine is work, sleep, and more work. Thrilling, I know."

"Purposeful. That's rare."

A commotion erupts from beneath the desk.

Luna crouches with a sigh. "Ricky! What are you doing in there?" She pulls out the chair to extract a medium-sized raccoon who reaches for her chest.

"Ricky, stop it." She tugs his small paws away and looks up at me with a smile. "Sorry. This is one of our resident raccoons, and he's a bit of a stinker."

Maren comes rushing into the room. "There you are, you little shit." She plants her hands on her hips, narrowing her eyes. "He snuck out when I was cleaning his cage. I've been searching for him for ten minutes."

"He was hiding under my desk." Luna stands and hands the raccoon to Maren.

"No banana sundae for you tonight, mister," she scolds as she walks away. "Damn it. Stop grabbing my boobs."

I raise an eyebrow at Luna.

"Ricky has a boob fetish."

"That's not something I ever thought I'd hear."

"You and me both."

She settles against the edge of her desk again, and I have to resist the urge to step closer, to cage her in against it.

"So, what are your thoughts on securing the sanctuary? The animals are my primary concern, but recent events have made me realize I also need to prioritize my own safety."

"I'd recommend a comprehensive system. Cameras at key points along the perimeter and on the exterior of all the buildings, inside all the sanctuary spaces, motion sensors, and upgraded locks. And to reiterate your point, given what's happened recently, your house warrants special attention."

"I don't want cameras inside my house. The idea of being watched makes me feel violated."

Oh, little doe. If you think the cameras will make you feel violated…

"Of course. But exterior cameras that cover vulnerable points of access are important. We can program them to capture only unusual activity, not everyday routines."

Luna hesitates, then nods. "And the cost?"

"I'll be donating your system, including monitoring."

Surprise flashes across her face. The expression makes me want to reach out and touch her, caress that smooth, flawless skin, and tell her she belongs to me and I'll give her anything she needs.

"I can't ask you to do that?"

"You didn't ask. I offered. I have a charitable foundation that donates to animal causes worldwide. Your system will be donated by the foundation. You're a 501(c)(3), correct?"

"Yes."

"Then it's settled. I'll send a detailed proposal today and have everything installed tomorrow."

"That quickly?"

"I'm the board chairman, Luna. I set the timeline."

And I want my eyes on you as soon as possible.

"Okay, tomorrow it is."

"I'll oversee the installation personally."

Luna shifts, and her eyes narrow. "Why would you do that?"

"Let's call it community service. I believe in hands-on support for local animal welfare efforts. And neighborhood watch efforts," I add with what I hope is an easy smile.

"That doesn't mean you need to install my security system personally. You must have more important things to do."

Luna is independent and stubborn. That's going to make her next encounter with the wolf a shock to her system. She'll surrender all that independence and stubbornness to me. She won't have a choice.

"I can always make time to help a beautiful neighbor. And your safety and the safety of your animals matter."

Her eyes soften, and satisfaction purrs through me.

"I also find puzzles compelling, and you present quite the puzzle."

She goes rigid. "I'm not a puzzle, Mr. Wolfe. I'm a veterinarian with a security problem."

"Damien." I'm tired of correcting her. "Everyone is a puzzle. Most are just tediously simple to solve."

"I'm not?"

I let my gaze linger on her face, studying every detail while allowing some of my real intensity to show through the mask I wear for the world. "You're delightfully complex."

A flush creeps up her neck, and she looks away first. She feels the pull between us, even if she doesn't understand it yet.

"I don't know how to thank you for your generosity, Damien."

"No thanks needed." I step closer, close enough to breathe in the scent of peaches and warmth that clings to her skin. Her scent haunts me even when she's not near. "I'm impressed with what you do here. It takes an exceptional person to heal those victims the law fails."

Her brow creases, and I wait to see if she'll connect my words to the note I left with Raymond Davis. Then her eyes snap to mine as recognition flares, but hesitation clouds it over. Like she's dismissing her suspicions before they fully form.

Intelligence, genuine compassion, and beauty are rare, seldom found in one package. But she embodies them all.

She clears her throat, stepping toward the door. "I should get back to it. The sanctuary doesn't run itself."

"Of course." I reach into my jacket, pulling out a different business card than the one Eleanor gave her. "Here are my personal numbers. Call me anytime. For any reason. I'll arrange for installation to begin tomorrow morning. It will take my team two to three days to complete."

Our fingers touch as she takes the card, and that electric spark passes between us again. Luna stares at our joined hands for a long moment before her eyes meet mine, something unreadable flickering in their depths.

"I'll walk you out."

Chapter Twenty-Four

Luna

The lobby door shuts behind us, and I'm aware of nothing but Damien's proximity. His hand hovers near the small of my back, not touching, but close enough for me to feel the warmth radiating through my sweater. Heat spreads outward from that point, rippling up my spine in waves that feel both thrilling and unsettling.

My girls dart up to us as if summoned, weaving their usual chaotic dance around my ankles. Sage butts her head against my shin while Willow and Juniper compete for prime ankle-rubbing real estate. I expect Damien to step back, maybe wrinkle his nose at the cat hair that's about to coat his expensive suit, but he sidesteps them with ease.

The way he moves is captivating—all controlled power wrapped in masculine confidence. I find myself looking at him longer than I should.

"The family." I work to keep my voice light despite the Olympic-level gymnastics routine my heart is currently performing. "Sage, Willow, and Juniper. They think they run the place."

"Don't they?"

"Pretty much." I try not to stare at the way his lips curve when he smiles, but it's like trying to look away from the sunset. "Even the wolves give them space."

He leans down and rubs his fingers down Juni's back. I watch, transfixed, as his large hand moves with surprising gentleness over her little chubby body. She arches into his touch, a purr vibrating through her. Those strong fingers stroking through her fur hold my attention in a way that makes my mouth go dry.

Jesus, Luna. It's a man petting a cat, not foreplay.

"You should feel privileged. She's very selective about who she allows to pet her."

He stands up, and damn, he's tall. I have to tilt my head back to meet those blue-gray eyes.

"I have a knack for coaxing purrs out of even the most temperamental of pussies with a single touch."

I choke on a surprised laugh. *Oh my God.* Maren would be so proud of that innuendo. But it's not only his choice of words that affects me. It's the way his voice deepens, taking on an edge that scrapes against something deep inside me. I swallow hard, my body responding before my brain can shut it down.

We reach his car, some sleek, expensive thing, and he extends his hand. "It was a pleasure, Dr. Foster."

The formal address feels wrong, too distant after the past hour of electricity crackling between us.

"Luna," I say, hoping my voice sounds confident even though my heart trips all over itself. "If I have to call you Damien, you have to call me Luna."

"Luna."

The way my name rolls off his tongue sends a familiar ripple of heat down my spine. His eyes never leave mine as he speaks, and I feel exposed, like he can see straight through to every dirty thought I've had about him today. And there have been quite a few.

"You have a very beautiful name."

My pulse jumps beneath his warm, calloused fingertips where they rest against my wrist. For a second, neither of us moves, and I'm drowning in those blue-gray depths that seem to spark in the afternoon light.

I withdraw my hand first, breaking whatever spell we've fallen under.

"I'll see you tomorrow."

He slides into the driver's seat in one seamless motion, his suit stretching across those broad shoulders as he settles in. The engine purrs to life—because of course it does—and I stand there like an idiot, watching until his taillights disappear around the bend.

Only then do I exhale, finally able to breathe freely for the first time in over an hour.

Damn!

Damien Wolfe is probably the most attractive man I've ever set eyes on. How the hell did I miss it during our almost-collision?

When I walked into the lobby today and looked up at him, the air vanished from my lungs. He was taller and broader than I'd realized outside the post office, but it was more than his physicality that made the small lobby feel cramped. It was him. The way he commanded attention without even trying, like gravity itself had shifted to revolve around him.

He looked distinguished in that dark gray suit that clung to his body like a second skin, managing to look both professional and casually devastating with his open collar and no tie. But it was his eyes that trapped me, that penetrating blue-gray that locked onto me the moment he extended his hand. Up close, they weren't completely blue. Amber flecks like tiny sparks nestled near the pupils, adding mysterious depth that made me think of storm clouds shot through with lightning.

Eleanor hadn't exaggerated about the silver streaks at his temples. Subtle but noticeable, my fingers itched to reach up and thread through those soft strands.

Everything about him radiated a contradictory aura of unapproachability that made me want to step back, but also an ease that made it impossible to look away. The odd flutter in my stomach had been a pleasant surprise that quickly settled lower, becoming something altogether more dangerous when our skin touched.

Now, standing alone in the driveway, that odd flutter still pulses low in my belly. There's something about Damien Wolfe, something familiar yet dangerous that I can't quite place.

Maren bursts out the door like a tornado the moment Damien's sleek black car disappears down the gravel driveway.

"You did not tell me he was that fucking hot."

She waves her hand beside her face as if she's trying to fan herself. "That man could make a woman come just from walking into a room."

I give her my best disapproving look because I'm not about to admit how affected I am by him. "Maren, control yourself. You're a thirty-two-year-old woman, not a horny teenager."

"Eighteen, thirty-two, fifty-two. It doesn't matter." She fans herself more dramatically, and I have to bite back a smile at her theatrics. "That man was put on this earth to make all women within his vicinity drop their panties and say, 'Give it to me, big boy.'"

I cringe at her breathy Marilyn Monroe imitation, though part of me, the part that's still tingling from his touch, wants to agree with her.

"Jesus, Maren." I look around to see if any of the volunteers are within earshot. "You can't say shit like that at work. You're going to get me sued."

She waves me off. "Whatever. Everyone here saw with their own eyes that he's a god among men."

"He's good-looking, but he's not that handsome," I lie, because she doesn't need more ammunition.

But could I sound any more transparent? Even I don't believe myself.

"You're right. He's not handsome. He's sex on a stick."

"Do I need to throw cold water on you?"

"No. That'll make my scrubs as wet as my panties."

"Jesus," I say again, shaking my head. "I'm going to have to lock you up when he comes back, aren't I?"

"You might. But you can lock him inside with me. Leave the handcuffs." She wiggles her eyebrows, and I laugh. "Eleanor wasn't lying about those sexy silver streaks. Seeing him might have brought out a daddy kink in me."

"I'm telling JT how you're behaving the next time I see him."

Maren snorts. "Girl, even JT would drop his boxers for that man."

Sage winds between my legs, and I lean down to pick her up. She settles against my chest, her motor vibrating.

"So?" Maren presses, not willing to let this go.

"What?"

"Aside from the panty-dropping face and body, what's he like? Is he as pretentious as that car suggests?"

I consider how to describe Damien Wolfe. Unexpectedly generous. Unnervingly handsome. Disturbingly perceptive. And somehow, despite his wealth, power, and overall serious demeanor, I'm drawn to him.

"He's... not what I expected."

"Meaning?"

"He's donating the system."

"As he should. I told you, he's richer than God and more beautiful than an angel from heaven." Her sigh is designed to annoy me, and she knows it.

"He's overseeing the installation personally. Says it's to 'support' local animal welfare efforts."

"Right..." Maren snorts. "The fact that you're gorgeous and single has nothing to do with it."

"It's not like that." Though even as I say it, the intensity of his gaze as his eyes scanned my face and the gentle touch of his thumb against my wrist still give me goosebumps.

"Honey, I saw how he looked at you when he thought no one was watching. Like he wanted to throw you over his shoulder, caveman style, take you back to his sex dungeon, and tie you up for days."

"Not everyone is as sex-obsessed as you."

"Yes, they are. Even you. Though I swear you're trying to break the record for the most days a woman can go without an orgasm. With another person, at least."

You have no idea how hard I came with another person last night, Maren.

I'm tempted to say that out loud, but I don't. The memory of those hands, that voice, the way my body had responded—it's too raw and too confusing.

"I think you should totally hit that. He's gorgeous and rich and probably fucks like a beast. I'm telling you, do not let that man pass you by."

"Alright, enough." I set Sage on the ground and turn to head back into the sanctuary, pushing thoughts of Damien Wolfe and how he would fuck out of my mind. "What do we still have to do this afternoon?"

Maren keeps pace with me as we head toward the building. "You mean other than talk about Mr. Hottie Billionaire Sex on a Stick?" I ignore her as we enter the lobby. "Gertie needs her medicated bath, and Winston is constipated."

"Which one do you want to take?"

"I'll take getting drenched giving a goat a bath over giving an opossum a suppository any day."

Of course she would.

***

The rest of the afternoon passes in a blur, but my mind wanders constantly. Every time it does, I see those blue-gray eyes with their amber flecks. I imagine his hands on my skin, his low voice whispering my name in the dark.

By evening, exhaustion has settled deep in my bones, but it's the restless kind that comes from too much thinking and not enough resolution. After a quick dinner of reheated soup that I barely taste, I need air and space to think.

The front porch is out of the question. So, I grab my glass of wine and climb through the window to the balcony again. Shadow follows and lies at my feet as usual, but his ears remain alert, head constantly swiveling toward the surrounding forest. I follow his gaze into the darkness.

"Is he out there, baby?"

I haven't felt my watcher's eyes on me all day. I tell myself I'm relieved that whatever madness possessed me to respond to him the last two nights has passed. But in the quietest corners of my mind, I admit the truth.

I miss the feeling.

My thoughts drift to Damien. I received an email from him before I left the office with the security proposal he promised. It was detailed and beyond generous. Seeing the dollar amount that was zeroed out at the bottom made my head spin, like my mortgage and student loans had. The system he's proposing is worth more than I make in three years.

I grab my tablet from beside me, bring up a browser, and search "Damien Wolfe Colorado." Results flood my screen. Tech magazine profiles, business journal features, and charity gala photographs, where he looks devastating in black tie. The man has an impressive digital footprint. MIT graduate, founder of Wolfe Technologies at age eighteen, and a pioneer in surveillance systems and security AI. Current estimated net worth: $32.2 billion.

"Jesus."

I scroll through images of him at various events. In every photo, he commands attention, that same magnetic presence I'd experienced in person radiating through the screen. What is someone like him doing installing security systems at a tiny sanctuary in rural Colorado?

A plaintive meow interrupts my research, and Willow appears at the window, having climbed through after me. She jumps onto my lap, and I take a sip of wine as she circles before curling up.

Shadow rises beside me, growling, his posture rigid. His behavior has been so abnormal lately. From protective, to trusting of complete strangers, to deference to a man who radiates both lust and danger. My heart pounds as I follow his gaze, peering into the darkness between the trees.

"I know you're there. You might as well show yourself."

For one breathless moment, I think I see movement, but when I blink, it's gone.

With a shaky sigh, I usher Willow and Shadow back through the window and follow them inside, securing the latch behind me.

By the time I finish my shower, Sage and Willow have already claimed their spots on my bed, while Juniper lies on the windowsill. Her green eyes reflect the moonlight as she stares out into the darkness.

I hesitate before closing the curtains. I know he's out there. He's watching, and despite everything rational in my brain screaming at me to close them and forget about last night, I leave them open.

If he wants to watch, let him watch.

Sleep comes fitfully, dreams merging reality with fantasy in ways that leave me gasping and restless. In them, two men pursue me through endless forests. One wears a silver wolf mask, his touch demanding and rough; the other is in an expensive suit that does nothing to hide the predator underneath. Both with similar intense eyes that see too much. Both wanting something from me, I'm not sure I can give.

I drift between consciousness and dreams, never fully surrendering to either.

Chapter Twenty-Five

Luna

"**D**on't even fucking say it." Maren points at me as I curl up on the porch swing, tablet balanced on my knees, and my second cup of coffee in my hand. The wooden stairs groan under her stomping feet, and I bite back a laugh at the sight of her, banana walnut oatmeal splattered across her shirt and smeared on her forehead like war paint.

"Ricky get you again?"

The chuckle escapes despite my best efforts. For the last month, they've been locked in a battle of wills over the oatmeal we feed him and Zorro twice a week to regulate their digestion. And she loses every single time. Zorro eats it without issue, but Ricky makes it his mission to get more on Maren than into his belly.

"I'm done. D. O. N. E. Done." She flings the front door open. "You're on oatmeal duty from now on."

"I told you not to give him the bowl," I call after her retreating form. "One spoonful at a time, remember?"

Her grumbled curses drift down from upstairs, but I'm still laughing as I follow her inside. I shouldn't because he's launched his breakfast at me plenty of times too.

After a night of fractured sleep, dreams jerking me awake every hour, I'm dragging this morning. Every time I closed my eyes, I saw my watcher standing in the shadows of my room. But when I woke, heart racing and pulse throbbing between my legs, the room was empty.

I put my mug in the dishwasher and check the clock on the wall. I have five minutes until Damien arrives with his security team, so I swap my slippers for Skechers, trying to ignore the flutter in my stomach.

The shower turns on upstairs. Maren keeps half of her wardrobe here for situations like this. Next time I'm in Estes, I need to pick up her favorite chocolate-covered Bavarian pretzels from the Rocky Mountain Chocolate Factory as a small peace offering for everything she puts up with here.

My watcher didn't come last night. The realization sits in my chest like a stone, heavy and wrong. I should be relieved. I am relieved.

So why am I disappointed?

Shadow and I both felt his eyes on us before bed. But then nothing. Maybe now that he got what he wanted, there's no reason to come back. Except I don't believe that. He said he'd be back. He's not finished with me. This feels like a pause, not an ending.

My stomach twists. I should be celebrating his absence. He's a stalker, a serial killer, who's fixated on me for reasons I don't understand. Fear should be the only thing I feel. But my traitorous body remembers his hands and his mouth, the way he coaxed pleasure from places I didn't know existed. Pleasure so intense it bordered on pain. Heat creeps up my neck at the memory.

And the primal fear of both him and Damien chasing and hunting me in my dreams had me waking up flushed and aroused. I couldn't get my hand in my panties fast enough, but the orgasm was weak and unfulfilling compared to what he did to me.

I step back onto the porch as a large, black pickup truck pulls up the driveway, followed by two matching vans with "Wolfe Technologies" emblazoned on their sides. My pulse kicks up a notch when Damien steps out of the truck, and I have to grip the porch railing to steady myself.

Gone is yesterday's polished businessman. Dark jeans cling to his powerful legs, and a charcoal sweater stretches across his broad shoulders. This version of him looks untamed and dangerous in a way that makes breathing require conscious effort.

He opens the passenger door and lifts out a gorgeous pit bull with a muscular build and a distinctive blue-gray coat. And is that a pink bow around her neck? He sets her on the ground, and her ears perk up as she takes in her surroundings, her tail wagging.

The contrast should be jarring, but it isn't. If anything, seeing him with this rescue dog makes him more attractive. Those silver streaks at his temples catch the morning light as he directs his crew, and I have to swallow back the drool pooling in my mouth.

Maren's right. Older men are my kryptonite, and Damien checks every box on that fantasy list. Confident, intelligent, and with enough silver to suggest experience without fragility. He's in his mid-forties, so it's premature gray, but those salt-and-pepper strands would feel perfect wrapped around my fingers while his head moves between my—

Jesus Christ.

I've never been this horny in my life. Maybe my hormones are out of whack. I should probably get blood work done.

"Right on time." I hope my voice doesn't betray the direction of my thoughts. My hands smooth down my shirt, and I hate that I still need the turtleneck to hide the bite mark on my collarbone. Each step toward him takes concentration to appear normal. "You brought a friend!"

"I value punctuality." He hefts two heavy equipment cases from his truck bed as if they weigh nothing. "This is Athena. I didn't want to leave her home alone all day. I hope that's okay."

"Of course." I drop to one knee, extending my hand toward her. "Hey there, beautiful girl." She sniffs my fingers before leaning into my touch, her tail picking up speed as I scratch behind her ears. Scars mar her face, but her eyes are bright, open, and trusting.

"She's gorgeous." I look up at Damien. "What's her story?"

Anger flickers across his features, there and gone so quickly I almost miss it. "I rescued her from a dogfighting ring. Took some time to help her trust again, but she's come a long way."

Pain twists in my soul thinking about what this sweet girl survived. "Fucking bastards." I run my hands along Athena's scarred but powerful shoulders. "How could anyone hurt something so beautiful?"

"They can't anymore."

I look up at the venom in his tone, but his expression is impassive.

Athena seems to have decided I'm acceptable, pressing her head against my thigh with a soft whuff of contentment.

"She likes you."

"The feeling's mutual."

I stand ready to offer help with his equipment when the front door of the house bangs open. Maren bounds out, dressed in clean scrubs, her wet hair twisted into a messy ponytail.

She skids to a stop when she sees Damien, me, and Athena by the truck, and the sly smile that spreads across her face makes me want to throttle her.

"Well, well, well..." She draws out each word like she's savoring it. "If it isn't Mr. Tall, Dark, and Mysterious. And he brought backup." She bends down, offering her hand to Athena. "Hello there, gorgeous."

Athena greets Maren with as much enthusiasm.

"Ms. Rodriguez." Damien gives her a slight nod, his expression unreadable.

"Maren, don't you have something to do?" My voice carries a warning she's immune to after fifteen years of friendship.

"Sure. I'll leave you three to it. It's kinda hot out here, anyway." She chuckles under her breath as she walks away.

As soon as she's behind Damien, she starts fanning her face, mouthing "so hot" at me. I shoot her my most vicious glare. The one that has zero effect on her.

When she's gone, Damien looks down at me with a smirk that says he missed nothing. "Is your friend okay? She looks a little flustered."

"Nothing another cold shower won't fix. So, where do you need to start?"

"How about your office? That's where we should set up the hub. Unless you want it in your house."

"My office is fine. Need help?"

"I've got it. Though if you could get the door..."

I watch the graceful way he carries the weight as he passes me, Athena trotting along beside him. He smells different today, his cologne stronger, though not overpowering, the vanilla and amber scent making that spot below my belly button clench.

I lead him toward my office, trying to keep my thoughts professional. Ricky goes scurrying across the treatment area, Tate hot on his tail.

"That raccoon is a bit of a troublemaker, isn't he?" Damien's lips quirk. Athena's ears perk forward with interest, but she stays at his side.

"You have no idea." I push open my office door. "So you said the installation will take two days?"

He sets his equipment case on my desk, while Athena settles onto the floor nearby. "Yes. Today I'll focus on getting the hub set up, the system in your home, and the perimeter cameras."

"Is the house a priority?"

"Given recent events, your personal spaces are of utmost importance."

I nod, trying not to stare at the way his sweater stretches across his broad chest. "I have a few animals to check on, but I'll be in and out. Maren or one of the interns can also help if you need anything. Just ask. And don't worry about Athena. She's welcome to roam around. Most of our animals are used to dogs."

"I prefer to work uninterrupted." His tone isn't rude, more matter-of-fact. "But I'll find you if questions arise. And Athena will stay with me."

"Fair enough." I hesitate at the door. "There's coffee in the kitchen if you want. Second door on the left. And there's a water bowl in there for Athena too."

The ghost of a smile touches his lips.

"Thank you."

※

Throughout the day, I find myself inventing reasons to pass by my office. I tell myself it's professional curiosity, but the truth is I'm drawn to watching him work. Damien's movements are economical and practiced as he drills, wires, and programs, surprising for someone of his wealth and status. I find myself mesmerized by the flex of muscles in his forearms as he installs mounting brackets and the slight furrow of concentration between his brows. Athena proves the perfect companion, staying out of his way but alert to his every movement.

During one pass, I'm so distracted by my thoughts that I nearly collide with him as I round the corner, arms full of charts.

"Sorry!" The word bursts out as his hands come up to steady me, gripping my upper arms.

Heat spreads from where he touches me, racing up to my shoulders and down to my fingertips. The same sensation as yesterday. I lift my eyes to his face, searching for some sign he feels it too.

There's only careful neutrality in his gaze. "No harm done." He releases me, stepping back to a professional distance that feels both disappointing and relieving. "I was heading to my truck for additional hardware."

"Right." I clutch the folders tighter against my chest as I move to the side. "How's it going?"

"Efficiently." He glances at his watch. "We're a little ahead of schedule, so I should get to the main building connections today."

"That's... good."

Apparently, I've lost the ability to speak like a normal person.

He excuses himself, and I take a moment to catch my breath before giving Athena a treat from my pocket. The pull I feel toward him is powerful and confusing. I only met the man yesterday, for Christ's sake.

I shake it off and go about my way. The next thing I know, I've completed my evening rounds and darkness has fallen. I'm tired and looking forward to a hot shower before calling Shadow in from his run. As I walk toward the house, I'm surprised to see Damien's black pickup still here and the lights on in the living room.

The front door stands ajar, spilling warm light onto my porch. I push it open. "Hello?"

"In the kitchen." Damien's voice drifts from the back of the house.

He's standing in front of an open panel on my kitchen wall, tools spread across the table. His sleeves are pushed up, revealing forearms corded with muscle and covered in tattoos I can't quite make out as he connects wires to my new security system.

Athena lies nearby, watching him work, while Sage has claimed her favorite perch on the dog's back, the same way she does with Shadow.

"You're still here." I lean against the doorframe, thinking about how right they both look in the space.

Where the hell did that come from?

He glances over his shoulder, those penetrating eyes finding mine. "Just finishing up. We got most of the system installed today. All the interior sensors in your house and the sanctuary buildings."

"It's past eight. You don't have to work these hours."

Damien straightens, turning to face me. "I do my best work at night."

Okay. That's an odd thing to say.

I move around the island, stepping closer, and his eyes track my movements.

"Is that the main control panel?"

"No, that's beside the front door. This is a secondary panel. There's also one in your bedroom, so you can arm or disarm the system from upstairs." He gestures for me to join him. "Let me show you how it works."

His arm is almost touching mine as he explains the system, and I'm too distracted by his proximity to understand any of it. Heat radiates from his body, and that vanilla-amber scent makes my head swim. He turns his head to look down at me, and my breath catches.

"Luna?"

My name rolls off his tongue like he's tasting it, drawing out each syllable.

"Yes?" The word escapes on a breathy exhale I didn't mean to release.

His eyes drop to my mouth, and the heat in his gaze makes my nipples tighten, but then he steps back, clearing his throat. His professional mask slides back into place. It's a bit unnerving how easily he does that, almost as if he's two separate people.

"If you have any problems with anything, or if anything doesn't work to your satisfaction, call me directly. You have my numbers. Call anytime. Day or night."

"Thank you, Damien. For everything."

"We'll finish with the exterior cameras and motion sensors tomorrow." He packs up his tools. "I won't be here. I have business at my Denver office, but my team will complete the installation. Once everything's finished, I'll stop by to ensure it's all working properly."

Athena rises when he lifts his equipment case, stretching in that leisurely way dogs do. Sage meows in protest at losing her warm perch.

"She's such a good girl." I crouch to give her another pet before scooping Sage into my arms. I follow them down the hall to the front door. "Hey, if you ever need to board her when you go out of town, I'd be happy to have her stay here. We're set up for it, and she seems to get along well with everyone."

His mouth curves, not quite a smile but close, and the transformation is breathtaking. He looks younger. Softer. "That's kind of you. I'll keep that in mind."

He hesitates at the door, looking back at me with an expression I can't quite read. The air between us feels charged, full of unspoken possibilities.

"Lock up behind me. And stay safe, Luna."

⋅•◦•⋅

My thoughts are in disarray, and my nerves are frazzled as I lock up and set the alarm. I'm glad I have the security system because, as the night goes on, I'm more convinced than ever that what happened with my watcher was complete insanity.

It can't happen again.

I'm playing Russian roulette with my life. It doesn't matter how drawn I am to him or how wet I get just thinking about what he did to me. I'm asking to get murdered.

I have to stop this. But how?

He's fixated on me. That's what creepy stalkers do. They obsess and watch and stalk until they finally knock you unconscious and take you to their murder lair and cut you into little pieces.

Okay, so maybe I'm being a little dramatic.

But probably not.

Now, I'm attracted to Damien. His quiet intensity draws me in, a silent pull that feels both exciting and unnerving. Maybe I'm in such a constant state of arousal that I'm attracted to everyone. Soon, I'll have the hots for Maren.

Knowing her, she'd probably like it.

I jump in the shower and let the water wash away my lingering unease, feeling safer knowing that I have a security system. But I should have told Maren about my watcher. Someone should know in case I vanish or my body turns up dead, wrapped in plastic.

What will I do if he comes tonight? At least the new system will keep him out. If he tries to break in, Damien's company will be alerted, and they'll call the sheriff. But will they make it here before he murders me? Or I have an aneurysm and end up in a coma from orgasming too hard.

I slip into an oversized t-shirt. A knot of fear tightens my stomach because I know with chilling certainty that nothing will stop him the next time he comes for me. Security system or not.

Against my better judgment, I look out my window for a long time before I crawl into bed, exhausted yet too wired to sleep. He's not out there tonight. His gaze is absent. I don't feel the familiar prickle on my skin that always comes when he's watching me.

I grab my phone from the nightstand, debating whether I should call Maren and confess. Maybe I should have asked her to stay tonight.

No. I don't know my watcher's true intentions with me yet, and I can't bear to put her in danger.

My mind drifts to Damien again, replaying his expressions, the restrained hunger in his eyes when he looked at me. It reminds me too much of my watcher.

The coincidence nags at me, but I push the thought away. It's too far-fetched. I'm just connecting them because of the wolf, or Wolfe, aspect. Damien Wolfe is a billionaire. He's not a masked stalker, creeping around the woods of Colorado and taking women against their will.

He's too refined, distinguished, and rich. My watcher is rough, almost savage. They're complete opposites, except in how my body reacts to them.

As my consciousness fades and sleep claims me, the weight of disappointment settles, like a heavy blanket in the night's stillness, because, even though I don't want him to, once again, my watcher doesn't show.

⸻ ◆ ⸻

Something jolts me from sleep. I bolt upright in bed, my heart hammering against my ribs.

What was that?

I strain, listening for whatever woke me. The house is quiet. Too quiet. At the foot of my bed, Sage, Willow, and Juniper sleep undisturbed, curled together in a pile of fur, while Shadow snores in his bed in the corner.

I look around my room, and nothing is amiss. But something isn't right.

I glance at the keypad next to the door. Damien insisted I have one installed in the bedroom. A solid red light signals that the system is armed.

So why does the back of my neck itch?

The creaking of the hardwood floor in the hallway outside my door sends ice flooding my veins.

Someone's in the house. It can only be one person.

I throw back the covers and slide out of bed. Shadow doesn't stir, which is odd. He should be freaking out if a stranger is inside the house.

I love him, but my wolf is really starting to disappoint me.

The keypad still glows red, which means no one breached any doors or windows. Damien's system is supposed to be breachproof.

I edge toward my closet, opening it to reach inside for the baseball bat I keep there. The one I should start setting beside the bed at night. The smooth wood feels reassuring in my grip as I tighten my fingers around it.

I pause at my bedroom door, listening.

Nothing.

The house is silent again.

Steeling myself, I turn the knob and step into the hallway, bat raised and ready. My pulse throbs in my throat as I scan the darkness, but there's no one there. The hallway stretches empty before me, moonlight filtering through the window at the far end, casting long shadows on the floor.

Still gripping the bat, I make my way to the gun cabinet. If my watcher is in the house again, I'm going to shoot him. And I won't miss this time.

When the door swings open, my stomach plummets.

The shotgun is gone.

"No, no, no."

I search the cabinet with frantic hands, as if the weapon might materialize if I look hard enough. But it's not there.

He took it. How did he know the combination to my gun cabinet?

I back away, clutching the bat tighter, and hurry back to my bedroom. I need my phone. I'm calling Karen and putting an end to this insanity.

When I reach my nightstand, my phone isn't there.

What the hell?

Shadow still hasn't stirred in his bed, which makes no sense. He should be going crazy right now. The cats remain unbothered as well.

What the hell is happening to my animals? Am I dreaming? I pinch myself. Nope, not dreaming.

My heart hammers so hard I can hear the blood rushing in my ears. He's in my house again, and he's taken my grandfather's shotgun and my phone.

What the actual fuck!

How did he get past my security system?

I take a deep breath, trying to steady my nerves, but it doesn't stop my arms from shaking. Clutching the bat with both hands, I move toward the bedroom door again. If he's here, I need to confront him. I need to end this game, whatever it is.

I close the door behind me because I won't take the chance that he'll shoot Shadow if he comes to my rescue.

The stairs creak beneath my weight as I descend them, one at a time. My muscles are coiled tight, ready to swing if necessary. The living room below is dark, but I can make out the familiar shadowy shapes of my furniture.

I freeze as I reach the bottom step.

He's lounging in the chair beside the window, like he owns the place. The silver wolf mask catches the moonlight streaming in the front window, making his visible mouth seem even more dangerous when it curves into an infuriating smirk.

My grandfather's shotgun lies in his lap.

"Looking for this?"

Chapter Twenty-Six

Damien

A myriad of emotions battle for dominance on her face. Fear tugging at the corners of her eyes, anger flaring her nostrils, recognition flickering in her pupils, and beneath it all, desire pooling in the flush of her cheeks and the parting of her lips. She's trying so hard to hide it, but her body betrays her, a series of subtle cues that tell me everything she won't say.

"How did you get in?"

Her voice quivers, and the sound shoots straight through me. Part of me wants to comfort her terror. Another part feeds on it.

"The alarm—"

"Was child's play. As advanced as Damien Wolfe's systems are, they're no match for me, Luna."

She squares her shoulders, but she can't hide the tremor that runs through her body. Her breath comes in short, shallow gasps. She's afraid, yes, but there's more. So much more.

"You need to stop breaking into my house. This twisted game is over, and I want you to leave."

I admire her courage as I lean forward, savoring the way her wide eyes track my movement.

"Breaking in implies I had to work for it." Annoyance sparks in her eyes. "And that's not going to happen, Luna. You let me taste you last night. Really taste you. There's no going back from that."

"I said get out." Her voice is firmer now, but her hands tremble as she raises the bat higher.

She has good form. I try to remember if Cade's background check mentioned her playing softball as a child, but I'm distracted. The sight of her t-shirt inching up, exposing her smooth, creamy thighs, fills my mind with images of them wrapped around me.

"I'll call the sheriff this time."

"With what?" I hold up her phone before placing it on the side table, never taking my eyes off the thighs I intend to be buried between in minutes.

"Stop looking at me like that."

I reluctantly drag my gaze up and meet her eyes through my mask.

"Like what?"

"Like... a wolf eyeing its dinner."

I lick my lips. "Oh, I am."

She tightens her grip on the bat.

"I'll scream. If I scream, Shadow won't defer to you. He'll attack."

It's an empty threat. I heard her close her bedroom door before she came downstairs.

"I don't think so." My voice is steady despite the fire growing in my veins. "We both know you don't want me to leave."

"You don't know what I want."

I stand, setting the shotgun aside. I've never needed weapons to feel powerful, but she doesn't know that. She takes an instinctive step back as I approach.

"I know exactly what you want, little doe." My voice turns rough. "I know because you showed me when you so beautifully came apart on my tongue."

"That was... That was a mistake."

"You said that about the night you shattered on my fingers too." Another step brings me closer. Her lips part, chest rising and falling in quick bursts as she presses against the wall. "If you really don't want this, why haven't you run or swung that bat?"

Her knuckles whiten as I reach for it. Our fingers brush, hers ice-cold and trembling. The bat slides from her grip. I drop it with a hollow thud on the hardwood and kick it aside. Her pupils dilate, dark pools expanding to swallow the hazel irises.

"It's time, Luna."

"Time for what?" A soft exhale escapes her lips.

"You know." I lean in until I can feel the heat radiating from her skin. Her eyelids flutter closed, then open. Her throat ripples as she swallows. "You know exactly what happens next."

She shakes her head, sending waves of hair cascading over her shoulders. My fingers trace the delicate line of her jaw. Her skin is soft and warm beneath my fingertips.

"Denying it won't stop me."

I trail my fingers down the column of her neck, feeling the rapid flutter of her pulse beneath her skin. It beats against my touch like it's trying to escape her body. My hand closes around her throat, a firm grip that sends a clear message.

Her eyes widen, fear flickering in their depths. Her breath hitches. Beneath my thumb, her heartbeat thrums, pounding with a genuine fear of me.

She reaches up, her fingers wrapping around my hand, trying to pry it away, but my grip is unyielding. Her nails dig into my skin in a futile attempt to break free.

"What are you—"

"I'm claiming what's mine."

I wrench her away from the wall. She stumbles as I spin her, her back colliding with my chest. I drag her against me until no space remains between us—her body pressed to mine, her warmth bleeding through my clothes. She arches away, her spine curving as she tries to create distance that doesn't exist. My arm locks around her waist, crushing her against me.

She's so small compared to me, so delicate, yet I sense the steel beneath her softness.

"Please don't kill me." Her pulse batters against my palm, frantic and uneven.

"I'm not going to kill you, Luna." My lips brush the shell of her ear. "I'm going to ruin you."

She claws at my hand, her nails scraping against my skin, her body thrashing in my grip. She tries to speak, but no words come out, only desperate gasps.

"Tell me you want this, Luna. Give me your consent."

I loosen my fingers but don't release her. She sucks in a deep breath as her lungs expand, a harsh, rasping sound that fills the silence.

"And if I don't, you'll just take it. Like you did last night."

"Yes."

She drops her hands. "Then why does it matter if I give you consent?"

"Because I know you want it. You want me to take you, Luna. Claim you. You want it as much as I do."

"I don't."

Liar.

I'll indulge her denial for now. She needs time to wrap her mind around it, to accept the truth of her desires.

"I'm not going to give you permission to rape me."

"It's not rape when you surrender willingly." I tighten my fingers again but don't cut off her air. "And you will surrender, Luna."

"Who are you?"

I hesitate. Names have power. The moment I speak it, I hand her a weapon, so my real identity must remain hidden. For now. Possibly forever.

"You don't need my name to come on my cock." My lips brush the curve where her neck meets her shoulder. "And you will come on me tonight, Luna. More times than you think possible. Your cunt's going to milk me dry. Then, when you're sure I'm done, when you think your body can't take anymore, I'll rut you so fucking deep you'll squirt all over me while you beg me never to stop."

"Jesus. Do you kiss your mother with that mouth?"

I chuckle at her feeble attempt at bravery. "My mother's dead. So, no. But the things my mouth is going to do to you would make even a dead woman blush."

"I'm sorry about your mother." She softens, her voice filled with sincerity. I pause, her words stopping me short. I know she lost hers at ten, but she can't fathom the cruel, neglectful, vindictive woman my mother was.

"Don't be. She got exactly what she deserved. Now it's time to stop stalling, Luna."

I release her throat, and she inhales a relieved breath, sagging against me. Her body trembles, a violent tremor that makes my dick throb against her spine.

I slide my fingers over her collarbone, then down between her breasts. Her heart pounds against my palm as I march her forward, toward the kitchen. Since walking through it the other night, all I can think about is bending her over the large oak table and fucking her raw.

"What are you doing?" She struggles. "Where are we going?"

"Somewhere I can spread you out."

Moonlight coming through the window over the sink bathes the kitchen in a soft glow. It makes her skin shimmer like a pearl as I walk her across the room. I spin her to face me before lifting her onto the table.

"Please don't do this." She tries to wriggle off, but I press my hands against the tops of her thighs, holding her in place.

"Stop fighting this." I pull her legs apart and step between them. "Lift your arms."

She glares at me, defiance more than fear flashing in her eyes now. They flit to the back door.

"Don't even think about it because you won't get far. Whether it's here on this table or on the grass in your backyard, you're taking my cock tonight, Luna. You're going to come all over me. Over. And over. And over."

She goes still. Her lips part enough for a quick intake of breath as she tries to disguise how my words affect her. But her body can't lie.

"Now lift your arms."

Her eyes trace the mask covering my face, almost as if she's trying to figure out who I am. I pinch the soft flesh of her inner thighs, and she jolts.

"Ow."

"Do it."

She raises her arms. I grip the cotton hem and pull the fabric up and over her head. The t-shirt lands somewhere behind me. She sits before me in nothing but pale lace panties, her skin flushed in the dim light.

My mouth finds her breast, lips closing around the tight peak of her nipple. My teeth graze the sensitive tip while my tongue traces patterns that make her breath catch. I cup the weight of her other breast in my palm, my thumb tracing lazy loops until her skin pebbles and tightens. Her head tips back, and a sound escapes—half sigh, half surrender—as her body yields to me, pliant and willing.

Her hands rise toward my face. I catch her wrists before she can reach me, my grip punishing as I pin her arms behind her back.

"No. My mask stays on!"

With a gasp, her spine curves, and her breasts push forward.

"I just wanted to touch you."

The words hang between us, raw with need.

"You don't fucking touch me unless I tell you to."

Those beautiful hazel eyes search my face, swirling with a mixture of confusion and want. Her brows draw together, lips parting as if to speak, then closing again.

"But how's this going to work?"

"Very simply. You're going to take my cock exactly as I give it to you." My thumb presses against the pulse in her wrist. "I touch you, little doe, not the other way around."

Fire flashes across her features. Her jaw sets, muscles tensing as she pulls against my grip.

"I'm not looking to be raped. If that's what this is going to be, you can leave."

Her defiance is so fucking beautiful, a challenge that I can't resist. I lean forward, tracing my lips along her neck with enough contact to make her shiver. Her pulse races beneath my touch. I bite down, and she gasps, back arching as I leave my mark. Her skin tastes of salt and a sweetness that makes me want to devour her whole.

My tongue traces the spot I've reclaimed. She turns her face to the side, exposing more of her throat, and her warm breath ghosts across the exposed skin below my mask. The warmth is unsettling, more intimate than I expect.

"Kiss me." The words tumble from her lips, her voice breaking on the plea.

I lift my head and look down into her face. "No. No kissing."

Her face crumples and then hardens again. "Why not?"

Silence stretches between us. I release her wrists and pull her from the table in one fluid motion. Her legs shake as she stands, surprised by the sudden movement.

Kissing her is not an option. It'll make it too personal, and I need to keep this—*her*—separate. She knows I'm a killer, and despite having opportunities to tell the police, she's kept my secret. But I can't be sure she won't change her mind if she knows my real identity.

My gut tells me I can trust her, but my mind, the part of me that has spent twenty-five years alone in the shadows, remains hesitant and unconvinced.

It's time she learns who's in control here.

Chapter Twenty-Seven

Luna

"Turn around."

His voice plummets to that low, authoritative register that makes my knees weak. It's obvious he's disguising it, but why?

I study his face, trying to see past that mask, desperate to glimpse the man beneath it, but all I see are eyes so dark they're almost black.

My fingers curl at my sides. Every instinct screams run. My muscles tense, ready to bolt or strike. Instead, I stand frozen.

Goosebumps race across my skin, each hair standing on end. Fear slithers up my spine, coiling in my chest like a living thing. But underneath it, something else unfurls, and a deep-rooted carnal desire awakens.

"Don't make me tell you again, Luna."

My name on his lips sounds like ownership, like he's claimed it as something that exists only in his mouth. My body responds with a rush of arousal that makes me dizzy.

Beneath that mask, his lips part, the bottom one fuller than seems fair. My muscles clench, and heat blooms between my thighs as I try to ignore how the mask makes his mouth look obscenely tempting.

He spins me. The world tilts, blurs, and when it stops, the kitchen table looms before me, its solid oak surface becoming the center of my world.

His palm spreads across my back, pressure building until I lean forward over the table. The wood is cool and smooth against my palms as I brace myself. My pulse thunders in my ears, each beat echoing through the silence.

He pushes me forward until my breasts meet the table. I gasp as my nipples press against the cold surface.

"Oh—"

His body cages me from behind, heat radiating through his clothes. His breath ghosts across my neck, then the silver mask touches my shoulder—ice against fire.

"Hands behind your back."

"Why?"

"Because you've shown you can't be trusted."

"I wasn't going to pull your mask off. I just wanted to slide my fingers into your hair."

"Well, you'll have to earn the privilege of freedom. Let's find out if your pussy can do that. Now, don't make me tell you again."

The rebelliousness I've worn like armor all night should rise to the surface. I should fight, argue, and push back. Instead, his voice dissolves my resistance. My wrists cross at the small of my back without conscious thought. The position sends a thrill through me that I try to ignore but can't. I jump at the bite of cool plastic against my skin.

"What the—"

I twist against the table, my muscles straining. He pulls, one swift motion, and a zip tie sinks into my wrists. Not enough to cut, just enough to mark. My pulse pounds against the plastic restraint.

I test the bonds, but my hands won't budge.

My eyes widen. This isn't his warm hands holding mine in place, pinning me down like I'd imagined. This is different. My throat closes. Air comes in short bursts, and a shiver of dread cascades over me. He could do anything. Anything at all. And I'm now completely at his mercy.

"Perfect." He sweeps my long hair to the side, and his hand traces the length of my spine, possessive and reverent. "You're so fucking perfect like this."

Despite how my body is screaming to let him do whatever he wants to me, my brain catches up with the reality of my situation. I'm bent over my kitchen table, almost naked, about to get fucked by my masked watcher, and I have no idea if he's going to kill me afterward.

"You know what? I've changed my mind. I'm not okay with this. Let me up. Untie me and get the hell out of my house."

His chuckle is low and dangerous.

"It's too late for that."

Warm fingers grip the lace waistband of my panties, a flush of embarrassment replacing my panic as he pulls them down my legs. His knee presses against my inner thighs a second later, a firm pressure pushing them apart. I'm bound and vulnerable, unable or unwilling to resist whatever he has in mind, and my heart skitters, torn between dread and an undeniable ache of want.

His hot breath floats over me, tickling my sex, and memories of his skilled mouth slam into me. I want nothing more than for him to move closer. He pushes my thighs wider, spreading me open. I pull air into my lungs and hold it there, muscles tense, waiting for the first touch of his tongue.

But he just breathes. In and out. The exhale warms my slick flesh. I squirm, trying to shift away, but his hands lock my thighs in place. His gaze burns into me, focused and intense, studying every part of me I can't cover. He's already spent hours with his face buried between my thighs, but this is different. My heart pounds against my ribs, and my face heats. Being open like this while he just looks—it strips something away that his mouth never touched. The vulnerability scrapes me raw even as my body pulses with need.

I try to push myself up from the table, but it's impossible with my hands bound behind my back.

"I'm serious. Let me up and get the fuck out of my house."

The heat of his mouth vanishes, and he stands, gripping the zip tie with one hand and pushing down on my back with the other, keeping me still.

"Relax, Luna. As long as you don't fight me, I won't hurt you."

"Please let me go."

"No. *You* need to let go. Let me show you what your body is capable of."

He gathers my arousal on his agile fingers, torturing me with slow, flicking strokes, and a moan tears out of me I can't suppress.

"Stop thinking." There's something almost tender beneath the command. "Stop fighting. Just feel."

My forehead drops to the table. I gasp for air but can't seem to pull enough into my lungs, and my legs tremble, threatening to give out.

"Oh, God."

My hips push back against his hand, chasing more contact, more friction. I bite my lip hard enough to taste copper. I should hate this. Hate him and myself for responding. But my body arches into every stroke of his fingers, greedy and desperate.

The sound of his zipper fills the room, and I turn my head to see. His cock springs free, standing thick and heavy, his skin stretched tight and flushed almost purple. My core clenches, empty and aching, and fresh arousal trickles down my thighs as my body readies itself to take him.

"I can't wait any longer, Luna."

A raw edge of desire roughens his voice as he lines up at my entrance, his head teasing through my slick heat. I gasp, every nerve inside me coming alive.

Pain and pleasure collide, and a cry explodes from my chest. Everything else falls away. There's only this. The shock of fullness and the burning stretch as he drives into me with one deep, possessive stroke.

Chapter Twenty-Eight

Luna

The initial invasion is a brutal, tearing thrust that splits me apart as he forces his way into me, every inch of him, hot and hard. Tears sting, and a ragged scream claws its way out of my throat, more pain than pleasure as he buries himself to the hilt.

"Fuck, Luna." The words rip from somewhere deep in his chest, as if torn from his soul.

He withdraws, only to slam back in, a white-hot burn searing my insides as he stretches me. Tears pour down my cheeks, my body struggling to accommodate his brutal intrusion.

His thighs press against mine, the denim of his jeans rubbing against my bare skin. Every ridge, every vein of his cock drags along my inner walls as he moves within me, stoking a fire that grows with each slow plunge, a desperate, fleeting moment of reprieve before the next inevitable thrust. My body responds, slickening, easing his path as he drives into me, and soon the pain dissolves into something more—a deep, pulsing ache inside my core that radiates outward.

Lightning races from my scalp to my toes as he fills me. My body stretches and reshapes itself around him. Thought fragments and scatters, the world narrowing to this—his weight, his heat, the way I come apart and rebuild in the space of a heartbeat. This moment of absolute surrender.

My head falls to the table, the cool wood meeting burning skin, a stark contrast to the fire raging within. Every thrust is a brand, a claim, and, God help me, I don't want him to stop.

His hands roam my body, rough and possessive, leaving trails of goosebumps in their wake.

"You feel so fucking good, Luna. I knew you'd feel like this."

His words are not for me but a confession wrung from deep inside him. Heat floods through me at the knowledge that I unravel him just as he destroys me.

His breath is hot on my back, his heart pounding against my spine. The storm of sensation pulls me under and drowns me. His thrusts are brutal and punishing, stealing my breath and my sanity with each drive of his hips. I watch our reflection in the window, his masked figure looming behind me, my body jerking with each movement. I want to see his face beneath that mask, see the expression that matches the raw, primal rhythm of his body, because we look feral and wild, and it takes my breath away.

My nipples drag against the wood, friction that shoots straight to my core. His hand slides around, fingers finding my clit, teasing the sensitive bundle of nerves until my breath catches in small, broken sounds that echo around us.

"I'm never going to stop fucking you, Luna." His lips are hot on my neck, his words a dark, erotic litany. "You feel like heaven on earth."

He picks up the pace, pounding into me harder, each thrust stealing my breath, stealing my soul, and it's frightening and exhilarating all at once.

My body trembles, the pleasure building, cresting, and threatening to consume me. His hand tangles in my hair, pulling my head back, exposing my neck. His other hand snakes around, finding my throat, and squeezing. Panic surges through me, my heart pounding, my lungs burning, and I thrash beneath him, tears again stinging my eyes. His fingers return to my clit, relentless, driving me higher, even as his other hand tightens around my windpipe.

Shit! He's going to kill me.

The silver mask hovers at the edge of my vision, a constant reminder of the enigma that is this man who is commanding my body so completely.

"Look at me." The words sound shredded, like they clawed their way out of his throat.

I turn my face, meet his gaze through the mask, and what I see there—possession, desire, something darker, and more dangerous—rips the last thread of my control and sends me spiraling over the edge.

My vision fractures, and my orgasm slams into me, a brutal, electrifying force, as his fingers release me. Air rushes into my lungs, and I'm coming again, right on top of the first one.

"That's it, baby, breathe." Convulsions wrack my body, and my climax goes on and on as he drives deeper, his rhythm faltering. "Oh, fuck, yes, you fucking squeeze me so good, Luna."

With a final, brutal thrust, he goes rigid above me, every muscle in his body drawn taut as he pulses inside me. I burst into tears, sobs wracking my body as he hovers over me. His lips find the curve of my neck, hands stroking, caressing, and soothing, while dark praise flows from his mouth.

"My perfect girl. So beautiful when you fall apart for me."

The tenderness in his voice splits my chest open. More sobs pour out, one after another, filling the kitchen's silence with wet, gasping sounds.

His weight pins me to the table, his cock still buried inside while my breath comes in ragged gasps that take forever to even out. When he finally pulls out, the drag of it makes me bite down on my lip. My inner walls clench, grasping at what's no longer there, and the hollow ache left behind makes me flinch.

Fabric rustles and a zipper rasps behind me, and then his fingers are tracing down my spine again, stopping at the small of my back.

"Don't move."

A laugh wants to bubble up but dies in my throat. Moving requires muscles I no longer have control over. My legs won't hold me, and my arms shake where they're still bound behind my back. I turn my face, resting my cheek on the table, watching as he walks across the kitchen to the sink. He grabs a dishtowel from the counter and runs it under the water.

He returns. The zip tie cuts into my wrists as he pulls me upright, lifting me to sit on the table again. The damp cloth passes over my face, cool against hot skin, as he washes away the evidence of my tears, my pleasure, and his claim, wiping salt tracks from my cheeks. I must look destroyed—eyes puffy, cheeks blotched, nose running. Yet his touch is gentle, tender, almost reverent, though something pulses beneath, an undercurrent of darkness, a promise of more to come.

He lowers the towel between my thighs. "I knew fucking you bare would be perfection."

Those words slice through the haze of aftershocks simmering inside me. "You didn't wear a condom."

He arches a brow, lips curling at one corner. "You're a bit late to the party on that one, beautiful. But no matter. I'll never wear a condom with you, Luna."

I shift toward the table's edge. His palms slam down on my thighs, fingers digging in to anchor me.

"Let me go. This was completely irresponsible. I can't believe we didn't use protection."

"I will only ever fuck you bare, Luna."

"I'm not having unprotected sex with someone who won't tell me who he is or show me his face."

His fist wraps around my hair, wrenching my head back, his mouth hot against my ear. "Are you on birth control?"

I hiss. Pain shoots through my scalp as I fight his grip. "Birth control doesn't protect against STDs."

"Do you have any STDs?" His tongue traces the length of my neck while his palm glides over my skin, fingers slipping between my thighs to stroke where I'm still raw. A spark jolts through me, and I suck in a breath.

"Maybe. You should have thought of that before you fucked me without a condom."

He chuckles again, a dark, sinful sound that makes my pussy clench. He groans as my body responds, coating his fingers with fresh arousal.

How can I be aroused again already?

"I've seen your medical records, love, and you're squeaky clean."

I pull against the zip-tie, trying to twist my hips away. His fist tightens in my hair, and pain flares at my scalp.

"How do I know you didn't give me anything? Please stop, that hurts."

His grip releases. My hair tumbles free, waves spilling over my shoulders. A shiver flickers up my spine as his fingertips trail a hot, feather-light path from my jaw to my ribs, tracing the hollow there before settling at my hip. "I'd never risk you like that, little doe."

"That's such a demeaning name."

"No, it isn't. It's full of adoration for the beautiful, gentle creature you are."

His words sink into me like honey through cracks, warming places I didn't know were cold. Then one finger parts my slick folds. The tip slides inside, pulling a gasp from my throat. My muscles grip him as his thumb finds my swollen clit, circling, each press setting off a tremor that surges down to my toes. I brace against the sensation, but my nipples tighten into hard points, craving the warmth of his mouth.

"Stop." Panic and heat mingle in my chest. "We can't do this again without a condom. If you don't have one, I have some upstairs."

What the hell? Did I just offer him condoms?

They're old, from the early days of Caleb's and my relationship. We used them for a few months at the beginning, then stopped once we decided to be exclusive. Shit, they're probably expired by now. But something is better than nothing.

"Well, we'll have to get rid of those, won't we?" His teeth graze the shell of my ear. His finger probes deeper, and my thighs tremble as a white-hot sting blossoms into pleasure. "I'll never wear a condom with you, Luna. I'll always come inside you, deep and thick, until it drips down your thighs."

Jesus Fucking Christ!

Need coils inside me, tighter than the restraint around my wrists. My body clenches, clinging to his teasing touch.

My heart lurches. Am I going to let him do this? Let him take me without a condom again?

"If your birth control isn't up to date, you'd better get that taken care of tomorrow." His breath is ragged against my neck. "But that won't stop me from coming in you tonight. Or tomorrow night. Or the next night."

He groans as he lowers his head and sinks his teeth into my nipple. A low moan rattles out from my throat before my mind can protest.

He slides a second finger inside, curling it. Heat roars through my veins. My bound hands clench behind my back. My head tips back, another moan tearing from my lips against my will, my body arching toward him.

Shit! Why is my reaction to his words, to the idea of having sex with him without a condom, so visceral?

"Why do you want to come inside me? Is this some twisted breeding kink?"

His lips curve, and he lifts his head. "No. I'm not interested in being anyone's father. But there will never be anything between us. Now, zip it, beautiful, or I'll gag you with your underwear, and believe me, you'll love how you taste when you're screaming for me."

He pulls his fingers free, and I whimper at the sudden void. I press my hands against the table behind me, wanting—needing—to somehow push back against the raw desire coursing through me.

I wrench my head up, searching the shadows behind his mask, aching to see the man underneath it. Wishing I knew his name. Wishing I knew why he burns all rational thought out of me.

"Lay back, little doe."

He guides my shoulders until I'm flat against the table, my hips tilting just enough to spare my wrists. He spreads my thighs wide, his shadow falling over me like a promise.

"What... what are you going to do to me?" My voice trembles between fear and desire.

His fingertips drift along my inner thighs, each caress igniting fireworks of sensation. He drops to his knees, breath hot, and his tongue finds my tender, battered flesh.

I arch into him, surrendering to the delicious destruction he vowed.

He promised to break me, ruin me, and with every trembling breath, I fear he just might have.

Chapter Twenty-Nine

Luna

The first rays of morning sunlight filter through my open curtains, pulling me from sleep. My muscles protest with a delicious soreness that brings back memories of last night.

Of him.

I sit up, wincing from the dull throb both between my thighs and deep in my abdomen. The man wasn't lying. He ravaged my body, leaving it bruised and aching.

After that first orgasm, when he choked me, the relief that I wasn't dead was so overwhelming that I barely registered him telling me how perfect I was. I know about erotic asphyxiation, but I've never experienced it before. It's frightening, not to mention dangerous. But it's heart-stopping too. The orgasm I had was so powerful, it felt like my soul left my body, and all I could do in response was sob.

After he laid me back on the table, he brought me to orgasm again with his mouth, then once more with his cock, before carrying me upstairs to my bedroom. He kicked out the babies, Shadow trotting away with a half-hearted growl, before he went down on me again while his body recovered.

What he did to me should be illegal. As I shift and a deeper ache in my ass makes itself known, I think it might be.

Anal sex is not my preference, though I tried it in college a handful of times when I drank too much at frat parties. But I don't remember my ass hurting this much the next day. Then again, "well-endowed" does not adequately describe my watcher.

The sheet falls away, revealing bruises all over my body, from both his hands and mouth. Hickeys cover my breasts, and a ghostly echo of his touch lingers where his strong fingers left their perfect imprints on my hips. I trace them with my fingertips, a shiver running through me.

Red welts wrap around my wrists, raw and tender to the touch. But there's something liberating, almost freeing, about being tied up. Strange as that sounds. I don't have to think. Just feel. And the feeling of him inside me, stretching me, claiming me, was like losing and finding myself all at once.

Shadow lifts his head from his bed in the corner, his amber eyes watching me. He knows what I did. What I let my watcher do to me.

The betrayal I felt at his calm acceptance of my masked watcher resurfaces, but I can't be mad at him. My watcher didn't hurt me. Not really. He could have killed me, but all he did was fulfill his promise to make me come harder and more times than I thought possible. I didn't know my body was capable of that kind of pleasure. Or pain. I shift again, an ache rippling through me.

"You knew he wasn't a threat, didn't you?"

Shadow yawns, stretching his massive body before padding over to rest his head on my lap, as if offering comfort or perhaps forgiveness for doubting his judgment.

"Is that why you didn't wake me? Because you knew I'd want what he did to me?" He only blinks at me. "If he murders me one day, I'm blaming you."

But I temper my words by hugging him around the neck. I trust my wolf as much as I trust Maren. If he thinks I'm safe, I must be, right?

"But he's a killer, Shadow."

I rest my forehead on the top of his, and he nudges my shoulder with his nose, his way of expressing affection.

My thoughts drift back to the wolf mask hiding my watcher's features. To his mouth, the only part of his face I could see, curving into that dangerous smile. And his voice—*God, that voice*—scraping against my ears. Nobody's voice dips that low and rough without effort.

I didn't ask him again who he was or if he'd take his mask off. I want to know, but I guess we exist in this strange space where intimacy doesn't require introduction. But what stings more than I care to admit was his refusal to kiss me.

I've never had sex without kissing, even with strangers, which I suppose he is. His denial of that intimacy sits wrong in my chest. As wrong as his refusal to get naked. He kept all his clothes on, even after we came upstairs to my bedroom. He just shoved his pants down far enough to free his cock and left everything else buttoned and zipped.

It felt humiliating at first, insulting, like I wasn't even worth the effort of removing his clothes. Then I remembered the hint of black ink that had peeked above his collar that night on my porch. I bet he's covered in tattoos, marks he can't let me see, so I can't identify him.

It still leaves me hollow inside, an ache that echoes in my chest when I think about it. I love kissing. I love the feel of another person's mouth on mine, the way breath mingles and becomes something shared.

I release Shadow, and my fingers drift to my hips again, tracing the tender spots where his grip branded me. I should be terrified right now, calling Karen and reinforcing my security system, not sitting here caressing the marks he left on my body like they're precious gifts.

My hand freezes against my skin. The security system. How did he bypass it?

I reach for my phone on the nightstand. It rings only once.

"Luna." His voice is smooth and cultured. "To what do I owe the pleasure of an early morning call?"

"Damien, hi." The words catch in my throat. "I'm sorry to bother you so early, but I'm a little worried about the security system. I'm not sure I armed it correctly last night. Can one of your guys check it when they come back today?"

There's a brief pause. "Is everything okay? Did something happen?"

"No, no." My gaze drifts to the marks on my body. "Everything's fine. I... I don't know if I paid close enough attention when you showed me how to arm it."

"I'll come by and check it for you."

His immediate willingness to help stirs a warmth that curls beneath my ribs. My fingers tighten around the phone. "I probably should have asked one of the techs when he got here, but—"

"No, that's okay. I told you to call me anytime." His tone remains even, like I haven't dragged him from sleep at the crack of dawn. "I'm in Denver getting ready for a meeting at nine, but I can stop by around noon. Would that work?"

"That would be perfect. Thank you."

"Anything for you, Luna. See you soon."

After we hang up, I slide to the edge of the mattress. My legs tremble when I try to stand, and I have to brace myself on the nightstand. When I'm steady, I grab my robe and wrap it around myself before heading to the bathroom. I look in the mirror, and I'm shocked at the purple fingerprints circling my throat like a twisted necklace.

Shit! That's going to be a bitch to cover.

My breath catches as memories of him choking me come rushing back. A ripple of desire runs through my body, settling like molten lava between my thighs.

I guess I'm into breath play. Who knew?

No one has ever touched me the way he did, like he was worshiping at an altar. Like my body held secrets he'd waited lifetimes to discover. As if he'd been starving for years, and I was the first real meal he'd tasted.

I step into the shower, letting hot water wash away his scent from my skin. When I'm done, I wipe condensation from the mirror and look closer at myself. My reflection stops me cold. The woman staring back at me looks different. Bruised, branded, exactly like what he promised he'd do to me.

I've never been the type of woman who wants to be "claimed" by a man. I've built my life around independence and self-reliance. My work at the sanctuary defines me, healing creatures who can't help themselves and advocating for those who have no voice.

Yet here I am, reveling in the marks left by a man who breaks into houses, leaves dead bodies as "gifts," and makes me feel more alive than I ever thought possible.

I dress in jeans and another turtleneck that covers the evidence of last night. I have work to do today. Animals to care for and a sanctuary to run. I can't spend the day lost in these dark, sensual memories.

My phone vibrates with an incoming text as I reach the bottom of the stairs.

Maren

Deer just dropped off. Hit on Rte 16. Stable but needs assessment. When are you coming over?

Me

Be there in 10

Work. Reality. Just what I need.

I feed Shadow and the girls while avoiding the large table that dominates the other side of the kitchen. My gaze keeps sliding toward it anyway. Less than six hours ago, I was spread across its surface. I'll never be able to eat at it again without thinking of him.

I head out the front door with Shadow at my heels, my eyes drifting toward the treeline. Is he out there now? The thought sends a thrill through me that's equal parts excitement and apprehension.

I should resist this, whatever this is between us. I should fight against this pull toward a man who represents everything I should fear.

But my body hums with want, despite how wrong I know it is.

For the first time in my carefully controlled life, I want to surrender to this wild, unexplainable connection. I want to fall deeper into this rabbit hole and discover where it leads. I want him, not despite the danger he represents, but perhaps because of it.

Is this what it feels like to be truly awake? To be shaken out of the comfortable numbness I've been living in?

As I reach the front door of the sanctuary building, I turn to face the woods. The breeze rustles the leaves overhead, and a hawk squawks somewhere in the distance. The air is growing heavy, thick with the scent of impending rain.

"I know you're there," I call out, surprising myself with my boldness.

Silence answers me, but I don't need confirmation. I know he's watching. My racing heart confirms it, drowning out everything except the weight of unseen eyes.

⸺◆⸺

"There you are!" Maren says as I push through the double doors to the main treatment area. "I was starting to worry."

"Sorry. I had a late night." The words scrape against my throat, my voice still hoarse from last night's... activities.

She gives me that look, the one where her eyes narrow and she's cataloging every detail. The way I'm holding my shoulders, the turtleneck in seventy-degree weather, and the rasp in my voice.

"You okay?"

I turn toward the sink, desperate to avoid her scrutiny. My hands shake as I reach for the soap dispenser. "Just tired. What's the deal with our new patient? Is it a buck or a doe?"

"Buck. And I don't think anything's broken, but there might be something with the right rear hoof. Deborah tranq'd him with xylazine, so he's out. I was about to clean his cuts."

I step into the exam room, and the young buck is lying quiet and still under sedation. Dark patches of dried blood mat his golden-brown coat, and road debris clings to his flank.

With him unconscious, I can see the full extent of his injuries.

"Poor guy. What did Deborah say happened?"

"Hit by an SUV. Driver called it in immediately. Said he rolled right off his hood and ran into the woods. Took Deborah and Roger an hour to track him down and dart him."

I pull on latex gloves and fall into the familiar rhythm of my work as I begin my exam.

Working on a conscious deer would be nearly impossible. They're flight animals, and even injured, they can seriously hurt themselves and us trying to escape.

I begin cleaning the worst of the scrapes, my mind drifting against my will. The way my watcher called me "little doe" with such tender possessiveness, watching me with those intense eyes behind his wolf mask.

Like we were predator and prey, hunter and hunted.

"Luna?" Maren's voice cuts through my thoughts. "I asked if you wanted me to start him on antibiotics."

Heat floods my cheeks. "Yes. Some fluids, too. And let's plan on some pain meds once the Xylazine wears off."

Maren nods, but she's studying me. "Are you sure you're alright? You seem distracted. You didn't find another dead body, did you? 'Cause I swear to God, if you did..."

"You'd know if I did."

"Then what's got you off your game today?"

I hesitate, my hands stilling on the buck's fur. Should I tell her? She's Maren. I've always been able to tell her anything. We don't keep secrets; at least, we never have before. But how can I tell her I spent half the night bent over my kitchen table, surrendering to a masked stranger? That every muscle in my body aches from positions I didn't know I could twist into with my wrists bound behind my back?

I know how she'll react. She'll love it. She'll eat up every dirty detail, eyes sparkling with delight. Until she finds out he's the man who's been stalking me and leaving corpses on my doorstep. Then she'll drag me to the nearest psych ward. After she schedules me an emergency appointment with my OBGYN.

Oh, shit! I forgot about that. My birth control won't protect me from STDs. I need to start a course of antibiotics as a precaution.

"I didn't sleep well. I'm fine." I focus on inserting the IV catheter, knowing that telling her would be like setting myself on fire.

I can't tell anyone.

She doesn't look convinced, but she drops it, busying herself with preparing the medications. Until she can't.

"Are you sure? Because you look like you got ridden hard and put away wet. And that can't be true. Otherwise, you'd be sharing those details with your bestie."

Her eyes rake over me like I'm a specimen under a microscope. She's always been way too observant for her own good. I need to throw her off the scent.

"Maren, I haven't even left the sanctuary in five days."

"So? That doesn't mean you're not partaking of the escort service in Estes Park."

"There's an escort service in Estes Park? Since when? Do I want to know how you know that?"

She gives me an innocent smile that's anything but. "A girl never tells her secrets. And nice attempted diversion technique, by the way."

Shit!

"There's also your hot new billionaire neighbor. He was still here when I left yesterday." Her eyes widen. "Did you and he..."

"I didn't have sex with Damien Wolfe." The words snap out quick and defensive. *But I am getting railed by a different wolf.* "He's coming by today."

"Why? I thought he was letting his team finish up."

"I don't think I armed the system right last night."

"Didn't he teach you how to do it yesterday?"

"Yeah, what's your point?"

Maren raises an eyebrow, handing me the antibiotic syringe. "That maybe the good doctor wants to see the hottie neighbor again."

I inject the antibiotic into the buck's IV line, watching the clear fluid disappear into his bloodstream.

"You have too active an imagination."

"Methinks she doth protest too much."

"That's not the right quote. Why do you always butcher quotes? Why not use the real ones? I know you know them."

"Stop trying to deflect." Maren snorts. "Seriously, though, you have that exhausted-sex glow all over you. I don't care what you say."

"I just need some uninterrupted sleep."

"I can start staying up here more often if you need me to. JT's only home for five days, then he's back on the road for two weeks. Give me a couple more days to get my fill of his magnificent cock, and then I'll come stay once he's gone."

My stomach clenches like a fist. As much as I love Maren and her company, that's not what I want. My watcher can't come to me if she's here.

Shit! Do I want him to come back?

"You don't need to, Mar. I'm fine."

"No, seriously. I don't mind. You didn't make the spare bedroom mine for nothing."

"Let's see how it goes." I adjust the IV drip, then smile at her. "You focus on JT while he's here, and we'll circle back to this when he leaves."

She shrugs, but concern still flickers behind her eyes.

"Okay. Let me get the portable X-ray in here."

⸻ ◈ ⸻

We finish up with the buck and get him settled in the recovery den. He'll need to be here for only one night. He's very lucky.

The door chime Damien installed yesterday echoes through the building.

"Showtime." Maren's lips curve into a knowing smirk. "Try not to jump his bones in the lobby."

I flip her off as I head toward the front, finding him standing there, tall and commanding in another impeccably tailored suit. His dark hair is perfectly styled, and his blue-gray eyes find mine the moment I appear. Something flickers in his gaze. Relief? Hunger? The intensity steals the air from my lungs.

"I'm sorry I'm late. My meeting ran long." His voice is smooth, sending a shiver through me.

I remember Maren's comment about my disheveled appearance, and I smooth out my shirt.

"That's okay. I was finishing up with a new patient. Thanks for coming by." I lead him toward the house. "I hope it wasn't too much trouble."

"Not at all. I was planning to head back up after my meeting." His gaze travels over my face like he's memorizing every detail. My pulse hammers against my throat. "You said you were concerned about the system?"

"Not concerned, but I wanted to make sure I set it correctly last night."

He goes straight to the security panel, his fingers dancing over the touchscreen. I watch him work, struck by how at ease he seems in my space. His movements, the way he carries himself, tug at the edge of my mind.

"Everything looks fine with how you armed it," he says after a moment, still studying the screen. "But it was disarmed at 1:07 AM and then rearmed at 1:08 AM. Then disarmed again at 4:16 AM and rearmed at 4:17 AM."

My heart races. Those must have been the times my masked watcher came and left. Three hours. He was inside me for three hours.

Jesus. No wonder my thighs shake when I walk today.

"Oh." I clear my throat. "I couldn't sleep, so Shadow and I went out to the porch for some fresh air. We were both a little restless last night."

The lie slides out with disturbing ease.

Damien's eyes find mine, and I feel exposed under his stare. "Was there anyone outside? The system didn't register any perimeter breaches."

"No, just Shadow and me." My cheeks warm under his scrutiny, and I resist the urge to touch my face. "Did the cameras catch anything?"

"Nothing unusual." He turns back to the panel, but I catch his reflection in the screen—still watching me. "But only the perimeter cameras were operational last night. It was more important to get the inside spaces wired yesterday. My team will be here shortly to finish installing the rest of the exterior cameras."

I nod, my thoughts spinning like leaves in a storm. How did my masked watcher get past the perimeter cameras? He always comes through the woods beside the driveway. The pieces don't fit, but Damien's presence scrambles my ability to think straight.

"Thank you again for donating all of this." I gesture to the security panel. "It's incredibly generous."

He turns to face me, and the space between us feels charged. "I have a vested interest in keeping you safe, Luna."

The possessive, almost hungry way he says my name sends a shiver down my spine.

He's standing so close that his cologne wraps around me, and my body wants to sway toward it, toward him. His gaze drops to my mouth, and for a heart-stopping moment, I think he might kiss me. Part of me wants him to close the distance, wants to lose myself in something that makes sense instead of this twisted desire for a man whose face I've never seen.

Damien looks conflicted, tension pulling at the corners of his mouth. Then he lets out a soft sigh and steps back, shattering the moment.

"Luna, would you like to have dinner with me?" The question tumbles out fast, and he blinks, like his brain is catching up to what he said. "There's a new restaurant in Estes, a farm-to-table place I think you'd enjoy."

The invitation catches me just as off guard. "I don't know, Damien. You've already done so much for the sanctuary."

"This has nothing to do with the sanctuary."

Part of me wants to lean into this, into whatever this pull is that vibrates in the air when he's near. But the other part recoils, shrinking back. Last night my watcher made me come until I cried. The ache still pulses between my thighs. How can I sit across a table from Damien when I'm still feeling the ghost of another man's touch?

"Damien, that's very sweet, and I appreciate it. I do. But I—"

"Just dinner. No obligations, no expectations. How about Friday?"

His face opens up, eyebrows lifted, and his mouth curves in a hopeful smile that makes him look almost boyish.

"Okay." The word slips out before I can stop it. "Dinner. Friday."

He grins, the expression spreading across his face and softening every hard angle. But before the smile settles, something else ripples across his features. His expression goes flat for a fraction of a second. Cold. Then warmth floods back in so fast the transition feels like whiplash.

My breath catches, and the hairs on my arms stand up.

What was that look?

"Well." I take a step back, needing distance from whatever just passed between us. "Thanks again for checking the system."

The strange look melts away, replaced by warm concern. "Of course. Anytime, Luna. I want you to feel safe."

He moves toward the door, then pauses. "And Luna? Make sure you set the alarm properly tonight. I'd hate for anything to happen to you."

On the surface, it's thoughtful. Protective, even. But tension radiates from his shoulders. That wasn't advice. That was a warning wrapped in velvet.

I stand there long after he's gone, my heart racing with confusion that makes my head spin. I stumble through the rest of the day, staring at the volunteer schedule until the names blur into meaningless shapes, feeding the animals without remembering which ones I've already done, and forgetting why I walked into the supply closet.

Every time I try to concentrate, my thoughts splinter in two directions—to my masked watcher's hands on my body in the dark and Damien's eyes burning into mine in broad daylight.

Two separate men, but something nags at the edge of my awareness. A similarity I can't pin down. The way they both look at me, maybe? Or could it be the way my body responds to each of them with that same pull low in my belly?

Chapter Thirty

Luna

I cradle the heavy laundry basket on my hip as I climb the basement stairs. It's late, but I have no choice. I slipped on my last pair of clean underwear after my evening shower. My still-damp skin clings to my pajamas—well, what passes for pajamas tonight. I've had to resort to wearing a short babydoll nightgown I haven't touched since I broke up with Caleb. He gave it to me for our second anniversary, but I only wore it once before our relationship imploded a few weeks later. I should've tossed it, but tonight, it's all I have.

My laundry schedule is a mess, thanks to the chaos my life has become. I need to get back on track so I'm not hauling wet clothes around at midnight. But in my defense, things have been a little insane lately.

I push open the door at the top of the stairs and enter the hallway that connects the kitchen to the living room. Darkness swallows me whole. Though they were on when I went downstairs ten minutes ago, all the lights on the first floor are off.

Outside, a distant crack of thunder rattles the windows, followed by a bright flash of lightning that rips through the sky. Heavy rain lashes against the enclosed porch windows, blurring the world outside.

My eyes dart to the alarm keypad next to the back door. The solid red light blinks at me. The system is armed.

But he's here. I can feel it in every nerve ending in my body.

I fumble for the wall switch, but when I press it, nothing happens. My throat constricts as I turn toward the living room. He's there. Like he belongs here.

Like he has every right to be in my house.

His now familiar silhouette fills the front window, his broad shoulders block-ing out the porch light with its irritating flicker. Behind him, rain falls in silver curtains, drumming a frantic rhythm on the roof, while the thunder rolls across the mountains. That damned silver wolf mask catches the lightning and throws it back at me in wicked flashes.

It's a scene ripped straight out of a horror film. My heart vaults into my throat, and cold sweat beads on my skin. Terror and rage crash together in my chest.

How the hell did he get in?

Damien's security system sucks.

My pulse hammers between my legs, desire and dread tangling into something that sets my skin on fire. The sight of him shouldn't make my heart race like this. Not this way. Not with breathless, quickened heartbeats. But my body has a mind of its own.

I set the laundry basket on the floor.

"I don't even know why I have a security system." My voice shakes, defeat wrapped around the raw edge of panic. Wariness threads through the words be-cause I'm not insane, but underneath it all coils this terrible, thrilling expectation that makes my skin feel too tight.

Lightning flashes through the window behind him. He takes several steps forward, each footfall heavy and measured, his body vibrating with raw power. I tilt my chin up to meet his gaze, my neck straining from the angle. His fingers flex at his sides, hands that could crush me.

He looms over me, breath sawing in and out of his lungs, rainwater dripping from his wavy hair. Tonight, there's a tension radiating from him, a new, palpable, unsettling energy. He doesn't speak, just stands there, chest heaving.

"What's wrong?" Fear thickens my voice until it barely sounds like me. "You seem—"

He's on me before I can finish. His fingers wrap around my throat in a vise-like grip, spinning me and pushing me over the sofa. My stomach slams against the back, and he yanks my wrists behind me, snapping zip ties tight around my skin. His hands are rough and demanding, yanking my nightgown up and tearing the delicate fabric. He shoves my underwear down, and I fight, panic surging as the sofa digs into my stomach.

"What are you doing?"

The intensity isn't entirely unexpected; he was rough and wild and completely consuming last night, but this feels different.

Angry. Punishing.

"Why are you so mad?" I gasp as he forces my legs apart with his knees.

He doesn't answer, and the silence is more unsettling than any harsh words could be.

"I—what the hell?" My voice is raw, but the question chokes off as he silences me with his mouth, tongue relentless, focusing on extracting pleasure from my body, whether I'm ready or not. My fingernails dig into my palms as his tongue drives me toward the edge with single-minded determination.

Before I can think, my body surrenders to his relentless assault, and my orgasm crashes through me like a tidal wave, violent and all-consuming. I cry out, the sound lost beneath another loud clap of thunder, my body convulsing as he holds me open, not letting me escape the intensity. When I try to pull away, overstimulated and shaking, he tightens his grip on my thighs.

Only when I'm trembling and spent does he stop, rising to his feet behind me, hips pressing against my ass, and his intention is clear. I struggle, but it's futile.

"Get the fuck off me."

He ignores my plea, gliding his fingers through my already slick flesh, harsh and demanding, as pain and pleasure twist together until tears slip down my cheeks. My body's betrayal of my own desire makes me want to scream, but I bite my lip as the sound builds in my throat. I swallow it back, refusing to give voice to this war between my mind and body.

His hand wraps around my throat, his thumb and forefinger pressing into the soft hollows beneath my jawline. Panic flares under my ribs, and my pulse hammers against his grip. My lungs strain, pulling in whispers of air as I force myself to breathe in shallow gasps, trusting him not to kill me. It's the only choice I have.

The pressure on my throat heightens everything, and the faint sound of his zipper confirms that, like last night, he won't bother undressing.

Then he's inside me, hard and claiming, and my teeth dig into the sofa cushion to muffle my cries. It's too much, too rough, but my body responds anyway, clenching around him even as I beg him to stop.

"Please." The gasp escapes with what little breath he's allowing me. "I can't—"

He slows down, but his thrusts remain forceful and deep. His fingers rub my clit, teasing with ruthless determination, until my pain tips over into pleasure. I shudder, crying into the cushion as another climax rips through me.

The cool mask against the side of my face sends a shiver cascading down my spine. The combination of his fingers on my throat, his rough possession, and the way he takes what he wants—it's intoxicating. My body surrenders, giving in to the ecstasy, the pain, and the fear.

It doesn't take him long. Whatever's got him so worked up catapults him to the edge of his own release. My body takes everything he gives me, jerking with the force of his thrusts, as bruises bloom on my throat and the front of my thighs. His thrusts become erratic, and I know he's close.

"Fuck!"

The first word he's spoken since he arrived is a roar that tears from his lips, close to my ear, as he comes inside me. The sensation sends me spiraling over the edge again. My pussy clamps down on his cock, a blazing third orgasm ripping through me as he releases his fingers and a blissful deep breath of air fills my lungs.

As the world comes back into focus, the storm outside rages, matching our ragged breaths.

"Get off me and get the fuck out of my house."

I twist my body beneath him, feeling the coarse fabric of his clothes against my back. Warm breath blows against my skin as he sighs.

"Do you have something you want to tell me, little doe?" His deep voice growls in my ear.

"No. Now let me go. I'm done with this. And—"

His fingers clamp around my throat again, cutting off my words. Panic flares as I force myself to take short, shallow breaths. I choke out, "I said, get out."

"How about we try this again? Do you have something you want to confess to me? A transgression, perhaps?"

"What... What are you talking about?" His grip on my throat is making it almost impossible to talk. "What do you want me to confess?"

His lips graze my skin with almost tender intent, and I shiver.

"Damien Wolfe." The name sounds like a curse. "I know you agreed to go out with him on Friday."

The words hit me like ice water, and I stop struggling. Damien and I were alone when he asked. Unless...

"How could you possibly know that?"

"I told you, Luna, I see everything."

"Did you hack into my security system?"

His lips curve against my ear. "Don't ask questions you don't want the answers to."

"That's illegal."

"So is killing, but that doesn't stop me."

He loosens his fingers, and I try to take a deep breath, but his weight pressing down on me makes it impossible.

"Let me up. I can't breathe. The sofa is digging into me, and my hands are going numb."

His compliance is surprising. He steps back and pulls me upright. The rage that burned in him has simmered to embers. I wish I could see his eyes better through the mask, and, almost as if the universe were listening, lightning lights the room again, but it's not enough. His eyes are still a mystery. Would seeing them help me understand the killer standing before me?

Do I even want to?

Right now, I want him gone. Erased from my life so I can return to the woman who didn't crave a killer's touch.

The torn nightgown barely covers me. My wrists strain against the restraints, come is dripping down my thighs, and my insides twist with desire and revulsion warring for control. But I won't shrink before him. He terrifies me, yet he knows what he does to my body. There's no hiding the way I respond to him.

"You have no right to invade my privacy. You have no right to come in here and take me against my will. Just because I let you fuck me last night doesn't mean you own me."

"That's where you're wrong. I do own you, Luna. And you need to come to terms with that."

"Fuck you."

His hand wraps around my throat again.

"You just did. And you will again before I leave here tonight. But we need to have a talk before I let you have my cock again."

"I don't want your cock. I want you to leave and never come back."

"It's amusing how you think you have a choice in this. Now tell me, are you attracted to him because his name is Wolfe and it makes you think of me?"

I flinch, and my throat tightens. His question scrapes against a raw place inside me, where conflicting desires for two men collide. My mind drags me back to Damien's introduction, his fingers sliding against mine, my pulse skipping, my skin warming at the contact. The way my breath stuttered when he'd leaned in to ask me to dinner, and how I stared at the curve of his mouth, desire unfurling in my stomach.

Much like my body's reaction to the man standing in front of me.

My nipples harden as he watches me, waiting for an answer. "That has nothing to do with it."

His jaw locks beneath the bottom of the mask. "So you admit you're attracted to him."

"I didn't say that, but even if I am, it's none of your business." My spine straightens, defiance flaring to life again. "You have no right to dictate my life."

The corners of his mouth curve upward—not a smile, something sharper. Predatory. Heat floods his gaze, the kind that comes before sex or violence or both.

My stomach drops, and I realize my mistake too late. He feeds on my rebellion, and I gave him exactly what he wanted. The realization should make me backpedal, choose softer words, and defuse whatever I ignited. Instead, my chin lifts higher. He wants a fight? Fine. I'll give him one.

"You will not go to dinner with him." His voice is harder now.

"Excuse me?"

Who the hell does he think he is?

"You will not go to dinner with him," he repeats, and there's no mistaking it for anything but a command. "You're mine. No one else touches what's mine."

"I'm not some possession with your name stamped on it. I make my own decisions. Just because I let you have my body doesn't mean you own me."

If he's going to repeat himself, so am I, but even as the words leave my mouth, my heartbeat betrays me, hammering against my ribs. I'm lying to both of us. He does own me. Has since that first night. In ways I refuse to admit. In ways that both terrify and electrify me.

"Yes, it does, Luna."

"No." His fingers flex against my throat, each heartbeat throbbing against his palm. "I don't even know your name. You won't show me your face. What makes you think I'm going to let you tell me who I see or what I do?"

He reaches behind me, seizing my bound wrists. Pain shoots up my spine as he pulls, forcing my back into a deep arch, my breasts thrust forward. The muscles between my shoulder blades shriek in protest, still aching from being restrained for hours last night as he ravaged me in a whirlwind of ecstasy and pain.

My back hits cool plaster. His six-foot-six frame dwarfs my five-foot-five body, his shoulders blocking the light, casting me in shadow. His breath warms my forehead while my eyes only reach his upper chest, a reminder of how he towers over me that sends butterflies scattering through my stomach despite everything.

"You betrayed me, Luna." The words slice the air, but underneath them I catch something raw, hurt bleeding through the anger. Even so, it's no excuse for the way he's treating me.

"I didn't betray you. We're nothing. All you want is to rut me like an animal."

"I am an animal."

"Yes, you are."

"You're mine, Luna." His voice drops to that rough growl that makes my core clench, my walls crumbling brick by brick.

"Say it."

"No." I refuse, but conviction has fled my voice. My body surrenders to his dominance, craving everything he promises.

His hand abandons my throat and fists in my hair, tight enough to draw a gasp from my lips. He cranks my head back, baring my neck as my pulse hammers beneath the surface.

"Say it." His mouth hovers above that frantic beating, his breath against my skin—warm, threatening, and promising.

"I won't." But even as the words leave my mouth, I'm melting into him, my body betraying every word.

He drags his mouth along my throat, and heat races across my skin. It's not enough. It's nowhere close to enough.

"Your body knows the truth. Even if your mind is still fighting it."

His hand slides down my side, fingers digging into my hip. The thin silk might as well be nothing. His palm burns through the fabric like he's touching bare skin.

This is madness. This whole twisted dance is insane, and I'm letting my body's hunger override every rational thought.

"Kiss me." The plea breaks from my lips. Every wall I've tried to build crumbles. I need his mouth. Need to know what he tastes like.

He pulls back, denying me what I'm begging for.

"I told you, no kissing."

"What's so terrible about kissing me?" Frustration bleeds through every word. "Why do you keep hiding behind that damned mask? And why won't you tell me who the hell you are?"

He presses his thumb against my bottom lip hard enough to make my mouth part. The touch is possessive and claiming, and it makes me want to bite him and beg him all at once.

"All you need to know is that you belong to me."

I close my eyes, the war between my sanity and my need tearing me apart. I want to keep some piece of myself untouchable, some part of myself that he can't claim, but the hunger in me is stronger than my pride.

"Why are you so jealous of Damien?" I ask instead. "What is he to you?"

He goes rigid, every muscle turning to stone. "You're going to call him and cancel."

I hesitate. Agreeing would betray everything I am.

"I already told him yes. I can't cancel without a reason."

The silence stretches between us, heavy with his displeasure. His anger builds like storm pressure, filling every corner of the room.

"Find one," he says, as if it's that simple. "Because if you go, I'll know. And I won't be pleased."

"Do you want to know where you can shove your displeasure?"

The threat makes me furious, heat blazing through every cell of my body as desire and defiance tangle into something that makes the world tilt.

"You can't appear in my life, refuse to tell me who you are, claim me as yours, and then punish me for trying to have a normal life."

"There's nothing normal about what's between us, Luna."

His fingers release my hair, leaving a rush of pins and needles across my scalp. The metallic rasp of his zipper cuts through my shallow breathing. His palms slide rough and hot against my skin, hoisting me up until my back presses flat against the cool wall. The denim of his jeans scratches against my inner thighs as he lifts me and positions himself.

Then he's inside me. My body yields to him, and a sharp intake of breath escapes me, catching in my throat before dissolving into a moan. My ankles cross behind him, my heels digging into his ass, pulling him closer, deeper, betraying everything my mind protests.

"There's nothing normal about what you need. About what I give you." A brutal thrust of his hips punctuates each word, pressing my bound hands into the wall.

God help me, he's right. These raw, twisted emotions I have for this man are consuming and dangerous. Everything a rational person would run from and report to the police.

But I haven't.

And I despise myself for it.

Chapter Thirty-One

Damien

My knees threaten to buckle as I unleash the last tremors of my release deep inside Luna. Her limbs tremble, hips convulsing as the final echoes of her own climax slip away.

I peel my teeth from the hollow of her neck, astonished there's no broken skin, already picturing the throbbing bruise that'll bloom by morning, joining the fingerprint marks.

She unwraps her legs from my waist and balances on shaky calves. I step back, the thunderous storm beyond the glass mirroring the tempest I've just stilled within me.

I should apologize, but I'm not that man. Vulnerability is poison to me, yet a part of me wants to expose my raw self to her. The urge unsettles me.

Instead, I slip a finger through the zip-tie and snap it open. I gather her wrists in front of me and examine the angry red marks that mar her skin. My fingers ghost over each emerging welt, an unspoken concession, the closest I can come to an apology. The little flare of surprise in her eyes tells me she understands.

Why the fuck did I ask her to dinner? The invitation spilled out before I could cage it. The plan was always simple. Keep Luna as my dark obsession, confined to stolen nights where I can take what I need from her body without the complications of daylight civilities.

But today, standing in front of her as Damien—no mask to hide behind, no terror widening her eyes—the careful separation I'd maintained cracked. She smiled at me. A genuine smile, warm and unguarded. I wanted her to look at me like that while knowing who I really am, and the desire felt foreign and uncomfortable

I don't want this. Don't trust it.

I adjust the mask.

Two faces of the same man. Damien Wolfe, who plays at being civilized, and the masked killer who embraces what lurks beneath his skin. She has no idea they're the same person, and that lie feeds my control over her. Or it did until I opened my mouth and asked her to dinner like some lovesick fool.

The thought of her with him, with the mask I wear in public, wakes something savage inside me. Would she want that version of me more than the one who claims her in the dark?

She was breathtaking tonight. I didn't expect her to agree to my demands. Even though the fear was pouring off her as thick as the rain outside, the fire in her when she defied me was a sight to behold.

That is what makes her different. She doesn't roll over. She fights first. Makes me work for her submission.

Makes it worth taking.

She walks around me, bending to pick up her discarded panties from the floor, scrunching them in her hand.

"What did you do with Shadow?"

"I locked him in the bedroom with the cats."

She nods and lifts the laundry basket from the floor. Without another word, she walks past me and up the stairs. A magnetic force I can't resist pulls me after her.

Shadow rushes through when she opens the door, weaving around her, sniffing, a low growl rumbling through his body as his gaze locks onto me.

"It's okay, baby. I'm alright," she assures him, stepping into the room and setting the basket on the bed. Shadow watches me, his hackles raised and teeth bared, before he lets out a huff and turns to follow Luna into the room.

I lean against the doorframe as she puts the clean laundry away. Shadow sticks close, trailing her every move from the bed to the dresser, the closet, and then back again.

She pulls the torn nightgown off, throws on a large Colorado Rockies t-shirt, and acts like I'm not even in the room.

"Luna."

Her eyes snap to mine, narrowing to slits, before her lips press into a thin line.

"You really are an asshole, you know." Though steady, the subtle tremor in her voice hints at the hurt she's trying to hide. "You didn't need to do that. You could have asked me about Damien like a normal person. But then again, you're not normal. You're a serial killer."

"And you're mine."

She laughs, but there's no humor in it. "I'm not anyone's. Especially not some masked freak who—"

She stops talking as I approach. Her muscles go rigid, her shoulders pulling back, and her weight shifting to the balls of her feet. Every line of her body screams flight. Shadow wedges himself between us, and her hand drops to his head, fingers curling into his fur.

"You hurt me." Her voice wavers. "And not just physically."

The tremor in those words hits me in the chest. I've heard pain before—screams, pleas, and broken sobs. None of it has touched me in decades. But hers hollows something out inside my ribs, makes me want to tear off this damn mask and tell her everything. Confess that I'm Damien, that I can't stay away from her, and why her saying yes to his invitation felt like swallowing broken glass.

Jesus, what the fuck is this woman doing to me?

"You had no right to treat me that way."

"I was fucking angry at you."

"That's no excuse." Her hand tightens in Shadow's fur. "I've had one abusive man in my life. I don't need another." The comparison cuts deep, drawing blood I didn't know I could still bleed. "And why? Because I agreed to have dinner with an acquaintance? It's dinner. It's not like I plan to fuck him, though I have every right to, if I want to."

Possessive rage rips through my chest, clawing up my throat until my vision tunnels, the edges going red.

"I will kill any other man who touches you, Luna." Each word is a vow. "Believe that."

"Leave Damien alone!"

Her face twists with anger, fear, and something protective that makes her voice shake as she shouts.

I press my mouth into a hard line, suppressing the smile that wants to emerge. She's defending him. Me. The contradiction shouldn't please me, but it does.

"Then cancel your dinner. Because if you think I'm going to stand by and let another man touch you, you haven't been listening to me."

"I can't have this conversation tonight." She drags both hands through her hair and grips the back of her neck. "Just leave Damien Wolfe alone." She presses the heels of her hands into her eyes. When they drop, the worry remains, carved into the space between her brows. "Everything aches, and I want you to leave."

"No."

I won't be dismissed.

The urge to reach for her battles with the fear of what she'll see in my touch. Tonight I was a storm, but even storms have eyes, calm centers they protect. She needs to know that no matter how angry I was, my intent was never to truly hurt her. But my tongue feels heavy and useless.

"Fine. Do what you want, but I'm going to bed. Do me a favor, reset the alarm on your way out."

She sets the laundry basket beside the door and turns to walk toward the bathroom. My hand shoots out, my fingers wrapping around her wrist. She jerks toward me, off-balance, and I catch her and walk her backward until her legs hit the mattress.

"What are you doing?"

"Get on the bed, Luna."

"You're not fucking me again."

"Don't test me, Luna. Get on the bed and lie on your stomach."

"No." She plants her feet, twisting her arm as she tries to wrench free. My grip tightens.

"Just lay the fuck down." I force the words out, restraining myself. "Keep pushing me, and tonight will end with my cock in your ass again."

Every muscle in her body locks. Her pulse hammers against my fingertips, rabbit-fast and frantic. It hurt at first when I fucked her ass last night, and I know she can't take me again any time soon, but that doesn't mean I won't hold it over her head like a threat.

She stops fighting, and I lift my free hand, tracing the curve of her cheekbone. "I'm not going to fuck you again. Not tonight."

Her eyes dart across what little she can see of my face, reading the shadows. Then, she nods.

I release her wrist and shoo the cats and Shadow out, easing the door closed behind me.

This time, when I touch her, my hands are gentler but still demanding. I coax her to her knees at the edge of the mattress and strip away her shirt, my palms skating over skin that bears the marks of my previous rough treatment.

When I turn her, easing her onto her stomach, she tenses.

"Relax."

I start at her shoulders, tracing the smooth line of her spine with my fingertips. My touch is firm but reverent as I map the landscape of her back, lingering on the slight dip at her waist and the gentle curve of her hips.

Her skin is soft beneath my hands. I lower my head and drag my lips across her shoulder blade. A tremor rolls through her when my exhale warms the side of her neck.

She releases a trembling breath. "What are you doing?"

"Feeling you."

I work my way down her body, using slow, firm strokes. She shudders, then sinks into the mattress with a soft sound. The tension drains from her muscles as my palms knead her lower back, thumbs digging into the knots buried there.

I've never touched a woman this reverently before. Never saw the point. But Luna makes me want to learn the shape of her bones, the give of her flesh, and the places where tension lives.

I massage down one leg and back up the other until her breathing evens out. By the time I reach her ass again, her body has gone slack, breath coming in gentle sighs.

She fell asleep with me still here, still touching her. The tightness in my chest loosens.

My fingers drift to the space between her thighs, finding her still slick with what I left behind. I trace the softness there, stroke the swollen folds, and circle the sensitive bundle of nerves without ever quite touching it.

Her breath stutters, and when I look up, she's watching me over her shoulder.

"I know I said I wouldn't fuck you again." I lean down, my mouth brushing her shoulder. "But can you give me one more?"

I ask, but we both know the answer doesn't matter. I'm taking it either way. But her answer surprises me.

"Yes." She pushes back against my fingers. "Don't stop."

I tease her until she's writhing, rolling her hips, until my control snaps. Then I'm pushing inside her, filling her in one thrust. We both groan as her body grips me, slick heat that makes my eyes roll back. The gentle touch from moments before burns away. I drive into her, each thrust rocking the bed frame against the wall. She pushes back to meet me, spine arching deep, the sounds coming from her shattered and incoherent.

Time stops meaning anything. It could be seconds, minutes—I can't tell anymore. Then my release tears through me, and I'm emptying into her, her body pulsing around me, pulling everything from me until there's nothing left.

"That's it, beautiful. You were made for my cock."

She flinches when I pull out, but her mouth stays closed, neither confirming nor denying what we both know is true.

I move toward the door. "Cancel dinner with Damien Wolfe. I won't tell you again."

"You don't tell me what to do."

That spark still burns in her voice, and my mouth almost curves into a smile. After everything tonight, she still thinks she gets to choose.

I open the door and turn back to her. "You have two choices here, Luna. You can accept this, or you can fight it. But make no mistake, you're mine. That doesn't change because you want it to."

She pulls the sheet up to her chin and rolls toward the wall, giving me her back.

"I'll be back tomorrow night. And the night after. And the night after. If you don't want that, call the sheriff. Tell her what I've done to both you and the others."

It's a risk, but one I'm willing to take because if she doesn't, when she doesn't, I'll have my answer.

"But know this, I've been meting out justice to monsters for twenty-five years. Some small-town sheriff won't be the one to stop me."

Chapter Thirty-Two

Luna

I crouch beside the wolf enclosure as I check the healing wound on Willie's leg. The large gray wolf, brought in a few days ago after his leg got caught in a trap, watches me with wary yellow eyes. But he's grown to trust me. His gaze follows my every movement, alert but no longer defensive.

"How's our boy doing?" Maren stands at the gate, her body blocking the exit as she keeps watch. Not that she'll be able to stop him if Willie decides to make a break for it, but she's a deterrent.

Shadow and Ghost both lie on the ground beside her, casual but alert to Willie's demeanor, watching over me as I treat him. Since Ghost left recovery, Shadow has taken the hybrid under his wing. Right from the start, there was no aggression or competition between them. I think Shadow sees the same thing I do in him. A creature that's a blend of two species, never belonging to either. Shadow's imprinting on me and the way I raised him makes him similar. He's neither completely wild nor truly domesticated.

"The infection's about cleared up." I probe the area around the wound, finding that the swelling has reduced. "Another few days of antibiotics and he should be good to release."

Willie gives a low rumble—not quite a growl, more like a grumble of protest at being handled. Shadow responds in kind. A warning. I respect Willie's tolerance. Wild wolves don't typically allow this kind of examination without sedation.

Sometimes it seems like I treat more wolves than any other animal, but I've always felt a deep connection to them. Though they were extinct in Colorado for decades, a formal reintroduction program a few years ago has brought them back.

But Shadow started it all seven years ago. His mother carried him down the ancient migration routes from Wyoming when he was still nursing and into the crosshairs of poachers. Other wolves followed, periodically trickling down from the north, until three years ago, when a breeding pair slipped across the border and gave the state its first wild-born pups in generations.

They've become my specialty. Word travels fast in the wildlife community, and when a wolf needs help anywhere in Colorado or the surrounding states, the call comes to me.

"You're being so good." I scratch behind Wille's ear in the spot I know he likes. "Almost done, handsome."

Maren snorts. "You and your wolf-whispering. It's honestly freaky how they all just submit to you."

"Not all of them."

I think of the masked wolf I take inside me. Like he promised, or threatened, he comes back every night, has for the last two weeks, and I submit to him, not the other way around.

He was right. I never called Karen. One day, I might regret it, but right now, even though I know he's a killer whose actions go against everything I stand for, I can't stop myself from hungering for his touch.

I finish my examination and back away from Willie, maintaining eye contact until I'm beside Maren. We exit the enclosure together, securing the double-gate system that prevents escapes.

"So, I got confirmation that three families are bringing their kids to our Elk Fest booth. The Kellermans, the Yamadas, and the new family that just moved here from Denver."

"That's great!" I smile, my mood lifting. Elk Fest is one of my favorite events. It's a chance to introduce children to wildlife conservation in a fun, educational way. "Which animals are we taking?"

"I was thinking Flower and Honey for sure," Maren says, referring to our two most social rabbits. "Maybe that new barn owl, if she's ready for a controlled introduction to crowds? And definitely Gertie."

"What about Winston? Kids love him." Tate's voice drifts over from the paddock, where he's brushing the horses.

I laugh. "Winston, the one-eyed opossum who hisses at his own shadow? That Winston?"

"Hey, he's got character." Tate leans over Patches' back, and his glasses slide down his nose. He shrugs his shoulder up to push them back into place. "And he's a great teaching opportunity about how even 'ugly' animals deserve protection and respect."

"He's not ugly, just unique." I crouch to give both Shadow and Ghost scratches. "Let's see how he does with our test run this week. If he can handle Maren in a good mood, he might be ready for actual children."

"I'm delightful!" Maren protests, but she's grinning. "Ask JT. He thinks I'm absolutely charming."

"We don't need to know why." I motion towards Tate. "There are young ones present."

"But Tate's almost old enough to drink now. He's twenty."

"Tate's been drinking since he was a freshman in high school," he says, but he's laughing. "And Maren's lack of filter is nothing compared to the house full of frat boys I live with now."

"I can't believe you're in a frat, Tate. That you pledged. How did you even make it through rush? You're..." Maren gestures with her hand, searching for words without saying what she means.

"A nerd?" Tate shrugs, eyes warm beneath his glasses.

"Well..."

I smack Maren on the leg with a frown. "You're not a nerd, Tate. Don't listen to her."

"No, she's right, Luna." He laughs again, unbothered as he moves to Patches' other side. "Every frat needs a token nerd. That's me."

"Do you have any idea what I used to do with frat boys?"

"Maren!" I slap her leg again. "Boundaries. This is not a workplace conversation. Save the confessions for after hours."

"What—"

She cuts off at the familiar sound of Roger's county truck, the engine's diesel growl growing louder as it reaches the circle drive, kicking up a cloud of dust that makes me squint. I stand, wiping my hands on my jeans.

"Please tell me it's not another python." Maren drops her head back. "I can't handle one more 'oops, my pet got too big' situation."

Roger's truck door slams shut, and he moves around to the passenger side with slow steps, like he's carrying something precious. My stomach does that familiar flip it always does when we're about to get new arrivals. Hope and dread in equal measure.

"Luna!" Roger's face is serious as he approaches. In his arms is a small carrier, the kind we use for kittens. "Got something special for you here."

"Define special." Maren crosses her arms. "Because your last 'special' was that skunk family that moved under our storage shed."

Roger ignores her sarcasm, which is wise. He's learned over the years that Maren's bark is worse than her bite, but only barely.

"Found these little ones on the Lily Lake trail." Roger lowers the carrier to the ground, both hands steadying it. "Six baby black-footed ferrets. Hikers spotted them yesterday afternoon, probably abandoned. We waited overnight to see if Mama would come back, but she didn't."

My heart stops. Black-footed ferrets. One of the most endangered mammals in North America. I drop to my knees beside the carrier, peering through the mesh. Six tiny forms huddle together, unmoving. They're so small, only a few weeks old at most, their eyes still closed.

"Jesus." My fingers find the carrier latch, fumbling with the clasp. "How long have they been alone?"

"At least eighteen hours, maybe more. They're in rough shape."

"Let's get them inside." I stand, lifting the carrier. It weighs almost nothing, which terrifies me. These babies should be heavier. "Maren, grab the small mammal emergency kit."

We sprint across the driveway, my mind already racing through protocols. Dehydration will be the first concern, then nutrition. These little ones need specialized formula, warmth, and round-the-clock care. My hands shake as I push open the door with my hip. This building has seen so many arrivals over the years, so many battles fought and won. And lost. I push that thought away and focus on the task at hand.

We move into the examination room, and I put the carrier down. Maren appears at my elbow with the emergency kit, her movements as efficient as mine.

I open the carrier, and my heart clenches. The babies are so still. Their tiny bodies are dehydrated, skin tenting when I pinch it. But they're alive. That has to count for something.

"How the hell did they survive out there?" I murmur, more to myself than anyone else. "Coyotes, hawks, owls... any one of them should have found these babies."

"Maybe someone was watching over them." Maren prepares a syringe with electrolyte solution. "Sometimes the universe saves the special ones."

Roger hovers near the door with Tate. "You think they'll make it?"

I don't answer. I'm focused on the smallest one, a little female who's not responding to my touch. Her breathing is so shallow, I strain to catch the rise and fall of her chest, each breath a whisper of movement.

"We'll do everything we can."

It's what I always say. It's never a promise, just a commitment to fight.

"I'll leave you to it then. Call me if you need anything. Anything at all."

The door closes behind him and Tate with a soft click, leaving Maren and me alone with our six tiny patients. I pick up the smallest one, feeling how light she is in my palm.

Come on, little one. Fight.

For the next two hours, we work in near silence. IV catheters smaller than toothpicks, warmed formula administered drop by drop, and heating pads adjusted to precisely the right temperature. It's delicate work, the kind that requires steady hands and steadier nerves.

The first five babies respond well. Their breathing strengthens, and their tiny bodies warm under our care. But the smallest one, the little female I noticed first, isn't rallying the way she should.

"Come on, sweetheart." I hold her against my chest. "Come on, fight for me."

Even as I say it, I can feel her slipping away. Her breathing becomes more labored, more erratic. I know this rhythm. I've felt it too many times before.

"Luna." Maren's voice is gentle and understanding.

"No," I say, working over the tiny body, refusing to give up. "No, we can save her. We can—"

The breathing stops.

The silence that follows is deafening. I stare down at the still form in my hands, this tiny life that never had a real chance. The weight of failure crashes over me like it always does, bringing me to my knees.

"No," I whisper, then louder, "No, no, no."

The sob that escapes me is raw, torn from somewhere deep in my chest. After five years of running this sanctuary, you'd think I'd be used to this. You'd think the losses would hurt less. But they don't. Every single one feels like a piece of my heart being ripped away.

I'm aware of Maren moving around me, taking the baby from my hands. She doesn't say anything. There are no words for this kind of loss, no platitudes that make it better. There's just the raw, devastating grief.

I sit there on the floor, surrounded by the equipment that saves lives and the knowledge that sometimes, it's not enough. Sometimes, despite everything we do, everything we know, and everything we give, it's not enough.

The other five babies squeak from the incubator, alive because of our intervention. But all I can see is the one we couldn't save, the one who needed a little more than we could give.

When Maren returns, she's carrying a small box with a paint marker and a round, flat rock resting on top. I'm still sitting in the same spot, watching the five surviving babies sleep in their incubator. Their tiny chests rise and fall in perfect rhythm, and I find myself counting each breath like a prayer.

"Luna?" Maren's voice is soft. "Are you ready?"

"Ready" is a relative term. Am I ready to say goodbye to another life cut short? No. Will I do it anyway because that's what we do here, because every creature deserves dignity in death as much as in life?

Yes, I will.

We walk out the back door into the late morning sun. The Gator sits parked right outside, with the keys already in the ignition. Maren climbs into the driver's seat while I settle beside her, cradling the box in my lap like it contains something precious. Which, I suppose, it does.

The ride to the back of the property is quiet except for the rumble of the utility vehicle's engine and the whisper of wind through the tall grass. The sanctuary spans forty-seven acres, and the cemetery sits on a gentle rise overlooking the valley below. It's peaceful here, surrounded by wildflowers and the occasional deer that wanders through, unafraid.

Tate kneels beside a small, rectangular hole he's dug in the earth, his shovel resting against a nearby tree. His blonde hair catches the sunlight as he looks up at our approach, and there's something achingly young about his face.

"Hey." He stands as we climb out of the Gator. No elaborate condolences or forced pleasantries. Just acknowledgment. I love that about him.

I walk over and wrap my arms around him in a hug that he returns without hesitation. He smells like earth and honest sweat, and for a moment, I let myself lean into the comfort of him.

"Thank you." The words come out muffled against his shoulder. "For this."

"Always."

Maren joins us, looking down at the hole with approval. "Perfect depth, as usual. You can head out now, Tate. Thanks for doing this."

"I can stay and help fill it in." He reaches for his shovel.

"No." Maren pats his arm. "This is what Luna and I do."

Tate nods, understanding. He's been volunteering here for over a year now, long enough to know our ways, our unspoken rules about death and mourning.

"Go take your girlfriend out for lunch or something," Maren adds with a small smile.

As Tate walks back toward the main buildings, I turn to Maren with raised eyebrows. "He has a girlfriend?"

"Oh, yeah." Maren settles down beside the small grave. "I saw them in Estes Park last weekend. Cute little brunette. Way out of his league."

"That's not nice. You really need to stop calling him a nerd."

"But he is. That doesn't mean I don't love him."

"He's not that bad."

"The guy tried to impress that group of kids from Estes Middle School last week by demonstrating his 'special bond' with Finley. He ended up with talon marks in his scalp and had to explain to a bunch of kids why our resident falcon doesn't actually want to be anyone's best friend."

The mental image makes me laugh, which feels strange and necessary at the same time. Leave it to Maren to find the perfect moment to lighten the mood, enough to make this bearable.

We kneel beside the hole, the box between us. The dirt smells rich and dark, mixed with the scent of wildflowers and pine needles. This place has become sacred to me, holding the remains of every animal we couldn't save.

"What's her name? She was a girl, right?"

"Fiona." I always name them. Every single one. They deserve that much—to be remembered as individuals rather than only statistics in our loss column. "Her name was Fiona."

I place the box in the hole, with care, my hands lingering on the cover. Such a small container for a life, even one that barely began.

"Goodbye, Fiona. I'm sorry we couldn't do more. I'm sorry the world wasn't kinder to you."

Maren places her hand over mine. "Rest easy, little one. No more hunger, no more fear."

The words hang between us, simple and honest. We've said variations of them dozens of times over the years, but they never feel routine. Each goodbye is specific and personal.

I lean against Maren's shoulder, grateful beyond words for her steady presence. She's been my anchor since the beginning, the one person who understands this calling that drives us both to exhaustion and heartbreak on a regular basis.

"You know," she says after a moment, "I was thinking we should get Tate a helmet if he's going to keep trying to commune with birds of prey."

I laugh despite the tears tracking down my cheeks. "You're terrible."

"I'm practical. Brain damage is expensive."

The lightness fades as quickly as it came, leaving me staring down at the small grave. How do I keep doing this? How do I keep opening my heart to creatures that might not survive, that might leave me kneeling in the dirt saying goodbye to another box, another name, another piece of my soul?

The losses pile up sometimes. Not only the animals, though those are the hardest. But the people too. Grandpa, five years ago now, taking with him the last of my family, the last person who knew me before I became the woman who runs a wildlife sanctuary and lives alone except for her best friend and a bunch of misfit animals.

My parents died when I was ten. Grandpa raised me after that and taught me about strength and resilience and the importance of fighting for things that can't fight for themselves. But even he couldn't stay forever.

Most days, I'm fine with the solitude. I have Maren, I have the work, and I have purpose. But sometimes, kneeling beside tiny graves, the weight of my aloneness is a physical burden, impossible to ignore.

Except I'm not alone anymore, am I? There's him. My watcher, my secret, the man who comes to me in the dark and sets my body on fire with his touch. I don't know his name, but I know the sound of his breathing in my ear, the weight of his hands on my skin, and the way he whispers that I'm his.

Only his.

The memories of his words send heat flooding through me, even here, even now. I've never belonged to anyone, never wanted to. I've been my own person since I learned no one can live forever, no matter how much you want them to. But with him, in those dark hours when the world disappears and there's nothing but heat and hunger, the sound of his voice, and his body claiming me, sometimes I wonder what it would be like to belong to someone. To have someone belong to me.

What would it be like to have dinner with him? To hold his hand in public, to wake up beside him in the morning light instead of finding empty sheets and the lingering scent of his skin? What would it be like to share this grief with him, to have him hold me while I cry over baby ferrets and the endless cycle of loss that defines my life?

Those are dangerous thoughts. He's not the kind of man to offer comfort, and he's made it clear that what we have exists only in shadow, only in secret. And maybe that's safer, anyway. People leave, people and animals die, and hearts break.

"Come on." Maren interrupts my spiraling thoughts. "Let's get this finished."

We begin covering the box with handfuls of moist earth, working in silence. The dirt falls with soft pattering sounds, covering cardboard and one small life that deserved so much more than it got.

When we're done, Maren marks the spot with the small stone she paints with Fiona's name. It joins dozens of others scattered across this hillside, a constellation of memory and loss.

We stand together for a few more minutes, looking down at the fresh grave. The wind whispers through the grass, carrying the promise of afternoon storms building over the mountains.

"Ready?" Maren asks.

I nod, though I'm never ready to leave them behind. But the living need us too, and five baby ferrets are waiting back in the recovery room for their next feeding.

Chapter Thirty-Three

Luna

The afternoon sun filters through the canopy above as Shadow and I follow the narrow deer path deeper into the woods. He pads beside me, pausing now and again to investigate a scent or sound that my human senses can't detect. I need this—the quiet, the space to breathe, the familiar comfort of Shadow's presence without the constant demands of the sanctuary.

"I couldn't save her, Shadow." The words taste bitter in my mouth, heavy with a week's worth of guilt. "Little Fiona. She was so tiny, and I... I couldn't fix her."

Shadow's eyes flick to me before returning to the path ahead. As much as I sometimes think otherwise, I know he doesn't understand my words, but there's something in his posture that suggests he's listening anyway. And that's what I need right now. That's the thing about animals; they hear everything, even the things we can't say.

"I know what you'd tell me if you could talk." I step over a fallen log. "The other five lived. But losing even one..."

My phone buzzes against my hip, and I ignore it. If it's important, Maren will call, not text. I need this time to process, to grieve, to remember why I do this work despite the heartbreak it brings.

"And then there's him." The words slip out, and Shadow's ears prick forward like he knows who I'm talking about. "My life used to be simple, you know? Just you and me, Maren, and the other animals. Now everything's complicated."

Now everything's twisted into knots I can't untangle.

That silver mask. Those rough hands that know exactly how to make me surrender. The way he possesses me in the dark, claiming me with a hunger that should terrify me but instead sets my blood on fire.

I press my palm against my chest, where my heart pounds. What kind of person am I that I can want someone I know is a killer? I know it's wrong. Everything about him goes against every moral code I've built my life around, and I've never been someone who looks the other way, who makes excuses for the inexcusable.

But then I think about the people he hunts. The ones the legal system fails to stop, over and over again. In the darkest corners of my soul, a voice whispers inside me, not with horror but with something that feels dangerously like satisfaction.

And that terrifies me more than wanting him does.

Lost in my internal war, I don't realize how far we've wandered until Shadow slows, his posture shifting to something more alert. I look up to see the familiar stone pillars that mark the western boundary of the Morrison Estate.

The Wolfe Estate now.

"Oh." The word escapes as a whisper. I haven't been here in years.

The Victorian mansion rises from the overgrown landscape like something torn from a nightmare and dropped into the Colorado wilderness. Its grand arches frame windows that stare down like hollow, accusing eyes. Some are still glazed with the original leaded glass that catches the afternoon light in fractured rainbows. Others are replaced with newer versions to match. The towering spires pierce the sky, their weathered slate tiles in the process of being replaced, the areas still needing updating creating jagged gaps like broken teeth.

The property still looks abandoned, wild, and overgrown in most places. But there are signs of change. Sections where the grounds have been cleared of the worst undergrowth. Scaffolding clings to the mansion's walls, where workers have been replacing rotted siding, though no one is working today. The ornate wraparound porch sags in places but is being shored up, its intricate gingerbread trim carved with roses and thorns bleached gray by decades of mountain weather.

It's still creepy and run-down, but beneath the decay and abandonment, the bones of something magnificent hide in plain sight. The soaring rooflines, the elegant proportions, and the intricate stonework around the foundation all speak of a time when this place was someone's dream of perfection.

And Damien is taking the first tentative steps to reclaim this Gothic monument from the wilderness, but he has a long way to go.

Shadow whines low in his throat, pressing against my leg. He's not afraid, but there's wariness in his posture. This place has too much history, too much darkness soaked into its bones.

Why would Damien buy a place like this?

There's no car in the driveway, so I let my curiosity get the better of me and move closer to the house.

"Just a quick look. We're not really trespassing. Much. Are we, baby?"

We reach the tall windows, and I cup my hands around my eyes and peer inside. The room beyond appears to be a study or an office. Mahogany desk, covered in computer screens and high-tech equipment, leather chairs, built-in bookshelves that stretch to the ceiling, and a massive stone fireplace in the corner. It's an odd mix of modern and traditional that somehow works.

"Enjoying the view?"

I spin around so fast I nearly lose my balance, my heart hammering against my ribs. Damien stands on the front porch steps, one shoulder leaning against a column, arms crossed. There's amusement in his stormy blue eyes. But the way they track a slow path down my body and back up, like he's already peeling away my clothes in his mind, makes heat bloom everywhere it touches. I think he's the one enjoying the view.

Shadow moves to position himself in front of me, not aggressive, but protective, his stance watchful, the way he gets when around unfamiliar men.

"I... God, I'm sorry." Heat floods my cheeks as I stammer. "I was hiking with Shadow, and we ended up here, and I was curious about what you were doing with the place. I wasn't trying to—"

"Spy on me?" He pushes off the column, moving down the steps with that easy confidence of his. "Peer into my windows like some kind of Peeping Tom?"

"I'm really sorry—"

But then I catch the subtle curve of his mouth, the way his eyes crinkle at the corners. Some of the tension leaves my shoulders.

"You're teasing me."

"Am I?" He closes the distance between us, stopping ten feet away, his eyes flicking to Shadow before they meet mine. "It's hard to be upset when I find you on my doorstep."

"Technically, I knew about this place first."

"But I bought it. Possession is nine-tenths of the law."

I laugh despite the awkwardness of being caught red-handed. The way the afternoon light catches the silver streaks at his temples and how his smile reveals that slight dimple in his right cheek puts me at ease. My heart still pounds against my ribcage, my skin burns, and my lungs can't seem to hold a full breath, but it's a different kind of heat than what my wolf ignites. It's comfortable.

Damien extends his hand toward Shadow, palm facing the ground. He waits with the patience of someone who knows wild things can't be rushed. There's an alpha confidence in his posture that speaks to something primal in Shadow. My wolf tilts his head, considering, before stepping forward. He accepts Damien's scratch behind his ears and even leans into the touch.

"Good to see you again, Shadow." My wolf, who keeps himself between me and strange men, who takes weeks to accept new people, just melted under Damien's hand.

As if summoned by the sound of voices, Athena comes bounding out of the house, her tail wagging so hard her entire butt wiggles with excitement. And she's wearing her trademark pink bow around her neck.

I crouch as she barrels towards me, accepting her enthusiastic greeting. "Hello, beautiful girl."

She lavishes my face with kisses while I scratch behind her ears, her entire body vibrating. Shadow tolerates her exuberant attention with the dignified patience of an elder sibling, but soon she's dragging him away from his guard duty for a game of chase across the yard.

I straighten, wiping dog slobber from my cheek. "I thought you were still out of town."

"I got back this morning." He gestures toward the house. "I've been working out of my office here."

"The one I was spying on through the window." I wince.

"The very one." His voice holds a dangerous playfulness, like he's savoring every second of my discomfort. "Though I have to say, most Peeping Toms are considerably less attractive."

The compliment is unexpected, and my pulse quickens in places it shouldn't.

"How have you been, Luna? How's everything at the sanctuary? The system working okay now?"

That's a loaded question. Should I mention how poorly his system keeps out certain predators?

No. That would open a door I'm not ready to go through, especially since I no longer believe my watcher wants to hurt me. Still, it would be nice if he knocked once in a while.

"Yeah. I just needed to get used to it."

Amusement sparks in his eyes as he nods.

"How's everything else?"

I'm surprised by how much I want to tell him about Fiona, about the weight of responsibility that sometimes feels crushing, and about the guilt that follows every loss despite Maren's reassurances that I did my best.

"I lost a ferret kit last week," I hear myself saying. "Fiona. Mom abandoned her and her siblings. Or was killed. But she was too small, not strong enough..."

"I'm sorry. That must have been devastating."

"It was." I swallow hard. It helps to say it out loud to someone who isn't trying to fix it or explain it away. "I know I can't save them all, but knowing something up here—" I tap my temple. "And feeling it in here—" I press my hand to my chest. "Are totally different things."

"You saved the other five, though."

I blink at him, startled. "How did you know there were five others?"

A look flickers across his face, too quick to identify. "Eleanor mentioned it when I stopped at the post office this morning. Said you'd worked miracles with the survivors."

That makes sense. I told Eleanor and Frank about the ferrets at Nancy's Diner two nights ago. Small-town gossip travels at light speed.

"They're thriving now." Saying it out loud lifts some of the grief. "But they still have a long way to go."

"See? Just because one couldn't be saved doesn't diminish what you accomplished with the others."

"Thank you. Sometimes I need to hear it from someone who isn't paid to make me feel better."

"Does Ms. Rodriguez have difficulty managing your guilt spirals?"

I laugh, surprised by how easily he can shift the mood. "Maren gets paid to deal with my medical crises, harassing animals, and terrible jokes. The emotional support is a bonus, required by her best friend status."

"And here I thought all that came free with friendship."

I motion toward the mansion, needing to redirect before I do something embarrassing like step closer to him.

"So what's the story here? Why did you buy it? I mean, with its history and all."

His expression doesn't change, but he follows my gaze to the mansion's imposing facade. "You mean Jeremiah Morrison?"

"What happened here is well known." I study his profile, trying to read his expression. "It's not exactly the kind of place most people would choose for a weekend retreat."

Damien walks toward a section of the porch where new support beams have been installed, running his hand along the fresh wood. "That's exactly why I bought it."

"Because of the history?"

"Because of what it represents. Morrison took something beautiful and twisted it into something dark. He let evil poison this place, turning it into a monument to suffering. But underneath all that darkness, the bones of something grand still exist."

He moves along the porch, his hand trailing over ornate carvings that have weathered decades of neglect.

"Most people would have torn it down."

"Most people can't see past the surface." He pauses at one of the towering columns, looking up. "They let fear and superstition blind them to the potential underneath. I prefer to take something viewed as evil and broken and give it new life. New meaning. Besides," he continues, his voice lighter now, "the isolation is perfect for my work. No neighbors, no distractions. Just me and my projects."

"What kind of projects require this much seclusion?"

His smile turns mysterious. "The kind that change the world. Or at least, certain people's worlds."

A chattering sound from overhead interrupts before I can ask what he means. A family of squirrels has appeared in the old oak tree beside the house, and one of them is decidedly different from the others.

"Sassy?"

I'd recognize that stubby tail anywhere. I haven't seen her since I released her. Almost as if she knows her name, she stops her chattering and fixes her black eyes on me. For a moment, we stare at each other across the space between the ground and the branches. Then, to my amazement, she makes her way down the trunk.

"Do you know that squirrel?" Damien asks, sounding incredulous.

"I treated her at the sanctuary months ago." I crouch as Sassy approaches, moving with the fearless confidence I remember from her recovery. "Her tail got cut off in a weed whacker accident."

Sassy reaches my outstretched hand and allows me to scoop her up, her small body warm and vibrating. She sniffs my fingers and settles into my palm like she belongs there.

"That's incredible." Wonder fills Damien's voice. "She remembers you."

"Animals remember kindness." I stroke Sassy's soft fur with one finger. "Especially when they're in pain and someone helps them."

"What happened to her? You said it was an accident?"

The sharpness in his tone makes me look up. His expression has gone cold, and there's a dangerous stillness about him that reminds me of a predator scenting blood.

"Old Man Henderson was trimming weeds along his fence line. He didn't see her in the tall grass. When he realized what he'd done, he was devastated. Brought her straight to me."

The tension in Damien's posture eases, but his eyes remain sharp. "So it was genuinely an accident."

"Completely. Henderson wouldn't hurt a fly on purpose. He brings me vegetables from his garden and asks about Sassy every time he sees me." I smile down at the squirrel. "He's the one who named her. Said she was too sassy to let a little thing like losing her tail slow her down."

"And he was right, it seems."

Sassy launches herself back toward the oak tree, rejoining her family with typical squirrel drama. The spell of the moment breaks, and I realize I've been kneeling in the dirt communing with a squirrel while Damien Wolfe watches me like I'm the most fascinating thing he's ever seen.

"Sorry." I brush off my knees as I stand. "I get a little excited about my animals."

"Don't apologize. It's remarkable. The connection you have with them." He pauses. "I've never met anyone quite like you, Luna Foster."

My body leans forward without permission. Just a fraction, but enough that I have to pull myself back.

"So." The word comes out breathy. I clear my throat. "What are your plans for this place? Beyond reclaiming it from the wilderness?"

"Complete restoration. The structural work is nearly finished. Then comes the fun part."

"Fun part?"

"Making it mine." He leans against the porch railing in a move that seems casual but somehow brings us closer together. "New kitchen, modern bathrooms, but keeping the original character. I want to honor what it was meant to be before Morrison corrupted it."

"That sounds like a massive undertaking."

"The best projects usually are. I'm bringing my designers back next month. The structural work needs to be finished first."

"What's your vision for it?"

"Something that honors the craftsmanship while adding modern conveniences. I'm too much of a techie not to have all my toys."

I run my fingers along a section of gingerbread trim, marveling at the detail carved into the wood several centuries ago. "It must have been amazing in its day."

"It will be again."

"Sounds like you've thought this through."

"I always think things through very carefully, Luna." He steps closer. "I don't make impulsive decisions."

"Never?"

"Almost never." His eyes drop to my lips for a moment before meeting my gaze again. "Though you seem to inspire some... unusual impulses."

My breath catches, and the air between us hums. The isolation of this place presses in around us, a reminder of how alone we are. My lips part on their own as I imagine erasing the distance between us, pressing my mouth to his, and finding out if he tastes as sinful as he looks.

Instead, I step back, putting a safer space between us. "When do you think it'll be finished?"

If he's disappointed by my retreat, he doesn't show it. "Six months for the major work, maybe eight if we run into complications. Historic houses always have surprises buried in their walls. I'll have to have you over when it's finished."

"I'd like that." The words are out before I can consider whether they're wise.

"Good." He steps closer again, and this time I don't retreat. "I wanted to apologize again for having to cancel our dinner so abruptly."

"It's okay. I understand business doesn't always follow convenient schedules."

"I'd still—"

My phone rings, interrupting him. The sound is jarring in the quiet afternoon, and I fumble to pull it from my pocket. Maren's name flashes on the screen.

"I should take this."

"Luna!" Maren's voice comes through the phone before I can even say hello. "We got a call from animal services. Rhonda is bringing in a coyote that was hit by a car on Trail Ridge Road. ETA fifteen minutes."

My stomach drops. That stretch of Highway 34 is notorious for wildlife collisions, especially during fall dispersal season, when pups, born in the spring, leave their dens to establish their own territories and find mates.

"How bad?" I already know from Maren's tone that it's serious.

"Probable internal bleeding, definitely multiple fractures. I'm prepping for surgery now. I know you needed this afternoon to yourself, but without Ethan, I need you here."

"On my way." I end the call and look up at Damien with regret. "I have to go. Emergency at the sanctuary."

"Of course." The disappointment shows in the way his shoulders drop. "Go save another life."

"Shadow, come." But he's already at my side, sensing the shift in my energy.

"Luna." Damien's voice stops me mid-turn. I pause, torn between the crisis calling me back and the pull to linger here in his presence. "Do you need a ride?"

"No. I know all the shortcuts. It'll be faster on foot, but thanks."

"Well, be careful out there. And thanks for stopping by." His expression shifts, his mouth quirking into a half-smile that borders on wicked. "Feel free to peep through my windows anytime."

I meet his eyes and mirror his obvious smirk with a matching one of my own before I turn and head toward the woods.

Turns out there's more to Damien Wolfe than brooding intensity and storm-cloud eyes. The man has a sense of humor hidden under there somewhere.

Shadow keeps pace beside me as we run through the familiar paths, my mind already shifting to what needs to be done when the coyote arrives. But I can't shake the memory of how natural it felt, standing there talking with Damien among the ruins of the Morrison Estate.

Behind us, the Gothic mansion disappears, but I can still feel the weight of Damien's gaze.

Chapter Thirty-Four

Damien

The streets of Estes Park are packed to the breaking point, the annual Elk Fest turning this small mountain town into a tourist circus.

The crowd presses against me from all sides, bodies and voices blending into an assault on my senses. I push through the chaos, my jaw clenched tight as I scan face after face.

None of them matter. None of them is Luna.

Under normal circumstances, I'd be miles away, holed up in my fortress where the noise can't reach me, as multiple monitors track Luna's every movement. But she's here somewhere, and that single thought drives me forward like a man possessed.

Heat courses through my veins as images from last night flash through my mind. Her hands zip-tied behind her back, my fingers wrapped around her throat, the way she begged for more as I bent her over her dining room table.

Twelve hours. It's been twelve hours since I was buried inside her, and my cock is already aching for her again.

But that wasn't Damien. It was her masked wolf.

She's the only woman who's ever been able to withstand the relentless intensity of my fucking. The only one who can take everything I give and still want more.

I've always had a short refractory period between erections, and I can usually last several hours before my cock falters, getting and maintaining multiple erections in that time, as long as I pace myself.

Most women tap out long before I'm done, their bodies giving up before my hunger is satisfied. That isn't why I've never had a normal, successful relationship with a woman. It's not my overactive sex drive that prevents it, but my inability to connect on any level, in or outside the bedroom.

I once asked my doctor whether what I experience is normal. His hearty laugh, firm handshake, and advice not to look a gift horse in the mouth still make me chuckle.

But Luna... she meets me stroke for stroke, taking every brutal thrust and every possessive mark I leave on her skin.

The brazenness of openly stalking her in broad daylight should concern me. But I need to see her like this, interacting with the world, smiling in the sunlight, not just writhing beneath me in the moonlight.

I spot her tent near the center of the festival, her sanctuary's banner fluttering in the breeze. The coil in my chest that's been wound tight all day loosens at the sight of her blonde hair catching the sun, the way she moves with easy confidence as she talks to the families gathered around Shadow. Even from here, I can see the massive wolf's adoring gaze fixed on her.

It's a feeling I understand all too well.

I hang back, ducking behind a rack of antler souvenirs, close enough to watch but hidden in plain sight. The faded jeans she's wearing hug every curve I traced with my tongue last night. Her sage-green sweatshirt conceals the constellation of marks left on her breasts by my lips, and beneath it, a turtleneck hides the bruises I left on her throat, fingertip-shaped reminders of my possession.

"Do you think we should have brought Ricky?" Maren's voice carries across the space as she puts a one-eyed opossum back in his cage.

"No. His paws can't be trusted in public." Luna's laugh washes over me, bright and unguarded. "We've got to find something to distract him. My breasts can't take much more."

Jealousy flares hot and irrational at the mention of that raccoon's obsession with her breasts. The absurdity of being jealous of a raccoon registers somewhere in my rational mind, which tells me I'm losing my grip.

As the families drift away, I edge closer, using a large tree for cover. Luna and Maren are alone now except for their animals, and I'm close enough to hear their conversation.

"So." Maren bumps Luna's shoulder. "I've been meaning to ask. Have you heard from Damien since he caught you creeping on his house?"

I stand motionless, curious for her reply.

"I didn't creep on his house. Shadow and I stumbled on it during our hike."

"Yeah. Sure. Says the woman who can navigate those woods with her eyes closed. Did he bring up anything about your canceled dinner date?"

My teeth grind together. Luna ignored my demand to cancel. Even though it pissed me the fuck off, I have to respect that she didn't cower to my threats. But when that Thursday came and went and she still hadn't called it off, I took matters into my own hands and texted her about an unexpected business trip.

That night, I waited to see if she'd tell me about it. When she didn't mention it, I asked her outright, ready to punish her for lying. But she told me the truth, that Damien had canceled, not her. I should have known better. Luna is good and honest. Even though she's keeping my secrets from everyone she trusts, she's not an outright liar.

I still took my disappointment and anger out on her, fucking her until she was raw. She accepted it all, giving me her tears and her orgasms with equal abandon.

The memory of it still makes me throb.

"Just that he was sorry he had to cancel."

"Have you heard from him since?"

"No." Luna's lips curve into a thoughtful frown.

"Hmmm."

"Why are you saying, hmmm?"

"He just seemed really into you when he was at the sanctuary. And he asked you out the next day. Why's he ghosting you now?"

"He's not ghosting me. He was fine when I saw him at his place. And I'm too busy to worry about it, Mar." Luna busies herself rearranging their display table.

"Look, I like Damien. I do. He's a nice guy. But I have a lot I'm juggling right now."

"What you need to juggle is his dick. Or better yet, ride it."

And that's enough.

I can't listen to another word without doing something that will blow my cover. Taking a breath, I step out from behind the tree and approach their booth, forcing my expression into something resembling casual interest rather than the storm of possessiveness and desire raging inside me.

"Ladies." Luna's smile widens at the sight of me. "Impressive setup you have here."

"Well, look who it is! Mr. Missing in Action." Maren nudges her elbow into Luna's ribs hard enough to make her stumble sideways. "Perfect timing. We were just talking about—"

"How great the turnout has been today." The look Luna shoots her friend is subtle but unmistakable—stop talking—and I have to fight back a grin.

Shadow rises to his feet as I approach, studying me. For a moment, we regard each other, and after a long beat, he sits back down, accepting my presence. He never gives away that he recognizes me from my nightly visits to his mistress.

Luna leans down and strokes Shadow's ears. "I never imagined seeing you here. Elk Fest doesn't seem like your kind of vibe."

I look around and try not to flinch. "I have to admit, the crowd isn't exactly my usual scene."

"No kidding." Maren snorts out a laugh. "You look like you're about two seconds away from buying the whole festival just to thin out the crowd."

"It's crossed my mind. But I figure I should try to get to know the locals. When in Rome and all that."

Luna's eyes twinkle with mischief. "No offense, Damien, but you stick out like a Ferrari in a parking lot full of pickup trucks."

"Here I thought I was doing a decent job of blending in."

The banter comes easier than expected, her teasing drawing out a side of me I'd forgotten existed.

"I didn't realize you spent so much time up here. It's a different energy than Denver."

"Maybe I like the peace and quiet. The city can be overwhelming sometimes."

"So, you plan to spend more time than only weekends in Aspen Ridge?"

"I do now."

The blush creeping up her neck is subtle but satisfying.

In truth, I haven't left Aspen Ridge since I first tasted Luna on my fingers. Only kills and essential office meetings have pulled me away. Even my Denver penthouse sits empty while work gets handled through video calls and encrypted messages.

"So, you've had a good turnout, huh?"

"Better than expected. We've had several donation pledges and three potential volunteer applications."

"I should check on Winston and Gertie. I think they need water." Maren gives Luna a meaningful look before moving to the other side of the tent.

Left alone with Luna, as alone as we can be in a crowded festival, I step closer. Being this close to her and not being able to touch her is torture of the worst kind.

And so, I lose my mind.

"Well, I guess I'll take advantage of her absence." Luna's eyes find mine, and that familiar pull sparks between us like it always does. "I was hoping we could try again for dinner?"

What. The. Fuck.

This is why I shouldn't be allowed near her in the daytime.

She studies me with those piercing hazel eyes, like she's solving a puzzle, getting closer to the pieces I've kept buried.

Shadow's growl vibrates the air. Low, steady, and dangerous. His hackles stand straight up. He's locked onto someone moving toward us, someone Luna hasn't noticed yet. I follow his gaze to the man approaching—heavyset, red-faced, radiating the kind of barely controlled violence I recognize intimately.

"You fucking bitch." He jabs his finger at Luna. "You took my horses."

Every muscle in Luna's body goes rigid, but she doesn't retreat an inch.

"Watch your fucking mouth." My facade cracks and falls away as I move in front of her. She glances at my face, eyes widening for a fraction of a second, then steps around me.

I don't stop her, but my body crowds the space behind her to intimidate the approaching asshole with my size.

"Mr. Pearson, your horses were malnourished and showed signs of physical abuse. The court agreed with our assessment."

"Two years of work down the drain because of you!" Spittle flies from his mouth. "Do you have any idea how much money you cost me?"

"Those animals were suffering. You should be grateful you're not facing criminal charges."

Shadow growls louder, positioning himself between Luna and the threat, but Pearson's focus remains locked on her.

"You think you're so fucking righteous. But you're just a stuck-up cunt who—"

He lunges for her arm, and rage explodes out of me. I move without conscious thought, grabbing Pearson's outstretched arm and twisting it behind his back. Using his momentum against him, I drive him face-first into the ground, my knee pressing into his spine with enough force to make him grunt.

"Touch her, and it will be the last thing you ever do."

Pearson struggles beneath me, but I increase the pressure until he whimpers like the pathetic piece of shit he is. Shadow's massive frame vibrates with contained violence beside me. The surrounding crowd has gone silent, staring in shock.

"Damien." Luna's voice cuts through the red haze clouding my vision. "Damien, that's enough."

I blink. The festival comes back into focus—the crowd, the families, the children staring. I'm supposed to be Damien Wolfe here. Not the version of myself that knows how to make a man stop breathing.

I release Pearson and step back. He scrambles to his feet, nose bleeding, and eyes wide with fear.

"You're fucking crazy." He backs away, gasping. "Both of you."

Two deputies push through the crowd. "What's going on here?"

Luna steps forward, composed despite what just happened. "This man was threatening me and attempted to assault me. Mr. Wolfe intervened."

"I saw it too." Maren steps up beside Luna as she glares at Pearson. Several other bystanders chime in, confirming the events that took place.

One of the deputies looks at me while the other escorts Pearson away as he complains that he wants to sue me for assault. "Sir, I'm going to need you to come with me to the station to make a statement. You too, Luna."

He gives her a look like this isn't the first time she's had a run-in with an overbearing asshole abuser.

"Jerry, I can't leave the booth right now. I can stop by later."

"I can handle it for a while." Maren rests her hand on Luna's arm. "Tate should be back with our lunch in a few minutes anyway."

"No, I'll stop by the station after the festival ends."

Jerry gives a reluctant nod, then his gaze returns to me. "Since you were one of the participants in the altercation, I need you to come now, sir."

"I'll follow in a few minutes."

"Now, sir. I don't want to arrest you, but I will if I have to."

"Do you even know who this is?" Maren asks with disbelief, and if I wasn't so amped up over Pearson, I'd chuckle.

"I don't care who he is."

"Jerry." Luna says his name again, and I don't like the familiarity in it. How well do they know each other? "Damien is an upstanding member of not only the Aspen Ridge community but also Denver. You can trust him to follow if he says he will."

I pull a business card out of my wallet. "I'll be right behind you, Deputy."

He glances at my name, and recognition flashes in his eyes before he looks at Luna.

"Don't make me chase you down for that statement, Luna." He tucks my card in the front pocket of his shirt and looks pointedly at me. "I'll see you at the station shortly, Mr. Wolfe."

After he walks away, Luna looks at me, and everything inside me goes still. The look on her face freezes the blood in my veins. Recognition, confusion, suspicion. She saw what I did. The speed. The violence. How natural it was for me.

"Are you okay?" I try to rein in the beast still snarling beneath my skin, not wanting her to see him.

She nods, but her eyes never leave mine. "That was intense. I've never seen that side of you before."

She has, just not with this face.

"I have zero tolerance for anyone who threatens women."

Luna takes a small step closer, studying me with an intensity that makes me want to run. I stand my ground as she searches my face.

"There's something familiar about the way you moved. The way you sounded."

The wheels are turning behind those beautiful eyes, and I need to get out of here before she pieces together what she's really seeing.

And before she says yes to my dinner invitation. What the fuck was I thinking? The whiplash of my dual identity is going to be the death of me.

"Well, I should keep my word to Deputy Jerry and head over there." I suppress my distaste as I say his name. "Do you intend to press charges against Pearson?"

I hope not, because I have much bigger plans for him. Not that it will interfere. I'll just have to be more strategic in my approach.

She shakes her head. "He didn't touch me, so probably not. That's not the first threat I've gotten, and nothing ever comes of pressing charges." Worry shines in her eyes. "I hope it won't be a problem for you, though."

"My lawyers eat people like Pearson for breakfast. You're my concern. I don't like that he threatened you."

"Happens all the time in my line of work, unfortunately." She shrugs, but there's heaviness in it. "I'm sorry you got mixed up in it."

"I'm not. I'm glad I was here." My fingers brush her elbow, drawing her gaze back to mine. "I'll give you a call soon, Luna."

I force myself to walk away, but my body fights the distance growing between us. The need to stay close to her and protect her sinks hooks into my chest.

My mind is already calculating as I disappear into the crowd. I memorized Pearson's face and his name. I know what he did to those horses. He was already on my kill list, but now he threatened Luna.

That bumped him to number one.

Chapter Thirty-Five

Damien

The night shrouds me like a second skin as I wait outside Pearson's ramshackle house on the outskirts of town. It's nearly 1 AM. The isolation of the property makes it perfect for my plan. No neighbors to hear. No witnesses to remember.

His wife left this morning to visit her sister in Phoenix. This is a fortuitous turn of events because I'm not taking him back to my basement. He'll die here, where he committed his sins.

I've spent the two days since the festival preparing. Reviewing his file. The man has a record. Three arrests for animal cruelty, but only one conviction that resulted in a slap on the wrist. The system failed, as it so often does.

I don't fail.

Dressed in black, my wolf mask secured over my face, I'm the hunter. The executioner. The darkness Luna both fears and craves.

Thank fuck, I was at the festival on Saturday. I shudder to think what might have happened with Pearson if I hadn't been. Though Shadow seemed like he might have had it under control. He was ready to rip Pearson's face off. But if he'd attacked the man in public like that, it would have resulted in his being taken from Luna. That would devastate her, and I'll never let it happen. My protection of her extends to everything and everyone she loves.

Pearson's truck sits in the dirt driveway. I creep across the overgrown yard. Empty beer cans litter the porch, and through the grimy windows, a television flickers in the living room. The security is laughable. A single deadbolt on a door that looks like it could be kicked in with minimal effort.

But I choose finesse.

The lock gives way to my tools. I slip inside, and the television masks any slight sound I make. The smell of stale beer, unwashed clothes, and rancid food infects the space. This is where care goes to die.

Pearson sprawls on a threadbare couch, holding a beer, with glazed eyes as he stares at the screen. He fails to sense the predator in his home until it's too late.

My hand clamps over his mouth before he can scream, the rag covering his nose. His eyes widen in terror as he sees the wolf mask looming over him before they roll back in his head.

When he comes to, he's shackled to a post in his barn, chest bare, arms chained above his head. The same barn where he abused his horses.

It's poetic justice, really.

Mouth gagged and eyes wild with terror, he registers his predicament. On a blood-stained plank, his instruments of cruelty are lined up—knives, whips, and prods.

"Remember me?" I lean in, close enough to see the sweat beading on his forehead. "No? It's the mask, isn't it? No matter. But more importantly, do you remember her? Luna Foster? The woman you threatened two days ago?"

Pearson's eyes track me as I move around him, following the glint of the knife in my hand. Walking around a victim always fucks with their head. They lose track of you, even for a second, and that second is everything. Straw, mud, and manure crust the floor beneath my boots, releasing a thick, pungent stench. Luna's sanctuary doesn't smell like this. This is the unmistakable odor of neglect.

He tugs at his rough bindings, but the effort is futile. The stench of his fear grows stronger with every step, making my heart race, and a dangerous grin spreads across my face.

"The body tells stories." My voice is casual, even though I'm barely holding back the urge to carve him open. "The horses Luna rescued from you? Their bodies were maps of your cruelty. Scars upon scars. Evidence of systematic torture."

I bring the blade to his face and drag the tip along his jaw. He whimpers, a strangled sound as pathetic as the man himself.

"I wonder what your body might tell me. What stories can we write on your flesh?" I tilt the knife, savoring the way his eyes go even wider as it pierces the skin. "Now it's your turn to bleed."

I don't drag it out tonight, but I don't rush either. In the privacy of my basement, I can take my time, but I'm late because I was inside Luna. A mere two hours ago, I was in heaven. Now I'm in hell.

White-hot rage crawls over my skin like needles. Dealing with this festering piece of shit pulled me away from her. But he'll pay for it as surely as he'll pay for his other sins.

I start with his Achilles heel, slashing the serrated knife over the rope-like tendons, hobbling him, like he did to several of his horses. His body convulses, legs buckling, shoulders wrenching upward until the joints pop, leaving him unable to stand.

Choked screams erupt behind the gag. The sound washes over me, a full-body experience that leaves my limbs buzzing with wild energy, like touching an electric fence. Adrenaline floods through me, a searing, burning sensation that makes my heart pound against my ribs.

Next, I carve his horses' names across his hairy, sweat-slicked chest, each letter a tribute to those he maimed. The steel slices through skin and muscle with ease. Thick ribbons of dark crimson blood coat my hands and snake down his trembling torso. His screams, muffled by the gag, ricochet off the rafters, a symphony of agony that sends the three barn cats I discovered earlier scuttling into the shadows. Their eyes catch the light as they watch from their hiding spots, but I'm undeterred, focused on the task at hand.

He scrambles sideways like a wounded crab, blood drenching the yellow straw, turning it slick and treacherous beneath him, but the rusted chains locked around his wrists keep him tethered in place no matter how hard he struggles. Every futile attempt to escape spatters my boots with fresh red droplets that join the faded ones from the past.

I cut away his filthy jeans and switch to the whip, its worn handle smooth against my palm. It hisses through the air with each strike against his bare skin. With deliberate cuts, I rip flesh from his quivering thighs and calves, mirroring his own calculated cruelty back onto him.

My hands are steady, and my resolve unbreakable. I'm not driven by cruelty or revenge. This is retribution. A balancing of scales that have tipped too far for too long. But because he threatened Luna, I want him to suffer more. I want to drag it out, even though I'm on the clock.

I pause, wiping sweat from my brow with my forearm. His once-arrogant face contorts with fear and regret, tears cutting wet tracks through the layers of dirt and blood caking his skin. But the remorse came too late. The fear came too late. None of it will save him now.

I charge the cattle prod. The device hums to life, vibrating, heavy in my hand as I size up Pearson's shredded, bloody body, looking for the most sensitive spots. My mouth waters, satisfaction just out of reach. His eyes widen with dread when I zero in on the first spot.

I press its prongs into the hollow of his knee, closing my eyes in concentration. The current lances through him, up my arm, and into my shoulder. My eyes pop open when he howls, an inhuman sound as muscle and bone convulse. I hunt for fresh spots, pressing again and again. Each scream that pours from him feeds the beast in my chest, a haunting cacophony of pain that rolls over me in waves, resonating deep in my soul.

These walls have heard worse, but never the sound of a man tearing apart from within. A slow drip-drip-drip of blood cuts through the silence. My pulse hammers in my ears like war drums.

He chokes, and I pull off the gag. A hoarse squeak tumbles free. Squeezing his cheeks, I force his mouth open, clamp forceps on his tongue, and yank it taut. With one swift cut at the root, I sever it. He spasms, and blood splatters my wrists, neck, and chest. The warm, sticky blood saturates my shirt, and the copper scent fills the space between us as it cascades down his body.

I step back, taking in my work with an artist's clinical eye, noting every detail. The barn is silent now, save for his ragged, gurgling breaths. I'm done, and judging by his slumped, battered body, Pearson is too.

I plunge my knife into his gut, but he barely reacts. I pull it out and hook it under his chin, lifting his face.

"Open your eyes, Pearson." My voice is harsh as I slide the bloody knife up his cheek, and his eyelids flutter open.

I lift my mask. Something flickers in his eyes. A shadow of recognition, perhaps, but I can't be sure. It doesn't matter. My face is the last one he'll see.

I thrust the knife through his right eye and twist, and his body jerks one final time before it goes still. My shoulders relax, and a wave of peace washes over me, the calming sensation smoothing every nerve.

Justice has been served for those horses, all of whom lived. Luna kept one, a mini horse, barely three feet tall, with a coat like a patchwork quilt that earned him his name, Patches. Local families adopted the other horses and now treat them with the kindness they never knew.

I take Pearson's belt buckle, stained with his blood. The perfect souvenir for Luna. Before I give it to her, I'll scrub it clean since she deserves better than his filth.

Collecting the cats takes patience, but I lure them from the rafters with treats before loading them into carriers I have in the Range Rover. They'll find their way to Luna's doorstep before dawn, and she'll take them in.

Pearson's body gets wrapped in plastic, then I drive out to Odessa Lake, where I dump it on a trail that's not for the faint of heart. At this time of the year, there will be few hikers, so it may take days or weeks for anyone to find him. I walk away, leaving behind the cooling corpse of a man who thought animals were objects to be abused.

Luna's gift burns in my pocket. Anticipation thrums through me at the thought of giving it to her. She'll struggle, relieved he's gone but tormented by that relief.

But that's why she needs me.

So I can rid the world of the filth that makes her cry.

The sanctuary's main building is quiet. I disable the door chime before slipping inside. I'm earlier than usual tonight, having just finished a kill. A dirtbag I picked up last night outside of Salt Lake City, Utah. Cade was with me, his military buddy providing a discreet airstrip for the helicopter. He's handling the cleanup, but I couldn't wait another second to see Luna. I've been coming earlier lately because it's clear my visits are exhausting my little doe. My waking her in the middle of the night is disrupting her sleep cycle. So, I make it a point to come earlier now so I can fuck her and tuck her into bed by a decent hour.

She's in her office, bent over paperwork, her silky blonde hair falling around her face like a curtain. She hasn't heard me yet. I pause, drinking in the sight of her, before I let the floor squeak under my boots.

Her head snaps up, eyes widening as they find me in the doorway. For a heartbeat, fear flickers across her features. Then recognition smooths it.

"You're early." Her voice trembles—relief, desire, and guilt all tangled into two simple words.

I step into the small office, closing the door behind me. In the dim light of her desk lamp, I appear more shadow than man.

I pull the silver belt buckle from my pocket and place it on her papers with a soft clink. The recessed horse in the center catches the light, its metal flanks gleaming.

Luna stares at it, her breath quickening as she recognizes the logo. Horror and turmoil wage war in her eyes—the healer battling the vengeful woman. Morality wrestles with darker impulses.

"Is that Odell Pearson's?" Her voice is steady despite the way her pulse jumps at her throat.

I nod, watching her face tighten.

"Did you kill him?"

Another nod, and she narrows her eyes.

"Have you lost your ability to speak?"

A slow smirk stretches across my lips.

She stands, pacing the small space, fingers raking through her hair. "Do you know what you're making me an accomplice to?"

"He hurt those animals. He would've hurt more. His life was forfeit the moment he threatened you."

She stops, exhaling a sharp breath. She doesn't ask how I know things anymore.

"Are you even listening to yourself? Who appointed you the arbiter of life and death?"

"I did."

She runs a hand down her face, exhaustion seeping into her features. "You didn't bring the body here, did you?"

"No. You told me not to. I do as you ask." She arches a brow. "Sometimes."

"Will they ever find his body?"

"Eventually."

She drops her voice low, the words meant for herself more than me. "I guess I'll be getting another visit from Karen." Then she looks up. "Were those his cats I found outside the other morning?"

"Yes. They were the only other animals on his property. I couldn't leave them to starve."

Her eyes soften. "I hate that you've put me in this position."

I know she hates it, but she crossed that line the moment she accepted my violence, my darkness, and my body inside hers.

Her gaze drops to the belt buckle. "Those horses. What he did to them. They were so afraid. So broken. Patches still jumps whenever the barn door slams." Her hands clench. "Part of me is glad he's dead. What does that make me?"

"Human."

The rigid line of her shoulders slumps, and a tremor runs through her jaw, the last threads of resistance snapping. She closes the distance between us, hands fisting my shirt.

"I hate that I want you." The confession hisses out as she presses her body against mine. Tonight I let her, because she's having an epiphany, and it's a brutal, beautiful sight. "I hate that I wait for you every night. I hate what you make me feel."

My hands capture her wrists, and I back her against the desk. "No. You hate that you *love* what I make you feel."

Darkness swallows her pupils, lips parting on a shaky exhale. Every logical defense her mind has built dissolves under her body's honest response. I release her wrists and step back.

"Strip."

She hesitates for only a heartbeat, then reaches for the buttons on her shirt. It's an old flannel she wears sometimes, and I think it might have been her grandfather's.

Her eyes never leave my mask as she works each button with careful fingers, and each revealed inch of skin is an offering. Her collarbone, the gentle swell of her breasts in a simple black lace bra, and the flat plane of her stomach. My blood roars through my veins.

The fabric slides from her shoulders and pools at her feet. Her hands move to the clasp of her bra, and I watch the play of muscle beneath her skin, the way her shoulders shift as she reaches behind her back. The bra follows the shirt, and then she's pushing her jeans down over her hips, the soft rasp of denim against her skin filling the room.

When she straightens, completely bare, she doesn't try to cover herself. Naked, she's perfection, all curves and shadows, skin like cream touched with gold.

I cross to her in three steps and guide her to sit on the sofa. My hand slides into her hair, blonde silk that catches on my rough fingers. The strands are warm, and they smell of vanilla shampoo mixed with her natural peach scent. I wind them around my knuckles, feel their texture and their weight, and force her to look at me.

"I'm not binding your wrists yet. You're going to need them."

Her eyes darken, understanding my intent.

I lean down, bringing my face close to hers. The space between us shrinks to nothing but breath and heat. My lips hover over hers, so close I can feel the whisper of her exhale. I'm playing with fire. Her mouth is right there—soft, parted, and waiting. My heart pounds with the temptation to kiss her, to taste those soft lips.

I've kissed women before, but not for a long time. Not since I embraced the darkness inside me. It's not that I don't enjoy kissing, but it's too intimate, too much like offering a piece of my soul. I prefer to just fuck, leaving the woman's mouth free to cry and scream as I ravage her. I don't need kissing.

Until Luna. I want to kiss her too much. That's why I can't allow it. If I lower my guard, I won't be able to maintain the separation between her wolf and Damien.

I turn my head at the last second, my mouth finding her cheek instead. My lips drag along the curve of her jaw and find the shell of her ear. "I've thought about your mouth all day."

A tremor runs through her. I release my grip on her hair, and she lifts her head. Her eyes are dark pools, pupils blown wide with want.

"Don't make me regret not tying your hands, Luna."

She nods, and her lips curve at one corner, a ghost of a smile she tries to hide but can't quite manage. Her eyes spark with gratitude mixed with anticipation.

"Now, let me fuck that beautiful mouth."

My thumb traces the soft curve of her lower lip. She shivers, and I step closer until my belt buckle almost touches her chin. Her fingers work to release me, the metal teeth of my zipper parting with a slow hiss that echoes in the quiet. My cock springs free, hard and pulsing, a bead of moisture already gathering at the tip.

She pushes the denim down my thighs, then pauses, eyebrows lifting.

I shake my head. "No. It stays on. Tuck it behind."

A crease forms between her brows, but she complies, lifting the cotton hem and resting it behind where I stand rigid against my stomach. She doesn't understand why I don't undress. But the shirt is a shield, protecting her from what lies beneath. Ink that spells out my damnation.

"Look what you do to me, Luna? How hard you make me."

Her tongue darts out, a quick flicker of pink, wetting her bottom lip. Her fingers hover for a heartbeat before wrapping around me, tentative at first, then firmer as her breathing quickens. My legs tremble, and my ragged breaths match hers. One hand cradles my shaft while the other glides upward, collecting the moisture at the tip, her thumb circling the sensitive skin.

"How the hell does this fit inside me?" She whispers, her breath warm against me. She's asked herself that more than once while close to my cock. I want to tell her we're made to fit together, but I stay silent, fearing my real voice will emerge if I speak. I'm also afraid I might whimper.

She leans in, her tongue darting out. The first contact almost buckles my knees. Her mouth curves into a smile against my skin as she traces a wet path up, then down, her tongue exploring every inch of me. My fingers find her hair, tangling in the silken strands.

"Take me in your mouth, Luna." The command fractures, morphing into a plea. I tighten my fingers in her hair, and she retaliates by gripping my balls, a silent reminder that she holds power too.

She's so fucking perfect.

When her lips finally part and envelop me, my heart stutters in my chest. She takes me deep, her mouth a warm, wet haven that threatens to undo me. She hums, a low vibration that resonates against my skin. The sensation is heaven and hell. Pleasure and torture.

For endless minutes, there's nothing but the slick sounds of her lips and tongue and our mingled breathing filling the small room. The world narrows to the burning heat of her mouth, the flick of her tongue against that spot beneath my crown that makes stars burst behind my eyelids.

"Here it comes, Luna. Be a good girl and take all of me."

Her whimper vibrates against my skin. My hips jerk forward of their own volition, my body chasing my release. Her throat constricts around me as she struggles not to pull away, her eyes watering at the corners, lashes clumping together like wet spikes.

I erupt, my release volcanic, a hot, pulsing rush that fills her mouth. A drop escapes from the corner of her lips, trailing down her chin. The muscles in her neck strain as she swallows, her throat working to take all of me.

I loosen my grip, and she pulls back with a gasp that fills the silence between us. Her jaw works side to side, wincing as she rubs at the muscles. Those eyes, soft with satisfaction, look up at me. I want to lean down and kiss her, to whisper my devotion in her mouth, but I stop myself.

Her thumb catches the wetness at the corner of her mouth, a quick swipe that she follows with a flick of her tongue. Her gaze travels to my covered stomach and lingers. Then she looks down. Disappointment bleeds across her features, subtle but unmistakable, there and gone before she can stop it.

But I see it. I always see it.

I pull out the zip ties. "Now it's my turn. Hands."

She stands and extends her arms behind her, a silent gift of surrender. The willing gesture makes my heart slam against my ribs. I loop the zip tie around her wrists and pull it tight, the ratcheting sound loud in the quiet room. My fingers linger on her bound hands before sliding down, tracing the curve of her bare ass.

"You don't have to do this anymore." Her voice is soft but steady. "I won't betray your trust."

"I know." I lean in, pressing my mouth to the side of her neck. Her pulse hammers beneath the skin, fast and wild against my lips. "But this. Being bound. Being mine. You crave it. As much as I do."

"Yes." The word melts from her lips, surrender wrapped in invitation.

I guide her around the desk and bend her over its smooth edge. She gasps when her bare skin meets the surface, her body jerking away from the chill before settling. Her cheek rests against the cool wood, the silver belt buckle inches from her face, papers rustling under her breasts as she gets comfortable. She breathes in shallow gasps, a flush spreading across her skin. Her eyes follow me as I grab her chair and roll it behind her.

"What are you—" Her question dissolves into a breathy moan as my intentions become clear.

I rest my palms on her skin, and she sighs beneath my touch. This craving owns me now. The sweetness I find between her thighs and the way she breaks apart when I use my mouth on her. It's become my addiction.

My fingers grip her thighs, thumbs brushing the damp seam of her sex. There's power in this, in making her come apart with my mouth, in hearing those sounds she makes only for me.

I need her ready and wet because I need to ride her hard tonight. Killing makes me primal and brutal. I don't want to hurt her, so I need to make sure her body is prepared to take what I'm about to give her.

I lean in, my tongue teasing a slow path around her clit, tasting the salty sweetness of her arousal. She shivers, hips lifting toward me, her moans muffled against the desk's surface, until they turn to desperate whimpers. Papers scatter beneath her as she writhes against the wood.

"Please." Her voice is tight with need. "I—"

I don't stop until she shudders against my face, release washing through her, the words "God, yes" dying on her lips as a strangled cry. Only then do I stand, shoving my pants down.

I slide my hand between her legs. Her wetness coats my fingers as they trace her entrance. Luna's breath catches, and her legs tremble as they part wider. She's ready.

Her body's welcoming heat wraps around the tip of my cock, and I'm powerless to resist. I drive forward, her body yielding, taking me to the hilt in one motion. The desk scrapes against the floor. Luna's nails dig crescents into her palms, her head thrown back as a raw sound tears from her. I grip her hips, withdrawing almost fully before slamming back in. The wet sound of our bodies colliding fills the room, punctuated by the harsh rhythm of my breathing and the desperate, broken way she gasps.

"Mine."

The word rips out of my throat, guttural and raw, torn from some primitive part of me. Not Damien's smooth voice. Not the wolf's controlled menace. Just me. Stripped down to the truth under the mask, the deception, and the double life I've built. A man who needs this woman more than his next breath. A woman he can no longer live without.

"Yours." She gasps it between pants, her body clamping down around me.

She rarely says it, usually defiantly refusing, but it seems each night she comes closer to accepting it, even if she fights it.

The word pushes me closer to the edge. I reach beneath her, my fingers finding her clit, flicking in a tempo that will send her over. Her inner muscles clench around me as she comes, crying out against the desk.

I follow seconds later, burying myself deep inside her as release crashes through me.

For several heartbeats, we remain frozen like this—her sprawled across the desk, me still inside her, and both of us breathing hard in the aftermath. I'm reluctant to pull out, to sever this moment where nothing stands between us.

When I pull away and free her wrists, she turns to face me, naked and unashamed. She dresses slowly, eyes on the belt buckle.

"Take it with you. I don't want it here."

I pocket the grim souvenir. "He'll never hurt another animal. Or threaten you."

Luna looks at me, and for a terrifying moment, I again wonder if she sees through the mask to the man beneath. If some part of her recognizes Damien in the set of my shoulders or the timbre of my voice when passion overtakes caution. A flicker of something—recognition, perhaps—shines in her eyes, then slides away behind her usual composure.

"I still have some paperwork to finish up."

Did she dismiss me?

"Will you come back later?"

She keeps her voice casual, but her teeth catch her bottom lip, and her hand moves to her throat, fingers pressing against her pulse point.

"Do you want me to?"

Her answer is immediate. "Yes."

I nod and turn to leave. A soft chittering sound draws both our attention to the doorway. Ricky sits there, beady eyes fixed on us.

"Ricky! How long have you—" Mortification colors Luna's cheeks. "Oh, my God. How did you get out of your cage?"

The raccoon tilts his head, chittering again as if commenting on the scene he's witnessed.

"Quite the voyeur you've got there."

Luna's eyes widen at my unexpected humor, caught between embarrassment and absurdity.

Ricky scurries forward, climbing onto the chair I'd abandoned, makes a determined grab for her breast, and Luna lets out a startled laugh. She pushes his paws away. "What am I going to do with you, Rick?"

The raccoon looks so affronted by her rebuff that I can't help but laugh, a genuine sound that strips away the darkness of my masked persona. Luna's gaze flicks to me, surprise in her expression. A shared moment of simple joy passes between us that's more intimate than the passion we just shared.

"He has good taste."

She shakes her head. "He has terrible boundaries. Like someone else I know."

Ricky climbs onto the desk, flops onto his back, and perches atop her scattered files like he's claimed a throne. Luna scoops him up, holding him like a furry, squirming baby. "Maybe he's the universe's way of keeping me sane."

The moment of levity passes, but its warmth lingers.

"I'll be back in an hour. I want you spread out naked on your bed when I come to you."

Her breath hitches, and she licks her lips, nodding.

Good girl.

Chapter Thirty-Six

Luna

The afternoon sun shines, and the unseasonably warm fall day is perfect for giving Mr. Snuffles his much-needed bath outside rather than wrestling with him in the cramped indoor washing station.

I adjust the hose nozzle and test the water temperature against my wrist. "Tate, can you check the water heater? This feels barely lukewarm."

"You got it." He jogs toward the barn with that eager energy that reminds me why I love having college interns. At twenty-one now—his birthday was last week—Tate has all the enthusiasm in the world for veterinary work, even if he's still figuring out that animals don't always cooperate with textbook procedures.

Mr. Snuffles seems to sense what's coming. The potbellied pig eyes the outdoor washing station with deep suspicion, his tail twitching as I coax him forward with gentle words and a handful of apple slices.

"Come on, buddy. You'll feel so much better once we get you cleaned up."

The moment the first spray of water hits him, Mr. Snuffles decides this is the perfect time to demonstrate his escape artist skills. He bolts sideways, slamming into my legs, sending me stumbling backward into the muddy area around the washing station.

"Whoa there!" I steady myself, laughing as Tate returns.

"Water heater's fine. The temperature should pick up in a minute." He grabs the other side of Mr. Snuffles' harness as the pig makes another break for freedom. "Jeez, he's stronger than he looks."

I redirect the hose, finally getting a steady stream on his back. He settles down, though his suspicious grunting continues.

"How's school going? I feel like I haven't asked in weeks."

Tate's face lights up. The guy loves talking about his studies. "Really good, actually. I'm taking animal behavior this semester, and right now we're covering the neural basis of behavior, which is amazing. Though I have to admit, working here has taught me more about animal psychology than any of my classes."

"That's the thing they don't tell you in vet school. Half of being a good vet is understanding that animals have personalities just as complex as people do."

Mr. Snuffles chooses that exact moment to prove my point by shaking and showering us both with soapy water.

"Perfect timing." I wipe suds from my eyes as Tate snorts.

"At least he's getting clean." Tate tries to hold the pig steady while I work shampoo into his bristly coat. "Even if he's getting us dirty in the process."

Tate's interaction with Mr. Snuffles is gentle and confident. The pig is relaxed now, enjoying the warm water and the attention.

"You're good with them, you know. The animals here trust you."

Tate scratches behind the pig's ears. "What's his story? He seems pretty healthy for a rescue case."

"He's not an abuse case." I scrub a stubborn patch of mud on his back. "His family loved him, but they had no idea how big potbellied pigs get. He's over two hundred pounds now, and they live in a small suburban house with a tiny backyard. They couldn't handle his size or his feisty personality."

Tate nods. "That happens a lot with exotic pets. People think they want something unique until reality hits."

"Yeah. So now we need to find him the right home. Somewhere with enough space for a pig his size and people who can appreciate his attitude." I smile as Mr. Snuffles snorts at me, as if he knows we're talking about him. "He needs a place where he can be himself without being too much for his family."

"Wait." Tate looks surprised, pausing in his rinsing. "You're not keeping him? I mean, you keep so many of the animals that come in. I figured Mr. Snuffles would be a permanent resident."

The question hits hard. I focus on working the soap through Mr. Snuffles' coarse hair, buying myself a moment before answering.

"That's exactly why I can't keep him. If I kept every animal that I could find a good home for, I wouldn't have room for the ones that are too broken to ever be adopted out. The ones that need this place to be their forever home."

My throat tightens, and Tate's expression softens.

"It's one of the hardest parts of this job. Loving them enough to let them go when they're ready for a real family. Or back into the wild where they belong. But that's what this is supposed to be about, right? Helping as many as we can, then setting them free to live their best lives."

The emotion catches me off guard, and I have to stop talking. Mr. Snuffles seems to sense my mood and leans against my legs, offering comfort in his own piggy way.

"Plus, Maren will absolutely wring my neck if I keep another adoptable animal."

Tate steps closer and wraps his wet, soapy arms around me in a spontaneous hug. "You're amazing, you know that?"

I melt into him, hugging him back, grateful for the support. He's the best hugger. Tate steps back, and we both start laughing as we realize how completely soaked we are. He grabs the hose again.

"So, Maren mentioned she saw you and your girlfriend in Estes Park a few weeks ago. How's that going?"

Tate's expression falters, and he focuses on rinsing Mr. Snuffles' left side. "We, uh, we actually broke up."

"I'm sorry, Tate."

"It's okay. She was way out of my league, anyway." He shrugs, trying to play it off, but I can hear the hurt underneath.

That's what Maren said. I keep that observation to myself. She has many wonderful qualities, but tact isn't always one of them.

"Hey." I catch his eye. "Don't sell yourself short. And don't let what Maren said about you being a nerd get to you. You're handsome, smart, kind, and passionate about what you do. Any girl would be lucky to have someone like that."

He smiles, though it doesn't quite reach his eyes. "Thanks, Luna. And I know Maren is only teasing. That wasn't why Courtney was out of my league. She liked my geeky side. But that means a lot coming from you."

If only I could take my own advice. Here I am encouraging him about finding love while I'm having anonymous sex with my masked stalker every night.

For the last month, I've settled into an unexpected routine that would horrify anyone who knew the truth. I spend my days with the usual: caring for the animals, taking in a few regular rescues like Mr. Snuffles, and a couple of new abuse cases. All of them are horrible, but one particular one—a llama who was skin and bones when Roger brought him in—gutted me. Karen arrested his owner, but she later had to release him because she couldn't make the charges stick.

Two days later, his body was found at the Longs Peak Trailhead, wrapped in plastic with a purple Rocky Mountain Columbine bloom pinned to his chest.

Karen came to see me again, asking questions I couldn't and didn't want to answer. When my wolf, as I've started calling him, because "watcher" just didn't feel right anymore, came to me that night, he didn't deny killing the man when I asked. Instead, he distracted me, his hands and mouth driving me to four explosive orgasms before leaving me trembling and naked in my bed. His last words before he left were a promise to make every one of my animals' abusers pay for their crimes. And for making me cry.

He comes to me almost every night, the exceptions so rare I can count them on one hand. We've learned how to work around Maren on the nights she stays over. I sneak back downstairs after she's asleep, and we close the pocket door at the entrance to the kitchen. More often than not, he has to gag me, muffling my sounds with his hand or my underwear pressed between my teeth.

My body shivers with the memories—his hands worshipping every curve, lifting and positioning me as if I'm weightless, pressing me against walls, over counters, across every surface in my house until they all bear the invisible imprint of our encounters. He always demands more from me, pushing my body past limits I didn't know I had. Even when I don't think my body can give it, it always does.

He still takes me from behind, his preferred way to claim me, his body clothed while I'm naked and bound beneath him. He hovers above me but never lets his full weight press down. His name remains a mystery locked behind his lips, and he never removes the mask. And still, after almost two months, he's never kissed me. Every part of me knows his touch except my mouth, which he guards against like it might break whatever spell keeps me his and elevate this to more than just anonymous fucking.

That's the most heartbreaking thing of all.

But with him, I've discovered a version of myself that I never knew existed—desired beyond reason and wanted with an intensity that borders on worship. Every previous sexual experience pales in comparison to the raw hunger he awakens in me.

It shocks me that I have no hesitation about giving my body to him—a stranger—night after night, bare and unguarded, with nothing between us. But how can someone who knows my body better than I do still be a stranger?

The familiar ache between my thighs pulses like a second heartbeat. My hand drifts there each morning now, pressing against the tender reminder of his possession, welcoming the sweet soreness that proves the previous night wasn't a dream. Is it weird that I'm getting used to it?

I don't recognize the woman staring back at me from the mirror anymore. I'm a constant disheveled mess. Exhaustion weighs on my shoulders from hours spent beneath him, but I wouldn't trade a single moment.

Except I'd give anything to have his mouth on mine, his full weight pressing me into the mattress, his face revealed in the morning light, and his real name whispered against my ear.

I guess there's a lot I would change if I could, even as I tell myself I'm content with what he gives me.

But if I'm honest, there's something thrilling about not knowing, about surrendering to a man whose face remains hidden. He binds me, bends me, takes what he wants, and makes me his in ways that feel both forbidden and inevitable. The anonymity and darkness surrounding his identity only amplify the fire he ignites.

I still haven't told Maren any of this, and she's stopped commenting on the dark circles under my eyes and the way I always move like I'm sore. She sees through every excuse I come up with but gives me space, waiting for me to crack, knowing it will only be a matter of time.

What I'm doing is beyond reckless. It's certifiably insane. He could kill me at any moment, and no one would know until someone discovered my plastic-wrapped corpse with a purple columbine pinned to my body.

But I don't fear him. Not like that.

Not anymore.

The contradiction makes no sense even to me. He doesn't hurt me, not really. He pins me down, chokes me until my vision blurs, and fucks me until I can't walk straight. But it's not the same as being hurt. Some nights, though, something darker radiates from him. The air between us feels charged with violence he's keeping on a leash. His grip tightens harder on those nights. His movements turn rougher and more punishing. Like he's trying to exorcise some inner demon through my body. My hips and throat bruise where his fingers dig in, my wrists ache from his hold, and purple marks bloom across my thighs.

But he never crosses the line into actual harm or something I can't handle. Never breaks me in a way I can't recover from.

Even the choking, when his hand closes around my throat and my lungs scream for air, somehow tips me over the edge. The orgasms that rip through me are so intense my vision goes black, then white, and for those suspended seconds, I'm untethered from my body, existing somewhere consciousness can't reach. Only sensation and ecstasy.

I turn at the sound of tires on gravel and see Karen's SUV pulling into the driveway. My stomach drops. I'm starting to hate that sound. It's nothing but a harbinger of bad news.

I slip through the gate. "Can you finish up with Mr. Snuffles? I'll be right back."

"Sure thing."

I walk toward the driveway, water still dripping from my clothes.

Karen exits her vehicle with that stern expression I'm too familiar with now. I meet her in front of the porch, aware of how ridiculous I must look—soaking wet, covered in soapsuds and pig hair, with mud caked on my boots.

"Luna."

"Karen. What brings you by today?"

"I need to speak with you about Odell Pearson."

My mouth goes dry. I've been waiting for this day, rehearsing this moment a hundred times, but now that it's here, I'm drowning.

"What about him?"

"His body was found this morning at Odessa Lake. Wrapped in plastic with a Rocky Mountain columbine taped to his body."

Why can't my wolf stop dumping bodies on trailheads?

I force my expression to remain neutral. "Again?"

"Yes. There was no note this time, but..." Karen hesitates. "Luna, I need to know about that day at Elk Fest. And what happened with Pearson and Damien Wolfe."

The mention of Damien's name makes my chest tighten. "Why don't you ask him?"

"I will. But I wanted to get your side of the story first."

My mind races. Damien had nothing to do with Pearson's death. I know exactly who killed him, and it wasn't my rich, handsome neighbor.

"Like the report says. Mr. Pearson tried to attack me. He was drunk and aggressive and tried to grab me, so Damien intervened."

"Intervened how, exactly?"

"He pinned him to the ground."

Karen nods, scribbling something in her notebook. "Have you ever witnessed Damien act violently before?"

"We don't know each other well. We'd only met a few times before that day."

Karen peers at me over her glasses. "What was he doing at your booth?"

"He was at the festival and stopped by to say hi, I guess. You really should talk to him if you want to know." I cross my arms, feeling defensive. "But what are you getting at with this, Karen? Why are you asking all these questions about Damien? You don't think he killed Odell Pearson, do you?"

"I'm investigating and following all leads. That's what I do, Luna."

"Well, you're going down the wrong path. Damien didn't kill him."

Her eyes narrow. "How do you know?"

"Because he's Damien Wolfe," I say, as if his name alone should explain everything. "He's a billionaire tech mogul who has no connection to Pearson or me, other than being in the wrong place at the wrong time."

"It sounds like it was the right time. Pearson weighed twice as much as you, Luna. He could have really hurt you."

"I'm grateful he was there. But you can't seriously think it's him. This is clearly the same person who killed all the others. Damien didn't even know me or the sanctuary when Daryl Rawlings and the Meyers were killed."

"But he moved to Aspen Ridge months prior, into a dilapidated house owned by a previous serial killer. That's a little odd for someone of his stature, don't you think?"

"Just because someone buys a property once owned by a serial killer doesn't make them one too."

"It's just interesting." Her tone is deceptively casual. "All these bodies started showing up right around that time. First on your property, then at remote locations around the county. That's quite a coincidence."

"It is a coincidence." My heart pounds so hard I'm sure she can hear it. "Karen, you're mistaken. Damien isn't capable of this."

The defensive edge in my voice surprises me. Why am I protecting him? Because he's innocent, yes, but also because... because I like him. More than I should, given my nighttime activities with my wolf.

"As you said, you hardly know the man. How can you be sure?"

"Because I do." The words sound petulant even to my own ears, but I double down anyway. "You're reaching, Karen."

The front door slams, and Maren's voice cuts through the tension.

"Morning, Sheriff Mills. This a social call or official business?" She bounds down the porch steps with her usual energy, but there's wariness in her eyes as she takes in the scene.

"Odell Pearson was found dead," I say.

Maren freezes on the bottom step. "Shit! Are you freaking kidding me? When? How?"

"This morning. Same MO as the others," Karen replies.

Maren's face darkens. "Good fucking riddance. That piece of shit had it coming."

"Maren." I shoot her a look, but she flicks her hand at me.

"What? I'm supposed to pretend I'm sad that the animal abuser is dead? Fuck that."

Karen doesn't react. Maren's outbursts stopped surprising her years ago.

"You were there when Pearson and Damien Wolfe had their altercation, correct?"

Maren glances at me, then back at Karen. "Yeah."

"Did you notice anything unusual about Mr. Wolfe's behavior?"

"Aside from how he took Pearson down like the Hulk in action?"

"What exactly does that mean?"

Why is she pressing this?

"It means that when that piece of shit lunged at Luna, Damien had him on the ground before any of us could even blink. It was hot as hell, honestly. Why are you asking about Damien, though?"

"She thinks it's odd that he moved here only a few months before our abusers started being killed. And because he was there when Pearson came at me, of course, that means he could be a suspect."

"I didn't say that, Luna." Karen gives me a look of disapproval. "Damien Wolfe has an impeccable reputation and no motive I can discern. I'm just asking questions in the normal course of investigating." She closes her notebook. "Now, I know I've asked you this before, but are you sure you can't think of anyone else who might harbor a grudge against you? Or want to harm you?"

Maren goes still beside me, biting her bottom lip. That nervous tell she's had since we've met. *Shit!* I know what that means.

"Luna." Maren's voice takes on that careful tone she uses when she's about to drop me into a shitstorm. "Do you still feel like someone's watching you?"

My vision blurs for a second. I shoot Maren the most murderous look I can manage, but she's already committed to this path. The traitor.

Karen's head whips toward me. "What?"

"It's nothing." The words tumble out too fast.

"Luna." All pretense of casual inquiry vanishes from Karen's voice. She's Sheriff Mills now. "What exactly have you been feeling?"

What I feel is both women staring at me, waiting. The air crackles with tension, and the silence stretches out like a rubber band about to snap. I'm going to murder Maren for bringing this up now.

I exhale. "For a while I felt—*emphasis on felt, past tense*—like someone was out in the woods, watching from the tree line. But it was around the same time you told me about the poachers. I'm sure that's what it was."

The lie rolls off my tongue like I've rehearsed it a hundred times. When did this become who I am? Someone who lies without flinching?

"Why didn't you tell me this before?" Karen's voice rises with frustration. "Luna, this is exactly the kind of thing I need to know about!"

"Because it was nothing! Woods surround my property, and woods are creepy, especially at night. I can't call you every time I get creeped out, Karen. You'd never get any real work done."

"The hell you can't! It's five bodies now, Luna. And you thought someone watching you was irrelevant? That feeling is not paranoia. That's your instinct trying to keep you alive."

Maren nods. "She's right, Lu. I know I teased you at first, it might be sexy to have a stalker, but this shit is getting disturbing as fuck now."

"You're only finding this disturbing now?" Karen stares at Maren like she's lost her mind.

Maren has the good sense to look sheepish, but I want to strangle her for starting this.

Karen turns back to me. "Has your security system caught anything unusual? Any footage of anyone on your property?"

No, because my stalker keeps hacking in and erasing the recordings.

"Nothing."

"I need you to be very careful, Luna." Karen's voice softens, taking on an almost maternal tone. "Keep your doors locked at all times. Make sure your cameras are always on and recording. And if you notice anything unusual—anything at all—or if you feel like someone is watching you again, you call me immediately. Day or night, I don't care. Promise me."

"I will." Another lie, so smooth it scares me.

But I'm not in any danger. My wolf poses no danger to me, but I can't tell either of them that.

I'm going to kill Maren for this, and I'm going to kill my wolf for continuing to single me out. He needs to stop and understand that these "gifts" are drawing too much attention.

"I mean it, Luna." Karen tucks her notebook away and fixes me with a serious stare. "Promise me you'll be smart about this."

"I promise." This time, I almost mean it.

As soon as Karen's SUV disappears down the driveway, I whirl on Maren with all the fury I've been holding back.

"Why the hell did you bring that up to her?"

"Because you didn't." Maren crosses her arms, jutting out her chin. "I warned you I'd tell her if the feeling didn't stop, and you said nothing."

"It did stop! I told you I've felt nothing for weeks. There's no one watching me, Maren."

She steps closer, her voice dropping to that dangerous level she uses when she's really pissed but trying to stay calm. "But there's another body, Lu. Whoever's doing this is obsessed with you and your animals. I don't give a flying fuck he's killing off those worthless sacks of shit. But I do care if whoever it is might be a danger to you." Her voice breaks on the last words. "He'll have to go through me to get to you, Luna. I swear to God. Over my dead fucking body."

The raw emotion in her voice, the way she'd put herself between me and danger without hesitation—this is why I'll love Maren until my last breath. I surge forward and wrap my arms around her, crushing her against me. My face presses into her shoulder.

"I love you. Even though I want to kick your ass for ratting me out to Karen."

"I fucking love you too, you stubborn bitch. Now get off me." She pushes me away with a laugh and an exaggerated gagging sound. "You're all wet, and you smell like pig shit and Mr. Snuffles. You need a shower."

I wave my hand over my body. "I just got one."

"A real one. And now you've gotten me wet, damn it."

Maren heads to the house to change, and I make my way back to where Tate is finishing up with Mr. Snuffles. The pig looks considerably cleaner and seems quite pleased with himself, while Tate looks like he's been through the ringer—clothes soaked through and glasses sitting crooked on his nose.

"How'd it go with the sheriff?" He squeezes water from his shirt.

"The usual. More questions about things I don't have answers to." I grab a towel and start drying Mr. Snuffles, who leans into the attention. "Thanks for handling him while I was gone."

"No problem. Though I think he enjoyed getting me soaked more than getting clean."

I laugh, and for a moment, the normalcy of it—working with animals, mentoring an eager student, the simple pleasure of caring for creatures that need us—almost makes me forget about the complex web of lies I'm weaving.

Almost.

But as the sun climbs higher and I think about the long day ahead, my mind is already racing toward tonight and the conversation I need to have with my wolf about his body-dumping habit.

Chapter Thirty-Seven

Luna

I step out the front door after my shower to see Maren strolling up the driveway like she doesn't have a care in the world, our resident mountain goat Gertie trotting beside her on her bright green leash.

A smile tugs at the corners of my mouth. Maren has her phone balanced in one hand, thumb swiping across the screen, while Gertie does her own thing—sniffing at every blade of grass and trying to eat Maren's shoelaces.

Then Gertie spots me, and her ears perk up. She lets out an excited bleat that makes my chest warm. Before I can even call out to her, she's pulling Maren toward me with surprising determination.

"Whoa, whoa!" Maren yelps, nearly dropping her phone as Gertie drags her forward.

"Hey there, pretty girl." I laugh as she reaches me, running my hands over her soft ears as she pushes her face into my stomach, her warm breath seeping through my sweatshirt as she bleats a happy hello that vibrates against my ribs.

Maren tucks a strand of dark hair behind her ear and grins at me. "I swear this goat has separation anxiety when it comes to you. Very clingy. Reminds me of that guy I dated in college who—"

Roger's truck barrels up the driveway, kicking up dust behind its wheels, and rescuing me from yet another retelling of Maren's collegiate exploits. I know them all because I lived through every wild adventure right beside her.

"He's making a habit of showing up here, driving like an F1 driver."

Her playful demeanor evaporates as she leads Gertie toward her enclosure, securing the gate before running back to stand beside me, her face already set in that focused expression she gets when shit's about to hit the fan.

Roger screeches to a stop in front of us, gravel spraying everywhere. He's out of the driver's seat before the engine stops, and his expression makes my heart rate spike because whatever's in the back of that truck is bad. Really bad.

"Luna! Thank God you're here." He rushes to the back of his truck. "Got a male black bear, about four hundred pounds. Shotgun wounds to the hindquarters."

My stomach drops. "Hunters?"

"Yeah. Rich assholes hunting on private land." Roger's voice is tight as he yanks the back doors open. "Tranq'd him on site, but he's lost a lot of blood."

"Black Bear Rifle season ended three days ago." Maren gives me a hand as I jump into the back of the truck to help Roger. Inside lies an enormous black bear, its glossy fur matted with blood around its massive haunches. Even sedated, he's a breathtaking beast, powerful muscles rippling beneath his coat with each shallow breath.

Maren exhales. "Now that's a big boy."

I'm already calculating what we'll need. "Mar, go get Ethan from inside. Tell him to grab the heavy-duty gurney. Then, prep the cell for surgery. We need fluids, antibiotics, and the portable X-ray."

"On it!"

She runs toward the building while I assess the situation. The bear is a behemoth, easily four hundred pounds of solid muscle and fur.

"How long has he been under?" I ask, checking his breathing as we wait.

"About forty minutes," Roger says, sweat beading on his forehead. "Had to dart him twice. First dose didn't fully take."

"What happened?"

Roger's face darkens. "Sheriff got a call from a landowner about gunshots on her property. Found these city types with a guide. Four men trespassing, hunting without permits, didn't give a shit that the season was over. They'd already wounded the bear when she arrived on the scene and immediately called the sheriff. Sheriff called me."

"How'd you get him in the truck on your own?"

"I didn't. Rhonda was there, and the owner's handyman helped. But then dispatch called about a pack of coyotes running loose in downtown Estes, so she had to detour there."

"Shit."

Ethan rounds the corner from behind the building, maneuvering the gurney over the uneven ground. He halts, running his hands through his sandy hair as he spots the bear. "What's the damage?"

"Multiple shotgun pellets to the hindquarters. We need to get him into the reinforced cell for surgery."

Ethan nods. We built the cell a year and a half ago, after I treated a grizzly and it almost mauled me. It's designed to handle large, dangerous animals while still allowing us to provide medical care.

"Did Karen arrest them?"

We position the heavy-duty gurney outside the truck's doors.

"You bet your ass she did. She's got them in custody right now. But you know how this goes. They'll probably just get a fine and a slap on the wrist."

The familiar rage bubbles up inside me. "Of course they will. Some rich guys looking for a trophy, and this beautiful animal pays the price."

The bear's vitals are stable but weakening with each passing minute.

"Roger, if you can help us get him inside, we should be good," Ethan says.

"You bet."

We move the gurney as close to the truck as possible. Even with the three of us, moving four hundred pounds of unconscious bear is going to be a bitch.

"On three." I grip the heavy tarp beneath him, and my muscles tense in preparation. "One, two, three!"

We slide the massive animal onto the gurney with grunts of effort. The bear's weight settles with a heavy thud that makes the steel of the reinforced stretcher creak.

"Christ, he's heavy," Ethan mutters.

We roll him toward the building's rear entrance, where we can go right into the medical area. The wheels strain against the weight, requiring all three of us to push.

"Thanks for getting him to us, Roger," I say as we navigate through the double doors. "I know it wasn't easy."

"Just save him. Those bastards don't deserve to win this one."

Maren has already transformed the reinforced cell into a surgical suite. The cell itself is built like a fortress—steel bars thick enough to contain a grizzly, with a door that can be locked in seconds. Inside, she's set up everything we need: surgical table, lights, monitoring equipment, instrument trays, and IV stands.

"Beautiful work, Mar," I tell her as we transfer the bear onto the surgical table inside the cell. Like the gurney, it's also custom-built, reinforced steel that can handle the weight and movement of large animals.

Roger helps us get the bear positioned, then steps back. "I'll leave you to it. Call me when you know how he's doing."

"Will do," Ethan says, pulling on surgical gloves.

I locate a vein in the bear's massive foreleg and slide the IV needle in. Its fur is coarser than it looks, and finding the vein through all that muscle takes concentration.

"Blood pressure's low," Maren says, attaching monitoring equipment. "Pulse is steady but weak."

I put on my headlamp and examine the wound. Multiple shotgun pellets have torn through the bear's flesh, leaving a ragged, bloody mess. Some are lodged deep. I can see them glinting under my light like malevolent stars.

"I need to get these pellets out before infection sets in."

"I'll assist." Ethan takes a position across from me. "Maren, monitor his vitals and keep an eye on the sedation level."

"Got it." She settles at the monitoring station we've positioned outside the cell door. Close enough to help, far enough to run if things go sideways.

I think of my wolf. Would he go after these men if he knew about this bear? The thought sends an unwelcome thrill through me, even in the middle of this crisis.

"Luna?" Ethan's voice pulls me back to the present. "You ready?"

I push away thoughts I shouldn't be having and concentrate.

"Let's do this."

I extract pellet after pellet, dropping them into a metal dish with soft pings that keep my anger simmering. So much damage from a few seconds of human cruelty. Ethan's hands are steady as he assists, holding retractors and passing instruments with the seamless coordination we've developed over years of working together.

Hunting is a way of life in Colorado. I've come to accept that, but I hate trophy hunting. I hate that gunning down animals for sport is legal anywhere. Hunting for food, for sustenance, for survival, is one thing. I understand the necessity. But killing just so a person can hang a trophy on their wall or spread it across their floor as a rug has always warred with my need to save and protect these animals.

The bear's massive paw twitches, and we freeze.

"Maren. Check the sedation level."

She glances at the monitors. "Should be fine for another thirty minutes, at least."

But the bear's breathing has changed, becoming shallower and more irregular. Another twitch, this time more pronounced. My heart rate spikes.

"He's waking up," Maren says, her voice tight with alarm. "His metabolism's burning through it faster than we thought."

"Mar, push more sedative into that line." Ethan's voice is low and steady, but tension radiates from his shoulders. "How much time do you still need?"

"Two pellets. Both deep. Two minutes, maybe less."

The bear's entire leg convulses, and I jerk my hands back. Adrenaline crashes through my veins.

"Luna, you need to step back. The IV line is clogged." Urgency sharpens Maren's voice.

"Give me ninety seconds." I focus on the glint of metal deep in muscle tissue.

A growl builds in the bear's chest, low at first, then louder. The sound vibrates through the cell and through my bones. Every hair on my neck stands up, a primal response to a sound humans are evolutionarily programmed to fear.

"Luna." Ethan's voice is deadly calm. "Back away. Now!"

I should listen, but I'm so close. One last pellet, and he'll be clear of the worst debris.

"Almost there." Sweat drips down my temple as I maneuver the forceps. "Almost—"

The bear roars. His eyes snap open, and four hundred pounds of terrified, wounded predator explode into motion on my surgical table.

Everything happens at once.

The table collapses beneath his weight. Instruments scatter in a metallic symphony of chaos, and Maren shouts over the din.

"Luna, get the fuck out of there!"

Time slows down. A massive paw swings toward my face, three-inch claws that could disembowel me with a single swipe gleaming under the overhead lights. Fear freezes me in place, my body refusing to process the command to move.

Something slams into me from the side as Maren tackles me, throwing us both to the floor as the bear's claws tear through the air where I stood a heartbeat earlier. White-hot pain explodes across my shoulder as one claw catches me during the fall, tearing through flesh like it's paper.

"Out! Out! OUT!" Ethan grabs both of us, rolling us toward the door.

We scramble out of the cell in a tangle of limbs, and Ethan slams the steel door shut with a resounding clang. The lock engages with a solid click as the bear lunges toward us, his massive paws hitting the bars with enough force to make them ring like bells.

Tate bursts through from the reception area. "What the hell happened?"

For a moment, we all stand there panting, watching the furious black bear pace inside the cell, roaring in anger and pain. He's magnificent and terrifying, wild eyes fixed on us through the bars.

"That was too fucking close." Ethan forces the words out between ragged breaths.

"Luna!" Maren grabs me as my knees buckle. Her face fills with horror. "Shit. You're bleeding bad."

I look down at my shoulder. The bear's claw has left a deep gash from my collarbone across my shoulder. Blood is flowing freely, warm and sticky against my skin. The adrenaline starts to ebb, and pain floods in to replace it.

"Not arterial," I say through gritted teeth, professional assessment kicking in even as my knees threaten to buckle again. "Just messy."

"We need to get you to the hospital." Ethan guides me to a chair, pressing a large towel against my shoulder. "Maren, keep the pressure on that."

"No hospital." I can't deal with the thought of having to drive all the way to Estes Park, sit in an ER for hours, and explain what happened. "You can stitch me up here."

"Luna—" Maren starts, biting her lip as her gaze darts between my face and my shoulder.

"No hospital." My words are final as I cover her shaking hand with mine. "You can stitch me up, Ethan."

A silent conversation passes between them, and Ethan's jaw tightens before he sighs. They both know that fighting my stubbornness is a losing battle.

"Fine, but we're doing this properly. Full sterile protocol, and if there's any sign of complications, you're going to the ER whether you like it or not."

"Deal." Relief floods through me even as the pain digs deeper.

"Maren, take her into the OR. Start an IV with morphine and prep the suture kit. Let me get this guy back under."

She nods and takes a breath as her professional mask slips back into place, but I know Maren; she's going to crash once this is all over.

"Tate, help me."

At her request, Tate crosses the room in three strides. He scoops me up like I weigh nothing. Pain tears through my shoulder, white-hot and vicious. A scream rips from my throat. He carries me across the hall into the small operating room, moving as gently as someone carrying a bomb. Sweat slicks my forehead. I bite down hard when Tate lowers me onto the table, but a cry still escapes. Everything blurs, tears flooding my vision. The adrenaline drains away, leaving nothing but fire, and each heartbeat sends another wave of agony from my shoulder blade to my fingertips.

"Thanks, Tate. Can you watch things up front while we take care of Luna?"

"Yeah. Let me know if you need anything."

He squeezes my hand once, worry etching lines onto his face. Then he's gone. Maren grabs scissors and cuts through my sweatshirt. Panic flutters in my chest for a second as the fabric falls away. What if she sees the marks my wolf leaves on my throat, the fingerprints that betray our twisted nights together? But his touch has been gentler this week, less brutal since he hasn't killed anyone. My skin is clear and unmarked, and the relief that washes through me is almost as powerful as the pain.

She finds a vein on the first try and inserts the IV with steady hands, pushing the morphine through. I have to strangle the scream building in my throat, grinding my teeth together until the drug spreads through my system and my muscles finally surrender to the table beneath me.

The bear's claw ripped clean through my bra strap, so Maren pins the loose fabric under my arm to keep me covered. She switches out the bloody towel, guiding my other hand up to hold it in place.

"Press on that. You're losing too much blood, Lu." Her hands are steadier now. "I need to get the suture kit prepped."

I do the best I can as I watch Ethan through the open door extend an injection pole and deliver the sedative into the bear's massive hindquarter. The bear swipes at the pole but misses.

"That should keep him out for a while." Ethan rushes into the operating room. "Long enough for us to patch you up and finish the surgery. Do you have a pair of sterile forceps?"

Maren nods. "Yeah. I ran everything through the autoclave yesterday."

She disappears into the walk-in closet where we store sterilized equipment.

Ethan moves to the sink and scrubs his hands while looking back at me. "I don't want to put in staples because we're too close to bone, but I want to get some internal sutures in there to reduce some of the tension on the outer layer."

Maren comes back with several vacuum-sealed packages and sets them on a tray beside me. Then she takes Ethan's place at the sink as he walks over to me, snapping on latex gloves. He pulls the towel back to examine the wound. "It actually doesn't look too bad, Luna. I still want to put internal stitches in because it's your shoulder."

Pain drowns out most of his words, but I nod, trusting him to do what's right.

"First, we have to irrigate and clean. I need to get a better look at it."

Maren steps up beside the table. "Okay, babe, we've got to be quick about this, and it's going to be painful and bloody as fuck, so I need you to be brave." Maren squeezes my hand, as much to encourage herself as me. She bleeds along with the people she loves when they're hurt, but being strong for them is her superpower.

I squeeze back. "You guys got this."

Ethan starts cleaning the wound, and the world explodes. A scream tears from somewhere deep inside me. My eyes roll back, and everything goes black.

⸺◆⸺

The next time I surface, Maren's brushing my sweaty hair from my forehead, her fingers cool against my fevered skin. I turn my face toward her palm, seeking the relief of that coolness, leaning into her touch.

"All done. You missed all the excitement, Lu."

"How bad is it?" I try to crane my neck, hissing through clenched teeth. Pain shreds through me.

"You're incredibly lucky it didn't hit anything vital." Ethan appears beside me. "Few inches to the left, and he would have caught your throat."

"Lucky me."

My tongue feels thick. The words come out slurred.

Ethan says something to Maren about the morphine level. His mouth moves, but the words don't quite register.

"Hey." I give them both a dirty look. "Don't pull that back."

"We're not. I'm having her up it a little. You can take oral meds tonight, but we need to stay ahead of the pain."

"Yeah, you think it's bad now; it's going to hurt like fuck once the adrenaline wears off."

I grab Maren's hand and kiss it rather than reply. The new dose hits my system like a warm wave.

"You lie here and rest while we finish up with our cranky patient."

Ethan walks out as I struggle to sit up. "No. I want to—"

"Lu, you need to rest." Maren places a hand on my uninjured shoulder, trying to guide me back down. I shrug her off, swallowing a cry as pain lances through my arm.

"I can observe."

"You're such a fucking control freak." Maren shakes her head but slides an arm around my waist to support me. I lift her hand to my lips in apology.

She sets me up in a chair outside the cell, covering me with a blanket and adjusting the morphine IV on its stand beside me. Then she and Ethan work together to complete the surgery. It kills me not to be helping, but I know my limitations. One-handed surgery while under the influence of narcotics is a recipe for disaster.

As they clean and dress the wound, I study the bear's massive form. Even unconscious, he radiates power and wildness. This is why I built this sanctuary, why I push myself beyond exhaustion day after day. For creatures like him, who have no voice against human cruelty and selfishness, even when they try to kill me.

"Those fuckers better get jail time."

I mutter it more to myself than anyone else. Neither Ethan nor Maren pays attention to me. They're too focused on the bear.

Thirty minutes later, with Tate's help, Maren leads me back to my house.

"Nappy-nappy time for Luna. And yes, that's a medical term."

I snort against Tate's neck as he carries me up the stairs.

As Maren helps me into my pajamas and tucks me into bed, I can't deny the dark truth growing inside me. The wound in my shoulder throbs with each pulse of blood, and beneath the pain lives something else. Hope. The twisted kind. That somehow the news will reach my wolf. That he'll know what happened before he comes to me tonight. That vengeance will find those hunters without me having to voice the desire out loud.

Chapter Thirty-Eight

Damien

The numbers on my screen blur as I stare at the acquisition proposal, but my mind isn't on the tech company we're discussing. It's on Luna. It's always on Luna. I've been so busy going over these documents with Cade this morning, I haven't even checked the cameras to see how her day is going.

"The valuation seems fair." Cade riffles through a stack of papers on his desk. The sound drags me out of my thoughts of Luna. "Guardian Matrix Solutions' AI algorithms would integrate perfectly with our existing infrastructure. This deal is solid. No red flags at all in their docs. And the price is right."

I nod, forcing myself to focus on his words. Athena lifts her head from her bed in the corner, her scarred ears perking up. She's better than any security system. She senses when someone's coming long before I do.

"The board meeting is scheduled for—" Cade stops mid-sentence as his eyes narrow at something on his screen. "You've got company."

I turn toward the window as Sheriff Mills' SUV pulls to a stop in front of the house. I press the speaker button on my desk phone. Tiffany, my executive assistant, picks up on the first ring.

"Yes, Mr. Wolfe?"

"Did Sheriff Mills call looking for me?"

"Yes. She said she had some questions about the incident at Elk Fest. I told her you were working out of your office up there today. I sent you a DM twenty minutes ago to let you know she was on her way."

I glance at the screen to my left, where my DMs appear. I was so wrapped up in the call with Cade, I missed their coming in.

"Okay. Next time, call me in addition to sending the DM.

"Yes, sir."

I hang up, then rise to my feet, shoving my chair back so hard it hits the wall behind me. "I'll call you back."

"Damien, wait—"

I disconnect the call and smooth my expression into something appropriately curious and welcoming. By the time Karen Mills knocks on my front door, I'm the picture of an innocent billionaire, willing to answer any question she may have.

"Sheriff Mills. My EA told me you'd be stopping by."

She studies my face with those keen cop eyes of hers. Karen Mills is good at her job—I've done my research—but she's also predictable in the way most law enforcement is. They look for patterns, for evidence, for logical connections. They don't look for monsters hiding in plain sight, wearing expensive suits.

"Mr. Wolfe, I was hoping we could chat about what happened at Elk Fest. With Odell Pearson."

"Of course." I step aside to let her in.

She follows me through the dilapidated hallway, her eyes taking in the peeling wallpaper and scuffed woodwork. I can almost hear her thoughts. Why would a billionaire live and work in a place like this? The answer is simple but twofold: because this house holds ghosts that understand me and because it's close to Luna.

Her expression shifts as I lead her into my office, a stark contrast to the rest of the house. Athena pads over to investigate our visitor, her tail wagging.

"Beautiful dog," she says, extending her hand for Athena to sniff.

"Rescue." I watch as my girl decides Karen is acceptable.

She settles into the chair across from my desk, pulling out her notebook. "I've read the reports, but I wanted to get your account of what happened with Mr. Pearson that day."

I lean back in my chair, projecting casual confidence. "It was pretty straight-forward. I was visiting Luna's booth, and Pearson started harassing her."

"Harassing her how?"

"Verbally at first. Calling her names, getting aggressive. Then he lunged at her. Tried to grab her." My jaw tightens at the memory. "No one should ever lay a hand on a woman like that."

"So you intervened."

"I did what anyone would do. I stopped him." Our eyes lock across the desk. "I won't apologize for defending Luna, Sheriff. Pearson was twice her size and clearly violent."

She scribbles something in her notebook. "According to witnesses, you took him down quite efficiently. Do you have any military or law enforcement back-ground?"

I almost smile at that. If only she knew the kind of training I've given myself over the years. "I work out regularly."

"Have you had any other interactions with Pearson? Before or after that day?"

"None. I'd never seen him before in my life. Why?"

"He was found murdered this morning."

I keep my face neutral. "What does that have to do with me?"

"Nothing at this point. What about the other individuals who've been found dead recently? Daryl Rawlings, Thomas and Bertha Meyers, Raymond Davis, and Calvin Whitmore?"

I let confusion cross my features. "I'm sorry, what about them?"

"Did you know any of them?"

"No. Should I?" I lean forward. "Sheriff, what exactly are you getting at here?"

She closes her notebook with a snap. "Probably nothing. Just following up on all leads." She stands, and I rise with her. "Thank you for your time, Mr. Wolfe."

"Of course. And Sheriff?" I pause at the door, letting my voice soften with practiced concern. "I hope you catch whoever's doing this. Luna doesn't deserve to live in fear."

After I escort her out and watch her SUV disappear down the driveway, I return to my office. I reach for the keyboard to call Cade back, but when the screen lights up, his face is already there.

"You never disconnected." He's so fucking nosy sometimes.

Cade's expression is grim as he leans forward. "I heard every word. Damien, this is fucking reckless."

I drop into my chair, the leather creaking under my weight. "She doesn't have anything on me."

"She doesn't need to have anything on you right now. She's asking questions, connecting dots, and you're making it easy for her by dropping bodies around like fucking party favors."

"You need to get over this. I told you I know what I'm doing."

"They're evidence." Irritation sharpens Cade's words. "Evidence that's going to lead back to you if you keep this up. You're acting like a lovesick teenager leaving dead roses on his crush's doorstep."

"Watch it."

"No, you watch it. You think Luna's worth throwing away everything we've built? Everything you've accomplished?"

An animalistic snarl erupts from my chest at the mention of Luna's name.

"She's worth everything!"

I turn to stare out the window toward the woods that separate our properties. He's right. For twenty-five years, I've been meticulous. Every kill planned to perfection, every body disposed of, vanishing from the world. And no one ever suspected me.

Then Luna walked into my life with her fierce protectiveness, her righteous anger, and her beautiful soul. And I started making mistakes. Started taking risks.

"The sheriff has nothing. She's fishing."

"She's a good cop doing her job. And good cops eventually catch criminals when they get sloppy." Cade's voice loses its bite. "You're not sloppy, Damien. You never have been. Don't start now." He pauses. "Should I hack into the county law enforcement database and see what she has?"

"No, don't waste your time. I'm telling you, she has nothing. I've left no traces."

He nods, but I know that look. He'll do it anyway because protecting me, sometimes even from myself, is what he does.

"You have to reinstate proper disposal protocols for all your targets, even Luna's."

"I'll think about it."

"Damien—"

"I said I'll think about it. Move on."

Athena pads over and rests her head on my foot. I crouch and scratch behind her ears, and she wiggles her body in response, her tail thumping against the floor.

"Well, think hard because I'd prefer we both stay out of jail." He glances at the screen to his right. "I have to go. MJ is calling me."

After we end the call, I sit back in my chair, staring out at the tree line. Luna is less than half a mile away. I could be there in minutes, but I have to wait until dark to go to her. I hate not being able to see her during the day because I lose my fucking mind and ask her to dinner, or try to, every time I do.

That doesn't mean I can't watch her.

I switch the monitors over to the sanctuary's cameras, expecting a glimpse of her usual routine. Instead, my heart stops.

What the fuck!

Luna is sitting outside the reinforced cell she showed me during my tour of the sanctuary, slumped in a chair like a broken doll. A massive black bear is inside with Maren and the other vet. But it's Luna who has my full attention. She's covered with a blanket, under which she is clearly shirtless. Her left arm is secured in a sling, and her face is pale with shock and pain.

My hands shake as I lean closer to the screen, every protective instinct I've ever possessed roars at me to get to her. She's alive, but she looks like she's been through hell.

Before I lose my fucking mind and tear over there like a lunatic, I force myself to rewind the footage.

I watch the events of the last couple of hours in fast forward, stopping at intervals to listen and see more closely. Even with Luna sitting safe in that chair, the images on screen steal the air from my lungs.

I skip ahead to the current feed. Luna is outside the cell, looking like a bear attacked her, yet she refuses to leave until she knows the bear is fine. That's my Luna—bleeding and broken but still putting everyone else first.

This is a new kind of rage for me. Not the cold, calculated anger I feel toward the animal abusers I hunt. This is pure, primal fury, the kind that makes men tear apart mountains with their bare hands.

I should have been there.

I find her standing in front of the living room window, moonlight bathing her in an ethereal glow that makes her look angelic. Even with her arm in a sling.

The sight of that fucking thing fills my entire body with a fresh surge of fury. The world went silent, and my heart froze when that bear woke and swiped at her. For a split second that felt like an eternity, I watched my entire life crashing down in front of me until Maren tackled Luna out of the way just in time. The sound I made while watching it, something between a roar and a whimper, still echoes in my ears.

For saving Luna, that woman will receive anything she wants for the rest of her life. A house. A car. Hell, her own fucking island if she wants it.

I want to tear that bear limb from limb for what he did to Luna. But I don't hurt animals. He's wild, and wild animals act on pure, untamed instinct. It's how they're made, and blaming him for his reaction today is like blaming him for breathing. It was an accident, but it could have easily ended in tragedy. Tragedy that would have driven me to do something I vowed never to do. But if he'd killed her, I would have destroyed him without hesitation or remorse.

The assholes who shot that bear have now vaulted to the top of my list.

Luna turns and sees me, and she startles, the hand of her uninjured arm flying to her chest.

"Jesus, you have to stop creeping up on me like that."

I step further into the room. The mask feels heavier tonight somehow, like it's weighing down more than my face. I study her through the eyeholes. Her eyes are glassy, pupils blown wide, and her posture is more relaxed than usual, loose and fluid. How she usually is after I've fucked her into oblivion.

"What kind of fun drugs have you taken, little doe?"

Her lips curve into a crooked half-smile. There's something beautifully unguarded about her like this, with her walls lowered by pharmaceutical intervention.

"Ethan gave me a script for Oxy. I don't usually take anything for pain, but I needed it. Getting swiped by a bear hurts like a bitch."

"I imagine it does."

She tilts her head. "You don't seem surprised by my sling."

"I'm not."

Because I've been watching the footage on a loop, rewinding, watching her get hurt over and over again like some kind of masochistic ritual. Just to feel that soul-deep relief that she's alive rush through me like a drug.

Her face scrunches up into a frown that's somehow both adorable and indignant. "You're such a creep, hacking into my cameras. I should shut them off."

"Don't you fucking dare, Luna."

Not that it would matter if she did. They'd power back on within seconds. I have backups for my backups, layers of redundancy she can't begin to fathom.

"Damien Wolfe's firewalls suck. I should tell him."

She's talking to herself now, which pulls a smile from me. She's endured my spying since the first day, hating every second, but she's never disabled the cameras. What amuses me is her debate about whether to inform me... about me being a spying creep.

She walks toward me, her pace slow and unsteady, but even drugged, her body moves with that sultry sway that makes my mouth water and my cock twitch. The space between her eyebrows pinches, and her nose and mouth scrunch up again in an adorable little pout.

"I've got enough good drugs in my system, but you can't bind my hands tonight. It'll tear my stitches open and probably send me into shock from the pain."

Does she really think I'm going to fuck her?

The notion that she expects me to use her body when she's injured causes the beast and the man to wage war inside my chest.

"As much as I love you coming on my cock for hours, Luna, I think your body needs a break tonight."

Her face falls, disappointment warring with the haze of medication. "I can probably suck your cock. Since you only let me touch it sometimes, I can do it without my hands." Sadness laces her voice as she says the words. It hurts her that I deny her that intimacy. "Then I can lie back, and you can go down on me if you want."

I always want, little doe.

I came here to check on her, with no intention of anything else happening tonight, but the hopeful look on her face nearly undoes me. She needs our connection as much as I do, even when she's in pain.

I should deny her. A gentler man wouldn't even be tempted to take her like this, wouldn't consider using her body when she's hurt. But I'm not a gentle man.

For the first time, I want to be one. For her.

"Where's your friend? Didn't she stay with you?" I close the distance between us.

"Sleeping. She refused to leave me alone. Put me to bed a while ago. But I couldn't sleep, so I came down to wait for you."

My hand finds her face, fingers tracing the line of her jaw before settling against her cheek. Her lashes flutter once, then fall closed. She turns into my touch, her breath warming my palm as she exhales—a sensation that goes straight to my cock.

"I love when you touch me."

I love it too, Luna.

"Are you alright?"

My ribs feel like they're closing around my lungs as I take her in. She's wearing a loose button-down pajama top that's slid off her shoulder, exposing the edge of the bandage beneath the fabric. Blood has seeped through the dressing, a small dark circle spreading across the white material.

She shrugs and winces at the movement. "It's not the first time I've almost been mauled. I doubt it'll be the last."

I understand that what she does, especially in the mountains of Colorado, puts her in contact with dangerous animals. But this woman needs to take her own safety more fucking seriously.

She needs to be more careful about protecting what's mine.

I unbutton her nightshirt with careful fingers, pushing it to the side so I can see the bandage, and discover she's naked underneath. Somehow, I don't think Maren put her to bed without underwear. The bandage stretches the entire width of her collarbone and shoulder, stark white against her pale skin. I brush my fingers across it. She trembles under my touch, goosebumps rising on her exposed flesh.

"You need to take better care of yourself, Luna."

"I try."

"Try harder."

My voice comes out harsh, edged with the fear that's been a living thing inside me all afternoon. She flinches at the harshness of my tone.

"Oh, oh, oh!" She holds up one finger like she remembered something important, her drug-addled brain jumping tracks. "You need to stop dropping bodies everywhere."

My lips curve at her demand. "Oh, yeah? Why's that?"

"Because Karen came to me today."

I know this because I watched that footage after I saw the bear footage.

"She was asking about Mr. Pearson. They found his body."

"I know."

She huffs, the sound adorable even as her eyes flash with annoyance. "Of course you do. She thinks Damien Wolfe might be the killer. You have to stop. You can't let him be blamed for it because he defended me."

"Don't worry about Damien Wolfe, Luna. He can take care of himself."

Her features scrunch up into a scowl. "He's nice, and he shouldn't be sucspec… suspet… suspected of your crimes. I mean it. Stop."

The word trips over her tongue. Her need to defend Damien—to defend me from myself—makes my jaw clench. The absurdity doesn't make it less irritating.

"I won't stop killing them."

She sighs, her eyes betraying her internal conflict—how my actions clash with her Hippocratic oath.

"Fine, but stop leaving them to be found. God, don't serial killers have secret ways they dispose of bodies? Get it together and come up with something better to get rid of the evidence."

I chuckle under my breath at her pragmatic take on my crimes. "I'll stop leaving the bodies around, little doe. Will that make you happy?"

"Yes. I don't want you to get caught. But I also don't want Damien to be accused of something he didn't do. He's innocent."

He's not innocent. We're the farthest thing from it.

"Come on." I take her elbow and guide her up the stairs. "Time for bed."

"We should fuck down here so Maren doesn't hear." She leans close, drops her voice to what she believes is a conspiratorial whisper. Instead, it's loud enough to wake the dead.

"Shh. You're going to wake your friend. And I told you, no cock for you tonight."

She pouts as we reach her room and step inside, closing the door behind us. Her cats and Shadow are all settled in for the night, none of them worried about me being here with her. Her wolf lifts his head and gives me a look before resting it back on his paws.

Luna turns to me, swaying on her feet, as she eyes the bulge in my jeans. "Are you going to let me suck you? I need more meds first, but as soon as they kick in and the pain goes away, I'll be good to go."

"I said, not tonight."

Who knew I'd be the one to refuse sex? This woman has turned my world upside down in ways I'm still discovering.

"So, I can't come on your face, either?"

She sighs, pouting again as I re-button her shirt, before leading her to the bed. Her pajama bottoms and underwear lay discarded on the floor beside it.

"Hi pussies," she coos at the cats huddled at the foot of the bed. "That's what Maren calls them. I think she just likes to say the word pussy."

She snickers, and the sound is so genuine and unfiltered that it makes me smile.

I help her sit on the edge before picking up her pants. When I look back at her, she's lying on her back, slithering her body up toward the pillows, wriggling her naked ass against the sheets as she tries to get comfortable.

I guess no pajama bottoms.

The cats slink up the mattress and tuck themselves beside her. She turns her face and presses a kiss to the fat one that's settled next to her head.

I toss her pants aside. "Where are your meds, Luna?"

She points to her bathroom.

I grab the bottle, filling a cup with water, before returning to the bedroom.

She's sprawled in the middle of the bed, the soft satin covering her torso, but her lower half bare. Her thighs are parted, and the sight tempts me to give her what she asked for. Then, a soft snore escapes her mouth.

Her perfection takes my breath away.

I give her a gentle shake. "Luna, you need to take your meds."

Her eyes flutter open, and she glares at me. "I'm trying to sleep."

I sit on the bed beside her and urge her to sit up.

"You can go back to sleep as soon as you swallow this pill."

She opens her mouth, and I put the pill on her tongue. She takes two deep swallows of water, some of it dribbling down her chin, before handing the glass back to me.

I help her lie back so she doesn't jostle her shoulder. The cats resettle around her. Then I maneuver the duvet over her while she grumbles something about stupid masked wolves cockblocking her. But she's already drifting, the medication making her eyelids heavy.

"Sleep, beautiful." I brush a strand of hair from her face.

I move to the chair across the room, watching as her breathing deepens and evens out. In sleep, she always looks younger than her thirty-two years, more vulnerable. The fierce wildlife vet who faces down bears and animal abusers is gone, replaced by this soft, trusting woman who lets a masked stranger into her home and her body.

I've been telling myself this is just sex, an arrangement that satisfies us both. But today, something changed. I can't define it, but the crushing weight in my chest when she was hurt and the icy fear that gripped me when I thought I might lose her went far beyond mere lust.

This feeling is foreign to me because I'm incapable of love. But as I sit here watching her, I can almost pretend otherwise.

Chapter Thirty-Nine

Luna

The Rocky Mountain Roadhouse is packed tonight, a typical Friday in Estes Park when tourists and locals alike seek refuge from the mountain chill in alcohol and conversation. Maren and I claim two stools at the far end of the bar, away from the worst of the noise but still within sight of the small dance floor where a few couples are already swaying to country music.

"To not getting eaten by bears!" Maren raises her tequila shot with a wicked grin.

I laugh and lift my own. "To having friends who know how to drug you and stitch you up afterward."

We clink glasses and down the shots. The tequila burns a path down my throat, sending warmth through my limbs. My shoulder still aches, but I've taken just enough pain medication to keep it manageable without interfering with the alcohol. No more narcotics, only high-dose prescription NSAIDs. One night of drinking with Maren won't hurt me.

"God, I need this." Maren signals the bartender for another round. "Do you know how long it's been since we had a proper girls' night?"

"Too long." The tension in my shoulders starts to ease. Between the sanctuary's constant demands and my wolf, social outings have fallen off my radar. Just thinking about him sends a flutter through my stomach, and I push the thought away. Not tonight. Tonight is about normalcy.

Maren studies my face with narrowed eyes. "There's something different about you lately."

I resist the urge to fidget under her scrutiny.

"Must be all those adrenaline rushes from nearly dying." I accept my second shot from the bartender. "Nothing like a bear attack to put some color in your cheeks."

Maren snorts. "Right. That's definitely it." She leans closer, lowering her voice. "I was hoping you'd say Mr. Sexy Superhero finally came over and fucked your brains out."

I choke out a laugh. "I've barely been able to lift my arm in weeks, Mar. What makes you think I'm up for the horizontal tango with anyone?"

But I've been having plenty of sex since nine days after Huck, our huckleberry-loving black bear, attacked me. My wolf went easy on me the first two weeks, using his mouth more than his cock while I healed. Then, when we'd both reached our breaking point, he was careful with my shoulder and stitches. He laid me on my back and spread my thighs with his hands as he plunged into me until my body gave him everything he demanded.

But yesterday my stitches came out, and last night, for the first time in weeks, he zip-tied my wrists behind my back and took me apart piece by piece. The pleasure tore through me so hard I sobbed, relief and ecstasy tangled together. I hadn't known how much I'd been starving for his control until I had it back.

One orgasm was all I could handle before the pain broke through and my body protested. But it was enough to restore something between us. Thank God for prescription pain relievers.

Maren hands me another shot. "Getting mauled is the worst kind of cock-blocking, isn't it?" She lets out a dramatic sigh. "Shame, though. That man is walking sex."

"He is hot," I agree, because denying Damien's attractiveness is futile at this point.

I flag the bartender down and ask for a glass of water. I need to stay hydrated so I don't get too drunk.

"His loss." Maren scans the room before looking back at me. "Seriously, Luna, I know I've said this a hundred times, but you need to hit that." She's grinning now, warming to her subject. "Any man who looks like that, carries himself like that, and has a package below the belt like his—"

I give her a pointed look, and she throws up her hands in mock surrender. "I didn't break the best friend code. I can't help where my eyes go sometimes." She motions to the bartender for another shot, then leans closer again. "But any man with all those attributes could fuck a woman until her head popped clean off."

I burst out laughing; the absurdity of her statement is exactly what I need right now. "Now that's an image."

"I know, right?" She laughs with me. "But it would be a hell of a way to go."

I don't feel jealous when Maren jokes about Damien this way. I don't feel possessive or threatened because despite his good looks, obvious interest in me, and my undeniable attraction to him, Damien and I are nothing. We've exchanged pleasantries and had a few conversations. He asked me to dinner, which we have yet to be able to coordinate our schedules to have, and yeah, he defended me from Pearson, but that's it. I'm insanely attracted to him, but I have no claim on him.

But if Maren had made those comments about my wolf, I'd be furious. The realization hits hard. I'd be seething with jealousy and burning with possessiveness. Because he's mine.

Mine.

The thought is so primitive, so unlike my rational, scientific self, that it takes my breath away. But it's true. Just as he whispers to me in the dark that I belong to him—that he's claiming me, branding me, making me his—I've been doing the same. In my mind, he's mine. My body is his, but his pleasure is mine to give. His groans of satisfaction are mine to elicit. His obsession is mine to cultivate.

"Earth to Luna." Maren waves a hand in front of my face. "Hello? Where'd you go just now?"

I blink, realizing I've been staring into space, trapped in my own forbidden thoughts. "Sorry. Just thinking about the sanctuary."

"Liar," she says, but there's no heat in it. "But fine, keep your secrets. For now."

Two men sidle up to our corner of the bar. They're both in their early thirties, handsome in that outdoorsy Colorado way, with well-groomed stubble and expensive North Face jackets over jeans. The taller one has intelligent eyes that crinkle at the corners.

"Ladies." His voice comes out deep, confident without tipping into arrogance. "Can we interest you in another round?"

Maren's eyes light up with mischief. She loves this game, even though we both know how it ends.

"Depends." She turns to face them. "Are you guys rescue workers? Because my friend here just survived a bear attack."

Their eyes widen as they both turn to me.

"No shit?" The shorter one leans against the bar beside me. His voice has a slight East Coast accent. "That sounds like a story worth hearing."

"She's a wildlife vet. Has her own sanctuary." Maren loves bragging about me and what we do. "Saves wild animals for a living and occasionally gets mauled for her trouble."

"That's impressive." The taller one slides onto the empty stool beside Maren. "I'm Brian, by the way. This is Mark."

We introduce ourselves as Mark grins at me. "I suddenly feel like my corporate job is painfully mundane."

"What do you do?"

"Environmental law. Less exciting than wrestling bears, but we occasionally take on some big, bad corporations."

"That's important work. The sanctuary deals with the consequences of environmental degradation every day."

Brian nods to the bartender. "Four of whatever these ladies are having, please."

Mark's attention stays on me. "So, the bear... did you have to fight it off single-handedly?"

I laugh, shaking my head. It's been a long time since I've engaged in this kind of casual flirtation. "Not exactly. He was sedated for surgery but woke up too soon. Calculating anesthesia for a four-hundred-pound bear can be challenging when you don't know how long it will take to remove the shotgun pellets in his flank."

"She got these heroic battle scars, though." Maren gives my shoulder a gentle tap. "Ten stitches. I helped by shooting her up with the good drugs while Ethan stitched her up."

The bartender delivers four tequila shots. Mark raises his glass. "To the badass woman who survives bear attacks."

"And her dealer." Brian nods toward Maren.

We all laugh and chug our shots. My pleasant buzz intensifies. It's nice being here, being normal, being admired by these attractive men who see only what I show them. The brave veterinarian with an interesting story. If they knew what awaits me in the darkness of my bedroom, what I let a killer do to me, what I beg him to do, would they still look at me with that admiration?

"So, you both work with animals?" Brian asks, his body language subtly angled toward Maren.

"I'm just a humble vet tech." Maren twirls a strand of hair around her finger. "Luna owns the whole sanctuary."

"That takes serious dedication." Mark's eyes study me with interest. "How many animals do you care for?"

"Currently? Twenty-seven. Mostly native wildlife. Wolves, raccoons, foxes, a few birds of prey, a mountain lion, and a one-eyed opossum. We also have some horses, a goat, and a few domesticated animals. Cats and such. All rehab cases."

"By rehab, she means animals too injured to return to the wild or too broken to be adopted out," Maren adds. "She gives them a forever home."

"Nice," Mark says. "My sister works for an animal conservation organization in Seattle. She'd love what you're doing."

"I'd be happy to have you over sometime. The sanctuary, I mean. We're always looking for supporters."

"I'd like that." Mark's smile is easy and open. "Maybe we can grab dinner after?"

This conversation is speeding into territory I can't navigate. "I'm kind of involved with someone."

Maren's gaze whips to me, and she narrows her eyes. She hates it when I turn down opportunities to get laid, especially when she knows I'm not dating anyone. And I'm not. Dating is not what my wolf and I do.

Mark looks disappointed. "Lucky guy."

"What about you?" Brian asks Maren, smoothly pivoting. "Seeing anyone?"

Maren holds up her phone, displaying her lock screen. A picture of her wrapped in the arms of a broad-shouldered man with a beard. "Two years and counting. He's on the road right now, though."

"Long-haul trucker?" Brian guesses.

"Got it in one. But we can still be friends, right?" She winks, and I hide my smile in my drink. This is Maren's favorite part. Flirting shamelessly while staying completely faithful to JT.

"Friends, it is." Brian clinks his glass against hers. "So tell me, what's the weirdest animal you've ever treated?"

⚬

The conversation flows after that. I laugh more freely than I have in months, as alcohol and easy company lift the weight of the sanctuary's constant demands and my moral dilemmas.

Mark keeps the conversation engaging without being pushy, occasionally letting his hand rest near mine on the bar. Close enough to suggest interest, but not so close as to be presumptuous. Each moment of proximity sends conflicting signals through my body, a flattering warmth at his attention colliding with an almost guilty thrill at the thought of my wolf's reaction.

But then I feel it, a prickling sensation that starts at the back of my neck. That feeling of being watched that I'm so familiar with now. I glance around, scanning the crowded bar, and freeze.

Damien stands at the far end of the bar, dark eyes locked on me. He doesn't move. Doesn't acknowledge me with a smile or a nod. But his expression shifts, and the danger in it is subtle enough that I doubt anyone else catches it. The change reaches across the space between us and wraps around my throat.

Familiar butterflies take flight in my stomach. He's devastating in dark jeans, a blue button-down, and a black pea coat hanging loose on his shoulders. Like he didn't try. Like he never has to.

The crowd between us might as well not exist. Every sound around me—the music, the laughter, the clink of glasses—fades to white noise. I grip the polished wood as a force tugs at my ribs, urging me toward him. Then he moves. Pushes off from the bar and walks toward us.

"Well, well." Maren's eyes follow my gaze. "Speak of the sexy beast."

There's something predatory in the way he moves through the crowd, his dark eyes never leaving mine. It stirs memories of another predator I know too well. I shove the thought down, bury it deep.

"Luna." A smile spreads warm across his face, but his eyes burn. "What a lovely surprise."

My pulse hammers in my ears. I keep my voice even through sheer force of will. "Damien. I'd never have pegged you as the country bar type any more than the Elk Fest type."

"I'm full of surprises." His gaze slides past me to Mark and Brian. The air shifts. He steps closer, not aggressive, but deliberate, claiming space that wasn't his a moment ago. "I hope I'm not interrupting anything."

Mark's posture changes. His eyes trace Damien's expensive coat, the confident set of his jaw, and the way he speaks like someone who's never been told no. Understanding flickers across Mark's face.

"Actually, we were just heading out." Mark's frown deepens. "Nice meeting you, Luna. Maren."

Brian nods, and both men melt back into the crowd, taking the hint. I should feel sorry for them, but my body has other ideas as I stand here watching Damien and what he just did with nothing more than his presence. My thighs press together against the ache building low and steady in my belly.

"Friends of yours?" A possessive edge sharpens the question.

"Just some guys we met tonight." Maren answers before I do. "They were buying us drinks and being appropriately charming." She clears her throat. "I think I need to visit the ladies' room. All that tequila is catching up with me." Her nudge is far from subtle. "You two play nice while I'm gone."

She saunters away, leaving Damien and me alone at the bar. The silence stretches between us, charged with an energy that gives me goosebumps. I take a sip of my water, trying to calm the nervous flutter in my chest.

Damien signals the bartender and orders a whiskey. "So... how are you? It looks like you're recovering well from your bear encounter."

Word of what happened spread through Aspen Ridge. Eleanor mentioned it to Damien, and he texted to check on me. The memory of those texts still warms me. His genuine concern had been touching.

"Good as new." I move my shoulder to emphasize the point, immediately regretting it. Though healed and stitch-free, the area is still sore and stiff, especially after last night. "So is Huck. We released him last week."

"Huck?"

"That's what we named him. Bears love huckleberries, and it was his favorite snack."

"Do you always name animals you don't keep?"

"Yes. Everyone deserves a name. Even if it's just for a little while."

"You look beautiful tonight."

His stare holds me captive. I swallow against the tightness in my throat. "Thank you. It's a nice break from the constant wolf fur and antiseptic that I'm usually wearing."

"You're always beautiful, Luna." His eyes move over me, taking their time. "Especially covered in wolf."

No deception shadows his face. There's nothing but sincerity, but the words drip with double meaning. The way his voice drops on "wolf" sends heat crawling up my spine.

"Luna, I wanted to apologize for what happened at Elk Fest." He shifts closer. "I shouldn't have lost my temper like that. I don't regret stopping Pearson, especially after he threatened you, but I could've handled it better."

"It's okay. He was a jerk who got what was coming to him."

The words are out before I realize what I've said, voicing my secret thoughts.

Damien's eyes flash, surprise flickering in them first, followed by dark, pleased satisfaction. Like he's just won something.

"Did Sheriff Mills talk to you about what happened that day?"

I've been wondering about it ever since Karen's visit.

His face changes, the muscles around his eyes tightening. "Yes. She came by after they found his body. Makes sense, I suppose. I was the last one to have a public altercation with him." His lips curve. "I suspect she thought I had something to do with his untimely demise."

He sounds like he's telling a joke only he understands.

"I told her it was ridiculous."

He lifts his whiskey and takes a slow sip. "I appreciate your defending my character."

"Well, the idea of you being a killer is ludicrous."

"Yes." He swirls the amber liquid in his glass. "The method of death sounds identical to the victims discovered on your property. It appears there's a serial killer on the loose in Aspen Ridge again." He pauses. "What are the odds of that?"

That private amusement creeps back into his voice, like he's savoring a punchline I'm not getting.

I grab my water and drink. "At least he's not killing innocents like Jeremiah Morrison."

My hand freezes halfway to setting the glass down. Did I just say that? Out loud?

Damien's gaze locks onto mine. The intensity there makes me want to look away.

"The sheriff seemed satisfied after we talked. I think she realized pretty quickly that a serial killer and the head of a Fortune 500 company aren't exactly the same demographic."

The tension in my shoulders eases. But Jeremiah Morrison's family was wealthy, one of the wealthiest in the county at the time. That's one reason he got away with killing those girls for as long as he did. I press my lips together and keep that thought to myself.

"No, I suppose they don't."

"Besides..." He takes another sip of his whiskey. "Why would I need to kill anyone when I have so many other ways to deal with problems?"

The way he says the words sends a chill through me, though I tell myself I'm reading too much into them. Damien is rich and powerful. Of course, he has resources most people don't. That doesn't make him dangerous. Not like my wolf.

"Anyway." Damien's voice shifts, losing its edge. "Before Pearson interrupted us that day, I was going to ask you to dinner again, but I wasn't sure if you'd be interested in rescheduling."

"I would have." The admission slips out before I can second-guess it.

His guarded intensity dissolves. His whole face transforms, and he smiles like I've just given him a gift he didn't think he'd receive. "Good. Are you free tomorrow night?"

My heart pounds as I think of my wolf. He seethed when I agreed to that first dinner with Damien. What will he do if I say yes now? Over a month later?

An internal battle rages inside me. But something else stirs too. A tiny spark of rebellion. Why shouldn't I have dinner with a handsome man who's interested in me? I'm a grown woman. I make my own choices. My wolf doesn't own me, no matter what he whispers against my skin every night.

"Actually," I say before I can overthink it. "Would you like to come to dinner instead? We have a family of foxes in the recovery den that needs monitoring. Ethan was nice enough to stay tonight so Maren and I could have a girl's night, but if you want to come over, I could cook."

"I'd like that very much. What time should I be there?"

"Seven?"

"Perfect. I'll bring wine."

We're interrupted by the sound of loud laughter from across the room, and I look over to see Maren at a small table with Mark and Brian, three shot glasses in front of them.

"I should probably go stop that before it gets out of hand."

Maren's going to hate herself in the morning when her hangover rears its ugly head.

"I'll drive the two of you home."

"That's sweet of you, but we can take an Uber." I wave the bartender over.

"Luna, it's late, and you've been drinking. Let me drive you."

His tone rubs me the wrong way. An assumption of authority that reminds me too much of someone else.

"I appreciate the offer, Damien, but we'll be fine."

"I insist." He hands his black AMEX to the bartender, telling him he's paying our tab too.

"Thank you, but I insist we can handle ourselves." I stand up to face him. For a brief, alcohol-fueled moment, I wonder if he and my wolf could be the same person. The commanding presence, the possessive streak, the way both men seem to think they have a right to make decisions for me. But that's ridiculous. The alcohol is turning coincidence into conspiracy.

Damien studies my face for a long moment, then nods. "All right. But text me when you get home."

I smile but have no intention of doing it.

"I'll see you tomorrow night."

I'm already turning toward Maren's table before he finishes the sentence. "Night, Damien."

The heat on my neck as I walk through the crowded bar tells me his eyes are following. When I reach their table, Maren's face lights up.

"There she is. I was just telling Brian and Mark about the time you had to give a porcupine an enema."

That particular story never gets less humiliating.

"This is why I don't let her drink tequila."

Brian laughs. "Sounds like veterinary medicine has its prickly moments."

I groan, but I join in their laughing. "Maren's rubbed off on you already."

"I've been saving that one since she told me," Brian says, not looking remotely ashamed.

"He's been making wildlife puns for the last five minutes. I'm impressed with his originality."

"Time to go." I grab her purse and help her to her feet. "Before you do something JT will have to forgive you for."

"But we were just getting to the good part!"

"The good part is where we both wake up tomorrow with our dignity intact."

Mark and Brian wave us off, and I get Maren outside into the crisp night air.

"So..." She's slightly more coherent now that we're away from the noise. "Damien Wolfe... showing up and going all caveman on poor Mark."

"He wasn't that bad."

"Luna, sweetie, that man took one look at Mark and Brian and basically pissed on you to mark his territory. Very alpha male." I think about denying it, but she's not wrong. "As much as my feminist side finds that macho posturing offensive, it's also kinda hot."

"He's coming to dinner tomorrow night."

Maren's eyes light up. "Finally! Are you going to fuck him?"

"Maren!"

"What? It's a legitimate question. You need a good, hard railing, Lu. It's been too damn long."

The tequila lowers my inhibitions, and for a moment I teeter on the edge of confession. Everything inside me wants to spill. About all these emotions I can't name, and the tangle of guilt and ecstasy that defines this relationship that exists only in shadows. How he makes me his possession while somehow making me feel like a goddess. The way terror and exhilaration dance together in my bloodstream until I can't tell which is which. And how fear and desire have become indistinguishable in the dark corners of my heart, tasting like freedom when it's mixed with his touch.

But something holds me back. Speaking of it in daylight or outside a dark bar after tequila shots might strip away the perfection and break the spell.

"I'm not sleeping with Damien on our first date. I'm not twenty-five anymore."

Maren studies my face, then shrugs. "Fine. But when you do, I want every dirty detail."

My chest loosens as she lets it drop. "Noted. Now, can we please get an Uber to your place? My shoulder's throbbing, and I've hit my limit of social interaction for the month."

"Such a hermit."

She arranges for our ride, and I stare into the darkness of the forest surrounding the small mountain town, wondering if he's out there watching.

It sends a shiver through me, dampened only by the knowledge that tonight, my bed will only have Maren in it, kicking me in her sleep. Tonight, I won't feel the cool metal of his mask between my thighs.

Maren appears beside me and links her arm through mine. "Our ride will be here in five minutes."

I lean against her as we wait. "Thanks for dragging me out tonight. I needed this."

She squeezes my arm. "Getting you drunk and trying to hook you up with hot, age-appropriate men are what best friends are for. At least until a sexy billionaire silver fox shows up."

I laugh. "He doesn't have much gray in his hair."

"It's incredibly sexy, though."

"Yeah... it is."

Our Uber arrives, a middle-aged woman in a sedan who beams at us as we climb in and asks about our night. Maren regales her with an exaggerated version of my bear encounter while I rest my head against the window, watching the town lights blur past.

The alcohol is making me philosophical, and I think about the two very different men in my life. Damien, with his wealth, power, and undeniable attraction to me. And my wolf, with his mask and darkness and the way he makes me feel like I'm burning alive.

As we reach the edge of downtown and drive through the quiet rural roads, that familiar sensation of being watched settles over me again. I glance out the back window but see nothing except distant headlights in the dark. Still, the feeling persists, making me wonder if somewhere out there, he's watching.

Tomorrow, I'll return to my sanctuary. And tomorrow night, I'll have dinner with Damien. But after he leaves, when darkness falls, my wolf will come to me again.

How am I supposed to reconcile the growing attraction I feel for one man and the burning desire I have for the other?

Have I made a mistake by inviting Damien over? The last thing I want is to provoke my wolf's anger, but part of me wants his reaction. I want him to lose control.

Under different circumstances, the shuddery feeling I get around Damien would make me want to pursue something real with him. But my life isn't simple, and my heart isn't free. That doesn't mean I can't enjoy dinner with a man who makes me almost as breathless as my wolf.

For tonight, though, I'm just a woman slightly drunk and pleasantly tired, heading to her best friend's apartment after a normal night out.

Just for tonight, I can pretend that's all I am.

Chapter Forty

Luna

"Why didn't you tell me you're making dinner for him?"

The accusation blares from my phone, and I can picture Maren's face. That look she gets when she thinks I'm holding out on her.

"I told you last night."

I rest my phone on the counter and bend to look in the oven. The lasagna is almost done. Fifteen more minutes at most.

"I woke up with my head on your boobs this morning, Lu. Like I remember anything about last night."

"You really don't remember Damien showing up at the bar?"

"Yeah... a little. I guess. I think. Maybe?"

"That's probably because you were so busy regaling Brian and Mark with stories about porcupine enemas."

"Shit! I don't remember that either."

I lift the place settings I left on the counter and walk to the table to set it. "Good thing today was your day off."

"Estella came over right after you left, so my day was anything but off. So what are you wearing?"

"You sound like a 1-800 sex line. Do they even have those anymore?"

"Don't make me laugh. My head's still pounding. Seriously, though, are you wearing the crotchless panties I gave you for your thirtieth birthday?"

I walk to the fridge and pull out the fixings for a garden salad. "It's dinner, Maren. Not dinner and sex."

"Uh-huh." I can practically hear her eye-roll. "You can lie to yourself, Lu, but I know you. Once you get Mr. Billionaire Sexy Silver Streaks in your house, Luna's secret slut is coming out." She makes a sniffling sound. "I'm so happy my baby's vag is gonna get some action."

"I don't even know why I told you. I'm hanging up now."

"Don't you dare," she snorts as I chop the veggies. "And you better jump on his dick, or I'm going to be pissed at you. But be careful, because even though he's hot as fuck, he does give off an intimidating, might-be-a-serial-killer vibe every once in a while."

The knife nearly slips at her words. My hand trembles before I steady it.

"He's not a serial killer." *That would be my wolf.* "He's just intense, but he's also sweet, in a next-door-neighbor kind of way."

That makes my panties wet. I keep that last part to myself.

"Yeah. Jeffrey Dahmer's neighbors said he was sweet, too. I hope he doesn't chop people up and put them in the freezer. That would totally ruin the mood when he has you sprawled out on your dining room table for dessert."

"Maren."

How does she have such clear subconscious knowledge of how I spend my time? Though it's my kitchen table, not the dining room.

"What? You've got to throw me a bone here. JT doesn't get back for three more days."

"I thought he was coming home tomorrow."

"Yeah, me too." She can't hide the disappointment in her voice. "I was ready. Handcuffs out, new bottle of lube, but he called and said he got held up with a mechanical issue and won't be home until Monday night now. Hey, do you need handcuffs for tonight? I can jump in the car and bring them up real quick."

"I don't need handcuffs, Maren."

I use zip ties.

"Whatever, your loss. But I still think he's looking for more than just a mediocre home-cooked meal."

I sigh, tossing the vegetables into the salad bowl. "I have no plans to have sex with him. It's just dinner. And thanks for the vote of confidence in my cooking." Shadow's low growl from the next room saves me. "I've got to go. Talk tomorrow."

I hang up before she can protest, walking down the hallway to the living room. He stands alert by the front window, ears forward. Ghost stands beside him, equally still, but far less tense.

Please don't be another dead body. I'll kill him! Or at least not let him inside me without a fight.

"What is it, guys?" I peer into the gathering darkness. The purple sky fades behind black mountain silhouettes.

A sleek black car pulls up my driveway. Shadow's hackles rise, a louder growl building in his chest. Not Damien, then. His Range Rover is unmistakable and not due for another half hour.

Ghost starts to growl too.

"Okay, you two, dial it back."

But then my stomach drops as the car approaches. I'd recognize that vintage Mustang anywhere. Caleb's pride and joy, restored with Daddy's money. The same car he once pinned me against while shouting that I cared more about "fucking animals" than our relationship.

"Shit."

I check my reflection in the hallway mirror. I'm dressed for Damien in slim jeans and a soft green sweater, with hair loose around my shoulders. Nothing like my usual work scrubs.

I consider calling Karen. The restraining order is clear, but something in me hesitates. It'll take at least half an hour for her to arrive. I can handle this myself.

I open the door before Caleb can knock.

"What the hell are you doing here?"

He stands on my porch with that familiar cocky smile, still conventionally handsome, with his sandy blonde hair and green eyes. In one hand, he holds a bouquet of red dahlias—my favorite. Once, that gesture would have melted me. Now it feels calculated, another manipulation tactic he'd perfected before I even realized he was doing it.

"Hello to you too, Luna." He holds out the flowers. "Can't a guy visit his favorite ex?"

"Most exes respect restraining orders." I make no move to accept the flowers. Shadow and Ghost growl beside me.

Caleb's smile falters. "Down, boy." He flicks his fingers at Shadow in dismissal, then notices Ghost flanking my other side. "You've got two wolves now?"

"Ghost is a hybrid." I bite my tongue the second the words leave my mouth. He doesn't deserve explanations.

"You look amazing." His gaze slides down my body, and revulsion crawls across my skin like ants. I resist the urge to cross my arms over my chest, forcing myself to stay still. I won't give him the satisfaction of seeing me retreat.

"What do you want, Caleb?"

"Can I come in? It's freezing out here." He feigns a shiver.

A thin layer of fresh snow from a brief overnight storm covers the ground. It feels like more is coming, but it isn't cold enough for him to shiver.

I check my watch. Twenty-five minutes until Damien arrives. "This isn't a good time, Caleb. The restraining order—"

"Is just paper." The words snap out, hard and fast, before he reins it back in. His features soften and rearrange into something apologetic. "I'm not here to cause trouble. I just wanted to stop by and apologize for everything that went down between us."

He holds up the flowers again with a hopeful smile. "Five minutes? For old times' sake?"

Against my better judgment and every warning bell in my head, I step aside, pulling Ghost and Shadow by the collars. "Five minutes. Then you leave, or I'm calling Sheriff Mills."

Caleb whistles as he enters, taking in my renovated space. "You've done a lot with the place. Still living your Dr. Doolittle fantasy, I see."

I bristle at his dismissive tone. "It's not a fantasy. The sanctuary is thriving."

"Right, right." He wanders into my kitchen, eyeing the half-prepared meal. "Expecting company?"

"I'm having a friend for dinner." I move behind the island, keeping it between us. Shadow positions himself on one side and Ghost on the other. They both keep a close eye on Caleb, Ghost following Shadow's lead. "What did you want to say? Your five minutes are almost up."

Caleb sets the flowers on the island, his expression shifting to one of sincerity. His eyes, once so captivating, now seem hollow, the performance behind them transparent.

"I've been thinking about us, about my mistakes."

"There is no 'us,' Caleb. There hasn't been for over a year. And the 'mistakes' you made were assaulting me. Repeatedly."

He flinches. "That's not fair—"

"Not fair?" My voice rises despite my intention to stay calm. "The bruises weren't fair. The black eye when I said I was working late wasn't fair. The broken ribs that nearly punctured my lungs weren't fair."

"I was under pressure at the firm. You were always here with your animals, never making time for us—"

"Don't you dare blame me for your violence. You made your choices."

"I know I hurt you. I was immature, focused on the wrong things. But I've changed. I'm seeing a therapist, working on my anger issues."

"People don't change."

"Some do when they realize what they've lost." He steps around the island, his cologne bringing back unwelcome memories. "We were good together, Luna, before things went wrong."

"We wanted different things." I step back until I hit the counter. "You wanted me to give up the sanctuary, move to Denver, and be the perfect wife."

"I was wrong to pressure you. Your work here is important. I see that now."

Shadow growls, moving between us. Caleb shoots him an irritated glance. "That wolf still doesn't like me."

"He's a good judge of character. He remembers you kicked him."

Caleb's pleasant mask slips, revealing a familiar temper as he snarls. "That thing tried to bite me."

"Only after you hit me. He was protecting me."

"Look, I'm trying here. Could you at least pretend to be civil?"

"I am being civil. But that doesn't mean I'm interested in revisiting anything." I check my watch. "Your five minutes are up."

Instead of leaving, he steps closer, his expression hardening. "There's someone else, isn't there? Is that what this is about?"

My heart pounds harder as I calculate the distance to my phone. "My personal life is none of your business anymore. You're violating the restraining order."

His eyes narrow. "Who is he? Eleanor mentioned billionaire Damien Wolfe's interest in you. Is it him?"

"When did you see Eleanor?"

"I stopped by the post office the other day. She always has the gossip. But she told me to get lost, that you had a new boyfriend. Is it Wolfe?"

"That's none of your business. And you need to leave. Now. Or I'm calling Karen."

He ignores me, his gaze sweeping the kitchen again, landing on the wine glasses. "You're making him dinner. How cozy."

"That's enough." I move toward the door, Shadow and Ghost at my heels. "Whatever you came for, the answer is no. We're done."

Caleb's hand clamps around my wrist before I reach the hallway, his fingers digging into bone. "You think you can do better than me?"

Fear and rage explode in my chest, but my voice comes out ice-cold. "Let go."

"You were mine for over two years." He yanks me closer. "You think I'm going to stand by while you spread your legs for the first rich prick who comes along? After you ruined my life?"

Shadow lunges with a snarl. Caleb releases me to shove him away, sending him skidding across the floor. Ghost moves to take his place in front of me, baring his teeth.

"Get out!" I shout, rage overriding fear. "Before I let these two show you what they think of men who abuse women."

Shadow recovers, hackles raised, positioning himself between us again.

Caleb raises his hands in mock surrender, eyes cold. "We're not finished, Luna. You might think you've traded up, but men like Wolfe don't waste time with small-town vets unless they want something."

"The only thing I want is for you to back the fuck away from Dr. Foster."

My head whips around at the menacing voice coming from the hallway. Damien's massive form fills the doorway. His normally composed features are tight with controlled fury, eyes locked on Caleb with lethal intensity.

The air in the room drops ten degrees.

"This is a private conversation." Caleb straightens to his full height, but he's still half a foot shorter than Damien.

"Not anymore." Damien steps inside the kitchen. He looks from Caleb to me, his gaze softening. "Are you alright, Luna?"

"I'm fine." But my voice trembles, giving me away.

Damien nods once, then turns back to Caleb. "You're leaving now."

"Who the hell do you think you are?"

"Someone who respects restraining orders. And someone who doesn't appreciate men who put their hands on women."

Caleb's face flushes. "You don't know what you're talking about—"

"Multiple domestic violence charges. Two dropped by previous girlfriends after mysterious settlements. One restraining order filed by Dr. Foster after you put her in the hospital with three broken ribs."

My breath catches. How does he know those details? Aside from Maren, Karen is the only other person I told about the hospital when I filed the restraining order.

"Who the fuck do you think you are, investigating me?"

"I make it my business to know about potential threats in my vicinity." Damien takes another step forward. Despite his impeccable clothes and composed demeanor, there's something savage in his stance.

For a moment, I see a flash of something else. The dark silhouette of my masked wolf superimposed over Damien's features. The resemblance is so striking, I gasp aloud. Same height, same powerful shoulders, same effortless authority.

It can't be.

It's just my mind playing tricks, associating two intense men in my life.

"You have thirty seconds to get off this property before I show you what happens to men who don't understand boundaries."

Violence hums beneath every syllable, and Caleb's bravado cracks.

"This isn't over." Caleb backs toward the door. "She'll get tired of you, too. That's the bitch's pattern."

Damien strikes like a snake, faster than my eyes can track. Between one heartbeat and the next, Caleb is pinned against the wall, Damien's fingers wrapped around his throat.

"The next time you come near her, they won't find enough of you to identify."

Those cold, calculated words send ice down my spine. This isn't empty male posturing. It's a promise delivered with the certainty of someone who knows how to fulfill it.

Caleb's face pales as Damien releases him. He stumbles toward the door, casting one last venomous glance before disappearing into the night.

Silence falls between us as Damien turns to me. His expression shifts, the deadly look fading from his face, replaced by the sophisticated businessman I'm familiar with. But I've seen what lies beneath, and the revelation both excites and terrifies me.

"I apologize for just walking in unannounced." He straightens the sweater beneath his open jacket. "I arrived early and heard raised voices."

I search his face, looking for any trace of the violence I just witnessed. The savage thing that pinned Caleb to the wall. "You didn't have to do that."

"Yes, I did."

Shadow approaches Damien, pressing his head against the man's hand. The gesture is immediate and trusting, and Damien scratches the top of his head. Ghost stays pressed against my leg, watching from a distance.

"Thank you." My lips tilt upward, and the tension melts from my body. "For stepping in."

Damien's eyes soften, though the dangerous edge remains. "No one should speak to you that way. Or touch you without permission."

I turn away, needing a moment. I move back toward the counter and toss the flowers in the trash. "Dinner is ready. I hope you still have an appetite."

"Starving, actually." He holds up a bottle of wine I missed before. "How about I pour?"

I hand him the corkscrew, and he works the bottle open, but his eyes don't leave me, and the look in them tightens everything low in my body in a way I'm not prepared for. My wolf looks at me like that. Like I'm prey, he's finally cornered.

Then his lips curve into a genuine, warm smile, and I dismiss the wild theory forming. My imagination is running away with me, creating connections where none exist.

Still, as I hand him the glasses and turn to the oven, a whisper of suspicion lingers, too persistent to dismiss.

Chapter Forty-One

Damien

Luna reaches for oven mitts patterned with cartoon animals and removes a lasagna from the oven, but my blood is still hot from the confrontation with her ex. My hands ache to do more than just throw him out. They want to crush, punish, and eliminate the threat he poses to her, but I force myself to appear calm as she makes her way around the kitchen, her movements still tense.

Shadow and the hybrid have retreated to the other room, comfortable with me here.

"You shouldn't have had to deal with that." Her voice is quieter than usual. "I'm sorry about Caleb."

"Don't apologize for him." I lean against the island, the wine glass cool against my palm. Heat burns in my throat, but I take a long swallow to cool it. She should never apologize for that asshole.

Luna's hands tremble as she carries the lasagna to the table, where I savored every inch of her skin last night. Tomato sauce and herbs fill the kitchen, but all I can think about is how she trembled beneath my tongue right there on that wooden surface.

"Are you sure you're okay?"

"I'm fine." She sighs. "No, that's not true. I'm rattled. I haven't seen him for over a year."

Every muscle wants to correct her, to say it's been one year, two months, and eleven days since she filed the restraining order against Caleb Hunter. But Damien Wolfe wouldn't know these things.

"Do you want to talk about it?" I ask instead, keeping my voice gentle.

She busies herself with the food, avoiding my eyes. "No. I don't want to spoil our dinner. Now don't get too excited." A self-deprecating smile tugs at her lips. "My cooking skills are subpar at best, but I can manage Italian basics."

I can't take my eyes off her. She dressed up for me tonight, with subtle makeup enhancing her natural beauty, and her hair loose around her shoulders like silk I want to fist in my hands.

The domestic scene stirs something dark and possessive inside me. The part of me that visits her at night burns with irrational anger. She made this dinner for Damien and prepared herself for him when she belongs to me.

But then I realize how fucking ridiculous that is. We're the same fucking man.

"It looks perfect." I move to the table and pull out her chair. "But you're deflecting."

"It's not exactly first date conversation material."

"Is that what this is?" I let a smile touch my lips, testing the waters. "A date?"

Pink spreads across her cheekbones as she tucks a strand of blonde hair behind her ear. "I guess that depends on how the lasagna turns out."

I take the seat beside her, close enough that our knees almost touch. Near enough to smell that sweet scent that drives me wild every night.

"I take it you weren't expecting your ex to show up tonight?"

"You don't give up easily, do you?"

"Not when it matters. And your safety matters."

Luna takes a breath. "Caleb and I met three years ago at a wildlife conservation fundraiser. He seemed perfect at first. Passionate about environmental causes, charming, attentive." She picks up her fork but doesn't eat. "We dated for a little over two years before he started to change. The pressure of making partner consumed him. He was working long hours, but it didn't bother me because I was so busy here. He started to resent the time it took away from him. He wanted my attention on his terms. I also think he developed a drug problem, though I'm not entirely sure."

My jaw locks. I know the kind of monster that hides behind Caleb Hunter's cocaine-sniffing, polished exterior.

"The violence didn't start until about six months before we broke up." Her voice drops, eyes fixed on her plate. "Just grabbing my arm too hard at first. Then a shove during an argument. He was always so sorry afterward, swore it would never happen again."

"Until it did."

She nods. "The night I ended it, he lost control. Said if I left him, he'd make sure I had nothing left. Threatened the sanctuary, my animals." Her voice hardens with the steel I recognize and admire. "That's the night he broke my ribs, and I knew I had to get out, no matter what. I filed for a restraining order the next day."

I take a careful sip of wine, using the moment to control the fury simmering under my skin. The beast inside me wants to howl, wants to hunt him down tonight and tear his throat out.

"And today? What did he want?"

"He claims he's changed. In therapy. Found God." Bitterness colors her laugh. "Said he wanted to apologize in person."

"And you believe him?"

"No. People like Caleb don't change. They just find new masks to wear."

I nod. She sees through his performance, the monster beneath his facade.

So why doesn't she see mine?

Maybe she does. But why does she accept him?

"How did you know the details in my restraining order? The hospital visit?"

Fuck!

I freeze, cursing my earlier slip, revealing too much of what I know about her life.

"Restraining orders are public record and your ex has a history of violent behavior. It was relevant to your security needs."

"So you did a background check on me?" There's curiosity in her voice, not accusation. Yet. But I catch the subtle shift in her posture, the way her shoulders pull back like she's bracing for something.

"Standard procedure for anyone who purchases our systems."

"That sounds a little invasive." She tilts her head. "I remember seeing something in the fine print on the contract I signed, but is that even legal?"

Luna Foster is too damn smart for her own good. It's one of the qualities that make her both impressive and dangerous to underestimate.

"It's not a formal background check. But we verify whether a customer has a criminal history to make sure the system won't be used for anything illegal." I pause, letting my mouth curve. "You don't, by the way. Have a criminal background."

She doesn't look convinced, but she lets it slide. "Well, I appreciate you showing up when you did tonight. Caleb can be unpredictable when he's angry."

His grip on her wrist burns fresh in my memory, and I force myself to uncoil the tension in my shoulders. "He won't bother you again."

"You sound very certain of that."

"I am."

It's not a promise; it's a guarantee. Caleb Hunter just moved to the top of my kill list.

"Well, thank you again for throwing him out."

"I'd do far more than that to protect you." The words slip out before I can censor them, too much truth bleeding through.

Her eyes shift, and her brows draw together. "You barely know me, Damien."

She has no idea how untrue that statement is.

"I'm a good judge of character. And you're worth protecting."

I steer us toward safer ground as we begin to eat. The lasagna is quite good, though I barely taste it, still consumed with thoughts of her ex and the many ways I could make him disappear.

Luna relaxes as we talk. She lights up, gesturing with her hands, passion burning bright in her voice, when she describes treating a lynx last week. It wasn't a case of abuse but a bold rescue of a cat that was returned to the wild the next day. She's breathtaking when she's animated like this.

"You're good at this."

She glances up from her plate, confusion creasing her forehead. "At what? Eating lasagna?" Her mouth twitches at one corner. "I mean, I'm decent with a fork, but I wouldn't call it a talent."

My laugh is easy and natural. She has this way of deflecting compliments with humor that makes me drop my guard. She's the only one who can do that.

I narrow my eyes at her in mock disapproval. "I meant your passion for healing. Your eyes light up when you talk about your work."

Her lips curve into that soft smile that makes my throat tight. "It's the only thing I've ever wanted to do. Even as a kid, I was always bringing home injured birds, foxes, squirrels, and stray cats. Drove first my parents and then my grandfather crazy."

"Tell me about him." I refill her wine glass, though I already know everything about Theodore Foster from Cade's report. I've done a deep dive into her family history, seen satellite images of the bridge collapse that killed her parents, read her grandfather's obituary, and know exactly what he left her in his will. But I want to hear it from her lips, want to understand the forces that shaped the woman next to me.

Her expression turns wistful. "He was a wild soul. Spent most of his life traveling the world photographing endangered species. This property had been in my family since the Colorado gold rush. It was supposed to be his retirement place. When my parents died, he settled here to raise me, but he never lost that wanderlust." She smiles at some private memory. "He taught me that every creature deserves compassion, even the ones that seem dangerous or beyond saving."

"He sounds like an extraordinary man."

"He was. When he died during my second year of residency, I felt like I'd lost everything again. But he left me the property, and I knew exactly what I wanted to do with it."

"Is that why you do this? Take in the lost causes?"

"They're not lost causes. Just misunderstood. Most wild animals act from fear or pain, or they're protecting their territory." Her hazel eyes find mine and hold. "People aren't so different."

The observation hits a little too close to home. Does she see through me? Has she connected the pieces?

"Some predators are made, not born."

I watch her reaction.

She considers this, twirling her wine glass. "Yes. Some of them have reasons, even the most vicious ones, for what they do. Understanding those reasons doesn't excuse the behavior, but it helps explain it."

"What about those who hunt other predators?" I'm walking into dangerous territory, but I can't help myself. "Where do they fit into your worldview?"

Luna goes still. "You mean like vigilantes?"

"For example."

She's quiet for a long moment, weighing her words. "I believe in justice. But justice and vengeance aren't the same thing."

"Sometimes the system fails." I'm reminded of the hundreds of animal abusers I've killed after they walked free from the courts. "Sometimes the only justice available is the kind you take for yourself."

"That's a slippery slope." She leans forward, engaged now. "Who decides what crimes deserve punishment? Who appoints themselves judge, jury, and executioner?"

"Someone who understands both predator and prey." Our conversation has shifted from the hypothetical to something much more dangerous. "Someone who's seen the darkness up close."

The air between us crackles with unspoken meaning. Luna's pupils dilate, whether from the wine or the dangerous turn in our discussion. I can't tell. But I recognize the signs of arousal in her body. The quickening pulse at her throat, the slight parting of her lips.

Is this conversation turning her on?

"Is that how you see the world, Damien? Predators and prey?" Her voice has dropped to something intimate and husky.

I hold her gaze. "I see a world where the strong prey on the weak until someone stronger stops them."

"And you? Which are you?"

"What do you think?"

She studies me with those shrewd eyes that are starting to see more than they should. Then she stands and grabs our empty plates. The spell breaks as she moves to the sink.

"I'm still figuring you out. I thought I had you pegged when you first showed up at my door. Clean-cut, professional, safe." She pauses, puts the dishes in the sink, and then leans against the counter. "But after what happened with Odell Pearson. And tonight, the way you handled Caleb like you knew exactly what kind of man he was. There's something else beneath all that polish. Something that makes me think you don't just stand by when someone is being victimized."

⸻ ✦ ⸻

I insist on helping Luna with the dishes despite her protests, and we make quick work of them. She suggests we move into the living room to finish the wine I brought. We settle on the sofa, and she turns toward me, tucking one leg beneath her. The movement draws my attention to the curve of her calf, and I force myself to focus on her face instead.

"So... Enough about me." She smiles, the wine warming her cheeks and eyes. "We've been talking about me all night. Tell me about the mysterious Damien Wolfe. Maren's internet deep dive turned up articles calling you a reclusive genius, but they don't say much else."

"Not much to tell." I give her the curated version of my past, the one that explains Damien Wolfe without revealing the darkness beneath. "Born into wealth, parents more interested in their social standing than their son. Shipped off to boarding schools when I became inconvenient."

"That sounds lonely."

"I got used to being on my own."

The understatement of the fucking century.

I don't tell her the rest. The brutalities of my childhood and the things I witnessed or experienced at the hands of the people who were supposed to love me but didn't. The isolation that taught me to observe rather than participate. And how that isolation shaped me into the predator I am now. Her predator.

"What about after school?" She leans forward with interest. "How did you end up founding your tech company?"

"Tech is only one of my companies, but I've always been good with systems. Understanding patterns, predicting behavior. It started with security systems I designed to protect myself from bullies at boarding school. Later, I realized there was a market for that kind of technology."

Her eyebrows lift before she can school her expression. "You were bullied?"

A smile tugs at my lips. "I wasn't always this big. I was a pretty scrawny kid until I hit puberty. Then I grew over a foot in a year."

She blinks, processing this. "Jesus, that must have been brutal on your joints."

"The joints were fine. It was the cafeteria tables that suffered. I kept kneecapping myself every time I stood up."

She shakes her head, but her eyes soften. "You make light of it, but that couldn't have been easy. Being different at that age... it's hard enough without growth spurts and bullies." She takes a sip of her wine. "So, are your parents proud of what you've built?"

"They died in a home invasion when I was sixteen." The practiced lie comes easily. The investigation produced no suspects. No one had scrutinized the grieving son, who was away at boarding school and who had both motive and, thanks to his specialized knowledge of systems, opportunity to cover his tracks.

"I'm so sorry." Luna reaches across the sofa to touch my hand, and the simple gesture of compassion hits me hard.

Her fingers are warm against my skin. I want to turn my hand over and capture hers, thread our fingers together, and pull her closer. Instead, I dismiss her sympathy for a loss I don't mourn.

"It was a long time ago."

"Still, losing parents is hard. I know that better than most." A shadow falls over her face. "I was ten when mine died. A drunk driver plowed into a bridge we were on. It collapsed, and they were both gone in an instant."

"That kind of loss is devastating, especially to a child."

"I don't remember the actual event. I only know what my Grandpa told me and what I read in the newspapers after I woke up from the coma."

"I'm glad you had him." I need to steer this conversation away from death and trauma. Topics I'm not equipped to handle without revealing too much. "So, Sage & Summit Sanctuary, what you've built here is remarkable, Luna."

I want to know everything about her and what makes her tick. I've researched the financials and know how she stretched her inheritance and savings to build the rehabilitation center. How she struggles some months to keep it afloat. It's why I paid off her mortgage and student loans. And why Cade now funnels money to the sanctuary through shell companies. Different amounts from different sources each month, designed to look like the kindness of strangers rather than the obsession of one man.

"It's not much compared to your empire." She gives me that humble smile, the one that makes me want to pin her against the wall and show her exactly how extraordinary she is. "But it's mine. My purpose."

"It's impressive. You've created something meaningful."

Luna studies me over the rim of her wineglass. "You sound almost envious."

"Maybe I am. You know exactly who you are and what you're meant to do. That's rare."

"And you don't?"

"I have my own purpose. Though it's not one I can discuss over dinner." I let a smile play on my lips, but her eyes narrow, and I realize I've said too much. Again. There's something about Luna that makes me careless with my secrets.

"No wonder people call you mysterious."

I lean forward, allowing some of my true intensity to show. "Everyone has secrets, Luna. Even you."

She shifts in her seat, a subtle tell that I've hit a nerve. "What makes you think I have secrets?"

"You live alone on a remote property, surrounded by animals most people fear. You keep your distance from people, preferring the company of those animals. And sometimes, at night, you stand at your bedroom window and look out into the darkness like you're waiting for something. Or someone."

Luna's face drains of color. "How would you know what I do at night?"

I recover quickly. "Nothing creepy. Just an observation from the night we finished your installation. Before I transferred the system to the mainframe for monitoring, I saw you looking out your upstairs window from the outside cameras."

"Oh." She relaxes, but suspicion lingers in her gaze. "You're very observant."

"It's what I do," I say with deliberate lightness, hoping she'll let it drop.

"You're not what I expected, Damien."

"Is that good or bad?"

She considers this, head tilted in that way that makes me want to kiss the curve of her neck.

"I'm still deciding. When people first meet you, you come off as this unapproachable, intense, and kind of scowly grump. Even the images of you online, you look the same way. All the time. But when you let someone under that facade, you're still intense, but you've got a soft center."

I choke on my wine and pretend to be offended. "Did you just call me soft? Like I'm some kind of marshmallow?"

"Pretty much." Her lips curve into a teasing smile. And fuck, I want to kiss her. "I mean, you're obviously a generous, kind man, wrapped in this intense package, but you have a subtle gentleness about you to offset all that intensity you project to the world. I like that about you."

I excuse myself to the bathroom, needing a moment to recalibrate. The mirror reflects a stranger, or rather, it reflects Damien Wolfe, the civilized mask I wear. But underneath, Luna's wolf is pacing, demanding to claim what's his.

The dual awareness of my separate identities is becoming harder to maintain in her presence. Every smile she gives Damien feels like a betrayal of her wolf. Every kind word she speaks makes me want to throw her over my shoulder and carry her upstairs, strip away every layer between us, and show her who she belongs to.

When I return to the living room, she sits motionless, firelight painting shadows across her face as she stares into the flames. I settle beside her, and she blinks before her hands move to the wine bottle, dividing what's left between our glasses. As she offers me mine, our fingers brush. This time, I don't let the moment pass. I capture her hand, feeling her pulse jump beneath my touch.

"Thank you for dinner, Luna. Despite the interruption."

She doesn't pull away, and the victory of that small surrender keeps the wolf prowling.

"I'm glad you arrived when you did. I don't know what would have happened if—"

"Nothing would have happened." I would have killed him before letting him hurt her. "You're tougher than you realize. You would've kicked his ass if you had to."

"Maybe." Her eyes drift towards Shadow and the hybrid asleep in the beds next to the fireplace. "But having more backup than just the wolves helped."

"I'll always back you up." The vow comes from every part of me. Damien and her wolf. She doesn't understand yet, but she owns me. She has my complete protection. My obsession. My devotion.

"Why me, Damien? You could have any woman in Colorado. In the world, probably. Why ask out a wildlife vet who lives in the middle of nowhere?"

Because you're mine.

"Because you're real. In a world of masks and pretense, you're exactly who you appear to be."

Once again, something in my tone or expression must betray the extent of my feelings, because Luna pulls her hand away and rises from the sofa.

"It's getting late." A hint of wariness creeps into her voice. "I have early rounds in the morning, and I need to check on the foxes one more time tonight."

I nod, respecting her boundaries. For now.

In a few hours, I'll return, and there will be no boundaries between us except the ones I put there. But first, I'll punish her for making dinner for another man. For entertaining thoughts of anyone other than me.

"Of course. Thank you again for dinner."

We walk to the door, and Luna pauses at the threshold. Her smile is tentative but genuine.

"Goodnight, Damien."

The porch creaks under my weight as I turn back. She stands in the doorway, her blonde hair curling around her face in soft waves, a gentle curve on her lips, and her eyes shimmering and glassy from her wine. The want that's been building all night crashes over me like a wave, demanding I stop pretending I can walk away.

"I don't think I can leave yet."

I step forward and lean down, capturing her mouth with mine. The kiss is fierce and hungry, nothing like the restrained courtesy I've shown her as Damien. This is a predator's claim, the kiss of her watcher, her dark lover, though she doesn't know it.

Luna stiffens, her palms coming up to brace against my chest. For a moment she fights it, her body radiating confusion at this shift from the respectful CEO she thinks I am and this sudden display of brutal dominance.

Then she surrenders with a soft sound that vibrates through my body, melting against me as her fingers curl into my sweater.

She kisses me back. Tentative at first, like she's touching something dangerous and forbidden. Then hunger takes over. The night air vanishes. Only heat remains, her lips and her tongue dancing with mine in a rhythm that burns away rational thought. Her body molds to mine, and emotions tear through my chest in opposite directions.

Triumph that she wants this. Wants me.

Fury that she would give this kiss to anyone but her wolf, even though he can never claim it.

The press of her body against me sets my blood on fire. Every inch of me comes alive where we touch. I want to sweep her up and carry her to that bedroom, where moonlight spills across her sheets. I want to strip away every barrier between us, skin against skin, feeling how perfectly she fits against me as we move together until our bodies drum out a single relentless rhythm.

I want to taste every breath she takes. I want to take my time and make it last until she's trembling and breathless and mine in every way that exists.

And I want to watch realization dawn in those beautiful hazel eyes. The moment she realizes that I'm her wolf. The man who owns her. Every last inch of her.

The fierce hunger I began with shifts as these emotions war within me. I soften the kiss, my palm cupping her cheek with unexpected gentleness. She trembles in my arms, her breathing stuttering at the shift from demand to devotion.

This is why I've avoided her lips, why I've never allowed myself this intimacy. Somehow, I knew that kissing her would change everything, would transform obsession into something far more dangerous.

I was right. This kiss is unraveling me, erasing the careful walls I've constructed between my public face and private darkness. The line between Damien Wolfe and her dark lover blurs as I taste her surrender.

I force myself to break away, both of us gasping for air, my forehead resting against hers as I close my eyes and try to piece together what's left of my control.

"I've wanted to do that since I first saw you."

Truth I've buried under layers of careful planning and justification slips out, though it's been burning in my chest from that very first moment.

My eyes open to find turmoil in hers. In her mind, she belongs to another man. She has no idea the man she thinks she's betraying is the same one holding her now.

The situation is so twisted it borders on madness.

Her lips part. "Damien, I—"

I silence her with another kiss, softer this time, my fingertips tracing her jawline as I taste her again. I can't bear whatever words might come next. I force myself back a step.

"Don't overthink it."

Her wide, uncertain eyes search mine. Want and confusion chase each other across her expression. The conflict playing out on her face satisfies the predator in me. She should feel torn. She's mine, has been for months, though only half of her understands the truth.

A sudden snap of a twig echoes from the shadows beyond her front yard. I turn my head toward the dark sweep of the woods, tracing the low ridgeline of the Henderson property. The night air carries the scent of snow, the faint musk of wet pine, and something wilder. Bears usually move uphill this time of year, but I trust my instincts more than habits.

I don't see anything. Still, I don't like the idea of Luna being outside if there's a bear around, especially after what happened a few weeks ago.

I turn back to look at her. She's biting her lip as she looks up at me with concern in her eyes.

"Is everything all right? Do you see something out there?" Her voice betrays a hint of anxiety. She thinks her watcher is watching us.

I give her a reassuring smile and lean down to kiss her again. She sighs into my mouth, and I have to force myself not to deepen the kiss, not to push her back against the door and take more.

"Probably an animal, but you should get inside." I step back, even though I want nothing more than to stay. "Goodnight, Luna. Lock your doors."

Her gaze follows me, thumb dragging across her bottom lip as if trying to hold on to the taste of our kiss. My pulse thuds in my ears. Each step toward my car requires conscious effort, aware of her eyes tracking every movement, hungry for answers I can't give.

As I drive away, I already know I'll be back within hours.

But tonight will be different. Something fundamental has changed between us. Between all versions of us. The barrier I built between Damien Wolfe and her dark watcher has crumbled under one kiss.

Chapter Forty-Two

Luna

I close the door behind Damien and lean against it, my fingers still tingling from where they touched his chest.

My lips burn with the memory of his kiss, first fierce and demanding, nothing like the polite, restrained man who shared dinner with me. Then it shifted into an achingly gentle caress that reached inside and stirred parts of me I'd buried and forgotten existed. The contrast leaves me reeling.

I press my fingertips to my mouth, still tasting him. Red wine underlaid with an edge that defies description, wild and untamed, like lightning before it strikes.

Shadow whines beside me, nudging my hand. I run my fingers through his thick fur. He tilts his head, those soulful eyes studying me, and I swear he smirks at me.

"I know, baby." I push away from the door.

I finish cleaning the kitchen on autopilot, loading the wine glasses into the dishwasher and wiping down the counter before flipping the machine on. My hands move through the motions while my brain replays the kiss on an endless loop. My stomach flutters with guilt braided through desire. I'm caught between the memory of Damien's mouth on mine and the weight of what feels like betrayal.

Because tonight, my wolf will come to me. My core clenches, arousal already gathering between my thighs. My body knows what's coming. It craves it. Craves him, even as my heart rebels against the complexity of wanting two men.

I walk Ghost back to the sanctuary building, letting him do his last business of the night. I tried to bring him into the house with us, but he resisted. His preference for solitude likely stems from his past life alone outdoors, and I respect his autonomy. He likes to greet Maren when she arrives in the mornings, so we set up a bed in the lobby for him.

The fox family gets a final check before Shadow and I make our way back to the house. I lock up, setting the alarm, but I don't know why I bother. It won't keep him out. I don't want it to, but I still arm it.

The air in my bedroom tonight is thick, charged with anticipation and anxiety. I move to the window, drawn by habit to look out into the darkness beyond. Shadows make the forest seem endless, thick, and impenetrable. Somewhere out there, he's watching. He's always watching.

Did he see what happened?

Of course he did. He sees everything. The knowledge that he witnessed my kiss with Damien makes my stomach knot with both dread and excitement.

I strip down to my bra and panties, then hesitate. Should I shower? Should I try to wash away Damien's scent, his touch? Or would that only make things worse?

In the end, I take a shower. I don't need to tempt his beast that much.

I wash my body, letting my hands skim over it, still thinking about Damien's kiss and how my heart thudded against my ribs while his mouth moved against my own. I slide my hands lower, slipping them between my thighs where I'm pulsing, my fingers sliding through the slick flesh. My eyes drift closed, Damien's face flashing behind my eyelids. The way he smiled at me tonight. Then my wolf's face replaces it, with his gleaming silver mask. My fingers pick up their pace as the image of him in my mind begins to flash, switching back and forth between the two men who seem to have a hold on me I can't explain.

I lean against the tile and slip one finger, then a second, inside. My moan echoes off the bathroom walls as I imagine my wolf's hands instead of mine, the way his fingers curl just so.

Then Damien's image breaks through, uninvited but impossible to ignore. How would his feel?

His cock had burned against my abdomen through the fabric of his pants, a brand that lingers even now. The echo of that pressure sends heat flaring under my skin with both guilt and longing. My wolf satisfies every physical craving, wringing pleasure from my body until I can't remember my own name. He knows exactly how to unravel me, how to build me up and tear me down until I exist only for his touch.

But rebellion stirs in my chest when I think of Damien, a dangerous curiosity that feels like cheating. Why am I imagining another man's hands, wondering how Damien's touch would compare? Whether he'd be gentle where my wolf is rough, patient where my wolf is demanding. Why am I wondering how he'd fill me, how his rhythm would differ from the relentless pace I've grown accustomed to?

The betrayal in these thoughts cuts deeper than what happened on the porch. At least then it was only my body responding. This is my mind choosing to stray, painting vivid pictures of a man who isn't mine to want.

My fingers move faster, and their faces swim together in my mind. My wolf's jaw tightening the way it does before he comes inside me, and Damien's crooked smile that never quite reaches his serious eyes. The mask's dark eyeholes versus storm-blue irises that hold me captive.

They morph back and forth from one to the other until they blur together.

One face.

Two sets of eyes.

The pressure builds and then breaks. My back arches off the tile as waves crash through me, my muscles contracting around my fingers in rhythmic pulses.

I slide down to the floor, my legs too weak to hold me. Water streams over my shoulders as my body trembles with aftershocks. My fingers trace idle patterns against the inside of my thigh as my breathing slows. I close my eyes, waiting for the familiar weight to press down, the tightness that should come.

Guilt for wanting the man who knows my body more intimately than I do now. Remorse for wanting a man I wish knew it as well.

But no crushing self-recrimination materializes. Only the breathless realization that settles in my chest like a stone.

I wish I could have them both.

⸺◆⸺

I step out of the shower and dry off, my body still humming, but, God help me, still craving more. I brush my teeth, washing away the memory of Damien's taste. Not that it will matter. My wolf won't kiss me. And that knowledge makes me feel hollow again.

Should I bother dressing? He's only going to strip me as soon as he gets here, tearing away whatever fabric dares to separate us. Should I just throw on an old t-shirt and call it a night? Or should I wear something that might make him pause, make him see me as more than only a body to claim in the darkness?

I slip into the nightgown I bought a few weeks ago from the Victoria's Secret catalog Maren brought to work to shop for a surprise for JT.

The silk slides over my skin like liquid, so soft it's barely there. Material this soft shouldn't exist, whispering across every curve as it settles just below my hips. Lace cups cradle my breasts in intricate weaves that reveal more than they conceal, and the thin straps feel like silk ribbons against my shoulders.

It's the same deep purple as the bedding my wolf bought to replace the sheets after our first encounter during my period. The first night it happened, he pushed me onto my stomach in the middle of my bed despite my protests and fucked me until the sheets looked like a crime scene.

Each night after that, he appeared with fresh purple sheets, a ritual both disturbing and considerate. The day my period ended, a delivery truck arrived with a new mattress set and plastic cover, accompanied by a simple note.

Be ready for next month.

I run my fingers over the silk covering my body, marveling at how it clings in all the right places. It's beautiful, flowing, and feminine. Everything I want to be for him, even if he'll tear it away within minutes of his arrival. I wear it anyway, a small act of defiance or maybe an olive branch wrapped in purple silk.

Am I being deceptive? The question gnaws at me as I study my reflection in the mirror. The nightgown transforms me into someone sultry, someone aware of her power. My nipples peek through the lace, and when I move, the silk parts at the front, offering tantalizing glimpses of what lies beneath. I want to distract him from my betrayal, yes, but more than that, I want him to lose control. I want him to see me in this whisper of fabric and be so overcome with lust that he can't think straight, can't do anything but tear it from my body and take me with the desperation that burns between us night after night.

My heart pounds, each beat echoing in my ears. An almost unbearable anticipation crawls under my skin. The not knowing whether he'll be gentle or rough, whether he'll punish me for letting another man's lips touch mine, or simply claim me harder to remind me who I belong to. Uncertainty sets my skin ablaze, making the silk feel like fire against my fevered flesh.

He vowed he'd kill any man who touched me, but I have to believe he won't. Is that why I'm dressing like this? To show him that the kiss didn't matter?

But it did.

Minutes stretch into an hour. Still, he doesn't come.

Doubt creeps in. What if tonight is the night he doesn't show? What if my kiss with Damien was the final straw, the betrayal that drove him away for good? The panic that grips me runs deeper than I want to acknowledge.

I've grown addicted to his touch, to the way he makes me feel powerful and powerless all at once. He's become as essential to me as breathing, and the idea of losing him is unbearable.

Chapter Forty-Three

Luna

I gasp as my door flies open. I didn't even hear the alarm being disarmed. Adrenaline surges through me, and my pulse spikes, excitement and nervousness warring in my chest.

His dark silhouette fills the doorway. His gaze travels over me, taking in every inch of silk and lace I've wrapped myself in. Fury radiates off him in scorching waves, but beneath that inferno, threading through it, lies a hunger so fierce it shimmers in the air between us.

I don't trust my voice, so I only watch him move closer. My eyes lift to his face when he's standing a few feet away from me.

"You invited another man into your house, made him dinner, then let him fucking kiss you?"

His low, rough voice cuts through the silence. The words themselves are calm, void of inflection, but I taste the storm brewing behind them, ready to break.

My mouth goes dry. He saw it all. Of course he did. That's probably who Damien felt lurking in the woods.

"Yes." I refuse to look away.

Silence.

He lifts his hand to my face. I flinch, expecting him to grip my jaw hard, but he only tilts my chin upward. His mask's eyeholes frame those black, unflinching predator eyes.

"Did you want him to kiss you?"

The question is a trap, and we both know it. If I say no, I'm lying. If I say yes, I'm admitting to wanting another man. Either answer damns me.

"I—" My throat constricts, but I force myself to hold his gaze. "Yes."

His hand drops, curling into a fist, and for a moment, I fear he'll lose control. Instead of being terrified, the barely restrained fury sends molten heat pooling between my thighs.

"Did you enjoy it?"

Another impossible question. But I've come this far with the truth.

"Yes."

He moves so fast I barely have time to gasp. One second, he's still. The next, his hands clamp around my thighs and lift me. My hands shoot towards his shoulders for balance, but I catch myself mid-reach, pressing them to my chest. I don't need to give him another reason to punish me. He crosses to the bed in three strides and drops me. I bounce, my nightgown fluttering.

"You're mine."

His body presses forward without touching, creating a cage of arms and legs that traps me beneath him. "Every inch of your body belongs to me, Luna. Your mouth, your ass, your cunt. All mine."

"I know."

The admission slips free even as guilt shreds my insides. When I kissed Damien, I was betraying this. Us. I want to say, "I'm sorry," but the words don't come.

His hand drifts down my neck, fingers ghosting over the skin, deceptively soft, until they wrap around my throat. I swallow as he tightens his fingers, cutting off my air.

My hands shoot up to his wrist, wrapping around it, but I don't struggle. I want this. I need this.

"You need a reminder of who you belong to."

Everything between my legs clenches tight as my body responds to the threat in his voice, craving it rather than fearing it.

"Yes."

It's all I can manage with my oxygen restricted.

Remind me. Make me forget everything but you.

His eyes through the mask are black. They bore into me, obsidian depths that strip away everything but his presence. My lungs strain, fighting for oxygen that won't come. The ache between my thighs intensifies, pulsing in rhythm with my pounding heartbeat.

Black creeps into the edges of my vision, and tears pool in the corners of my eyes. But then his fingers release me, and I gasp. My lungs fill with that first sweet breath of air.

He hauls himself up, seizing my wrists, yanking me to my feet as my body convulses with coughs and desperate gulps of air. I meet his eyes, and the pounding of my heart is deafening, a chaotic drumbeat in my ears echoing the anticipation of his wrath.

I just hope I survive it.

Chapter Forty-Four

Damien

She's wearing purple silk that matches the sheets I bought her. A babydoll that barely covers anything, lace so delicate it's practically transparent. My cock strains against my zipper, threatening to tear through the metal. But it's not just lust that slams into me. It's something deeper, more dangerous. Something that tightens like a fist around my lungs, sending tremors through my fingers.

I want to tear that silk away and claim every inch of her skin. I want to rip off this goddamn mask and show her exactly who kissed her less than two hours ago.

But I can't. Because I'm the asshole hiding behind metal and lies.

She rubs her throat, where fresh bruises will paint her skin by morning, coughing low and steady as she blinks away the moisture welling in her eyes.

But she doesn't cower. She never cowers.

Inside me, two beasts tear at each other. One snarls in rage that she kissed another man. The other throbs with the ache of her lips pressed against mine. The fury of the first wants to punish her. The hunger of the second can't unlearn the taste of her.

My jaw clenches until the muscles scream. I want to wreck her and worship her at the same time. Tear her apart, then collect the fragments and cherish them before putting her back together.

That kiss awakened something I thought long dead. I hate her for bringing it back to life, this soft and dangerous feeling that fills me with equal parts fury and desperation.

But it's seared itself into my memory. The way she tasted, the quiet gasp when my tongue met hers, and how she leaned in when she should have pulled away.

She makes me want more. Everything. Her body already belongs to me, but her heart and soul remain out of reach.

I'm losing my fucking mind.

"Tell me, did kissing him make you wet?" My tone is mocking, but my heart feels like it's tearing itself out of my chest. "If I slipped my fingers into your cunt right now, would I find you drenched? Wet from the feel of his lips on yours?"

Her eyes snap up to mine. Regret flickers there for a heartbeat before her expression hardens. Her chin lifts, exposing the pale column of her throat. She's breathtaking when she looks at me like that, like not even her fear will conquer her.

"Don't lie to me, Luna. I deserve your honesty."

That's a fucking joke. I'm the liar here.

"And what if I am wet? I'm always wet when you come to me."

"Yes. But it's usually *for* me. Not for another man."

She laughs, but it's brittle. "You want me to deny it? You know I kissed him." She holds my gaze without blinking. Moonlight glints off her tears. "I won't lie about it. But I won't be ashamed either. A man actually wanted to kiss me tonight. And maybe it was goddamn nice to be wanted that way."

The air between us shivers. "I don't make you feel wanted?"

Her lips press into a line. "In some ways, you do. In other ways, you don't."

My blood runs ice-cold. How could I have ever made her feel unwanted?

I need to know.

"What is it about him that made you want to betray what we have?"

"What we have? What exactly do we have? You come into my house at night, fuck me until my head spins, then disappear before dawn. We don't talk, we don't kiss, I don't even know who you are. So tell me, what exactly am I betraying?"

Her words slice into me. They're true. I've given her only my body. Never my face, never my name. Never my soul.

I step forward, hand closing around her neck again. She doesn't flinch.

"You know what this is."

"Do I? Because from where I'm standing, it looks like I'm just some convenient holes for you to stick your dick into. Maybe I wanted to know what it felt like to be with someone who actually sees me as more than that."

My hand tightens, pressing until her heartbeat thrums against my fingertips because her words gut me.

"Is that what you think? That you're just a fuck toy to me?"

She trembles, and for a fraction of a second, I think she'll crumble. Instead, she snarls, "What else am I supposed to think? You treat me like a dirty secret."

"You're the only thing that fucking matters." My voice drops to something dangerous. "And when you let another man's hands on you, his mouth on yours, it made me want to burn the whole fucking world down."

It's the truth stripped bare. Kissing her as Damien was torture twisted with ecstasy. Feeling her melt against me, knowing I created that response, but powerless to claim it. Powerless to make it mine.

"Then maybe you should have thought of that before deciding I wasn't worth anything more than anonymous sex. That I'm not worth your naked skin against mine. Or your weight on top of me. Or your lips on mine."

I take a step back and drink in the sight of her. The hardness in her eyes has dissolved. The guilt has fled. What remains is pain. Open, honest and devastating. It hurts her that I won't kiss her, let her touch me, or let her know me beyond the sex.

But that's what I'm trying to do as Damien!

I grasp her hair and tug her head back, forcing her to look at me.

"Is that what you want from him? His weight on you? His cock sliding deep inside you? For him to kiss you like it's the only thing he wants to do in the world?"

She tries to wrench her head free, but I won't let go. "Is there something wrong with wanting that? Wanting connection? Tenderness? Is that a crime?"

"I told you from the start I'm not a gentle man."

"You just want to fuck me against my will. Does that make you feel like a man? Is that what you need to get hard? Knowing the woman beneath you is forced to take you?"

"I don't force you. I take nothing you aren't willing to give me."

Her body arches, answering me as her eyes confirm the truth of my words. I tug her head back a little farther. She flinches.

"Ow, you're hurting me."

"Good." But I ease my grip to let her lift her head. "Because you fucking hurt me tonight, Luna. When you kissed him."

She blinks, and her lips part in surprise.

"You want to know why I kissed him? Because he's kind. And he looks at me like I'm more than a fuck."

Kind. She thinks Damien is kind. If only she knew that kindness is just another mask I wear, another lie in a life built on deception. This is the man I am, and though she accepts me in the dark, would she accept me in the light?

I snap the strap of her nightgown against her skin. "Did you want him to fuck you? Is that why you're wearing this little scrap of fabric that barely covers your pussy and puts your nipples on display, begging to be sucked?" I push her back onto the bed in one brutal motion.

I'm losing control. The precarious balance I've maintained for months is crumbling, and I can't stop it.

"Maybe I was tired of settling for a man who won't show me his face."

Then let me show you.

The words are right there, desperate to escape. But I can't.

I won't risk losing her.

"I give you my body, but you don't get to control my life. You don't get to make demands when you keep yourself hidden from me."

"I don't have to give you my name to own you."

The truth registers in her eyes, and her breath stutters. Her body recognizes its master, even if she doesn't know his name.

"I won't apologize for tonight. I'm not sorry I kissed someone who actually wants to kiss me back. Now, do you still want me?" Her chin comes up, daring me to answer. "Or are you just here to threaten me and mark my body?"

I press one knee between her thighs and lean over her. The moonlight slants through the window, catching the curve of her throat. I trace a fingertip along the bruises there, my finger trembling at the memory of how I made them.

"I always want you."

She looks at me, tears threatening to spill, but her gaze burns with defiant fire. "Then prove it."

The air is heavy with her challenge, and I'm incapable of denying her as she lies beneath me—beautiful, tempting and mine.

Mine.

The claim echoes in my head as my fingers trace the lace over her breasts. I graze the stiff peaks of her nipples with my thumbs, and her body quakes beneath my touch.

"This little scrap of nothing. So fucking beautiful." Need thickens my voice. "Did you put it on, thinking about him? What his hands would feel like on your skin?"

"No." She arches into my touch, breathless. "I wore it for you. Hoping you'd tear it off me."

Mission fucking accomplished.

I fist my hands in the delicate silk and tear it away from her body with one brutal pull. The sound of ripping fabric fills the air. She's bare beneath me, responding to the violence with a gasp. Hunger and possession explode in my chest, savage and all-consuming.

Mine.

She's naked, perfect, and shaking. I drop my head to her throat, lips blazing a path across her warm, pale skin. Her hands clench at her sides, proof she's dying to touch me, but she holds herself back.

Her back curves upward, resistance melting into need. I trail my fingers over every ridge and hollow. My hands splay against her hips, gripping as I push her up the bed, caressing her skin, and relearning curves I've memorized in the dark. She's so soft, so perfect, and I'm desperate to mark her, to leave evidence of my claim on every inch of her body.

I lift my head and look down at her.

"You're not a toy. Or a convenient fuck. You're the only thing in this world that makes sense."

It's more honesty than I've ever given. The hardness in her eyes cracks and falls away. What's left is wounded and desperate and hoping against hope. Tears gather on her eyelashes, catching the moonlight. I push up to my knees before she can speak.

"Now, let me show you what happens when you let another man touch you."

Chapter Forty-Five

Damien

S he trembles at the promise in my voice. The anger has burned away. How can I be angry with her for wanting all of me, not just the parts I'm willing to give?

"Hands above your head."

She inhales a quick breath and lifts her arms without hesitation. I loop the zip tie around her slender wrists and cinch it tight to the slatted headboard, leaving her trapped.

Helpless.

At my mercy.

My hands trace the curve of her ribs. My pulse hammers as she shudders beneath the whisper of my touch. Her skin feels like silk under my fingertips. My throat constricts. When my fingers close around her breasts, they fit my palms like they were made for my touch. Each pass of my thumbs over her nipples sends lightning through my veins, echoing the arch of her spine as a soft moan spills through her parted lips.

I lower my mouth, starving for her. A groan tears from my chest, vibrating against her breast. My tongue traces patterns learned over months of worshipping her body. But she keeps surprising me. Every gasp imprints itself on my consciousness. When I catch her nipple between my teeth, the desperate, shattered noise she makes echoes the violent rhythm pounding in my chest.

"Please."

"Please, what?" I lift my head. Her breath comes in quick, ragged bursts as she shifts against the cool cotton beneath her, desperate for any friction, hips pressing up in a silent plea. "Tell me, little doe?"

"Touch me. Please."

Almost nothing compares to the exquisite sound of her begging.

"Where?" My fingers hover centimeters above the bare skin of her stomach, deliberately out of reach, my fingertips quivering with anticipation. "Here?"

A soft whimper slides from her throat, an exquisite little sound, as she writhes, lips parting.

"Lower."

My fingertips skim the valley of her abdomen before stopping just above her hip.

"Here?"

She strains toward my touch, growling like an angry kitten.

"You know where."

I press my thumb to the soft skin above where she wants me most, barely brushing it. She gasps, quivering.

"Tell me."

She swallows, eyes fluttering.

"My cunt. Please touch my cunt."

A slow, satisfied smile spreads across my face. When desperation strips away her careful language, when she begs with crude words, those moments are worth everything.

I inhale, savoring the sweet, warm scent rising from her. "Don't you mean my cunt?"

Her pulse pounds at her throat as she nods. "Yours."

"Spread your legs."

She parts her thighs, letting them fall open, her skin pebbling where cool air meets warm flesh.

"Wider."

Her legs slide until they make a perfect V. She looks beautiful, desperate, and exposed, everything I've been craving since I first entered her bedroom.

"Look at you." The words scrape out of my throat. "So fucking beautiful."

I drop to my knees at the foot of the bed and tug her closer to the edge. My fingertip dips into the damp hollow of her outer lips, gathering slickness with a gentle sweep. She gasps, pressing down, but I pull away.

She trembles against her restraints. "Please, don't tease."

I lean in, voice low. "You gave up your right to make demands the moment you let another man put his mouth on you."

The first thrust of my fingers inside her is harsh, my anger at her kissing Damien flaring again. She's soaked. So smooth that her heat surrounds my fingers as they disappear. I curl them against that spot deep inside her, and her hips lift off the bed, a strangled cry escaping her throat.

"Tight." My thumb makes slow, circular motions on her clit. "But you're always tight for me, aren't you? No matter how many times you take me."

She gasps, her inner muscles clenching around my fingers.

"Not yet." I slow my movements, backing her away from the edge. "You don't get to come until I say you can."

"Please." Her hips chase my hand, eyes wild and desperate. "I need—"

"You need what I give you. Nothing more, nothing less."

The words push through my clenched teeth. She needs to know. Needs to understand that no one else can do this. I'm the only man who can tear her apart and put her back together. Push her past every limit.

I withdraw my fingers and bring them to my mouth. She whimpers, her head lifting off the pillow, her pupils blowing wide, the dark swallowing the light until barely any color remains. Salt and sweetness coat my tongue as I slide them between my lips. My gaze never leaves hers. Heat surges hot beneath my skin. I did this. I alone made her this wet, this desperate. No one else. The satisfaction rolls through my chest, escaping as a low hum that makes her thighs quiver.

"Sweet. But I think I need a better taste."

I lower my head, my tongue tracing slow paths through her folds. I've memorized every tender crease, but each time is intoxicating, the scent and taste making me want to drown in her. When I capture her clit between my lips, her entire body goes rigid. My hands press her thighs to the mattress as she dissolves into breathless gasps and silent tears beneath my mouth.

"Oh God." She strains against her bonds. "Please, I'm going to—"

I stop.

"Not yet." I pull back, wiping my lips. "First, I want to hear you say it again."

"Say what?" She gasps, need and confusion tangled together.

"That you're mine."

I've never been an insecure man, but I need her to say it, especially after tonight.

I rise to my feet, fingers fumbling with my zipper, desperate for relief from the painful constriction. A groan escapes my throat as I wrap my hand around my cock. The mattress dips beneath my weight as I position myself between her splayed thighs, her skin flushed and glistening.

"Say that you belong to me and only me, Luna."

"I'm yours."

"And the billionaire?"

Her body stiffens, and my pulse spikes.

Please, Luna. Tell me you belong to me. This me. And I'll find a way to give you all of me.

My hand continues its slow rhythm up and down my cock as I hover above her. Her expression softens, surrender washing over her features. My breath stops as I wait for her answer.

"I'm yours." Her voice breaks on the last word.

My chest seizes, pressure building behind my ribs. Love, unexpected and impossibly real, blazes through me at her words.

The revelation slams into me, stealing my breath. Love. I never thought myself capable of this feeling. Yet here it is, burning through every cell in my body as I look down at this woman who's somehow slipped past all my defenses. Past all the separation I put in place between us.

"Now it's my turn, beautiful girl. I need to be inside you."

I lean forward, my body drawn to hers like gravity, and for a moment I hover there. Her thighs tremble—still spread, still offering—against my hips. When I brush against her slick heat, the familiar jolt races up my spine, that first touch that always feels new. That's never enough. My breath catches as I press forward, the world narrowing to the single point where our bodies meet.

"I'm giving you one thing you want tonight, Luna. You'll get some of my weight." She gasps, and tears shimmer in her eyes. "But my mask stays on. My clothes stay on. No kissing. You want to feel me on top of you? I'll give you what I can, proof that you're not just a fuck toy, Luna. You're everything."

Her answering whimper tears straight through my chest, cracking it open.

I sink into her, a long, slow slide, watching her face transform with each inch. Her eyes flutter closed, lips parting in surrender. A groan tears from my throat as her heat envelops me. My fingers dig into her hips, not just guiding but anchoring myself to this moment.

To her.

I lower myself over her, arms braced but allowing my chest to graze her skin in the barest caress—contact so light it might be imagined. Her eyes fly open, startled and wide. My face hovers inches from hers, my mask a barrier between us while her expression—raw, unguarded, and desperate—burns itself into my vision. Her eyes drift closed, lashes like fans against her cheeks.

"Look at me."

The demand tears from my throat. I need her eyes on mine. Need her to see past everything else. Those lashes flutter open, and her gaze locks onto mine, eyes enormous and unfocused with desire, and lips parted around shallow breaths. The sight knocks the air out of my lungs. Her vulnerable expression echoes the turmoil within me, a silent recognition that this runs deeper than flesh.

I rotate my hips at the end of each slow, deep thrust, grinding into her. My hand slips between us, my thumb rubbing her clit. She lifts her hips, legs wrapping around me, pulling me deeper. My palm moves to her thigh, my fingers digging into her soft flesh as I find a deeper angle. Her moans rise higher, each one a surrender of control.

Her breath hitches. "There. Just like that."

Sweat trickles down my brow, beneath the mask, and my muscles quiver with the strain of holding back. I want to prolong this moment, this beautiful convergence of need and abandon.

I hold on, teetering on the edge, before I begin to unravel. My hips collide with hers, each thrust deeper than the last, as if I could somehow lose myself inside her. A shudder rolls through my entire body. She cries out as I return to the brutal rhythm she knows, the one that doesn't betray how much I need her. I bury my face in the curve of her neck, inhaling the salt of her skin, drowning in her scent until there's nothing left in the world but Luna.

I hover above her, muscles straining to keep space between us, but with each breath she rises to meet me, her spine curving. The gap I maintain crackles with a dangerous promise I'm terrified to keep. The arm bracing me over her trembles, not from exertion, but from the war between wanting to collapse onto her, surrender to her, and knowing I can't.

I'm giving you what I can, Luna.

My fingers slide back to her clit. A choked sob escapes her as her muscles tighten around me.

"That's right." I drive deeper into her, setting a punishing pace. "You're mine. Every moan, every gasp, every tremor belongs to me."

Mine, mine, mine.

The word echoes in my head, a chant that consumes me with each thrust. Her cries fill the air, mirroring the tremor in my limbs.

"Say it again, Luna." I dig my fingers into her hip, desperate to leave my mark. "Tell me you're mine."

"I'm yours." Her words are a drug, surging through my veins. "Only yours."

I press a tender kiss to the scar from her bear attack, then lower my mouth to her breast, worshiping her nipple with a reverence that belies my turmoil.

She lifts her head, her breath warm against the top of mine. For a second, I think she might kiss it. I've expected her to push that boundary when I worshipped her breasts, but she never has. She respects boundaries. Unlike me.

I know the damage I'm doing. Every night I come here, I'm tearing us both apart, but I can't stop. "I'm sorry." The words I never thought I'd say slip out before I can stop them, muffled around her nipple.

She stills beneath me. "What did you say?"

I can't repeat it. Instead, I focus on moving inside her, on the way she feels wrapped around me, trying to pour everything I can't say into the way I touch her.

The tension builds, coiling tighter and tighter until we both shatter. Her walls clench around me, and I follow her over the edge, burying myself deep as I come with a roar. She sobs beneath me. The zip-tie bites into her wrists as she strains against it, her orgasm tearing through her with violent beauty. Her release floods over me like liquid heat.

We linger in the aftermath, breathless and shuddering. I want to cut her bonds and gather her trembling form against my chest. Trace lazy patterns across her cooling skin until sleep claims us both. Whisper the words clogging my throat. Promises, confessions, and truths that could shatter everything.

But I remain silent.

"Thank you."

Her voice breaks, raw with the tears that track down her flushed cheeks. I look down at her, eyes glistening with a mix of euphoria and anguish. A contradiction that tears through my gut like claws.

I'm such a fucking asshole for denying her this. I'm destroying her with my selfishness. Destroying us both.

My chest constricts until breathing becomes almost impossible. I need distance before I give in to the urge to strip away every barrier between us.

Without a word, I reach up and snap the zip tie with a quick twist. The plastic falls away from her reddened wrists, and I step back from the bed where she lies like a fallen goddess, naked and beautiful among the torn remains of purple silk.

My seed, evidence of my claim, seeps from between her thighs, another mark of possession in a relationship built on taking what I can never truly have.

I pause at the door, turning to look at her. She's shifted onto her stomach, sprawled across the sheets, the curve of her spine catching the moonlight that filters through her curtains. Her hair spills across her pillow, her skin bearing the flush of release, and every line of her body speaking of satisfaction.

But the smile I'm used to seeing in these moments is nowhere to be found. Confusion clouds her eyes instead of the usual satisfied haze. Her lips part as if to speak, then close again. I can read the questions there as clearly as if she'd voiced them.

Are you leaving already? Why only once tonight?

She's learned my patterns too well, expecting the relentless hunger that usually drives me to possess her again and again until we're both wrung out. Tonight's restraint, especially after that kiss, confuses her and leaves her reaching for explanations I can't give.

The words stick in my throat like broken glass, and all I can do is memorize the way she looks at me. Beautiful and bewildered.

I refuse to look back again as I cross the threshold into the hallway.

I can't afford to. I'll break.

I'll tear off this fucking mask, speak my name, and damn us both to a future neither of us is prepared for.

Chapter Forty-Six

Damien

I make it back to the Range Rover in record time, my strides through the woods clipped and silent in the snow. Winter's coming assault will soon turn these woods into a white fortress around Luna's property, making it impassable on foot, and I need to figure out another route before that happens.

The taste of her is still on my lips, the scent of her still clinging to my skin and clothes. I grip the steering wheel as I navigate the short, winding road back home.

The duality of what just happened weighs on me like a physical presence in the car. Less than four hours ago, I was Damien Wolfe, kissing Luna goodbye on her doorstep. Now I'm returning from her bedroom, where I bound her hands and fucked her, reminding her—and myself—exactly who she belongs to.

My body still hums with desire for her. Taking her only once is not enough, but I had to get out of there because I was on the verge of blowing it all up and revealing myself to her.

I enter my house, pour three fingers of whiskey, and stand at the floor-to-ceiling windows in my office, staring into the darkness. My heart pounds so hard it feels like it's battering my ribs from the inside, trying to break free. The realization washes over me again and drowns me.

I'm in love with Luna.

This goes beyond want, beyond desire, and beyond the craving that's consumed me for months. I'm in love with her—a new and overwhelming emotion that shatters everything I thought I knew about myself.

It's been creeping up on me for weeks, but tonight, her expression when she looked at me as Damien, not with desire or submission, but with genuine warmth and affection, hit with the force of a wrecking ball. The way she returned my kiss on her doorstep, surrendering to Damien in a way she's never surrendered to me.

When this started, it was supposed to be simple. Take her. Claim her. Make her mine in the most fundamental way possible. Use her for both our pleasure until I ruined her for any other men, so she would be irrevocably mine. It was meant to be about control. About possession. About satisfying an obsession that had been beyond my ability to manage the second I laid eyes on her.

I didn't plan for her to affect me like this, didn't anticipate her burrowing so deep inside my heart that I feel like it will stop beating if I lose her.

Luna isn't like the other women I've known, the socialites and business associates who see only what I allow them to see. Or even the other women I've fucked over the years, who were simply a hot, wet body to satisfy my needs. She's genuine in a way that's both refreshing and terrifying. When she looks at me, I feel exposed, like she can see through every part of me.

And tonight, when I kissed her...

Fuck!

I run a hand through my hair, pacing in front of the window. That kiss as Damien had been everything the countless hours with her masked watcher hadn't been. Tender. Emotional. Real in a way that went beyond carnal want.

Tonight, her passionate and tender response to Damien's kiss ripped something open inside me, leaving me bleeding and exposed. I wanted to punish her for it. Wanted to brand into her body that she's mine, not some billionaire's she met a handful of times.

The irony would be comical if it weren't so fucked up.

I finish my whiskey and pour another, my mind replaying every moment of tonight. The way her eyes widened when I told her I knew she kissed him. Her confession that she'd wanted his kiss. Enjoyed it. The guilt and defiance warring in her expression as I bound her hands and claimed her body.

She came apart for me like she always does. Beautiful and desperate and completely mine.

For now.

The thought sends a chill through me because Luna is smart. And she's starting to notice things. I knew she would eventually.

How long before she puts the pieces together? How long before she realizes that her billionaire suitor and her masked lover share the same build, the same hands, and the same scent beneath the deliberate deception of different soaps and colognes?

Part of me wants her to figure it out. Wants to stop living this double life. The compartmentalization that once came so easily is fracturing under the weight of my feelings for her.

Another part of me, the part that's spent years learning that love is a weakness, is terrified of what will happen when she learns the truth.

Luna accepts me, her masked lover, for what I am. She knows I'm dangerous, who I kill and why, yet she still spreads her legs for me every night. She understands my darkness because she's seen firsthand the evil I eliminate from this world. Even as she struggles with it, in her mind, I'm almost a dark guardian angel.

Brutal but righteous.

But Damien Wolfe? He's supposed to be civilized. Refined. A billionaire philanthropist who donates security systems and charms her over dinner. When she realizes that the man who made her laugh over lasagna and wine tonight is the same one who binds her hands and fucks her into oblivion, will she see it as a betrayal?

Will she feel manipulated? Used? Or will she understand that both sides of me are real, that I need her to see all of me?

I set down my glass and move to my desk, where multiple monitors display feeds from Luna's sanctuary. The screens show her property from every angle, even her bedroom and bathroom. She knows her wolf watches her, but she has no idea how much or that I have cameras in her most private areas. She'd gouge my eyes out if she did.

I pull up the recording from earlier, turn up the volume, and watch from the beginning. From the time she returned to her room after Damien left, stripped and showered, and then brought herself to orgasm, with Damien on her mind, I'm sure.

Then, I watch as I come to her, furious and accusing, which I had no right to be. But she still surrenders and gives me everything. Every part of her. She holds nothing back. And all she wants is for me to do the same.

Despite how furious and hurt I was tonight, she doesn't deserve my anger because my deception isn't her fault.

Now, after taking her lips for the first time, I won't be able to live without them again. But I can't kiss her as the wolf. Not until she knows the truth.

So what the fuck am I supposed to do?

I have to pursue her as Damien. And I can't punish her if she accepts his attentions. That's not fair to her.

But when was life fucking fair?

Somewhere along the way, claiming, owning, and possessing Luna stopped being about obsession and started being about keeping the woman I've fallen in love with. The woman I may be in real danger of losing to... myself.

How did I fuck this up so badly?

On top of everything else, I have Caleb Hunter to deal with. Her piece-of-shit ex, who threatened her tonight, who dared to lay hands on her. He'll die because of what he did. But I have to be more careful this time. Luna can never know what happened to him. Can never connect his disappearance to me.

The kill will be easy. It's the lying that will be impossible.

First, I need to decide what to do about the fact that I'm living a lie that's becoming impossible to maintain. That I'm in love with a woman who doesn't even know that the two men in her life are the same person.

I close my eyes and lean back in my chair, remembering the taste of her lips as Damien, and the taste of her surrender as her wolf. Both encounters were real. Both versions of me want every part of her.

But which one does she want? The civilized man or the savage?

This can't continue. Soon, I'll have to make a choice. Reveal myself and risk losing her, or disappear from her life entirely.

Neither option is acceptable.

Maybe there's a third way. Maybe I can guide her to the truth, help her see the connections without shocking her with the full revelation. If I'm careful, if I'm clever about it, I can make her understand that both versions of me are real, that they're both hers.

That all of me is hers.

Or maybe I'm just a fucking selfish bastard who wants everything his way.

But the real question is... Will she still want to belong to me when the truth comes out?

And will I be brave enough to give her the choice?

Chapter Forty-Seven

Luna

My body aches in ways that remind me of every touch, every caress, every moment he made me forget my own name. The sheets beneath me are rumpled and twisted. My skin tingles with the ghost of his hands, the memory of his fingers wrapped around my throat as he punished me for kissing Damien. I can still feel the barest hint of his body pressing into mine, separated only by fabric and his iron restraint. Tears gather at the corners of my eyes as the images flood back, vivid enough to make my breath catch.

I roll onto my side, wincing at the pleasant ache between my thighs. He left after only fucking me once. No second round. No third. He never does that, even when he's angry. Especially when he's angry. I'm usually begging him, tears streaming down my face, telling him I can't take any more before he relents. But tonight, he left after taking me once, with barely a look back.

And it feels wrong.

The confusion sits heavy in my chest, mixing with the bliss still pulsing through my veins. I press my face into the sheets, breathing in the faint scent of him that clings to the fabric. That distinct clean, dark, woodsy scent that makes my pulse quicken even now.

My legs tremble as I push myself up, the reminder of his intensity sending aftershocks through my core. I need to clean up. Too often, I let myself fall asleep with his semen inside me, but the last thing I need right now is another UTI.

I lift the torn fragments of the silk babydoll, my lips curving and my body shivering at the memory of him tearing it from me like I hoped he would. His reaction was worth every dime it cost.

The bathroom tiles are cold against my bare feet, and I hiss at the contrast. Everything feels heightened, sensitive, like my skin is still buzzing from his touch. I toss the nightgown into the trash and take care of what I need to, my body protesting the loss of him even as my practical mind knows it's necessary.

When I catch sight of myself in the mirror, I pause. My hair is wild, my nipples swollen, and there are faint red marks along my throat and hips, on my breasts, and around my wrists from the zip ties. I look claimed and wrecked, and the sight sends a fresh wave of heat through me.

I wrap my robe around myself, the fabric cool and soothing against my flushed skin, and walk back into the bedroom.

Shadow sits in the hallway, his massive frame statue-still, eyes fixed on me with that patient expression he gets when nature calls. His tail gives a single thump against the hardwood floor.

"Really? Again?" I sigh, but there's no real irritation in my voice. He's been patient enough while I was... occupied. "Fine. Come on, baby. When you gotta go, you gotta go."

He bounds ahead of me as I make my way downstairs. The house feels too quiet, too empty all of a sudden, without the weight of my wolf's presence. I try to shake off the hollow feeling as I flip on the porch light and unlock the front door.

The cold hits me like a slap, and I grab my boots and coat from the closet. Snow crunches under Shadow's paws as he trots out into the yard, his dark gray fur stark against the white blanket covering everything. More flurries drift down from the heavy sky, catching the porch light like tiny diamonds.

I pull my coat tighter and lean against the doorframe, watching him sniff around his usual spots. The night is beautiful in that pristine way snow creates, muffling sound and smoothing over all the rough edges of the world.

But something feels off.

The sensation starts as a prickle at the base of my neck, that uncomfortable awareness that makes my shoulders tense. I'm used to being watched. My wolf's gaze is as familiar as my own reflection now. But this feels different. Heavier.

My eyes scan the treeline, and the feeling intensifies. It's coming from the woods across the property, not from his usual vantage point. And besides, he just left. Why would he leave and then watch me from the trees?

"Shadow," I call, my voice tight.

But he's already noticed something. His head snaps up from where he was investigating a snow-covered bush, and his throat vibrates with a growl. His hackles rise as he stares in the same direction that has my skin crawling.

"Shadow, come here. Now."

Instead of obeying, he takes a step toward the woods, his growl deepening. The sound raises goosebumps along my arms that have nothing to do with the cold.

"Shadow, no!" Panic edges into my voice as he starts toward the treeline, his massive form cutting through the snow. "Come back here!"

He pauses at the edge of the trees, his growl turning into something more threatening, more feral. For a moment, I think he's going to ignore me and disappear into the darkness. But then he turns and bounds back, placing himself between me and whatever lurks in those shadows.

His lips pull back to bare teeth that could tear a man's throat out, his eyes never leaving the woods. A continuous low vibration rolls from deep in his throat, a warning that makes my blood run cold.

The full moon breaks through the clouds, casting everything in a silver glow, and I swear I see movement in the trees. A figure retreating deeper into the shadows. But there's no metallic glint of a mask catching the light, no familiar silhouette that would ease the fear clawing at my ribs.

This isn't my wolf.

Could it be Caleb? No, he's got enough self-preservation to stay away once he's been warned off. And it can't be Damien either. He wouldn't skulk around in the trees. Plus, his estate sits to the east, and whoever I just saw was in the western tree line.

"Inside. Now."

I grab Shadow's collar, pulling him toward the door even though he outweighs me by almost fifty pounds.

He moves with me, his head still twisted toward the tree line. The growl rolls through his chest, vibrating up through my grip. I slam the door shut and lock it, my fingers shaking as I punch in the alarm code. The familiar beep of activation does little to calm my racing heart.

Shadow paces in front of the door, whining now, his instincts telling him there's a threat he needs to eliminate. I trust his judgment more than my own when it comes to danger. Wolves don't growl at nothing.

"It's okay."

I run my fingers through his thick fur. It's not okay. Someone else is out there, watching. Someone who doesn't belong.

I climb the stairs on unsteady legs, Shadow close at my heels, both of us listening for any sound that might indicate we're not alone. The house settles around us with its usual creaks and sighs, but every noise makes me jump.

In my bedroom, I check the window locks twice before closing the curtains for the first time in months. Shadow settles on the rug beside my bed, rather than in his corner.

As I climb back into bed, where my wolf's scent lingers on the sheets, I try to dismiss it as mere shadows playing tricks in the moonlight.

But the knot of unease in my stomach tells me otherwise.

I pull the blankets up to my chin and stare at the ceiling, trying to shake off the fear that something just changed. The now familiar safety I've found in the twisted dance between my wolf and me has been tainted by a darker, more dangerous presence.

I close my eyes, hoping the morning will bring answers.

Or at least make the fear seem less real.

Watch Me Burn

Read the Conclusion of
Luna & Damien's Story
Watch Me Burn
https://mybook.to/QNUPFxz

Please Review

Here's the thing about reviews—they're kind of a big deal for indie authors like me.

Reviews help our books get noticed, build momentum, and reach readers who might love them. They're one of the most powerful ways you can support an author, and trust me, we notice and appreciate every single one.

So if you enjoyed WATCH ME BREAK, I'd be incredibly grateful if you'd leave a review on Amazon, Goodreads, and/or wherever you share your reading recommendations. Even a few sentences go a long way.

Thank you so much for your support—it truly means the world!

Below are easy links for you.

www.Amazon.com/review/create-review?&asin=B0FFTHMLQT

https://www.goodreads.com/book/show/237395190-watch-me-break

https://www.bookbub.com/books/watch-me-break-a-dark-stalker-romance-watched-in-darkness-book-1-by-v-e-huntley

The BloodStone Legacy Series

Damnation

Atonement

Redemption

Watched in Darkness Series

Watch Me Break

Watch Me Burn

Watch Over Me Prequel Novella

Watch Me Bleed—Coming 2027

Sacred Sins—Coming 2027

Shadow Ice Brotherhood Series

Frozen Fury—Coming 2027

Frozen Wrath—Coming 2028

Frozen Savage—TBD

Frozen Sins—TBD

Frozen Vengeance—TBD

Frozen Menace—TBD

Strike & Surrender Series

Strike Hard, Surrender Softly—Coming 2027

Strike High, Surrender Deep—Coming 2028

Strike First, Surrender Last—TBD

Strike Fast, Surrender Slow—TBD

Strike Once, Surrender Forever—TBD

Strike Strong, Surrender Sweet—TBD

Follow Me

For more previews, deleted scenes and goodies, sign up for my newsletter:
Sign Up Here
https://vehuntley.com/

Connect with V.E:
https://www.facebook.com/v.e.huntley.author
https://www.instagram.com/vehuntley/
https://x.com/vehuntleywriter
https://www.tiktok.com/@vehuntley
https://bsky.app/profile/vehuntleyauthor.bsky.social
https://www.pinterest.com/vehuntleywriter/
https://www.goodreads.com/author/show/50245965.V_E_Huntley
Join my Whispers After Dark Facebook Group – it's a place we can talk about all
things books, especially naughty things
https://www.facebook.com/groups/v.e.huntleys.whispers.after.dark

Acknowledgements

There are so many people I'd like to thank—I don't even know where to start!

First and foremost, Hubby Chris—I couldn't do any of this without your love and support. Thank you for believing in me, even when I was convinced it would never happen and I should just become a professional cat mom instead.

Elle, I couldn't do this without you either! Thank you for kicking my ass (with love, of course), telling me I can do better, dig deeper, and reminding me that I have way hotter sex scenes and more brutal kill scenes lurking inside me. Spoiler alert: You're right every damn time.

To my incredible ARC team, street team, and all my amazing fans and followers—I would love to name every single one of you here, but let's be real... I'd 100% forget someone, spiral into guilt, and then dramatically refuse to leave my house for three weeks. So instead, I'm thanking you all as one beautiful, book-loving collective! Just know that I can't thank you enough for your support. Thank you for reading my books, loving them, and sharing them with the world. I'm so grateful to all of you!

And finally to Jessie, Geronimo, Casey, Arthur, Merlin, Lancelot, and Baby-Doll—your fur, purrs, and unconditional love have been my safe place. Also, thanks for judging me silently from across the room while I ugly-cried over my own plot twists. I miss you all so much!

About the author

I'm a retired producer who's spent most of my life telling stories in one form or another. Just ask my cats—they've endured years of me reciting entire dialogue scenes to them when all they desperately wanted was a nap.

My childhood fear of Dracula was so intense I couldn't sleep without the lights on and my mother standing guard at my bedroom door. Fast forward a few decades, and that terror has morphed into a full-blown obsession with all things dark and twisted.

After more than twenty years in film and television, I decided to follow my true calling—writing dark, steamy romance about anti-heroes who swear too much and have serious anger management issues, and the strong, spirited heroines who refuse to put up with their nonsense (but love them anyway).

When I'm not writing, I'm watching movies, reading, traveling, or adding to my husband's never-ending honey-do list (it's basically a part-time job at this point). You can find out more about me on my website, www.vehuntley.com.